D0915256

AMARI

AND THE

GREAT GAME

B. B. ALSTON

AMARI

AND THE
GREAT GAME

Illustrations by
GODWIN AKPAN

BALZER+BRAY

An Imprint of HarperCollins*Publishers*

Balzer + Bray is an imprint of HarperCollins Publishers.

Amari and the Great Game
Copyright © 2022 by Brandon Alston
Illustrations copyright © 2022 by Godwin Akpan
All rights reserved. Printed in the United States of America.
No part of this book may be used or reproduced in any manner whatsoever without
written permission except in the case of brief quotations embodied in critical articles
and reviews. For information address HarperCollins Children's Books, a division of
HarperCollins Publishers, 195 Broadway, New York, NY 10007.
www.harpercollinschildrens.com

Library of Congress Control Number: 2022935801
ISBN 978-0-06-297519-5 — ISBN 978-0-06-323026-2 (special edition)
ISBN 978-0-06-329158-4 (special edition)

Typography by Carla Weise
23 24 25 26 27 LBC 6 5 4 3 2

First Edition

*For my mom, Songa,
who taught me I could do anything*

BEWARE OF UNSEEN DANGERS

I SPRINT DOWN THE SIDEWALK, FLYING PAST DESIGNER BOU-
tiques, luxury shops, and a fancy art gallery. A few blocks
ahead lies the sprawling downtown campus of Whitman
Preparatory Academy. The main building's all-glass exte-
rior sparkles in the morning light, and a line of cars circles
the large fountain out front, dropping off kids who—unlike
me—might actually get to homeroom before the eight fifteen tardy bell.

Late or not, school is where I should be headed too.

Instead I stop in front of a run-down little shack that
looks like it's been crammed between two larger, much
nicer buildings. The faded sign out front reads *Marco's
Mini-Mart*.

Taking a few seconds to catch my breath, I pull out my phone to listen to the voicemail again.

Voicemail from Elsie
"Come to Marco's before school. Emergency!"

If there's one thing I've learned about Elsie Rodriguez during our first year as classmates, it's that the girl can exaggerate. When I say there's an emergency, then best believe something major has happened. But Elsie is another story—when she uses the word "emergency," it could just mean the delivery guy is late with the robot parts for her latest science project.

Either way, being best friends means showing up for each other no matter what—even if that requires blowing my perfect attendance record. Which I should've earned on Friday, I might add, but we've got to make up for that random snow day back in January.

I head into the store. If the outside of the building is sketchy, inside's even worse. The place is dimly lit, just bright enough to reveal sections of paint missing from the walls. This is *supposed* to be a convenience store selling drinks and snacks, but every time I've picked anything up, it's already expired. I don't think that soda cooler has ever worked.

And did I mention the store always has the faint smell of rotten eggs? Like, *always*.

I scrunch up my nose and cut through the candy aisle. Up ahead, some poor guy looks completely unimpressed by the chip selection. *Same here, mister.* I scoot past him and head for the register.

A big, bald bodybuilder guy in a *Muscles Win Tussles* T-shirt stands behind the counter. His eyes narrow at my approach.

I squint right back at him. Suddenly tufts of bright red fur appear on his head and neck, and two curved tusks jut from his jaw.

But then I blink, and he looks human again. That's the benefit of the more expensive glamours—even my True Sight eye drops only work for a few seconds before the disguising enchantment kicks back in. This one is definitely something from Vivi LaBoom's City-Camouflage Casual Collection.

I clear my throat and politely ask, "May I use your restroom?"

He crosses his thick arms and looks me over before grumbling, "And why should I let you?"

I grin and roll my eyes. "C'mon, Tiny. I'm already late for school."

A slow smile splits Tiny's face and he lets out a bellowing laugh. "No 'Hello' . . . No 'How is your day?' . . . Just 'Give me key.'"

"Pretty please?" I ask.

"Fine, fine. Anything for a fellow human."

I lean in, lowering my voice to a whisper. "Just so you know, we don't usually call each other humans."

Tiny scratches his bald head, his confused eyes flashing bright yellow before changing back. "But why? You are human, yes?"

I nod. "It's just . . . we assume everyone we meet is human, so there isn't any reason to mention it."

His shoulders droop dramatically. "So many things to remember to fit into human world."

I give him a reassuring pat on the arm. "You'll get the hang of it."

Tiny nods and reaches under the counter. I hold out my hand, and he drops the restroom key into my palm.

"Um, excuse me?" That guy from before pops out from behind the chips rack. "I asked about the bathroom a few minutes ago and you said it was out of order."

Tiny frowns. "Out of order for *you*. Perfectly fine for her. Any questions?"

The guy looks ready to protest, but an inhuman growl from Tiny seems to change his mind.

"Be careful," Tiny says to me in a low voice. "That one has look of a Watcher."

I bite my lip. Watchers are folks who're convinced there's more to the world than meets the eye. According to them, there's this huge global conspiracy to hide the fact that supernatural creatures from myths and legends are real and secretly live among us.

These guys have websites and chat rooms and members

all over. They try to find evidence that will prove to the world that they're right. Which is probably why Mr. Watcher guy is hanging around a convenience store that's clearly not *really* a convenience store.

Most people just think Watchers are conspiracy theorists and don't pay them any attention. But I kinda have to take them serious—because not only are they right, but I'm part of an organization, the Bureau of Supernatural Affairs, that's committed to making sure the proof they're so desperate to find never ever gets out.

Sure enough, when I glance back over my shoulder I find the Watcher guy's eyes on me. He fumbles through his pockets for a phone—then has the nerve to start recording us!

"Can you give me a distraction?" I whisper to Tiny.

He grins and steps from behind the counter. "This I *can* do well." He throws his arms open and shouts, "Congratulations, sir! You are big winner!"

The man furrows his brow as Tiny puts a thick arm around his shoulders and guides him toward the counter. "B-but I didn't enter any contest . . ." The poor guy whips his head around frantically, trying to find me, but I've already ducked down the candy aisle toward the restroom at the back of the store.

I ignore the giant *Out of Order* sign plastered across the door and stick the key in the lock. Then I take one more glance behind me to make sure the coast is clear.

The Watcher guy frowns up at Tiny. "You're saying I won . . . a mop bucket?"

"Quality mop bucket," Tiny answers. "Used many times and never leak."

I grin and twist the doorknob.

The real Marco's, the one behind this door, isn't just a different kind of store, it's practically a different world. Marco's Fine Desserts is only open to the city's supernatural community—meaning no disguises or glamours necessary—and it's got the best magical treats in Atlanta. Midas Milkshakes that stain your teeth bright gold, Stardusted Scones to give your skin a faint glow, and even the World's Best Bad Coffee, which tastes so awful it shocks you into perfect wide-awakeness. The moment I step inside, sweet smells fill my nose and I'm instantly in a great mood.

I squeeze between a couple of harpies, careful to duck beneath their wings. A tall yeti in a chef's hat literally barks a hello from behind the counter, and I wave back. "Hi, Marco!" But the distraction nearly causes me to trip over a boggart, which thumbs its hooked nose at me and mumbles something about "rude humans" before waddling off.

I spot Elsie at a table with another Bureau kid, Julia Farsight, whose heavy eyelids always make her look sleepy. I rush over.

"Okay," I say, slipping into the seat across from them. "What's so important that we needed to meet here before school?"

Elsie frowns. "I don't think I used the word *important*."

"You literally said it was an emergency."

"No," she says. "I said 'emerge and see.'" She grins

mischievously. "As in 'emerge and see' what I've got for you!"

Julia giggles.

"*Els* . . . this is going to cost me a perfect attendance certificate. And you know how much Mama cares about stuff like that. The lady has already got a spot picked out on her wall."

"Don't worry," she says. "Bear's bringing his dad's spare transporter so we can be at school in an instant. As long as we're on the bus when it leaves for the Georgia Aquarium, Mr. Ames will count us as present."

"Teleporting to school is allowed?" I ask. "Because I've been taking the city bus all year."

"*Allowed* might be a strong word," says Elsie.

"As far as I know, it's not *not* allowed . . . ," Julia adds in her singsong voice.

I wince. "I'm really looking forward to starting summer camp tomorrow, so maybe let's not get kicked out of the Bureau before then?"

Elsie just smiles and starts tapping on her cell phone. "Would they really kick out somebody who's getting headlines like this?" She flips the phone around and shows me all the search results for my name she's found on the othernet—the protected portion of the internet reserved for the supernatural world. "They're all *nice* articles."

"Even *Better Gnomes & Gardens* wrote about you," says Julia. "We've got a colony of gnomes on our property and it's a real pain to get them to talk about anything other than flowers, so that's a real accomplishment. You're practically a celebrity."

"Yeah," says Elsie. "Look around."

I don't have to, because I know she's right. Supernaturals around the dessert shop have been pointing and staring ever since I sat down. A few, I've noticed, even take pictures that I'm sure will end up on Eurgphmthilthmsphlthm—Eurg for short—the supernatural world's leading social media site.

Still, I pick up Elsie's phone and tap on the first link.

AMARI PETERS: THE GOOD MAGICIAN?

The controversial teenager returns to the Bureau this summer

Magicians are known for two things: off-the-charts magic levels and a long history as our world's greatest villains. Despite this, a thirteen-year-old girl seems poised to prove that magicians don't have to be bad. She's already saved the world once and gained fans across the globe in the process. But even that hasn't stopped critics from questioning her true motives. What else could the girl wonder accomplish as a force for good? One thing's for sure, the entire supernatural world is watching!

I frown at the word "villains." The Night Brothers—Vladimir and Moreau—are still who the supernatural world thinks of first whenever magicians are mentioned, and for good reason. Not only did those two start the Ancient War, but Moreau survived to commit horrible crimes for seven hundred years—until last summer, when he was betrayed by his magician protégé, Dylan Van Helsing. Someone I *thought* was my friend. Dylan managed to steal a powerful spell book for Moreau, only to turn on his mentor and keep it for himself. He offered to make me his new partner instead, but I refused. Our magic clashed and I won. Barely.

Even though the whole thing was considered classified, somehow word got out and the supernatural media started asking questions. So the Bureau finally released the footage of our fight, and the supernatural world got to see a magician choose *not* to become a villain. The video instantly went viral across the othernet. There's even memes of me clad in armor, reaching up to call down lightning.

I hand Elsie back her phone. "One viral video doesn't make you a celebrity."

Elsie raises an eyebrow. "Have you checked your follower count recently?"

I pull out my phone, open Instagram, and point to my twenty-three followers—two of whom are sitting at this table. "Not that impressive."

Elsie just rolls her eyes and lays her own phone onto the table. "You know what I mean." She pulls up my Eurg profile.

@Amari_Peters ✅
1.73 million followers

"I didn't know you had *that* many," says Julia. "You're even verified."

"The Ban All Magicians page has twice that many followers," says a grumpy voice over my shoulder.

Ugh. Bear.

This kid got his nickname because he's the tallest student at our middle school and an even bigger bully. He's also the fourth member, and only eighth grader, in our school's Soup Club—short for SUPErnatural club. It's for Bureau kids who know about the supernatural world. Lots of middle schools and high schools have them—sometimes they're even listed in the student handbook. Lucky for us, non-Bureau kids have zero interest in giving up their free period for a club named after soup . . . where you don't actually eat any.

"Bear . . ." Julia wags a finger. "Be nice."

Bear drops into the seat beside me, making sure to lean as far away from me as possible. As much as the supernatural world has started to accept magicians over the past year, there are still folks who will always hate me for being a magician like the Night Brothers. No matter what I do.

"We're all here," Bear grumbles. "What's this stupid meeting even about?"

Elsie shoots Bear a look before sitting up straighter. "*Well* . . . I just wanted to say that I've really enjoyed being president of Whitman's Soup Club. And I thought I'd gather the four of us together one last time before we're off to camp. I got you each a gift!"

Julia claps. "I love gifts!"

Even Bear perks up a bit.

But I recognize the look in Elsie's eyes—she's up to something. "What did you do?"

Elsie waves to Marco, and four plates come floating toward our table. "I ordered fortune cookies. *Real* ones."

I gape at the plates landing softly on the table before each of us. "But these things don't just reveal your fortune—they *cost* a fortune too."

Elsie nods. "Only because they're so difficult to make. You have to infuse the dough with used tea leaves from a successful prediction, a Magic 8-Ball has to be present in the room, the stars have to be in the proper alignment, the fire pit you bake it in has to have yielded at least three visions in the past year . . . and those are just the requirements I can remember. This totally drained my science fair winnings, but I happen to think you guys are worth it."

Julia grins and cracks hers open, pulling out the tiny slip of paper and setting it down. It's blank. But then she closes her eyes, whispering to herself before placing a piece of cookie in her mouth.

Suddenly red letters appear on the paper.

"What's it say?" asks Elsie.

Julia holds it up for us to see.

The grass isn't always greener on the other side.

"I asked the cookie if I should switch departments this summer," Julia says. "Guess I should stay in the Department of the Dead. Being a medium *does* make me a good fit."

I remember Julia going onstage at the Welcome Ceremony last summer to touch the Crystal Ball—gaining the ability to talk to ghosts seemed like the last thing she expected. But the Crystal Ball is funny like that; you never know which talent of yours will be upgraded to a supernatural ability. It could be something totally obvious, like turning my super-creative best friend into a mastermind inventor, or something you never imagined.

In my case, the Crystal Ball woke up the magic that had been dormant inside me my entire life. Except humans aren't supposed to have magic until *after* they get to the Bureau. Every member is given a small 10 percent dose at the welcome ceremony, just enough to give us each a supernatural ability. But since I already had magic (and a lot—as in 100 percent magicality), I was labeled a magician. And magicians can use their magic to perform seemingly impossible feats.

That didn't exactly go over very well, and the higher-ups at the Bureau freaked out—some of them even suggested erasing my memories or sticking me in a lab to be studied. Luckily I was given the chance to prove I belonged.

Bear tries his cookie next. He frowns when his fortune comes back as:

Sometimes the real enemy is in the mirror.

He crosses his arms and turns away from us. No chance he's gonna tell us what he asked.

Elsie is up next, and I already know what her question will be. Elsie's a weredragon—only she's never been able to fully shift. The closest she's come is blowing fire a few times. Between her books and her dragon expert adoptive mom, all she knows is that shifting for the first time requires a great act of courage. As the last of her kind, I know it's something that really bothers her.

My best friend closes her eyes and places the cookie into her mouth. She holds her breath as the letters begin to appear on the paper.

Your hard work will pay off.

That girl hollers so loud the whole place jumps.

"Does that mean—" I begin.

"I think so!" She beams. "I might actually shift into a full dragon this summer! *Finally.* Of course, the cookies are only right about seventy percent of the time, but I feel so much better now."

"That's amazing!" I say. "I'm really happy for you."

My turn! I break my own cookie. There's really only one answer I'm looking for.

The whole reason I joined the Bureau last summer was to find out what happened to my missing brother, Quinton, who'd been working there as an agent fighting supernatural crime for years. I eventually found him, but not before Moreau had already put a curse so terrible on Quinton that he still hasn't woken up from it.

At first it was easy to believe that he'd get better. That any day now he'd come home to me and Mama, and everything would go back to how it used to be. But that never happened, and now every day it's a little harder to keep my hopes up. Quinton's spent the last two months getting experimental treatments from cursebreakers in Sydney, Australia, but even they couldn't help.

I go back and forth in my head about whether I should ask. Because what if the answer is no? Would I be okay with that?

I blurt it out before I lose my nerve. "Will my brother ever wake up?"

Elsie grabs my wrist before I can eat the cookie. "Sorry—two things. You can't ask your question out loud. Also, um . . . it has to be about yourself for it to work."

"Oh," I say, deflated. I'm not sure what else to ask. So I place the cookie in my mouth and think. After a few seconds I shrug and ask, *Is there anything important I should know?*

Gasps sound around the table and I look down at my fortune.

Beware of unseen dangers.

2

ONCE WE FINALLY GET TO WHITMAN PREP, ELSIE AND I wait in the side parking lot with all the other students who signed up for Mr. Ames's famous last-day-of-school field trip. Which sounds weird, but Whitman Prep prides itself on making every day a learning day, so it was either visit the Georgia Aquarium or report to the school auditorium for day *five* of Mrs. Laurel performing dramatic readings of various Shakespeare plays.

Believe it or not, it wasn't an easy choice. That lady's acting is so over-the-top that even *Romeo and Juliet* feels like a comedy.

Elsie gives me a nudge with her elbow. "Still worrying about your fortune cookie?"

"It's that obvious?" I ask.

She nods. "Your aura is really yellow."

Reading auras is a perk of being a weredragon. Emotions give off certain colors, called auras, which Elsie can see. Even after a year of being her friend, I still forget sometimes.

"You guys got advice," I say. "But I got a warning."

A bright flash in the darkened clouds overhead shifts my focus upward. For the briefest moment, my mind wanders back to my battle with Dylan. My magic allows me to create illusions, so I still don't get how I was able to summon real lightning to beat him.

"Maybe the 'dangers' are just the normal stuff Junior Agents deal with every summer," says Elsie. "Everyone knows Supernatural Investigations is the most dangerous specialty in the whole Bureau. You're going to be literally fighting bad guys."

"That makes sense," I say. "But why would it say *unseen* dangers?"

Elsie's brow furrows and I can tell she's racking her genius brain for something encouraging to say. Finally she shrugs. "You'll have tons of other agents around whenever that danger does decide to show itself. So don't worry, okay?"

"But—"

TWEEEEP!

The sound of Mr. Ames's whistle has every kid covering their ears, but our biology teacher doesn't seem to notice. "It's nine o'clock! Everybody onto the bus!"

Bear shoves past us. "Clear the way! Eighth grader coming through!"

Elsie and I turn and follow him to the bus door, where Mr. Ames is taking attendance.

"Why the long face, Ms. Peters?" asks Mr. Ames. "Today's a day of excitement!"

I swallow. "I know, I just—"

BOOM! A clap of thunder makes me jump, and suddenly rain begins to pour down.

Me and Elsie dash up the bus steps and find a seat near the back. Through the window, I can see other kids scrambling to get inside.

"Okay, so I'm not saying your fortune was right," Elsie says worriedly. "But I am saying this storm is making me a little queasy."

Biting my lip, I squint through the rain at the black clouds above. Somehow the sky looks—no, *feels*—menacing, like the storm in this scary movie me and Quinton watched forever ago, right before the guy with chainsaw hands appeared.

Maybe I'm just overthinking.

After a nervous twenty minutes, something happens that finally takes my mind off that silly fortune cookie: Elsie yawns.

Which probably doesn't sound like that big a deal, but it's the reason I'm now sitting perfectly still, not making a sound. After two whole months, I'm finally going to win our bet.

Maybe.

See, Elsie's come *close* to dozing off a few times now. She'll give a great big yawn, her eyelids slowly drifting shut. But that's when my luck runs out—the bus will hit a bump in the road that jostles her awake, or somebody's phone will go off, or the kids in the seat in front of us will start another shouting match that no one with ears could sleep through. Last time it was about who would win an arm-wrestling contest between a gargoyle and the world's strongest man. Who even thinks up a question like that?

Besides, it's obvious the gargoyle would win—it'd simply turn its arm into stone and howl with laughter until someone declared a tie. Gargoyles are notorious pranksters who love hiding on old buildings making faces at people behind their backs.

This time, though, when Elsie's eyes close, they stay that way. And when the bus sways a few seconds later and her snoring head slides onto my shoulder, I can't help grinning. This is going to be so perfect—even better than the picture she got of me dozing off during that pep rally a couple months back. Head drooped, mouth open . . . I still don't know how she did it. I swear I only nodded off for a second.

Later at lunch, she bet me that I couldn't get her back. I took her up on that bet, even added to it—the loser gets their photo posted on the winner's Eurg, just in time for the #CaughtEmNapping challenge.

Carefully I reach into my pocket for my phone and then position it for the perfect selfie. I wait until she's right in the middle of a loud snore, then make my silliest face as I reach to snap the picture—

"FANTASTIC!" yells Mr. Ames out of nowhere, jumping to his feet. The bus makes a wide turn, and he stumbles, grabbing the back of a seat to stay upright. I don't think I've ever seen the guy so happy. He's grinning as if he just won the Georgia lottery or something.

Elsie's eyes pop open, and the moment she spots the phone, a smile spreads across her face. "Did you just get me back?"

"Almost," I say with a groan. "Your favorite biology teacher saved you."

Mr. Ames is coming down the aisle now, scanning the seats as he goes. As soon as he finds us, he squats and shows Elsie his phone. "Great news, Ms. Rodriguez! You got accepted—the dean just forwarded the email."

At first Elsie clearly has no clue what he's talking about. Then her eyes go wide. "Wait, you mean Oxford?"

"That's right!" says Mr. Ames. "You rocked the entrance exam and they're offering you a place in their specialist program for exceptionally gifted children. You'll be studying among the brightest minds in the whole world!"

Elsie just stares. "I'm really going to study science and mathematics at Oxford University . . . in England?"

Mr. Ames nods enthusiastically. "From seventh grade to Oxford! I'm so proud of you. What an accomplishment!"

Elsie squeals as she turns to me, and I try to give her my best smile—I really do. She's the most brilliant person I've ever met, but as happy as I am for her, I can't help the sinking feeling that I'm about to lose my best friend. This past school year at Whitman Prep has been the best I've ever had. Mostly because I got to share it with her.

Elsie's smile wavers as she turns back to Mr. Ames.

The guy sniffles and takes off his glasses to wipe his eyes.

"Are you crying?" asks Elsie, embarrassed.

"It's just been such a pleasure to teach you," he says. "The brightest student I've ever had." His eyes shift to me. "Your friend here is going to do amazing things, right, Ms. Peters?"

"Yep." I nod. "Amazing things."

He gets to his feet and gives Elsie another big grin before heading back to his seat.

I try to keep up my own smile, but I'm not sure how well it's going. My mind races with what Elsie leaving could mean for us. Will we even still be friends?

Elsie fiddles with her hands nervously and a long moment passes before she turns to face me again. "Okay, so what are you really thinking?"

"I'm happy for you," I say quickly. "You'll be one of those genius kids they show on the news who graduates college as a teenager. Then you'll go off and cure rare diseases or solve world hunger or something."

Elsie gives me a look. "Be honest, Amari. A blue aura is

the opposite of happy. And yours is *really* blue."

I shrug. "I just wish you'd have told me. I didn't even know you applied." I mean, sure, she's complained about how easy schoolwork is for her. And yeah, she's even mentioned skipping grades before. But how many thirteen-year-olds are applying for college?

"I know," she says. "But, honestly, I didn't take it seriously. I only took the entrance exam because Mr. Ames kept going on about it. I didn't think I had a real shot. Some of the kids in that program got in when they were, like, eight or nine years old. I'm pretty smart, but . . ."

"Pretty smart?" I say. "Elsie, you're *brilliant* and you know it."

Her cheeks go pink, and she grins. "Okay, maybe a little."

I start to laugh, but then another thought comes to mind. "Wait, if you're moving to England, does that mean you'll go to summer camp at the London Bureau next year?"

She opens her mouth to say no, then shuts it. "I didn't really think about that—"

Suddenly the bus begins to shake so hard it rattles the windows and bounces me in my seat. A chorus of nervous shouts goes up.

I turn to look out the window to see what's going on, but it's all fogged up.

That's when everything goes quiet—no more rattling windows, no more voices.

"Els, what's happening?" I ask, turning to her—and gasp.

Elsie's gone completely still, her body hovering a few inches above the seat. The confused expression etched on her face doesn't change. Not even a blink. And her long black ponytail floats motionless above her head. It's almost like I'm staring at a picture of Elsie instead of the real thing—like someone pressed the pause button on her.

I give Elsie a gentle nudge, hoping it might jolt her out of whatever's happening, but it's like touching a mannequin at the mall. She doesn't react at all to my touch—she's completely still.

No, no, no. This isn't right. Heart racing, I get to my feet, looking around the bus for help.

But it's not just Elsie—*no one*'s moving. The kids in the seat in front of us are frozen too, a tangle of arms and legs. And the girl across the aisle floats in midair, eyes wide and arms outstretched for a phone that hovers just out of her reach. Using my forearm, I wipe a bit of fog off the window and feel my heart skip. Even the raindrops are frozen in place.

It's like time has stopped completely. Well, for everyone except me.

Beware of unseen dangers. Is this what the fortune cookie warned me about?

3

My eyes dart frantically around the bus again until they land on Mr. Ames, who's crouched at the very front next to the driver.

I shake out my nerves and scoot past Elsie into the aisle. Maybe whatever is going on didn't affect him, just like it didn't affect me. But the closer I get, the less hope I have. Each row of seats I pass has frozen kids. So by the time I finally do reach Mr. Ames, I'm not surprised to find him and the bus driver frozen too.

I swallow. *Why is this happening?*

And then it's over. Suddenly, there's sound again— movement too. Everything goes back to normal so fast, I jump.

Mr. Ames startles when he turns to find me directly behind him. "Uh, Ms. Peters? Did you need something?"

With my heart still racing, I'm not sure how to respond. "Do you, um, remember what happened? Just now?"

He scrunches his forehead in confusion. "I'm not sure what you mean."

I just stare. How can he not remember being frozen?

Mr. Ames raises an eyebrow. "Is everything okay? Are you wanting to talk about something?" Understanding settles over his face. "Perhaps you're concerned about Ms. Rodriguez leaving?"

I shake my head quickly. "It's nothing. Sorry." I turn and head back to my seat, eyeing the other kids, who carry on joking and laughing with each other like nothing happened. Even if they don't remember being frozen, shouldn't they at least remember the bus shaking? It's all so strange. Only when I get back to Elsie and find her happily tapping away at her phone do I breathe a sigh of relief. I give her the biggest hug. "Thank goodness."

"Um, Amari?" she says. "I haven't made a decision about leaving yet, you know."

I look her in the eyes. "You too? You don't remember *anything*?"

"About what? The Oxford stuff?"

I shake my head. "After that. We were talking and everything just froze. Well, except me."

Elsie lifts an eyebrow. "Everything . . . froze?"

"I'm serious."

My phone starts to beep in my pocket like crazy. And then so does Elsie's. We lock eyes. That only happens for one reason. I pull it out and a notification flashes across the screen:

Red Alert!
Emergency!

Elsie's jaw drops.
"*Told* you," I say.
A text pops up on Elsie's phone.

New Text Message from Bear:
Meet me at the back of the bus.

Of course he'd only text Elsie and not me.

Elsie and I double-check that Mr. Ames isn't looking, then we sneak to the back row. Bear scowls when he sees me but slides over to the window to give us both room to sit.

"Checked out the red alert yet?" he asks, looking past me to Elsie.

Elsie and I both shake our heads. "We came straight back after we got your message."

He holds out his phone and taps on the notification. Elsie and I lean in close to read it:

RED ALERT
The Department of Magical Science confirms

that a massive time freeze occurred over most of Georgia today, with the Department of Half Truths and Full Cover-Ups moving swiftly to correct affected clocks. The cause of such an unprecedented and dangerous display of magic remains unclear.

"Magic?" whispers Elsie.

"That time freeze must've hit our bus," I say. "But—"

"Wait, what?" Bear interrupts, frowning. "I don't remember being frozen."

"Well, you were," I say. "I'm the only one who wasn't. Trust me, it was strange."

Elsie nods, distracted. "Time isn't something you can feel, even if it stops. What I don't get is why they think it's magic related. A magical time freeze that big shouldn't be possible."

"Isn't it obvious?" asks Bear. "Amari just admitted it didn't affect her. It's got to be another magician trick."

I roll my eyes at that. "Of course *you'd* think that."

Elsie looks between us and pales. "A freeze grenade can stop time around one person for maybe a minute, but even that takes an incredible amount of magic—and they take months to recharge. For something like this your magic would have to be off the charts, like . . ." She looks right at me as her words trail off.

"Like a magician?" Bear sneers and crosses his thick arms. "Think about it. Wouldn't it make sense for whoever set off the time freeze to make sure they couldn't be trapped by their own spell? For a magician to make it magician-safe?"

I glare at Bear. Mostly because that *does* make sense. A knot of dread starts to twist in my belly. This couldn't really be a magician's fault, could it?

Elsie drops her eyes. "We shouldn't just assume."

Bear doesn't seem to hear her. He's too busy frowning at his phone. "I'm missing the next update." He taps the screen a few times, and suddenly I hear the voice of Director Van Helsing, head of the Department of Supernatural Investigations. He adjusts the volume so that only we can hear.

Van Helsing: . . . magic unlike we've ever seen before.

Reporter: What can you tell us, Director?

Van Helsing: This was no harmless accident, but rather a targeted attack on our very way of life. It will not be tolerated and it will not *go unanswered.*

Reporter: Any idea what or even who could've caused it?

Van Helsing: Magic this dangerous, on this scale, has traditionally been the dark work of magicians. And it's with that in mind that emergency measures shall be taken to ensure the safety of our world.

The clip ends and Bear sits back, his smirk widening. "Hear that! Bet they got your jail cell in Blackstone already picked out."

"Just shut up, okay?" My knot of dread has bloomed into full-blown panic.

Bear just laughs in my face.

I turn to Elsie. "Can Van Helsing do that?"

It's Bear who answers. "You bet he can!"

"This isn't fair." Elsie's jaw tenses like it does whenever she gets frustrated. "Amari was sitting right next to me."

"You sure about that?" Bear asks. "Because when I got up to ask Mr. Ames something, *you* were dozing off. Matter of fact, it looked to me like Amari was watching you, waiting for you to fall asleep. Looking for her chance to cast that spell, I think."

I shake my head. "I was trying to win a bet! Besides, my magic makes illusions. I don't know anything about stopping time. You heard Elsie—magic that powerful isn't possible."

"That's the thing about you magicians," he answers. "You're always doing stuff that shouldn't be possible. Heck, everyone knows you stirred up a nasty thunderstorm last summer and brought down lightning on Dylan Van Helsing. That wasn't just an illusion, now was it?"

I don't answer. That spell may have started as an illusion, but the lightning was very real.

Bear continues. "I'll bet it's no coincidence that there's another bad thunderstorm outside right now. Maybe that's your secret—who knows what kind of magic you're hiding."

"I'm out of here." I get up and stomp back up the aisle, Elsie close behind me.

When we get back to our seats, Elsie says, "The fact that they're calling this an attack and not an accident means there's more to the freeze than they're telling us."

I nod. "What do you think Director Van Helsing meant

by 'emergency measures'?"

I don't have to wait long to get my answer. An email pops onto my phone. It's from the Bureau.

> Amari Peters,
> You are hereby UNINVITED to summer camp
> at the Bureau of Supernatural Affairs effective
> immediately.
> > —Office of the Deputy Minister of the
> > Supernatural World Congress

4

Turns out that awful storm knocked out the power to much of downtown Atlanta, including the Georgia Aquarium, so we end up turning around and heading back to Whitman Prep. As soon as we arrive, Mr. Ames disappears with Elsie to spread the Oxford news around school. The rest of us get sent to the auditorium to watch Mrs. Laurel wail inconsolably through the ending of *Macbeth*.

Not that I'm listening much. All I can think about is being uninvited to summer camp. If I'm not allowed back at the Bureau, how am I supposed to see Quinton? The only thing that got me through the months he spent receiving treatment in Australia was knowing I'd eventually get to see him this summer. What if he gets worse and I'm not there?

I need to talk to someone . . . like Maria Van Helsing. Dylan and I weren't the only magicians who got outed last summer. Maria, Dylan's older sister, was too. Turns out, the prestigious Van Helsing family had been secretly passing down their own magic to select members of the family for centuries.

Maria is also the reason I can't take all the credit for changing folks' minds about magicians. She's way more famous than me, not only as a Van Helsing, but also as one-half of VanQuish, along with Quinton. Before he got cursed, they were one of the most accomplished Special Agent teams ever. They've even got action figures.

If anyone can tell me more about what's going on, it'll be her.

But when I tap on the Eurg app, an error message pops onscreen.

Error! Othernet Access Denied

For a few seconds I can only stare. Being uninvited to camp is bad enough, but now I can't even use the othernet? It feels like I'm not just being kicked out of the Bureau, but the entire supernatural world. This is all so incredibly unfair. It makes me want to scream.

I settle for sending Elsie a quick text instead. She replies instantly.

If Elsie's mom is talking to the principal, does that mean Elsie's definitely leaving? And not only that, I was sort of counting on Elsie's driver to give me a ride home.

So now I've got to take the city bus.

It's just my luck that a pale-skinned orc sits down beside me. He's so huge he takes up like three seats. Nobody else pays any attention because people don't notice what they don't expect to see. Well, that and he's wearing a trench coat and a ton of Unsightly brand eye-repellent—it makes people not even want to look at you. It's also the bare minimum disguise the Bureau requires for supernaturals to go out in public. Only my True Sight eyedrops allow me to notice his wide, flat head and solid black eyes. His thick arms burst through his sleeves in places.

The orc catches me staring and snarls.

I've ridden the bus with enough supernaturals that I'm not offended. Sure, there are times when a snarl means "I'm going to eat you for lunch," but most of the time it just means something like, "It's a hundred degrees outside and I've still got to wear this trench coat!"

I just smile and point to the newspaper he's pretending to read, whispering, "You've got it upside down."

But that only seems to annoy him. He folds the paper and frowns. "Who do you think you are—"

I see the exact moment the orc realizes I'm Amari

Peters, the magician girl, as his words trail off and his whole body goes suddenly stiff. That snarl becomes a whimper as he gets up from his seats and slinks as far from me as it's possible to go.

Right, I think, *because I'm the scary one in this situation.* Does the Bureau blaming magicians for the time freeze mean everyone will be afraid of me again? Will this one thing—that isn't even my fault!—really erase all the good I did last summer?

Nearly forty-five minutes later, I step off the bus at the end of my block, my belly still doing anxious flips. That was a long time to do nothing but worry.

As stressed as I feel, it's the complete opposite of the mood at the Rosewood housing projects. Now that the rain has stopped, it's practically a block party here in "the 'Wood," with all the kids and grown-ups packing the sidewalks. Music booms from windows and car stereos, and people are out laughing and dancing and having a good time. Especially the little kids splashing in rain puddles.

A few people nod or say "what up" as I pass. Most folks in the 'Wood know me from being Quinton's little sister. He's practically a local legend for getting into two Ivy League schools, and for all the good he did with the neighborhood tutoring program. Of course, nobody around here knows what he *really* did after high school. The saddest part is that because of the curse, he's never been able to come home, so people still think he's missing.

But that doesn't stop people from celebrating him. To

my neighbors, it's enough that he was from here. One good story to go up against all the bad ones that outsiders like to tell about us.

Jayden, a friend from the neighborhood, waves at me from the other side of the street. If he were next to me, he'd swear all the people greeting me is proof that I'm just as big a deal as my brother was. But then that boy is always trying to boost my head up like that.

As if I wasn't already feeling awful about summer camp, seeing Jayden hurts big-time. Of all the things I accomplished last year, being able to nominate him for a tryout this summer is at the top of the list. Tomorrow will be his first time at the Bureau, and I won't even be there to look out for him like I promised.

I'm frowning as I reach my apartment building. Out of habit I glance toward Mrs. Walters's window and stop cold when I see that it's empty.

Mrs. Walters is *always* in that window. Doesn't matter the time or the day, she sits right there so she doesn't miss one second of everyone else's business. Even keeps a notebook to jot stuff down so she won't forget. That lady's the nosiest person I've ever met.

She also happens to be a witch disguised as an old woman—not that I had any idea about her real identity until last summer. Contrary to what people think, witches aren't human at all. That bright green skin is a dead giveaway.

An idea pops into my head. Mrs. Walters might just be nosy enough to know something about the time freeze.

Maybe enough to point me in the direction of who caused it.

It's a long shot, but it's worth a try. I jog past my doorway and give her door a soft knock. Even with all the noise in the street I can hear music coming from inside.

Nobody answers. But the door *is* slightly ajar. That's strange, and it makes me a little worried.

"Hello? Anyone here?" I push the door open just wide enough to peek inside. All the witch's belongings seem to be shoved into one corner. A bundle of broomsticks hovers in midair, and dusty old books fill up a large copper cauldron. But my eyes go directly to the shirt folding other shirts and packing them neatly into the suitcases. Kinda gives "work shirt" a new meaning.

What's going on? Is Mrs. Walters moving?

"Um, excuse you?" Mrs. Walters yanks the door fully open. "You lost or something?"

I can barely see her face behind a thick scarf and giant shades, then my True Sight kicks in and her brown skin shifts to its natural green. Her nose lengthens until it's pointy and crooked, and her chin juts out so far that her face looks like a half-moon from the side. Exactly like the Wicked Witch of the West.

It's not the first time I've seen her true appearance, but the change still throws me.

"I—I didn't see you in the window, and . . ." I tilt my head as I hear a familiar song coming from the other room. "Wait, since when do you listen to rap?"

Mrs. Walters smiles a wide gap-toothed grin and does

a little shimmy in the doorway. "These feet been cutting a rug for centuries, baby! We just having ourselves a lil going-away party."

Going away? I glance back to the luggage. *To where?*

"See if the girl knows how to play spades!" someone shouts from farther inside.

Mrs. Walters looks me over like she's sizing me up. "Well, do you?"

I'm almost offended by the question. Spades is practically the national pastime for Black folks in the South. You can't even show up to certain cookouts if you don't know how to play. I give her my most confident smile. "Of course. But—"

"Then come on in!" She pulls me inside and shuts the door.

"Uh, Mrs. Walters?" I say as she guides me toward the next room. "I really just came to ask you about the time freeze . . ."

"Girlie, hush that fuss and pull up a chair."

"But—" My mouth drops open. Two more identical-looking Mrs. Walterses sit at the dining table. It takes a few seconds before their glamours fade too and I can see the witches underneath. One is tall and skinny, the other short and stout.

"You're *all* Mrs. Walters?" Well, that explains how she's always in that window. I mean, there've been times when me and Mama were leaving the grocery store and Mrs. Walters was only just entering, yet she'd still be sitting in that window when we got home. Used to creep me out.

"That's right," says Short Witch. "We could only get our hands on one fake ID to be in this city, being wanted criminals and all—"

"Shh!" Tall Witch shivers. "There you go tellin' all our business. She works for the Bureau, remember? She could turn us in."

I glance between them. Did she really just say *criminals*?

Short Witch rolls her eyes. "Well, we leaving, ain't we? Besides, being a magician and all, I reckon this girlie's got much bigger concerns than four witches on the run."

"But you guys were wrongfully accused, right?" I laugh nervously. "Like, you didn't actually do anything . . ."

None of them quite meet my eyes. That answers that.

I take another glance around the room. "Didn't you say there are four of you?"

Tall Witch leans her head back and laughs. "That's Dottie over there in the jar."

"The frog?" I ask, eyes wide.

"That's right," says Short Witch. "House rules say you cheat, you get an hour in the jar. So I do hope you know how to play fair."

I swallow. What in the world have I been dragged into?

"Why don't you go over to the desk and pick out a deck of cards," says the Mrs. Walters who answered the door.

I decide to think of her as "First Witch" and make my way over to the desk. There's a red deck with menacing dark eyes etched on the back and a blue deck with a frowny face. "Either one?"

"They're both enchanted, so choose wisely!"

I glance back and forth between the blue and red cards. "Enchanted how?"

"Oh, girlie, a witch's deck is never harmless. Some cards bite!"

"Some cards fright!"

"And some cards set your clothes alight!"

They all burst into laughter. "And that's not all those cards do. But we wouldn't want to spoil the fun!"

I don't like the sound of that. I bite my lip for a second and think. I *do* need information, but there's got to be a way to get it without getting hexed. I decide to play along but promise myself to quit the game the second I get them to tell me whatever they know about the time freeze. They won't be sticking me in a jar with Dottie if I can help it.

I grab the blue deck and head back to the table. Tall Witch starts to deal the cards, and I'm just about to start asking about the time freeze when I notice one of my cards shimmying across the table toward Short Witch, who scoops it up.

"Hey, that's mine!" I say. "We're on the same team."

"Says who?" Short Witch taunts. "This here is Witch's Spades. Every witch for herself."

First Witch shakes her head. "Best mind your cards if you mean to play with us."

I frown at these weird rules. If stealing cards is allowed, then what's considered cheating?

When my next cards come, I form a neat stack and

cover them with my hand. A quick glance around the table tells me all three witches are taking this game super serious.

"So . . . ," I begin. "That time freeze was kinda crazy, huh?"

That seems to snap their focus. Short Witch frowns and shakes her head. "You *would* know all about that, wouldn't ya?"

"I don't know anything," I say quickly. "I hoped you might've heard something—like who caused it or how it was done."

"Don't know nothing," she snaps, "and don't wanna know nothing. Ain't my business."

Now I'm the one staring. *Since when has anything not been these witches' business?*

"Oh, I know what you're thinking," follows Tall Witch with a frown. "But even we've got our limits."

I glance among the three of them. "Do you think it could happen again? Another time freeze? Maybe somewhere else?"

"Ain't another freeze we're concerned with. It's all the funny business that's been going on with this one."

I lean forward in my seat. "Like what?"

"Like how we haven't heard from the Prime Minister yet. Any time something major happens, Merlin wastes no time hopping on the othernet to say everything's gonna be okay. But he ain't said a doggone word today, has he?" She leans closer, grimacing. "Instead, we hear it's that awful Deputy Minister making all the moves."

I think back to the message uninviting me to the Bureau. It was signed by the Office of the Deputy Minister.

Tall Witch makes a fretful face and places a card at the center of the table. It's a ten, but not in any suit I recognize. Instead of hearts, diamonds, clubs, or spades, this card has little jester hats.

"The ten of pranks," says First Witch, laying down a queen with the same symbol.

Short Witch follows with the king.

I quickly glance through my own cards. None are familiar, but I know enough about spades to know that the ace of pranks should win me the hand. So I play it.

The moment the card touches the table, giant buckets appear over the witches' heads, tipping over to drench them all with water. "Hold your breath!" one of them shouts through the downpour.

I cover my mouth, both in surprise and to keep from laughing, until it stops. "What just happened?"

"You won the hand," says Tall Witch, shaking out her dripping wet robes. "Prank cards are never fun. No rhyme or reason to what they'll do. It's on you to play the next card, girlie."

I nod, still a bit frazzled. "So, um, who *is* the Deputy Minister?"

"Bane," says Short Witch with a snarl.

Tall Witch shivers. "Don't much blame you for not wanting to keep a wretched thing like that in your memory."

"It begs the question, though, don't it . . . ?" asks First

Witch. "Only reason for the Deputy Minister to take charge is if the Prime Minister ain't available."

I sit up straighter. "Are you saying something might've happened to Merlin?" You'd never know it from his hunched figure and mottled tree-bark skin, but the old elf led the supernatural world's armies against the Night Brothers in the Ancient War, and he's been leading the supernatural world as Prime Minister ever since. "Isn't he, like, the most magical being in the supernatural world?"

"Was till *you* came along, wasn't he?" says Short Witch.

My cheeks burn. "I guess so." The difference is Merlin has had centuries to master his magic, and I'm still a beginner.

First Witch leans back in her seat. "If it ain't magicians behind all this, wouldn't surprise me one bit if that Bane fella is. He'll be calling himself *Prime Minister* Bane any day now, just you watch. And that'll be especially bad for everyone in this room."

"Really? Why?"

Short Witch leans forward and juts out her chin. "For all the carrying on about how smart you Peters kids are, you sure don't show it! You do know that Bane is a wraith, doncha?"

"Really?" I remember learning about them last summer. "They're cursed, right?"

Tall Witch nods. "One of the nastiest curses there's ever been. Imagine being ripped out of your body and forced to live on forever as a spirit, half in this world and half in the next, a flickering shadow of what you once were."

I don't have to ask who cursed them—the Night Brothers. During the Ancient War, a group of armored knights on horseback charged out to meet them in battle and Moreau unleashed a curse known as the the Living Death. Supposedly it was so awful to witness that the rest of the army ran away.

First Witch shakes her head. "Those wraiths have never forgiven magicians for what happened to them. Bane himself has craved revenge, as he was captain of that cursed squadron. But Merlin, being Prime Minister, held him in check to keep the peace."

It begins to make sense.

"And if Merlin ain't available—like we fear—that means Bane is in charge. He could go after anyone he wanted."

"That's why we're making ourselves scarce. Our coven was among those who broke with the Sisterhood of Witches and joined the Night Brothers. We were young and foolish, lured in by the grandeur of their magic. I reckon Bane will have a list of all those he wishes to get even with. If our names are there, he's gonna have to do some real hard looking to get hold of us."

A car honks outside.

"That's our ride," says Tall Witch.

Short Witch shakes her head. "Not until we finish the turn. You never played your card, girlie."

I offer a weak smile. "Noticed, huh?"

All three nod. "Cards get offended when you stop the game midturn. Can hold a mean grudge too. Punishments for losing will be extra nasty next time we play if the turn isn't ended correctly."

I play my best card, another ace, this one with a screaming-face symbol.

Short Witch and Tall Witch both sulk, unable to beat my card.

But First Witch smiles. "Ace of Horrors, eh?" She slams down a black card with a skull and crossbones. "Ace of Dangers."

If Witch's Spades is anything like real spades, then I've just lost. I wince, waiting for whatever comes next. The lights flicker overhead and sparks of electricity shoot across the table.

"Ouch!" shouts Short Witch, jumping back.

Tall Witch yelps and shakes her hand. "Danger cards are always the worst."

Their eyes turn to me. The electricity from the table skips over my fingers. Only I don't feel a thing. *Whoa.*

I meet First Witch's eyes and she grins. "Reckon that spark is nothing to a girl who commands lightning."

"What else can you do?" asks Short Witch in an awed voice. "I've always wanted to ask, ever since I seen the video of you taking on that Van Helsing boy."

Bear's taunt echoes in my head. *"Who knows what kind of magic you're hiding . . ."*

I swallow. "I honestly don't know."

5

I WAVE AT THE TAXI CARRYING AWAY ALL FOUR MRS. WAL-terses and then head inside my own apartment. I learned a lot from them about Deputy Minister Bane, but nothing that could help me get back into the Bureau. I do know I got uninvited because everyone is sure a magician is behind the time freeze. So the only way back in is to prove it *wasn't* a magician.

Even though my gut tells me that it had to be. As much as I don't want that to be true, why else wouldn't the time freeze affect me? Why would someone other than a magician make a spell magician-safe?

It's all so frustrating. I mean, there is one other possibility. But there's no way they'd be behind this—

"Hey, Babygirl!"

I'm so lost in my own thoughts the words barely register. I throw a half-hearted wave toward the kitchen. "Hey, Mama." I need to get to my room so I can think.

But the smell of Mama's cooking stops me in my tracks.

"Mm-hmm," she says. "I thought this might ungrumpy that face of yours."

"Sorry . . . just thinking about some stuff." I head for the kitchen and she smiles, stirring a long wooden spoon through what's got to be her famous spicy gumbo. My mouth waters like crazy, my belly growling in anticipation. Then it dawns on me why she's cooking so much food. Elsie is supposed to come over for an early dinner. With everything that's going on, I'd completely forgotten.

I text to ask if she's still coming.

New Text Message from Elsie:

On my way

Good. With a little more time together, I'll bet we could have all this figured out. For now, I'm not telling Mama about being uninvited to summer camp. Because then I'd have to explain why, and that would only make her worry.

Mama dips a smaller spoon into the gumbo, then hands it to me.

I let flavor dance over my tongue. It tastes so good I smile around the spoon and, for a second, forget all my problems.

Mama nods like that's exactly the reaction she was waiting for.

Then the aftertaste kicks in and I cough. "Um, you don't think it might be *too* spicy?"

Mama gasps and looks me up and down like I'm a stranger. "No such thing."

I bite down on my lip. "Sometimes you kind of overdo it with the peppers."

Mama's jaw drops, her hands going straight to her hips. "Doesn't stop you from getting seconds, and thirds!"

"But I'm *used* to it. Elsie can literally breathe fire, and she still ain't ready for your gumbo."

Mama tries her best to keep a straight face but she bursts out laughing. Then I'm laughing too.

It's hard to believe that this time last year we were barely speaking to one another. With Quinton missing and her working long hours to keep up with bills, things were just so hard. Thankfully Mama got a promotion that lets her be home more, and I found my brother, even if he hasn't woken up from that nasty curse yet.

I miss him so much. I've got to get myself invited back to summer camp so I can see him.

"Something smells good!"

I turn to find Elsie has just teleported into the living room wearing a bright blue Oxford University T-shirt and carrying a huge duffel bag. It's so big that if you didn't know her, you'd think the girl was moving in with us. But Elsie carries whatever inventions she's working on wherever she goes. Claims you never know when inspiration might strike.

"There you are!" says Mama, waving her over. "Come here and get some of this love." Elsie gives me a little wave and goes to let Mama give her one of those rib-busting auntie-type hugs.

After they embrace, Mama steps back to have a look at my best friend, her eyes going directly to Elsie's T-shirt. "I see you're already thinking about college. Never too early, especially smart as you are."

Elsie goes slightly pink. "Actually, I've already been accepted to Oxford for next fall. I just got the news today."

"My goodness!" says Mama. "I know your family must be so proud."

"They are," Elsie answers, but she doesn't look as excited as she did back on the bus. "This will be me and Amari's last summer together."

Mama's eyes move between us and she seems to catch on that Oxford is a sore topic. "Well, I've got to make a quick run to the corner store to grab some sodas. You two talk things out, okay?"

We both nod and watch her grab the keys and head outside. Then we just sort of stare at one another before I plop down on the couch. "So I guess you made up your mind?"

Elsie's face drops. "Not me—my mom. She pretty much *told* me I'm going. That it's a once-in-a-lifetime opportunity." She sighs and sits next to me. "She's already put in a work transfer for the London Bureau and rented an apartment near campus."

"Oh" is all I can think to say. This is really happening—I'm losing my best friend. "I'm surprised your mom let you come over, with all the time-freeze stuff."

"She refused at first, so I called my grandma and told her about you being uninvited to camp. Grams convinced her that I should be able to say goodbye in person."

I blink and turn my head as my eyes begin to well up. "Well, you said it."

"This *isn't* goodbye," says Elsie. "If this is going to be our last summer, then let's make it count. Let's spend it together at the Bureau."

That's my best friend, always optimistic. I wipe my eyes and meet her determined stare. "I'd love that. But how?"

Elsie's about to answer, but suddenly her phone's other-net app opens on its own. A lady's voice whispers through the speakers. "If possible, find a quiet location for an important announcement."

"What's up?" I ask.

Elsie scoots closer and shows me the screen. A man's stern face fills it up, colorless as a black-and-white photo, flickering and fading into view. At first I think something's wrong with her phone, then realize everything around him shows up crystal clear. The man's cold eyes stare back at us until finally his lips twist into a joyless smile.

A chill runs down my back. A wraith. This must be Bane, the Deputy Prime Minister.

"Once upon a time," he begins, "the supernatural citizens of our world felt safe. But last summer they watched as vicious half-human, half-animal hybrids destroyed the homes of the Bureau's oldest and greatest families. Today I regret to inform you of an even bolder, more sinister attack. Many of you are aware of the brief time freeze that occurred across the state of Georgia this morning. But that doesn't tell the full story. Because one location never unfroze."

Elsie gasps as an image of a giant circular room filled with supernaturals of all kinds appears onscreen. Some are seated at desks, others cling to walls, a few are even perched along the ceiling—all of them frozen in time. And right at the center, standing before a wide podium, his eyes wide and frightened, is Merlin—the Prime Minister.

Elsie and I turn to look at one another, stunned. "Els," I whisper, "the entire Supernatural World Congress is still frozen."

She swallows and nods. Bane continues his speech.

"The great leaders of our world are still trapped, perhaps forever. You may wonder how it came to this. How even the great Merlin himself has fallen victim to such a horrifying fate. And I will tell you how. We've grown *tolerant*."

Bane practically spits the last word.

"It was long ago decided that magicians and all who associated with them would be labeled as UnWanteds and rightfully denied any place in our world. Yet UnWanteds now live openly among us while nothing is done about it. Magicians walk freely about the Bureau, casting spells and calling themselves agents . . ."

My jaw clenches. He means me and Maria.

Elsie shakes her head. "I don't like this one bit."

"Those who are old enough to remember the Ancient War should be ashamed. And those too young should take heed. We must never forget the UnWanteds' crimes and we must never forgive. That is why I am invoking emergency powers to name myself Prime Minister of the Supernatural World, effective immediately. Rest assured, I will put right all that has been set wrong. I will bring these UnWanteds to heel. I will root out every magician scurrying in the shadows. And, above all else, I will restore order to our world. You have my solemn vow."

Bane lifts a hand in front of his face and balls it into a tight fist. "From this point forward, a crime committed by one UnWanted is a crime committed by all. A reckoning is coming!"

≋ 6 ≋

INTERNATIONAL LEAGUE
OF MAGICIANS

FLIP TO THE BACK FOR INSTRUCTIONS. THANKS!

ELSIE'S MOM STARTS BLOWING UP HER PHONE THE SEC-
ond the speech is over, so she heads into my room for
some privacy. If her mom didn't want her here before, I'm
sure it's ten times worse now.

While Elsie's gone, I reach inside her duffel and grab
her laptop. Since I'm banned from using my own othernet
app, it's the only way I can look up that "UnWanted" word
Bane kept using. I've seen it pop up in my Eurg comments
a few times, but I didn't realize it had any special meaning.

> UnWanted—Slang. Derogatory. Name used for
> magicians and other supernaturals who fought
> on the Night Brothers' side in the Ancient War.

Made popular by Abraham Van Helsing in 1315 during his campaign to exclude anyone associated with magicians from supernatural society, particularly those beings created by magicians, such as hybrids and boogeypeople.

I'm an UnWanted. No wonder Bane likes the word—it describes everyone he's come to hate. The witches were right—he's using the time freeze to justify a grudge he's carried for centuries.

But it's not fair! Nearly everyone who fought in the Ancient War has been dead for ages—that war was like seven hundred years ago! Aside from a few folks with really long lives, like the four Mrs. Walterses, it's the UnWanteds' descendants being punished now, and they didn't choose to be UnWanteds any more than I chose to be a magician. Yet we're considered illegal simply for existing.

"This is so messed up," Elsie says, coming back into the room. "My mom says I have to go home."

"Maybe you should," I say. "There's no way I'm getting back into the Bureau now."

"I say we fight back," says Elsie. "You've got over a million followers—you should post something in your own defense. Everyone's seen that video of you stopping Dylan. The supernatural world knows you're a hero no matter what Bane says."

"Except when I got uninvited from the Bureau, my

Eurg account disappeared too. That means I don't have *any* followers anymore."

Elsie's shoulders droop. "There's got to be something we can do."

"This'll sound pretty dumb now," I admit, "but I was thinking, if I could somehow solve the time freeze and clear my name, then maybe it would be enough to get Bane to back off."

My best friend just shakes her head. "Now that he's Prime Minister, I don't think anything will stop him from trying to get his revenge. Even if the supernaturals he's targeting haven't done anything wrong."

"Yeah," I say. "I realize that now."

"Still, figuring out the time freeze is a good idea. Especially if it turns out that an UnWanted didn't cause it. It'll show everyone that Bane's attacking UnWanteds for his own reasons and not to protect the supernatural world like he claims—" Elsie's phone starts buzzing again, but she just takes one look, frowns, and shoves it into her pocket.

"I don't think your mom is going to be too happy about you ignoring her calls."

"True." Elsie grins sneakily. "But technically she can only ground me till camp starts tomorrow."

I can't help but laugh at that.

"This calls for a whiteboard," Elsie announces. "You did get one, right?"

I've been telling her I would all year. "I forgot?"

Elsie shoots me a look. "You *know* you can't do a proper investigation without a whiteboard."

"Is that what this is?" I ask. "Are we officially starting another investigation?"

She grins. "Yep, and since my whiteboard is currently filled with useful equations, we'll need a new one." A few taps on her phone and suddenly there's a knock at the door.

I hop to my feet to answer, just in time for a lady with winged shoes to shove a box into my arms and dash off in a blur. I remove the tape and, sure enough, a brand-new whiteboard is staring back at me.

"I used my mom's Hermes account—instant delivery." She uncaps a black marker and adjusts her glasses. "All right, so who do we suspect caused the time freeze?"

I shrug. "Everyone seems pretty convinced it's a magician."

Elsie nods. "So the first step is to prove that it wasn't."

She makes a quick list.

KNOWN MAGICIANS AND WHY THEY DIDN'T CAUSE THE TIME FREEZE:

The Night Brothers—both deceased

Moreau's apprentices—all deceased except for the Moreau impersonator in Blackstone Prison

Amari—on the bus with me during time freeze

Dylan Van Helsing—locked away in the Sightless Depths

Maria Van Helsing—attending New Teachers meeting at the Bureau

"Did I leave anyone out?" Elsie shows me the board. "Because if not, I think we can safely rule out magicians."

"Actually . . . ," I begin, "there *are* other magicians I haven't told you about."

Elsie's jaw drops. "Wait, really? Who?"

"The League of Magicians. They've been around for centuries."

My best friend stares at me, speechless.

"I know I should've told you," I say. "But they made me promise I wouldn't reveal them to anyone. It just doesn't seem fair to keep it from you now when we're investigating magicians."

"Okay," says Elsie, still looking flustered. "So I'm guessing no one at the Bureau knows about these magicians either?"

"Maria Van Helsing would," I say. "She's a member."

"And you? How many members are there?"

"I was invited after the whole Dylan thing, but I never gave them an answer. I'm not sure exactly how many there are—a few hundred maybe?"

"H-hundred?" Elsie stammers. "There are hundreds of magicians out there that nobody knows about?"

"Um . . . yes?"

"Do you think any of them could've caused the time freeze?" she asks.

"That's the thing," I say. "They take being secret super seriously. There's no way they'd do something that could bring attention to themselves. Especially something as bold as freezing the leaders of the supernatural world."

"Well, is there someone you can ask? Is there like a special magic phone you guys use or something?"

"Hold on." I sprint into my room, drop to the floor, and reach beneath my dresser for a small white business card. It was given to me last summer by the League's steward. I head back into the living room and show it to Elsie.

She reads aloud, "'International League of Magicians.'" Then flips it over, where tiny writing is inscribed:

A MAGICIAN MAY PLACE THIS CARD AGAINST ANY MIRROR TO REACH THE LEAGUE STEWARD

"I still can't believe there's this whole society of magicians nobody knows about," says Elsie. "You have to ask this steward person if he knows anything about the time freeze!"

"I know, but it's complicated. Remember the video of me and Dylan's fight, when he was trying to recruit me to his side? How he made a really big deal about the two of us being born with magic? How it made us special? Well, the League of Magicians believes the same thing. I'm kind of scared what they might have planned for me. What if they turn out to be just as bad?"

Elsie nods. "I get it. You know I'm the biggest wimp in the world—"

I start to interrupt her, but she shakes her head.

"We both know it's true," she says. "It's the reason I've never fully shifted into a dragon. I've never done anything brave enough to make it happen. But that's not you. Amari, you're the bravest person I know. As many fans as you have now, I remember when everyone hated you just for being a magician. But you didn't let that stop you from saving the world. You're still the same girl you were then. Go and get the answers you're looking for. It's the only way we can be sure that magicians are innocent."

I suck in a deep breath, then blow it out. It really is the only way to be sure. "You're right, as always. It's time for me to be brave." If super-sweet Maria Van Helsing is a member, they can't be *that* bad, right?

Elsie smiles. "I'm also really curious to see how this card works . . . from a scientific standpoint, of course."

I grin. "Whatever you say."

We head into the bathroom and flick on the light. The card said to place it against the mirror to reach the steward. But reach him how exactly?

Elsie adjusts her glasses. "Do you think it's like Face-Time and his face will just appear in the mirror?"

I shrug. "Maybe stand in the doorway—just in case. You aren't supposed to know about them, remember?"

She nods and steps just out of view.

I decide to test the card out, letting it just barely touch the glass. To my surprise, the mirror ripples like water in response. Elsie and I exchange glances.

"The card said to place it against any mirror to REACH

the League steward," I say. "Maybe I'm supposed to . . . *reach* inside?"

Elsie gives me a thumbs-up.

Before I can chicken out, I push the entire card through the mirror. The surface swirls around my wrist, which suddenly feels cold and wet. I look to my best friend in alarm, but the mirror yanks me inside. One second I'm standing in my bathroom, and the next I'm pulled into freezing water that chills me to my bones. I try to snap my mouth shut, but it's already full. My eyes dart frantically back and forth.

I'm shivering like crazy, and it's pitch-dark nearly everywhere I look. But below me, far in the distance, something glows, so I kick off in that direction. *Please let me get there before I need another breath.*

It just seems so far away. Too far.

I concentrate on putting one arm in front of the other, kicking hard with my legs and willing myself toward the light. Everything burns—my muscles and especially my lungs. Until finally, *finally,* I get close enough to make out the shape of a man standing in a brightly lit doorway. He's moving his arms, and I realize he's waving me forward.

I use what strength I've got left to make one last push. Two hands reach out and pull me inside . . . where it's completely dry.

With a thump I land on the hardwood floor. I'm coughing and spitting up water, but I made it. Thank goodness.

Cosimo Galileo Leonardo de' Pazzi—Cozmo to those who know him—the steward of the League of Magicians, pats my back. "My dear girl, are you quite all right?"

I'm too busy inhaling a lungful of air to do anything but nod.

"It just so happens I was making arrangements to pay you a visit in the morning, and here you are. Impeccable timing."

"Why did your card try to drown me?" I ask as soon as I'm able.

Cozmo frowns. "That's a security measure, I'm afraid. There is always the chance that a nonmagician might find a card and try to use it. Had you provided some proof of magic, the house would've sucked you right through the front door."

"Proof of magic?"

"Literally a spell of any kind," he explains. "It's a real shame you haven't been taught our ways."

I'm not sure what to say to that. It's not like I've been very eager to explore my magician side. Though I'm sure Maria would've told me if I'd asked.

"What's done is done, I suppose. It's a wonder you made it through. Large, hungry things prowl these depths at night. Not the least of which is the Loch Ness Monster. Has a particular fondness for the taste of magicians, that one. Always swimming outside the windows with those glowing eyes."

"Where . . . are we?" I ask, glancing around at a fancy living room filled with expensive-looking furniture.

Cozmo looks confused. "Why, my lake house, of course.

You do realize you're at the bottom of Loch Ness . . . the lake . . . don't you?"

It takes me a moment to wrap my head around that. "How did the house even get down here?"

Cozmo ignores the question. "You know, I wondered whether or not I was doing the right thing by planning to go see you, but now that you're here there can really be no doubt. It's fate! It's entirely meant to be!"

I frown. "What's meant to be?"

"Follow me—and do hurry. The house throws a fit whenever guests arrive before it's ready to receive anyone. It can be quite a rude host when it's in a mood."

As if in answer, the whole building shakes in irritation. Brooms and mops and dusters glide out of the next room and begin to furiously clean the area around us.

Cozmo puts his hands on his hips and raises his voice. "Our guest doesn't care if you're still a bit messy, do you, Amari?"

I just stare.

"Tell it," Cozmo whispers. "Tell the house it's quite clean enough already."

"Oh, um, right." I nod along. "Wow, uh, this is one *clean* house. I sure wish my apartment looked this good." I'm not sure how convincing I sound, but the house at least stops its shaking, and the cleaning supplies glide back through the doors.

"Good," says Cozmo. "Things are already quite stressful

enough without having to deal with a self-conscious bag of bricks."

The lake house rumbles again.

"I'm kidding!" Cozmo winces and turns to me. "Let's get to the study before it starts rearranging the hallways in protest."

Cozmo starts to turn, but I reach to stop him. I came here for a reason, and it wasn't for a tour. I need answers.

"Before we go anywhere," I say, "I want to know if anyone from the League of Magicians is responsible for the time freeze."

Cozmo seems annoyed by the question. "I can say with absolute certainty that no League magicians caused that catastrophe. You should remember that magicians are far from the only beings with powerful magic."

As relieved as I am, that doesn't help me figure out who *is* responsible. I'm sure I know the answer to my next question, but I decide to ask anyway. "Is there any chance there are magicians out there who aren't part of the League?"

"Absolutely none," Cozmo says confidently. "There are only ever two born magicians in an age—you and Dylan now, and the Night Brothers before you. We in the League are magicians because Vladimir chose to share his magic and we have passed it down through the generations. Rest assured, should any League magician wish to leave our order, they won't be taking their magic with them."

If what he's saying is true, then magicians really aren't

behind the time freeze. "How would you explain the time freeze not affecting me? I was the only one on my bus who wasn't frozen."

Cozmo raises an eyebrow. "That *is* an interesting question. I have my theories, but that really is a conversation for another day. We have far more pressing concerns. Follow me!"

"But—"

He darts off toward a doorway, giving me no choice but to follow. Where are we even going? And what's more pressing than the time freeze when magicians are being blamed for it?

I trail him down twisting hallways, through a pitch-black room, across shifting balconies where we jump from one side to the other, and then into a great big dining room with a fancy twirling chandelier. Finally we reach a very short hallway with a dead end.

I bend over to catch my breath again. "What's . . . the rush?"

Cozmo isn't the least bit winded. "Disaster could strike at any moment! Ever since Bane declared his intention to root out hidden magicians, the League has been in an uproar. I'm doing my very best to advise calm, but it's only a matter of time before Bane gets too close. I shudder to think what might happen if a magician felt threatened and lashed out. It would be a disaster."

"Can't you just tell them not to?" I ask. "Aren't you in charge?"

"I am merely the League's steward, meaning my authority is temporary and hardly complete. I'm meant to guide magiciankind only until a born magician can take over as its rightful leader. It was my full intention to give you and Dylan more time to grow up, to become wiser and more skilled in your magic. To choose for yourselves whether you wish to bear this burden. But that is no longer an option."

So I *was* right to worry about the League's fascination with born magicians. But he can't mean what I think he means. "What's no longer an option?"

Cozmo bows low before me. "Amari Peters, I'm offering you full leadership of our order. To be yours until death."

He can't be serious. "You want *me* to lead the League of Magicians?"

"You must! The League is in disarray!"

"What makes you think they'll listen to me?" I say. "I'm *thirteen*!"

Again he ignores me and instead lifts his gaze to the ceiling. "House, reveal the Crown!" Suddenly the walls begin to slide away and the dead-end hallway opens up, revealing a small room with a pedestal at its center. A shimmering black crown sits atop it on a velvet pillow.

I feel myself moving toward it before I even realize what I'm doing. My head goes fuzzy, and warmth fills my chest just like it does when I cast a spell.

I shake my head to clear the haze. "What *is* that?"

"A treasure handed down from one of the Night Brothers: the Crown of Count Vladimir."

A memory comes crashing into my mind—the last time I was in the same room as something belonging to the Night Brothers. The Black Book that Dylan stole from the Bureau's vault.

"It's my duty to present it to you," Cozmo continues. "The League has passed down Vladimir's magic through the generations. But it's still Vladimir's—whoever wears his Crown can summon all of it. Your spells wouldn't merely draw upon the magic in your own blood as they do now, but on that of hundreds of magicians. I'd claim this power for myself if I could, but the Crown can be worn only by a born magician." He looks at me seriously. "Will you accept it? Take your place on the Midnight Throne and lead us against our enemies!"

He means Bane—and the agents he'll send after the magicians. "Is the Bureau your enemy?"

Cozmo's eyes grow hard. "You might possess some loyalty to the magician hunters in the Bureau of Supernatural Affairs, but my concern, first and foremost, will always rest with the survival of magiciankind."

I shake my head. "You want me to choose between the Bureau and the League?"

"I'm asking you to choose between what you'd like to be and what you already are—what you've always been. Being a magician is in your blood, child. You think you have magic now, but the Crown will grant you more than you even thought possible—you would be stronger than any magician who has ever lived. No one could stand against you."

The thrill in his voice stirs the growing sense of dread inside me. It's clear that I've made a terrible mistake coming here. How can I accept the Crown when I barely understand the magic I have? "What do you want me to do with all that power?"

"Defend us," says Cozmo. "Lead us into war if need be. Bane has forced our hand. Our very existence wavers on a knife's edge. It would only take the capture of one magician to reveal our existence to the supernatural world. We must act, and we must act now."

Suddenly I feel dizzy. Is Cozmo really asking me to turn against all the people I care about at the Bureau? Including Quinton?

Is he really suggesting a war?

My mind scrambles for some way out of this. "I—I need some time to make a decision. Please."

Cozmo frowns. "Time is the one thing we don't have."

"I don't care." My voice cracks with desperation—this is all too much. "It's what I need."

Cozmo shakes his head, a sad glint in his eye. "The others will hear of this. And I won't be the only magician to question whether you've chosen to place the Bureau above the League."

"Just listen to me," I say. "If I can figure out who caused—no, if I can figure out how to *end* the time freeze, then the

Supernatural World Congress would be free and Bane would lose his position as Prime Minister. Things would go back to normal, and no one would be hunting you."

Cozmo doesn't answer, letting my hopes dangle in the air.

"*Please*," I repeat. "I don't want anyone getting hurt in some stupid war. You can't want that either."

Finally he says, "I will give you as much time as I can." His expression hardens again. "But understand, refusing the Crown comes with grave consequences."

Relief pours over me. "I understand."

"No," he replies. "I don't believe you do. But I've a feeling you will."

≋ 7 ≋

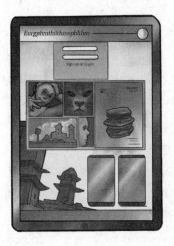

M AMA WAKES ME WITH A KNOCK THE NEXT MORNING, just as she always does on workdays. Only instead of heading back to the kitchen to heat up my Pop-Tart like usual, she hovers in the doorway, a smile on her face. "Your little *boyfriend* is waiting on you in the living room."

Boyfriend? I sit up, wiping the sleep from my eyes. "You mean Jayden? He's just a friend who happens to be a boy."

Mama shoots me one of those "whatever you say" looks before her face splits into a wide grin. "Well, go and see what he wants. Apparently, you promised to help him with something? I'm guessing summer camp stuff?"

I *did* say that. Like two weeks ago. But he swore he had it all figured out. "Okay, I'll go talk to him."

Mama turns and heads down the hallway. I blow out a long breath. A memory of the Crown and Cozmo's talk of war flashes in my mind, and I shudder. Elsie had already teleported home by the time I got back from Cozmo's lake house. Her mom was threatening to come get her if she hadn't. But we had a late-night FaceTime to talk about how scary things have gotten. We both came to the same conclusion—I've got to find a way back into the Bureau so we can continue our investigation. There's so much depending on us getting to the bottom of this. But how?

Not to mention, I can't hide being uninvited to summer camp from Mama much longer. We're supposed to report there today.

I close my eyes and suck in a deep breath. *One problem at a time.*

When I get to the living room Jayden has his Starter Kit all laid out on the coffee table. His face lights up when he sees me. "'Sup, superstar?"

I roll my eyes and try to hide my blush. "You're so corny."

Mama laughs from the kitchen, a knowing look on her face. I ignore it and plop down on the opposite side of the small couch.

Jayden holds up a True Sight eyedropper. The color of the liquid inside shifts from blue to red to green between his fingertips. "This stuff safe?"

"It's how we see past the glamours and disguises that supernaturals use. I know it looks strange, but you'll need it."

Jayden just nods. "So this supernatural stuff really ain't a joke, huh?"

"Was taking a flying ship to look at some underwater trains last summer a joke?"

He shakes his head and grins. "Nah, guess not. Just been so long, it kinda feels like a dream I had one night."

Jayden's excitement starts to dig up my own disappointment. Because I should be excited too. This would've been my first summer as a full Junior Agent.

"Don't worry," I say, trying to keep my voice cheerful. "It won't seem like a dream once you get to the Bureau. It's a pretty amazing place."

He nods, and I decide to see what's really brought him here so early. I lean closer. "I thought you didn't need my help?"

Jayden's grin turns sheepish. "I had planned on taking the drops right before I left. Told Ma about it and everything, and she was real excited. Said she'd find somebody to drive us down to the Vanderbilt Hotel." His face falls. "But then she leaves this note saying she goin' away all week. I don't even know if she remembered I was leaving today. Don't have any money to get there on my own and it's too far to walk."

"Oh." I should've known it was something like that. With how much his mom disappears on him, Jayden pretty much takes care of himself.

"Don't worry," says Mama, "you can ride with us when

I take Amari up there later this morning."

Jayden grins. "Thanks, Ms. P."

"W-well," I sputter. "You really only have to take Jayden."

Mama raises an eyebrow. "And why is that?"

I rack my brain for a good excuse. "Oh, um, because I'm . . . starting late because . . . well, it's top secret."

That's the best I could do?

Jayden meets my eyes. "Oh *yeah*," he says, realizing I'm stalling. "That thing you was, uh, telling me 'bout . . ."

"Yes," I say quickly. "Definitely that thing."

Mama looks confused. "And when were you going to tell *me*, exactly?"

"Oh, uh, I could've sworn I told you."

Mama looks between us and shakes her head. "Well, Jayden, you're still welcome to catch a ride with me. I've got a few errands to run on that side of town before I head in to work."

"Thanks again, Ms. P."

Once Mama turns her back, I whisper, "Thanks."

"Looked like you needed some help," says Jayden. "But why you ain't going with us?"

I glance to Mama and back to Jayden, and keeping my voice low, say, "I sort of got uninvited."

He frowns. "How you do that? And why ain't you tell me?"

I'm not sure how to answer that. Jayden is brand-new to all this. He doesn't know anything about magicians or the Night Brothers, and certainly not about the time freeze at the Congress Room that's got the supernatural world so riled up.

I settle on, "It's a long story."

His face falls. "If you're not there, I won't know nobody. Maybe I should just stay home too. If I'm being real, this whole thing been making me nervous anyway."

"No," I say quickly. "You should definitely go. Don't miss out on something this special because of me. Besides, I'll find my way there. Promise."

"Promise?" he repeats.

I nod. Though I have no idea how I'll be able to keep it.

As I twist off the top of the True Sight eyedrops, Jayden tells me Barnabus Ware showed up to his interview covered in dirt and freshly mowed grass, explaining that the natural look is all the rage this season. When I ask what badge Jayden got, he tells me copper, which is great, even though Barnabus had him pegged for notebook paper. Same old Barnabus.

For as big and tough as Jayden likes to pretend he is, this boy is a complete baby when it comes to these eyedrops. We waste the first one because he keeps closing his eyes at the last second. You'd think I was pouring lava on him the way he ducks away. Thankfully there's an In Case You Need It bag with an extra drop, and we finally get it done.

Then it's a matter of testing it out. It would've been easy enough if Mrs. Walters were still next door, but since she isn't, we've got to go a bit farther. Thankfully there's almost always one place to find a supernatural in hiding—the city bus.

There's one already turning the corner.

"Focus on the bus," I say. "Chances are, somebody inside is supernatural."

We wait patiently for the bus to cruise down the street, until finally it's right in front of the apartment.

"AHHH!" The way Jayden shouts, you could probably hear him a mile away.

But that's when I spot the zombie with its head twisted back the wrong way, just barely pulling off a disguise.

All I can do is pat Jayden on the back and swear to him that most supernaturals are actually pretty nice. Zombies get a bad rap from movies and TV shows. In reality, most are just as happy to nibble on a rare steak as they are on someone's arm.

When the time comes for Mama to take Jayden to the Bureau, I do my best to keep up a smile. Not only so she doesn't suspect anything, but also so Jayden doesn't lose his nerve or feel guilty for going without me. Seeing him drive off in the passenger seat makes it hard to keep the smile going, though. He really is going to be on his own.

At least I had Elsie last summer.

At eleven a.m. it becomes official—summer camp has begun without me. Everyone'll be getting rooms assigned to them and reuniting with their friends. I should be visiting

Quinton right now. The thought makes me slump farther into the sofa.

New Text Message from Elsie:
Working on something but don't want to get your hopes up.
Stay close to your phone.

I type a reply *so* fast.

From Amari:
Something to get me back into the Bureau???

She just sends back a winking-face emoji. I should've known Elsie would have my back. *Please* let whatever she's up to work out.

It's not until two that Elsie follows up:

New Text Message from Elsie:
Will be there at 3.

I quickly message back:

From Amari:
How come? Did it work?

But I don't get a reply. My heart beats so fast from anticipation. It must've worked if she's coming, right?

At 2:59 p.m., my best friend teleports into my living room, wearing a white lab coat with her name stitched on one side, and *Department of Magical Science* on the other. Her silver badge glints.

Elsie grins from ear to ear. "Pack your stuff!"

I scream and start to jump up and down but stop myself. "This isn't a prank, is it? Because that would be mean."

Elsie's smile just gets bigger. "Check your email!"

I pull out my phone, but there aren't any new emails. "I don't see anything—"

Something pops onscreen. It's from the Bureau.

> 1 New Email: From Bureau of Supernatural Affairs
> Amari Peters, please report to summer camp immediately.
> —Department of Half Truths and Full Cover-Ups

Happy tears skip down my cheeks and I spin around to Elsie. "How?"

Elsie's face makes an odd expression. "Lara Van Helsing, if you can believe it."

The name sends another jolt of emotions through me—anger, surprise, worry. It's the last thing I expected her to say. "The same Lara whose mission it was to make my life miserable last summer?"

Elsie nods. "Lara messaged me this morning about whether there was any proof that magicians were behind the time freeze, and I was like, 'Nope, everyone just sort of assumes it was.' So then we were talking about how you couldn't even post something on Eurg to defend yourself. Maria's page was taken down too."

"I didn't know that," I say.

"Me either! That's why Lara and I decided to do something on your behalf. We did a livestream this morning on Lara's Eurg page about how unfair it is to make you and Maria, two of the biggest heroes at the Bureau, unwelcome just because you're magicians. I repeated what I said about there not being proof, and Lara asked her three million followers to demand that you both be reinstated under the hashtags #VanQuish and #TheGoodMagician. Between her followers and yours, it worked!"

Now that my Eurg app is functional again, a quick visit shows me their livestream has been reposted tens of thousands of times in only a few hours. It's number three on the trending page, behind only Bane's speech and the photos of the time freeze. Big names across the supernatural world are using the hashtags too. Fashion designer Madame Duboise, with her pale green skin and signature rose-petal ponytail, posed in a T-shirt with me and Maria's faces on the front. And she's got over thirty-three million followers. Even the pop group the Shrieking Sirens shouted us out onstage during the Atlantis stop of their Shipwrecked, Hearts Mended tour.

"Nothing about it on the Bureau's official Eurg page or from Bane's account," I say. "I still can't believe it worked."

Elsie just shrugs. "Guess our new Prime Minister didn't

want more bad publicity when he's already got the time freeze to worry about. Plus, my mom says he's always been extremely unpopular."

As much as Bane's future reaction worries me, there's also something else bothering me right now. "Is it wrong to feel a little weird about Lara's part in this?"

Elsie shakes her head. "I totally understand why you'd have mixed feelings about who made it happen. But that doesn't take away from *why* it happened. You've got supporters, including me."

She's right. I've spent the last year downplaying all the support I've gotten, mostly because I get nervous and embarrassed by too much attention. Last summer, after I got so much hate for being a magician, I asked for people to give me a chance. Maybe I should give them a chance too. I give my best friend the biggest hug. "Thanks, Els."

"We should hurry, though. We're already late."

"Right." I gather up my stuff as quickly as possible and shoot Mama a quick text.

From Amari:
Catching a ride with Elsie to the Bureau. Love u!

8

I T'S NOT UNTIL WE APPEAR BEHIND THE ZEBRA PEN AT
Zoo Atlanta that I realize we aren't teleporting directly to
the Bureau. I scrunch up my nose at the smell. Elsie points me
toward a paved walkway and explains that the Bureau is on
lockdown after the time freeze, and so are all the surrounding
buildings and streets. They'd opened things up temporarily
for trainees' and juniors' arrival, but now that camp has officially started, the lockdown is back in place. So the only ways
into the Bureau are the supernatural entrances—the underground waterways, the special telescope transporter on the
International Space Station, and the Tubes.

"I thought only supernaturals could use the Tubes?"
I ask.

Elsie nods. "Normally humans are strongly discouraged. We can just drive up to the Vanderbilt Hotel or teleport directly inside, you know? No need to make already long Tube lines even worse. *But* Bureau personnel can use them as a last resort."

We follow the walkway around until we reach a door marked *Zoo Personnel Only*. A guy sweeping nearby puts up a hand to stop us as we approach.

"Off-limits."

"Not to us." Elsie flashes her silver badge first, and I follow with my moonstone one.

The guy nods and goes back to pretending to clean.

Elsie looks to make sure no one is watching, then we dash inside to find a long room filled with TV screens showing supernatural programming. Nearly all are tuned to news reports about the Congress Room and the supernaturals frozen inside. The more time goes by, the worse I feel for them. It's a reminder of just how much is at stake—if the time freeze isn't stopped, they might never get out.

A large sign flashes *Tube Station 21* overhead as supernaturals of all sorts form a lengthy line leading to a glass door at the end of the room. Besides the TVs and seating areas, there isn't much else here except a furry ogre behind the counter of a small diner. Sizzling on the grill is the largest bird I've ever seen—I'd be more afraid of that thing eating me than the other way around.

Elsie sighs. "We'll be stuck in this line forever."

"Maybe I can shout 'I'm on official Bureau business' and

get to the front right away?"

My best friend cranes her neck to look ahead. "I'm not sure that would work with this crowd."

I take another look. Elsie might have a point. In line are a pit troll, a family of frowning minotaurs, two sandmen, a banshee . . . and not one smile among them. I don't get the feeling they'd care to help two junior members of the Bureau be someplace on time.

Still, it's worth a shot. "Maybe we could ask nicely?"

"Sure." Elsie smiles nervously. "What could go wrong?"

I tap on the wide back of the pit troll in front of me. With a rumbling snort, the scarred, leathery-skinned supernatural turns its massive head, cold black eyes sizing us up as it flashes yellow teeth as big as my fingers. Its thick jaw snaps shut with a loud crack, and it grumbles, "Whaddya want?"

Elsie goes pale.

I swallow, then squeak, "Um, we were wondering if you'd maybe let us go ahead of you? We're running really late and it's our first day back to the Bureau—"

"Same Bureau that suspended my known world license for throwing some jerk's car into the woods after he cut me off? I don't care about no stinking Bureau!" The troll huffs. "And I sure as heck don't care about two blasted tween girls!"

"Actually we're both thirteen, so we're teens, not tweens—"

The pit troll snarls.

"Um, never mind . . . ," Elsie whispers.

The whole station goes quiet. Every supernatural in the room turns to watch us after my face appears on one of the television monitors above the words,

Teen Hero? Or Terrifying Time Freeze Suspect?
Curious Minds Want to Know!

"Magician!" something shouts.

And I watch the pit troll, a supernatural four times my size, shrink away from me in absolute terror. Others stumble back or fly off or even just shut their eyes. I don't feel triumphant or powerful, though—I feel awful. The last thing I want is for anything to be afraid of me. "I didn't do that. They're wrong about me."

But no one is listening. It's a reminder that even though a lot of supernaturals might support me, it's not everyone. It's probably not even most of the supernatural world.

"You said you wanted to use the Tube, so go ahead!" whimpers the pit troll.

Elsie's hand lands on my shoulder. "Let's just go, okay?"

"Fine."

We make our way to the front of the line. I'm almost relieved to find that the winged goblin manning the door and smoking a cigar doesn't seem impressed by me at all.

"Destination?" asks the goblin in a bored voice.

I start. "You aren't afraid of me?"

The winged goblin barely looks up from his crossword. "My kind are born inside erupting volcanoes. Gonna take a lot more than a little abracadabra with the clocks and what-not to ruffle these feathers. Comprende?"

I nod quickly.

"Good. Destination?"

I answer, "The lobby of the Bureau of Supernatural Affairs."

"All right, listen up. You're gonna wanna take two rights and then a left. Make sure you don't miss the second right."

I glance between Elsie and the goblin. "I don't know what that means." And from the puzzled look on her face, neither does my best friend.

"Don't worry," he says. "You will. Now go on inside, you're holding up my line."

"Can my friend and I go together?" I ask.

The winged goblin points over his shoulder to a small sign that reads *One at a Time Please.*

"You got this," says Elsie.

"I got this," I repeat.

The glass door opens, and I step inside. Then it shuts behind me with a thud.

The winged goblin holds up three fingers, then two, one . . .

"AYEEE!" Without any warning the floor drops away, and suddenly I'm sliding through a clear tube faster and faster. Lights line the top of the tube so that I can see every twist and turn as I zip along. It moves through stone and dirt, then up through a room with lots of wires and back down through the bottom of a swimming pool and still lower through the sewers.

From there it takes one especially long dive, moving me so fast that my belly feels like it's up in my throat. Finally I emerge in a large cavern where I just barely make out a maze of other tunnels heading in every direction.

The tube begins to flatten out, allowing me to see where it splits in two up ahead. I lean hard into the right tunnel and dive even deeper, so fast that I wonder if the center of the earth is nearby, but instead I emerge inside another large cavern, this one full of glittering gemstones that sparkle as I pass.

WHOA! Something enormous—hand? claw? talon?—grips the tube, giving it a hard shake that bounces me inside, and I spot the outline of something so massive I can't even see it all as the tunnel gives me the option of going left, toward the creature, or right, away from it. It's an easy choice to make.

Finally the tube begins to rise, up and up, and the last left I take drops me right onto a large cushioned pillow beneath a chute at the front of the main lobby of the Bureau of Supernatural Affairs. I get up and work out my wobbly legs until Elsie plops onto the same pillow thirty seconds later.

I help her to her feet.

She looks me right in the eyes and says, "Amari, let's never do that again. Like, ever."

"Agreed."

It doesn't take long for the excitement of just being here

to come back. My brother and I are in the same place for the first time in months. "Let's go see Quinton!" I suggest.

Me and Elsie rush across the lobby, which is being serenaded by cupids strumming golden harps high overhead. We zigzag through a small herd of centaurs before being stopped by a squadron of armored draugrs seeking directions to the Department of the Dead.

We tell them to follow us to the elevators, but as soon as we get close enough to point them out, a boy in a white uniform with a bright red sash steps in our path. His badge reads *Department of Half Truths and Full Cover-Ups*.

"Amari Peters," he says. "Please follow me."

"And who are you exactly?" I ask.

He sighs as if he's irritated. "Junior Double-Talker Khalil Ali. I've got instructions to bring you to meet our director."

Well, that didn't take long. I should've known I'd get in trouble for Lara's livestream.

I turn to follow Khalil back across the packed lobby to a small podium with a large engraving of a man with two faces—with his left face, the man speaks confidently and openly, but his right face whispers, shielding his mouth from view with his hand. It's supposed to represent the Department of Half Truths and Full Cover-Ups' dual mission to inform the supernatural world about what's happening within the Bureau as well as keep any supernatural activity quiet from the known world.

A knot of dread forms in my gut as I notice a group

of supernaturals with microphones and cameras waiting in front of the podium. Are they here for me?

Khalil brings us to the edge of the gathering and puts his hands on his hips, head whipping back and forth. "The director was supposed to meet us here. . . ."

"Amari Peters!" someone shouts. Next thing I know, the supernatural media are surrounding us.

"I have a question!" squeaks a floating pixie carrying a microphone as big as he is. Suddenly there's a camera in my face too. "How do you feel about being named a possible suspect in the time freeze investigation?"

"I . . . um . . . don't think it's fair—"

Another microphone pops into view, this time held by something shrouded by a veil. "Miss Peters, I represent the *Tomorrow* morning show on the Oracle network. What do you say to those who suggest that you and Maria Van Helsing are being given special treatment due to your celebrity? You're being allowed into the Bureau at a time when most UnWanteds have been told they must leave the city—that they don't deserve a place in our world."

I open my mouth to answer, but don't know what to say. Because I *did* get special treatment, didn't I? I'm not sure how to feel either, other than awful.

An arm wraps around my shoulder, and I look up to find a brown-skinned lady with bushy black hair and thick glasses beside me. Her golden director's badge shimmers against the bright red of her sash. She smiles and waves to the reporters as she guides Elsie and me through the crowd and over to the podium.

Before the reporters can start shouting questions again, the director says, "Allow me to introduce myself. I'm Elaine Harlowe, the new Director of the Department of Half Truths and Full Cover-Ups. The Bureau would like to make a public apology to Amari here, for what was *clearly* a rather unfortunate misunderstanding. We never intended for her to be uninvited to camp. In fact, it's our long-standing policy to celebrate all our high-achieving members—especially our juniors."

It's all I can do to keep my jaw from hitting the floor. A misunderstanding?

But Director Harlowe just smiles. "We'll take a few questions, but then we really must be going. These girls have a busy summer ahead of them!"

A yeti in a trench coat steps forward, and the others fall silent. He smooths the mop of curly fur on his head and barks, "Trent from the *Forest Lantern*. You've become famous for single-handedly stopping Dylan Van Helsing from using the Black Book—"

"I had help—" I begin.

But the yeti talks right over me. "Now that you're back, will you turn your attention to solving the time freeze next?"

I hesitate, then realize this is the perfect opportunity to reassure the supernatural world that I had nothing to do with the freeze. And not only that—if everyone knows about my investigation, then it'll be harder for the adults to ignore me when I ask to help with the Bureau's investigation.

"Um, first, I just want to say . . ."

The microphone cuts out. Harlowe steps in front of me and shouts, "Unfortunately, that's all the questions we'll be answering for today."

But we didn't actually answer anything?

A chorus of groans comes from the audience.

Harlowe swiftly guides Elsie and me away, her heels clicking loudly as we go. She doesn't slow until we reach a waiting elevator.

Once inside, we just stare at this lady in her bright white pantsuit and her thick red glasses that match her sash. Is she for real? We don't seem to be in trouble, but then maybe she's just waiting till we're alone to tell us.

Harlowe claps as the doors snap shut. "Wasn't that fun? Or as my kind like to say—'Wasn't that *faun*!'"

Her kind? I look her over, but she seems as human as I am. Until I glance down. Those weren't heels I heard clicking before—they were hooves. "You're a faun?"

"I am." Director Harlowe pulls back her bushy hair to reveal floppy goat ears. "No need to look so shocked. It used to be that fauns were allowed to work at the Bureau under the same 'Essentially Human' rule that allows your friend Elsie to be here. If you could go out in public without needing a glamour or disguise, then you could work at the Bureau. I only required the right pair of shoes. Quite a silly rule, to be honest—and yet one they couldn't wait to change once I touched the Crystal Ball. But that's a story for another time."

Faun or not, I've got questions. "Why wouldn't you let me tell them about my investigation?"

"What investigation, dear?" Harlowe's smile doesn't waver. "Have you learned something?"

"I—not yet, but—"

"Besides," Harlowe cuts in, "that was *clearly* a rather ill-timed microphone malfunction."

Elsie shakes her head. "You also said Amari being uninvited was a misunderstanding, but I saw the message myself. It was pretty clear."

Harlowe sighs. "Well, let's see, then. Show it to me."

I pull out my phone, but the message is no longer there. It takes a few seconds to find my voice. "It's gone!"

"The first thing to know about my department," says Harlowe, "is that we never let the truth get in the way of a good story. I hope there are no hard feelings. You're in for a wonderful summer."

I glance at Elsie, unsure what to say to that. My best friend just frowns.

"Lucy?" calls Harlowe.

"Yes, Director?" the elevator answers.

"Let's get Amari here down to Supernatural Health," says Harlowe. "I've got a feeling she's anxious to see her brother after so long away." She looks to me for confirmation, and I nod.

"I'm on it," says Lucy, and we drop down into the Bureau at a speed that used to seem impossibly fast before that ride through the Tubes.

Now that we're moving, I close my eyes and focus on my brother. *Quinton, I'm on my way.*

"Now approaching the Department of Supernatural Health," Lucy announces as the medical lobby slides into view. As soon as the elevator doors open, Harlowe says, "Check beneath your pillows when you get to your room."

I look back over my shoulder as Elsie and I step off the elevator and Harlowe waves an enthusiastic goodbye. What a strange lady.

I do my best to put the last ten minutes out of my mind as we head through the ICU—the Intense Curses Unit— to Quinton's room. Except my brother isn't the only person waiting for us. Agent Magnus and Agent Fiona, the trainers who had my back last summer, are here too, as well as Maria Van Helsing, Quinton's partner, who's beaming.

Seeing Maria lifts my spirits too because her magic lets me speak to Quinton, even while he's permanently asleep. I've also got a million questions for her—like what things have been like for her since the time freeze, and if she knows about Cozmo wanting me to lead the League of Magicians. But there's a warning behind her smile, so I keep quiet. For now.

Before I can ask what they're all doing here, Magnus says, "Had a feelin' this'd be your first stop." He gives me a big pat on the shoulder. "Glad to have you back, kid. We'll give ya a moment alone."

"Aye," says Fiona with a grin of her own. They head into the hallway with Elsie.

My eyes move to my brother lying still on the bed. I hate that he's stuck like this, unable to wake up. I'd do anything to cure him. For now, I guess, just being here with him after the months he's been in Sydney will have to be enough.

"Ready?" asks Maria, picking up Quinton's hand and offering her other hand to me.

I won't lie, it's weird having to speak through someone else, but I know that Maria can choose not to listen. As soon as I take her hand, Quinton's dorky voice echoes in my head. "How's it going, sis?"

Just the sound fills me up, sparking flashes of memories we've had together. Tears pour down my face as I answer him in my mind. *Oh, you know, being the best sister ever.*

His laughter echoes through my head. "I missed you."

I really missed you too. I'm going to try to see you a lot more now that I'm here.

"Enjoy yourself," says Quinton. "Don't spend all your time worrying over me, okay?"

I'll try.

"Good," he says. "Now, I think we're all gathered here for a reason. Magnus has something for you."

I look up to find Agent Magnus peeking into the room.

"That's our cue," Magnus says once our eyes meet. He steps back in, pulling a gray jacket from behind him.

Agent Fiona follows, Elsie at her side. "With camp shutting down early last summer, we didn't get a chance to give ye a proper Gray Jacket Ceremony. So we wanted to do it now. While we're all here."

"Well, what do you think?" Maria asks, laughing.

"That it looks just like my old gray jacket but darker?" I'm only half joking.

"This one's got a few tricks up its sleeves." Magnus winks. "Literally."

My heart soars. I worked hard last summer to become a Junior Agent. Even still, receiving this jacket almost doesn't seem real. Between the hate I got for being a magician, having a partner who betrayed me, and facing down one of the Night Brothers—I've *so* earned this.

Magnus holds out the jacket and I take it. "It's my honor to present you with a gray jacket, symbolizing you officially joining the ranks of Supernatural Investigations as a junior member."

"Put it on then, lass," says Fiona.

"Okay." I'm grinning so wide. It fits perfectly—like it's always been meant for me.

Maria takes my hand, and I hear Quinton say, "I'm so proud of you, Amari."

I'm proud of me too.

9

A S THEY LEAVE QUINTON'S ROOM, AGENTS MAGNUS
and Fiona offer to escort me and Elsie to the youth
dorms to get settled in, but I tell them to go on without me.
I really want to speak with Maria about magician stuff.

The moment we're alone, I say, "There's so much I need
to tell you."

Maria flushes, her blue eyes focusing on something over
my shoulder. I turn to find it's a guy in medical scrubs—a
Senior Cursebreaker. "Sorry, Amari—I'm supposed to help
with Quinton right now. The cursebreakers need me to talk
to your brother while they perform a few tests."

"Oh," I say.

"But don't worry," Maria adds. "We'll have plenty of

time tomorrow to catch up on *everything*. Just the two of us. Try to enjoy yourself until then, okay?"

As nice as that sounds, I don't know how much time I have before Cozmo tries to make me accept the Crown again. I glance at the cursebreaker, then back at Maria. It's not like I can just blurt out League stuff in front of a stranger. Especially here at the Bureau.

I don't have much of a choice but to do as she says. "Promise we'll talk tomorrow?"

"Promise," she says.

I give Quinton's hand a soft squeeze and then rush out to catch up with the others. I'm able to just make it onto their elevator, thanks to Elsie spotting me at the last second and holding the door.

"Thanks," I say as the doors slide shut. I may have struck out with Maria, but I doubt I'll get a better chance than this to question Magnus and Fiona. "So . . . how's the time freeze investigation going?"

Magnus lets out a frustrated grunt.

"That's a bit of a sore subject, lass," says Fiona. "The sad truth is, there is no investigation. Not by anyone at the Bureau anyhow."

There's no way I heard that right. "No one's investigating the time freeze?"

"Both Supernatural Investigations and Magical Science sent people over to the Congress Room as soon as it happened," says Magnus. "But then today that Harlowe woman came in ordering everybody back to the Bureau. Told us

Bane's office was taking over the investigation and that we aren't allowed to come back."

Elsie crosses her arms. "How does Director Harlowe get to give orders to other departments?"

"Same question we're all asking," says Magnus. "But Chief Crowe says that Harlowe speaks for the Prime Minister."

"It's all more than a wee bit odd," says Fiona. "Director Rub-Ish suddenly retires from Half Truths and Full Cover-Ups without so much as a warning, and out of nowhere Harlowe gets the job? On Bane's recommendation? She's never even run an outpost before."

"Did you find anything before Harlowe showed up?" I glance between Magnus and Fiona. "Maybe something that proves a magician didn't cause the time freeze?"

"Let's just say that particular point caused some friction between the departments," says Magnus, shifting uncomfortably. "We all agree this time freeze shouldn't be possible. But whereas Magical Science reckons that not even a magician could keep a spell like that going for this long, the agents think the more impossible it seems, the more it proves it had to be a magician."

I swallow, remembering how that electricity sparked across my fingers back at Mrs. Walters's apartment. Even I don't know everything my magic is capable of doing.

Elsie shakes her head. "It's true magicians can push the limits of magic, but the Senior Researchers are right—the calculations say it can't be a magician's spell. People are only blaming magicians because they don't have any other guesses."

When Elsie and I get off the elevator at the youth dorms, Bertha, our hall monitor, is waiting for us in her usual military fatigues. She's also wearing her usual annoyed expression, and the moment she spots us I just know she's going to make some rude comment. She's never been a big fan of mine, so I'm expecting the worst.

But Bertha just says, "Peters, Rodriguez, you're in the junior dorms now. Room 119." Then she's off, stomping after a couple of trainees and shouting about running in the halls.

If only everyone had that same reaction to seeing me back. Stares and whispers follow me through the halls. Being a magician makes you stand out, and on top of that, it seems half the supernatural world believes I might be behind the time freeze. But I'm feeling too good to let what anyone else thinks get me down—my brand-new Junior Agent jacket says I belong here just as much as anyone.

And as we continue, some kids *do* greet us. Brian Li from my trainee class gives me a nod, and Gemma, Elsie's lab partner from last summer, comes up and says a quick hello. It's not most kids, and maybe it never will be, but at least *some* are willing to give me a chance. All I can do is keep showing them who I am, and if they'd rather believe something different, then that's on them.

Turns out our new junior-level dorm is crazy cool—*way* better than our trainee room from last summer. First off, this one is only meant for two roommates: it comes with a pair of wide, fluffy beds instead of four skinny ones. And they're so comfy! Elsie and I take turns bouncing on them. Then there's one whole wall that's basically a giant flat-screen TV—it can be programmed to a thousand different real-world views. With the press of a button, we shift the image from a twinkling New York City skyline to a colorful rain forest, before eventually settling on a relaxing ocean sunset.

"Amari?" Elsie sits next to me on my bed. "How are we supposed to find a way to end the time freeze if no one from the Bureau is even allowed to investigate?"

"I don't know." I sigh. "But somehow I've got to find a way before Cozmo asks me about the Crown again. I don't want to lead the League into a war with the Bureau."

"What if you just said no?" she asks.

"Turn down the Crown for good?"

Elsie nods.

"Then he'll probably lead the League into a war without me," I say. "They're too scared of what Bane might do now."

"Okay, well, what if you accept the Crown and *then* command them not to go to war?"

I think on that one for a second. "That's not an option either. If Bane gets his hands on a magician and fighting breaks out, I'll be forced into leading them against the Bureau anyway."

"So ending the time freeze and getting Merlin back as Prime Minister is pretty much our only hope?"

"Yep," I say.

Elsie nudges me with her shoulder. "Some way to spend our last summer together, huh?"

I smile a little and nod. "I wish we could just spend it having fun. I'm sorry to drag you into saving the world again."

"Drag me into it?" Elsie puts on her most confident smile. "Helping is what a trusty sidekick is for. We'll figure this thing out, and have fun doing it."

"Els, you're nobody's sidekick. I wouldn't even be here without your help. You're a better friend than I could've ever hoped for."

Elsie goes pink, and she pulls me into one of her dragon-strength hugs. "Don't you go getting sappy on me."

I laugh and try to breathe at the same time. "Hey, who's hugging who here?"

It's not long before Bertha announces over the intercom that juniors are to head to the food court for early dinner. I barely hear Elsie asking me what I want to eat for my first meal back at camp, because I'm stuck in my own head—I haven't been able to stop thinking about Director Harlowe. If she's so close with Bane, who's made it clear how he feels about magicians, then why was she so nice to me? Her department sent the email that let me back into camp, after all.

Elsie waves a hand in front of my face. "Hello? You in there?"

"Sorry. I'm coming." But as we head for the door, I remember something. "Els, didn't Harlowe say we should check under our pillows?"

Elsie pauses and goes back to her bed, flipping over her pillow. Three cards are sitting there, and she plops down to read them. "Club cards!"

"Club cards?" I repeat.

"Now that we're juniors, we can officially join clubs at the Bureau." She holds one up. "This one says I'm eligible to join the Magical Science Fair . . . and this one's for the VanQuish Fan Club and . . . a prestige club! The Junior Genius Society!"

As she reads, I look under my own pillow. There's just one card there, with shiny gold writing.

THE ELITES
YOU HAVE BEEN CHOSEN
FOR A CLUB MOST EXCLUSIVE.
DIRECTORS, CHIEF DIRECTORS, AND A WHO'S-WHO
OF THE BUREAU'S MOST FAMOUS MEMBERS
HAVE ALL WORN OUR STAR PINS.
JOIN US AT THE BACK OF THE CLUB FAIR TONIGHT
TO TAKE YOUR PLACE AMONG THE STARS.

The card begins to fold and twist in my hand until it's the shape of a star. It's got tiny prongs on the back.

"Amari!" Elsie whisper-shouts. "You got invited to the Elites?"

"Um, I think so." I show her the star. "What kind of club is it?"

"A prestige club—it means you have to be asked to join. The Elites is supposed to be the most exclusive in the whole Bureau. I can't think of anyone who's been invited in only their second summer."

I sit down to think. "The invite makes it sound like really important members of the Bureau will be there. This is our chance to find out what the Bureau really thinks about the time freeze!"

Elsie crosses her arms. "Don't you think it's a little strange for you to suddenly go from being uninvited to summer camp to being chosen for the most exclusive junior club all in the same day?"

"Maybe," I say.

"Just maybe?"

I bite my lip. "Okay, it definitely is. Especially since Harlowe supposedly speaks for Bane."

"She's up to something." Elsie sighs. "I just know it."

"I still want to go. Somebody there has to know something that can help us."

I was kind of hoping that dinner would be a good chance to catch up with Jayden to see what he thinks about the Bureau so far, but the trainees were sent to dinner even earlier than us juniors. Makes sense, I guess. They've got an earlier curfew too. They'll receive their badges and new supernatural abilities first thing in the morning. If we skip breakfast, we might be able to watch him touch the Crystal Ball.

Elsie has spent most of the afternoon doing othernet searches on Director Harlowe. If there's one thing that girl knows how to do, it's research. Even now, when we're supposed to be eating, she's still bent over that phone.

"Your tacos are getting cold," I say, pushing her plate closer.

Elsie barely looks up. "Says here that Elaine Harlowe was adopted by Lord and Lady Harlowe, English nobility who immigrated to the States. On a hike, the couple found her wandering the woods alone as a small child. It caused quite the controversy when the Harlowes, having no children of their own, nominated her for the Bureau when young Elaine turned twelve. Initially her application was denied, citing that only humans are considered for membership. But Harlowe eventually won her case when she proved through human dress and hairstyle that she passed the admittedly loose requirements for being considered 'Essentially Human.' The ruling upset many who believed the 'Essentially Human' exception was strictly reserved for humans who could shift into supernaturals, and those with at least one human parent. Many feared that Harlowe's inclusion would encourage other supernaturals to join, and humanity would soon lose control of its only link to the supernatural world."

I remember something Harlowe said in the elevator. "Is that why they changed the rules after Harlowe got to the Bureau?"

"The article gets to that near the end." Elsie skims until she finds what she's looking for. "The laws were changed, however, when Harlowe touched the Crystal Ball and was granted a much higher-than-normal dose of magic due to the fact that the device didn't recognize her as human. The supernatural ability she received was noted as extremely dangerous—so dangerous, in fact, that it appears in no official record, and Harlowe may only use it in extreme circumstances requiring express permission from Merlin, the Prime Minister."

"So I wasn't the first person to have the Crystal Ball declare her ability illegal?" I ask.

"Guess not," says Elsie. "The difference is that Harlowe's welcome ceremony was in 1899."

"Harlowe's that old?" I ask.

"Yep," says Elsie. "Fauns can live for more than two hundred years. Says here that the controversy over hiding Harlowe's supernatural ability is why the welcome ceremony has been open to the supernatural public ever since."

"That's scary," I say.

Elsie nods and puts down her phone down. "Really scary. Try to learn as much as you can at the Elites meeting tonight, but maybe stay away from Harlowe. At least until we figure out the best way to approach her."

"That I can do," I say.

We both decide, at least for now, that we're better off focusing on our tacos. We've already gone back for seconds and I'm eyeing the line, considering thirds, when my best friend nods toward the other side of the room.

I follow her eyes. "What are we looking at?"

"Over by the bathrooms," she says. "Bear and his friends keep throwing fries at someone . . . is that Lara?"

I look a little closer and sure enough, Lara Van Helsing sits alone at a table in the far corner. She's not even telling them to stop—she just stares down at her tray as french fries whiz past her head. "What's going on with her?"

Elsie frowns. "Her aura looks awful."

It's strange watching Lara experience the same type of bullying that she put me through last summer. I see the way she shrinks away from Bear and his awful friends, her face bright red. It feels a bit like karma, but that doesn't mean it's easy to watch. So I turn away.

Elsie meets my gaze. "We should do something."

I roll my eyes. "You're not seriously suggesting we go over there."

"I know she isn't the most pleasant person in the world—"

I nearly drop my last taco. "Els, she made my life *miserable* last summer. I almost quit because of her. The girl literally jumped me in an alley!"

Elsie winces. "All good points. But I just think maybe part of the reason she's having such a tough time is because she stuck her neck out for you *this* summer."

"You mean she stuck her neck out for her sister Maria, which just happened to help me too."

"That's not fair," says Elsie. "She was happy to include you in the livestream."

"Well, I don't care," I say. "If you want to go over there, then—"

Elsie stands and scoops up her tray.

I'm so stunned, I just stare. Never in a million years did I think she'd actually do it. I cross my arms.

Elsie shakes her head. "You're better than this, Amari."

The disappointment in her voice hits like a hammer. Elsie starts toward Lara's table, and no matter how I might feel about Lara, I can't let my best friend face those boys on her own. Besides, deep down I know she's right about standing up to bullies; it's just hard when the person you're trying to save is a bully too. I rush to catch up.

Elsie grins. "I knew you'd come."

Annoyed as I might be with this whole situation, I can't help but smile too. "Of course you did."

Once we're closer, Elsie shouts at Bear and his friend. "Leave her alone!"

The boys turn, and Bear starts laughing. "What are you going to do if we don't?"

Elsie shrinks back and I hesitate, same as I always do whenever I consider using my magic. But not for long. I use my illusions to set my eyes aglow. "Try us and find out."

It's enough to send Bear's friends stumbling out of their seats.

But Bear knows me from school, so he isn't so easily frightened. He gets to his feet and crosses his arms, his height allowing him to tower over me. "You're bluffing."

I stare right back at him, making it clear I'm not afraid. I'm not the girl from last summer who runs and hides anymore. Elsie looks on, eyes wide.

Bear's expression sours, but before he can say something mean, Agent Magnus's voice rings out from a few tables away. "Don't know what the disagreement seems to be, but I do know it's over now. Y'all get on back to your dorms."

"This *isn't* over . . ."—Bear spits before turning back to Lara—"*magician lover.*" Then he jogs to catch up with his friends.

I nod my thanks and Magnus tips his cowboy hat before continuing toward the hot dog stand.

"You okay?" Elsie steps over to Lara, concerned.

Lara's lip quivers as if she's on the verge of tears. But then she looks at me and her expression hardens. "I had it under control." She straightens her clothes and lifts her chin before getting to her feet, then pushes her way past us and hurries toward the elevators. "Next time, mind your own business."

I give Elsie a look that says "I told you so." It's obvious that Lara still hates my guts. Why did she help me get back into the Bureau?

Nothing makes any sense this summer.

"Amari?" asks Elsie. "Lara failed her Junior Agent tryout last year, right?"

I nod.

"So why was she eating with us juniors?"

Good question.

≋ 10 ≋

AFTER DINNER, ELSIE AND I FOLLOW THE LARGE CROWD of juniors down to the Special Events floor, where the Club Fair is being held. I feel my jaw drop at the sight of the massive ballroom completely transformed. It looks like a giant street fair—kids in tall wooden booths holding up colorful homemade signs and passing out flyers as other kids walk from booth to booth around the floor.

The rows of booths are packed in tight, lining both sides of walkways that branch off in different directions. Farther into the ballroom, these give way to large tents with fancy electric signs displaying club names like *Young Detectives* and *Deep-Sea Explorers*. Beyond those, at the opposite end of the room, is a huge red tent with gold trim. The invitation to the Elites said to "join us at the back of the Club Fair," so ignoring all the kids calling out to us about their clubs, I head straight for that giant tent, Elsie on my heels. I'm here for a reason, and the faster I can get where I'm going, the more time I'll have to speak with the Bureau VIPs about the time freeze. I'll just have to make sure I keep my distance from Harlowe and her spooky secret supernatural ability.

We make it about a dozen steps before a small group of Junior Agents moves to block our path. A tall boy, around fifteen or sixteen, steps forward and says, "You must be Amari Peters."

"That's me," I say. "Now could you move? I'm kind of in a hurry."

He smirks. "Why? The Club Fair is open for like three hours. You've got plenty of time."

"The Elites tent," I answer. "I have an invitation."

His eyes move first to my moonstone badge, then to the paper star pin on the opposite lapel of my Junior Agent jacket. "In your second summer? That's impressive. I've actually been invited the last *two* years." He flashes a wide grin. "I'm Tristan Davies. You've probably heard of me."

He says it like I'm supposed to be impressed. I mean, the name does sound kinda familiar. But then I wasn't exactly hanging out with many Junior Agents last summer. It was hard enough trying to fit in with the trainees.

Elsie nods, though, looking starstruck. "I know who you are."

"Not surprising," says Tristan. "But whatever you've

heard, I'm even better than that." Then the boy actually winks.

I'm over his cocky attitude. "Can we go now?"

To my surprise, he steps out of the way, saying, "Anything for the sister of the great Quinton Peters. You and I should keep in touch this summer. If we're good enough to be Elites on our own, imagine what we could do together."

Wait, is this boy offering to be my partner? That's a huge change from last summer, when the popular kids wanted no part of being friends with me. Truth is, I *will* need a partner as a Junior Agent. All agents work in pairs, like Quinton and Maria, or Magnus and Fiona. With Elsie in a different department, it's the one thing she can't help me with. "I'll think about it," I say, trying to play it cool.

"You do that." He grins like he can see right through my act. "But you should know the Elites tent isn't open yet."

"Oh," I say. "When does it open?"

He just grins and steps around us, waving for the other Junior Agents to follow. "Trust me, you'll know."

Once they're gone, I ask Elsie, "*Should* I know who Tristan Davies is?"

She gives me the same look she gave me in biology class whenever I hadn't done the assigned reading.

"What? Is he important? Some blah-blah-blah's great grandson or something?"

"Actually he's a merit kid," says Elsie. That means he didn't get nominated by a family member like most kids here. He got in for doing something extraordinary, like scoring super high on the year-end exams or saving an old lady from a burning building.

"Before you," Elsie continues, "Tristan Davies was supposed to be the Next Big Thing in Supernatural Investigations. He was being mentored by VanQuish, even helped with the capture of the fake Moreau a few years back."

If he was mentored by Quinton and Maria, then he really must be good. I grin at my blushing best friend.

"What?" she asks. "Why are you making that face?"

"Can't you read my aura?" I tease.

"You know I can only see how you're feeling, not what you're thinking."

I laugh. "I was just thinking that you seemed pretty dazzled by Tristan Davies."

"What, no!" Elsie says, looking mortified. "He's cute, sure, but he's also extremely arrogant."

Elsie's mouth is saying one thing, but her reddish cheeks tell a different story. Still, I decide not to pick on her too much, and change the subject. "Do you think the Elites tent is really closed?"

Elsie nods. "Tristan was headed in the opposite direction, so probably."

"So what do we do until it opens?" I ask.

"Check out a few clubs?"

Turns out stopping by a few booths is exactly what I needed to shake off my nerves about my mission. I *need* to learn something useful tonight. We don't have any other leads.

As soon as kids notice the paper star on my jacket, it's like they forget that I'm Amari Peters the magician girl. My head whips back and forth trying to keep up with everyone calling my name. Everyone wants an Elite in their club, I guess. Whatever worries the time freeze stirred up about me seem completely forgotten.

The Duboise Fashion Club is my first stop, mostly because the girl out front rushes over and tugs me to the booth. She explains that the club gets a sneak peek at the upcoming fall style catalog. Then she wraps a strip of thin white fabric around my neck and tells me jungle scarves are going to be *the* must-have accessory this winter.

When I ask her what's "jungle" about a plain white scarf, she tells me to name my favorite furry animal. I say "tiger," mostly because it's the first thing that pops into my head. No sooner do I say the word than orange-and-black fur grows out from the scarf, until my entire neck is covered in thick tiger fur. It's so cozy.

"Cool, right?" the girl says. "You can name any animal in the jungle, and the best part is, no actual critters were harmed to make it!"

I couldn't help but accept one of her flyers after that. Farther down the walkway are even more fun clubs, like the Thrill Seekers, who travel on the weekends to the supernatural world's most dangerous places, and do things like sneak through booby-trapped tombs deep inside the pyramids or go hiking in the Famished Forest with its carnivorous trees.

Elsie steers me clear of some kid named Arthur, who's

standing in front of the VanQuish Fan Club booth, explaining that if he were to catch sight of Quinton's little sister we'd never get away. We make a brief stop at the Truth-Tellers club to say hello to Julia Farsight. She's wearing a *Unite for UnWanteds* T-shirt and explains that they have a podcast and do livestreams where they fight for those who can't fight for themselves. It's so cool to see somebody have the courage to speak out about the change they want to see in the world. And Julia is just a good person. Elsie and I promise to come to a meeting.

The tents in the other half of the ballroom are the department clubs, which Elsie explains are run by the different departments at the Bureau. For instance, the Junior Researchers are all eligible to join the Magical Science Fair, where members compete to win prizes at the end of summer camp. The poor kid with the sign-up sheet looked devastated at the sight of Elsie, asking if she was *sure* she wanted to join, and if someone with her list of accomplishments might rather be a judge instead. I might've been the one invited to the Elites, but that girl already has a reputation for being awesome.

The Young Detectives club is reserved for Junior Agents. They investigate famous unsolved cases like the theft of Excalibur, the magical sword of King Arthur (the thieves even took the stone it was buried in). I'd love to join, but they meet nearly every evening and I've already got my hands full with this investigation.

When we reach the international clubs with kids visiting

here from other Bureaus, Elsie and I get quiet. It's another reminder that she's leaving. And though I'd never admit it to her, I don't know if I'm okay with that.

"I, um, should probably go over and introduce myself to the London kids," says Elsie. "Since I'll be there next summer."

"Yeah," I say. "That's probably a good idea."

A lonely feeling settles over me as I watch her go. I honestly don't know what I'll do without her.

Thankfully, I don't get long to dwell on it because suddenly the lights go dim. A booming drumroll echoes throughout the ballroom.

Harlowe's voice comes over the intercom. "Elites are stars, and stars have a way of shining, don't they?"

The little pin on my jacket begins to vibrate, shimmering with golden light, until a streak of sparkles shoots straight up into the air, exploding above my head. Across the room more golden explosions go off, cheers going up around the ballroom each time one happens.

Finally the room is completely dark again. "Elites," Harlowe continues, "please come to our special tent for refreshments and congratulations."

Elsie comes back in a hurry—this is it. "Good luck. And be careful around Harlowe."

"Don't worry, I'll stay far away from her."

I move quickly through the Club Fair as the overhead lights begin to come back on. I'm one of the last to reach the red tent. Even from outside, it looks bright and welcoming.

Applause is the first thing I hear when I step inside. Everything looks incredibly fancy, from the plush rug we're standing on to the waitstaff in full tuxedos and a table decked out with silky table linens and topped with gleaming silver plates and utensils. There's *so* much food, and a whole table full of drinks in tall glasses.

It's the adults who are clapping for us. Directors, deputy directors, and even a few folks who look old enough to be retired already are all lined up in a row. Harlowe and Chief Crowe stand in front of the others, smiling. The Bureau's most important members are all gathered here. I can't leave without learning something.

We juniors crowd near the entrance. There's like thirty of us, two kids from each department.

Tristan steps up beside me, that same confident grin on his face. "I've already put in a word with Agent Fiona for us to be partners. Should be official tomorrow. One of the perks of being a gold star Elite is getting to choose who you're paired up with."

"Oh, um, okay." I didn't realize he was serious before. I'm not sure whether to be grateful or terrified that I won't measure up next to him.

Harlowe steps forward. "Welcome, Elites! This club represents the best the Bureau has to offer. Every one of you demonstrated uncommon excellence last summer, despite camp being cut short. In fact, we have one junior here today who is almost single-handedly responsible for ending the hybrid attacks and stopping Moreau and Dylan Van

Helsing's villainous plot. A special round of applause for Amari Peters!"

My cheeks burn as the room thunders with cheers and clapping in my honor. I sneak a glance at Director Van Helsing, who's practically sneering. He's never made it a secret how he feels about me. You'd think that after learning two of his kids—Dylan and Maria—are magicians, he'd be willing to change his opinion. But as far as I can tell, that hasn't happened. Guess preserving his worldview is more important.

My eyes return to Tristan. He's dropped his grin. Now he looks . . . nervous. But why?

"Now, then," says Harlowe. "Those of you who aren't first-timers know what comes next. Even among Elites, we aren't all equal. It's time to announce our gold star Elites— representing the *very* best in each department."

That must be what he meant earlier when he told me gold star Elites get to pick their own partner.

Harlowe rubs her hands together excitedly. "Count down with me. Three . . . two . . . one . . . Now look at your stars!"

Tristan and I both glance at his star pin.

It's silver.

"Impossible." Tristan stares down at his star like he can't believe his eyes. There's none of the smugness from before. He looks angry.

I look down to see that my own paper star is now glittering gold.

Did I just beat out Tristan Davies?

That's gotta be why he looked so unsure a moment ago. When Harlowe singled me out, he must've known I might be getting the gold star for Supernatural Investigations and not him.

"Second place to you?" Tristan mutters.

"I—I'm sorry," I say quickly, unsure of what else to do. But he turns and stomps off as the adults come over to offer their congratulations. *Why am I apologizing?*

Director Van Helsing is before me in an instant, arms folded. "*Congratulations.*" He practically spits the words. "Breaking the rules may have earned you that star, but snooping around investigations will *not* be tolerated this summer. That's a direct order."

I resist the urge to shrink away. That's what I would've done last summer, when I didn't feel like I belonged. But now I know that's not true—I've got a moonstone badge, I made Junior Agent, and now I'm an Elite.

I lift my chin defiantly. "Then I guess you won't be sharing what you've discovered about the time freeze?"

Director Van Helsing's expression darkens. "Listen, young lady—"

"Amari!" Chief Crowe interrupts, stepping over to wrap me in a big hug. "I'm so proud of you. An Elite in only your second summer! Not even your brother can say that."

Director Van Helsing storms off, and I give the chief my full attention. "I just wish there was something I could do to help Merlin and all those supernaturals trapped in the

Congress Room. It doesn't make sense that the Bureau isn't allowed to investigate."

"Heard about that, have you?" Chief Crowe shakes her head, the gills on her neck marking her as half-Atlantian opening and closing. "The situation is certainly less than ideal. I just hope Bane is taking this as seriously as he should. Investigations are hard work."

"Did you guys make any progress before Bane came and took over?"

Chief Crowe sighs. "Nothing significant. Why?"

"Oh," I say, realizing I might be too obvious. "Just curious."

Chief Crowe looks doubtful. "Stay far away from this case, Peters. Bane isn't to be trifled with. If you get caught doing something you shouldn't, I won't be able to protect you."

"Understood," I say.

Chief Crowe nods and moves on to congratulate another Elite. I glance around until my eyes settle on a bright white lab coat off in the corner of the room. I make my way over.

"Hi, Director Fokus," I say.

She readjusts her glasses and blinks at me a few times. "Oh, hello there."

"Do you remember me?" I ask.

"Of course," she says. "I don't suppose you would ever reconsider a few weeks beneath my microscope? Allow me to untangle the many mysteries of magiciancraft? I'm *fairly* certain you'd survive the testing."

I shake my head quickly. "Don't think so." Does this

lady really think I'll agree to being an Amari-sized guinea pig?

Fokus frowns. "Then what do you and I have to talk about?"

"Wait," I say as she turns to leave. "Everyone thinks a magician caused the freeze, but that's not possible, right?"

"You heard that from an agent, didn't you?" Fokus rolls her eyes. "There's not a scientific theory in the world they'd trust more than a good hunch. Allow me to put your mind at ease. You are the most magical being we've ever tested, and you've got enough magic inside you to maybe freeze time in this tent for two seconds. Does that help?"

"Definitely." I almost tell her about the time freeze not affecting me, but I've got a feeling she'll want to test that theory, and I'd end up trapped in her lab after all. Then where would my investigation be?

Fokus glances at her watch. "I promised the chief exactly ten minutes away from my lab, and since that time has come and gone, I must be going. Congrats again on your gold star."

As Fokus heads for the door I wander back toward the crowd, where a few retired members of the Bureau come over to offer their congrats. It's clear they don't know much about the time freeze, so I start to glance around for who else I can talk to.

That's when I notice Director Van Helsing approach Director Harlowe. He says something that makes her scowl. Is he complaining about me being an Elite? Or something else?

Harlowe holds up a finger and taps on a glass with her spoon to get everyone's attention. "We aren't here just to talk, let's eat!"

As the crowd moves toward the food tables, Harlowe and Van Helsing head for the exit.

I start after them. I know I promised Elsie I'd stay away from Harlowe, but this *feels* important. I slip through the crowd to follow, stepping outside just in time to see them both head around the side of the tent.

I tiptoe closer until I catch the sound of hushed voices.

". . . rubbing that Peters girl in my face, and I don't appreciate it," says Director Van Helsing. "When I offered my support, you promised she'd be uninvited!"

Harlowe sighs. "And the Prime Minister changed his mind, simple as that. The girl has a passionate following. He's got big plans for Amari."

Plans for me? What makes Bane think I'd do anything to help him?

"And who are you to speak for Bane?" asks Director Van Helsing. "You've been a director for all of five minutes. Maybe I should be looking into that. Something's not right with you two."

"Oh, come now, Victor," says Harlowe, her voice taking on an almost musical quality. "You don't want to make an enemy of me. Just forget about all that."

Van Helsing is quiet for a long moment. "But—"

"I said, forget about it."

My phone buzzes loudly and I hurry to silence it. A

second later Van Helsing and Harlowe are right in front of me. I'm *so* caught.

Van Helsing narrows his eyes. "What are you doing back here?"

I scramble for a believable excuse. "I . . . uh . . . was looking for Director Harlowe. They were asking for her in the Elites tent."

Harlowe grins. "Were they now?"

I nod.

Director Van Helsing shoves past me, grumbling, "I've got work to do."

Harlowe comes close and wraps her arm around my shoulders, squeezing a little too tight as she guides me back toward the front of the tent. "Van Helsing is gone. So, please, tell me what you're *really* doing out here. Eavesdropping?"

If anyone can spot a lie, I should've known it would be the director of Half Truths and Full Cover-Ups. I feel like a fly that's landed directly in the center of a spiderweb.

"Talk to me," Harlowe says. "We're friends, are we not? Friends don't lie to one another."

I got caught red-handed, so I might as well be honest. "I *was* listening."

"Of course you were." Harlowe smiles. "You've been digging for information about the time freeze investigation since you arrived."

I swallow. "How do you know?"

"You'd be surprised what one can learn by simply paying attention. Let me guess, the girl who got famous for saving the world now has her ambitious eyes on the time freeze, am I right?"

"No—I mean, yes . . . but it's not about being famous or wanting credit. It's more complicated than that. Merlin and the Supernatural World Congress need to be freed. It's important."

Harlowe nods. "And Bane knows that. It's why he's taken over the investigation. To ensure that it gets solved as quickly as possible."

"But wouldn't that mean letting agents investigate? It's what we're trained to do."

"Think back to your studies last summer," she says. "Why might a Prime Minister take an investigation away from the Bureau?"

"Usually if the Prime Minister thinks there's a chance the Bureau committed the crime." It hits me what she's suggesting, and I nearly stumble. "You think someone at the Bureau caused the time freeze? Who?"

As we reach the entrance of the tent, Harlowe sighs and stops short. "Let's just say we haven't ruled it out. Of course, many people are quite certain a magician is responsible—of which there are only two at the Bureau."

I shudder. "You think it was me or Maria? But Director Fokus says it couldn't have been a magician. The spell is too strong."

Suddenly that smile of hers turns ice cold. "And here I thought you understood that I never allow the truth to get in the way of a good story. The supernatural world wants to believe it was a magician—because magicians doing bad things makes sense. They don't want to think about the possibility that a new danger exists that could hurt them." Harlowe shakes her head. "And as your friend, I just wonder if people might start to get the wrong idea about why a teenage magician like yourself seems so obsessed with the time freeze. Why, some might start to believe you're trying to cover your tracks."

"But that's not true," I say in a small voice.

"You know that, and *I* know that. But would Bane see it that way? Would anybody? Perhaps it's best if you let the adults handle things this summer. Why give anyone a reason to doubt you?"

I don't answer. There's nothing I can even think to say.

"Good girl," says Harlowe after a moment. "I knew two friends like us could come to an understanding."

≈ 11 ≈

ELSIE AND I WAKE UP SUPER EARLY THE NEXT MORNING to watch Jayden's welcome ceremony on the TV wall of our room. I wanted to go in person, but Elsie told me that only nosebleed seats are available this late.

I haven't gotten a chance to talk to Jayden yet, so it'll be nice to know he's doing okay. I can't wait to see him accept that shiny copper badge.

Onscreen, Chief Crowe is at the podium explaining to the first-year trainees that becoming supernatural is necessary for entry into the supernatural world. That means touching the Crystal Ball and having one of their talents upgraded to a supernatural ability beyond those of ordinary humans.

My best friend and I are both seated on the comfy carpet between our beds surrounded by snacks. Usually, this would be a guaranteed good time. But things feel tense. I know Elsie feels it too because she keeps glancing over at me.

"I'm fine," I say to her. "For real."

"Are you sure?" asks Elsie. "Because Harlowe basically admitted she could blame you for the time freeze anytime she wants. That could land you in Blackstone Prison—or worse, the Sightless Depths. And you're acting like it's no big deal."

"It's definitely a big deal," I admit. "But I can't give up the investigation. And we both know why."

"What if we just put things on pause for a day or two? Until we figure out a way to do it without Harlowe finding out."

"Except I already promised Cozmo I'd start working to end the time freeze. Who knows when he'll ask me to take the Crown again? I still don't know how much time I have."

"I'm just worried about you," says Elsie.

"I know," I say. "If it helps, I can't do much with the investigation until I find a new lead. Fokus agreed that it can't be a magician, but that doesn't tell us who it *could* be."

Elsie doesn't respond, but I can see the relief on her face. We go back to watching the welcome ceremony, cheering when the camera pans to Jayden's section for a few seconds. He looks nervous, but also excited. It makes me smile.

The first kid Chief Crowe calls to the stage is a tall white girl with braces and a face full of freckles. She smiles for the cameras as she shakes the chief's hand and accepts her notebook-paper badge. Then it's over to the Crystal Ball, which glows faintly at her touch.

The large screen at the back of the stage reads:

Talent Enhanced to Supernatural Ability:
Honesty to Lie Detection

"That's actually a really great ability for such a low-level badge," says Elsie.

"So she basically becomes a human lie detector?"

Elsie nods. "Think how useful that would be in Supernatural Investigations or even Spies and Secrets. I bet a few departments would make an exception to let her try out."

Chief Crowe calls the next kid's name, but suddenly agents appear onstage. More appear in the aisles and near the exits. Harlowe's voice comes over the intercom. "The rest of this morning's welcome ceremony is hereby canceled, by order of the Prime Minister. No more trainees shall receive a badge or a supernatural ability until every child has been proven not to be a magician. All trainees are to report back to their rooms and agents will be around shortly with a Magic-Meter to ensure that no one has come to the Bureau already in possession of magic."

The intercom clicks off, leaving Elsie and me silent. They're actually checking for magicians.

"Can they do that?" I whisper.

"They just did," Elsie answers.

Wordlessly, we both climb back into bed. There's still a couple hours before breakfast starts.

My phone buzzes. It's a text message from Cozmo.

A ticking-clock emoji, followed by:

Still waiting for an answer.

Later, Elsie and I join the crowd clogging the youth dorm hallways to wait for an elevator. Even though the welcome ceremony was canceled, juniors still have to report for the start of training.

"How can you-know-who be rushing you already?" Elsie whispers.

"I don't want to lead the League," I say quietly. "Especially into a war."

"Then we keep trying," Elsie says. "But I'm really scared for you."

"Me too."

The line isn't moving. And the kids around us keep eyeing my Elites pin. I'm only still wearing it because, honestly, I earned it. Maybe Harlowe runs the club, but that doesn't mean what I accomplished should be ignored.

It isn't until an older girl—a Junior Curator from the Department of the Unexplained—comes up to me that I understand why my pin is getting so many confused looks.

"You know you don't have to wait in line, don't you?" she says.

"I don't?" That's news to me.

"You're one of us now," she says. "Elites have special permission to take Lord Kensington whenever we want."

"You guys get to ride the chief's personal elevator?" asks Elsie, looking stunned.

"Can I bring my best friend?" I ask.

The girl frowns. "Elites only, I'm afraid. If everyone brought their friends, that elevator would be just as full as the others."

"Oh," I say. "Um, maybe next time."

"Suit yourself." She shrugs and walks away.

Elsie says, "You don't have to wait here with me, you know."

"Because I should get used to you not being around?" I wince. That's not what I meant to say at all—even if it is what I was thinking.

Elsie drops her eyes. "Amari, that's not fair."

"I know, just forget I said anything, okay? Let's both have a good first day."

Elsie offers a small smile. "We'd have to make it out of this line first."

She's right—at this rate, we'll never get where we're going. I watch that Junior Curator hop onto Lord Kensington with a few other Elites. That's when I notice an empty elevator at the far end. "What about that one?"

Elsie leans around the boy in front of us to look. "That's weird . . . maybe nobody else has noticed?"

"Let's not wait to find out!" I say. "Come on!"

"But—"

I run so no one else can steal our elevator. With Cozmo breathing down my neck about the Crown and the time freeze investigation off to such a slow start, the least I can do is get to class on time.

Elsie hesitates but follows anyway. "There's probably a reason no one's choosing this one."

Finally the elevator slides into view. My best friend groans. "Oh *no*. It's Beauford."

"What's wrong with Beauford?" I ask. "Is he new?"

"The opposite of new," Elsie replies. "He's *old*. The Bureau must've let him unretire again."

Beauford's elevator doors creak loudly as they struggle to slide open. A weary voice says, "Greetings, Junior, er, um— you know your own names, doncha? Where ya headed?"

"Supernatural Investigations and Magical Science," I say.

"Speak up!" the elevator shouts. "You youngsters and your whispery voices . . ."

Elsie frowns before clearing her throat. "SUPERNAT-URAL INVEST—!"

"Don't you raise your voice at me, missy!" says the elevator. "Respect your elders."

"She didn't mean it," I say quickly, ignoring the face Elsie makes. "It's just that it's our first day as juniors and it's really important we be on time."

"Reckon I can manage that. I've been called the fastest way to travel in the whole Bureau!"

"Really?"

"That's right," says Beauford. "Now come on in."

Elsie looks skeptical. "This seems like a really bad idea."

"We already got out of line," I say. "Unless you want to go all the way to the back?"

With a sigh, Elsie joins me inside.

The doors squeak shut and the elevator inches its way upward—like, literally. It takes us fifteen minutes just to reach the next floor, which is completely underwater. "Now approaching," says Beauford, "the Department of Undersea Relations."

"Um, Beauford? I thought you were the fastest way to travel."

"Sure was! Why, back in '77—"

"1977!" I exclaim. This elevator is older than *Mama*.

"Don't be silly! *1877!* I was the fastest 'cause I was the first and only elevator in the Bureau! Before me you had to take the stairs!"

I groan.

Elsie keeps tapping her foot, an "I told you so" clear in her expression. On both sides of us, other elevators zip up and down their tubes at blurring speeds.

I try to be polite. "Excuse me, Mr. Beauford. But is there any way you could speed up?"

"You need me to speak up?" he asks.

"No, *speed* up," I reply.

"I am speaking up!" shouts Beauford.

Elsie covers her face.

I clear my throat. "Can. You. Please. Go. Faster!"

"Faster?" the elevator scoffs. "I'm going as fast as I can! Ain't what I used to be, you know. That's the problem with this *new* generation. No patience. Everything's a rush. What's the hurry? You're already gonna be late."

"Yeah," I say, "because of you!"

But the elevator continues to drone on. We pass the library floor, which is covered completely in books—the floors, pillars, even the ceiling. Beauford doesn't even stop his lecture to announce it.

Zzz.

Elsie and I turn to look at one another. Did our elevator just fall asleep?

Suddenly we drop so fast that I feel my feet leave the ground. We're in free-fall! Elsie and I lock arms in midair, both of us screaming our lungs out.

A red sign appears on the wall of the elevator: *Emergency Features Activated.* The elevator slows, causing me and Elsie to come crashing down onto soft airbags, still screaming.

"What is all the commotion about?" asks Beauford sleepily. "Oh yes, now approaching the underground tunnels." The elevator doors shudder open.

My knees wobble as I get to my feet, and I reach out a hand to help Elsie up. This isn't our floor—in fact, we're as far away as possible from where we needed to go. But neither of us hesitates to get off while we've got the chance. "My . . . bad," I say, trying to catch my breath. "From now on . . . I'll take your advice."

"Honestly, I'm just glad to be alive," says Elsie.

Thankfully we're able to catch a ride back up to our floors with Lucy. I wave to Elsie over my shoulder as I dash into the lobby of Supernatural Investigations, a large black-and-white room with a statue of Abraham Van Helsing driving a stake into the heart of Count Vladimir to mark the end of the Ancient War. The statue even shows Vladimir wearing the Crown.

Like I needed another reminder.

I head through the lobby, presenting my moonstone badge to the scanner on the back wall. The doors open with a whoosh, and I step forward into the giant U-shaped main hallway. This place is always busy, and today is no different. The hum of chatter fills my ears, and fast-moving currents of grown-ups move swiftly in both directions. I stay close to the wall to keep from being run over.

I move past the Hall of Special Agents, with its glistening hardwoods and shiny gold trim, to a smaller hallway marked *Junior Agents*, then follow that until I reach the glass wall of a massive classroom. Around fifty teenagers of different ages, all decked out in their gray suits, fill the space, paired up at desks with laptops and gold nameplates in front of them.

Seeing everyone paired up makes me wonder if Tristan and I are still supposed to be partners. With the tantrum he threw in the Elites tent, my guess is probably not.

I head for the door. Seems like I'm the last to arrive.

Make that *almost* last.

Lara Van Helsing sits on the floor next to the classroom door, her arms around her knees. Just as Elsie and I suspected, somehow she's a Junior Agent despite failing last summer's tryout.

This is awkward. Part of me wants to step right past her into the classroom. This girl couldn't have been more awful to me last year. Still, I can't help feeling that maybe Elsie was right—I do owe her *something* for helping me get back into the Bureau.

"Everything okay?" I ask.

At the sound of my voice Lara goes stiff, her head whipping around. She quickly gets up to her feet, her face flushing deep red. "I—I was just . . ."

"Hiding?" I finish.

Anger flashes across her face. "Was not!"

"You sure about that?"

Lara starts toward the glass door, but I can see her hesitation—like she'd rather be anywhere else. Her face falls as she pulls open the door and the loud squeak makes every head in the room turn in our direction. I follow her inside, my heart splashing down into my belly as every eye seems to size us up.

"Peters! Van Helsing!" calls Agent Fiona from the front of the room. "I'm assuming ye both know you're late?"

"Must've gotten lost," I joke.

Fiona doesn't smile back. It's a reminder that Agent Fiona out of class isn't the same as in class. "That's no way to set an example now, is it?"

It feels strange to think that a room full of older kids would be looking to me to set an example. But I guess that's what comes with this gold Elites pin. "Sorry."

Fiona makes a face but softens a bit. "Go on and take your seats. Van Helsing, you're there at the back. We'll figure out what to do with ye soon enough. Peters, you're up here."

I rush forward, nearly tripping, which gets a few chuckles. Cheeks burning, I scan for my nameplate, but every seat seems to be taken.

"Up *here*, lass," says Fiona, pointing to a desk in the first row. An empty chair sits next to none other than Tristan Davies. I guess we *are* still partners.

I slip into the desk next to Tristan. He pretends not to notice.

"Skies *above*." Fiona shakes her head, exasperated. "Van Helsing, what on earth are ye doing still on your feet?"

I turn to find Lara still at the very back of the room. Her head is bowed and she's shaking.

"I . . ."

"Speak up, child!" Fiona calls. Laughter bubbles up around the room, but Fiona quiets it with a stern look.

"I don't have a chair," Lara calls.

"Only *real* Junior Agents get chairs," someone hollers. Snickers ring out.

"That's enough," says Fiona. "Van Helsing's chair better show up in the next thirty seconds or else you'll all be taking turns cleaning the cages in Creature Control. And you've not known agony like trying to get invisible poo off your shoes."

Tristan's hand immediately goes up. "I'm not admitting guilt, but I might have seen it in the boys' bathroom across the hall."

Fiona fumes. "Then somebody'd better bring it back here."

Tristan snaps his fingers, and Bear jumps to his feet like an obedient puppy and dashes out of the room. A few seconds later he returns, dropping the chair loudly at Lara's desk.

Tristan flashes another winning smile. "Just having a bit of fun with the fresh faces is all. We didn't mean any harm."

"It costs ye nothing to be kind," Agent Fiona tells the class. "And I don't think I need to remind ye who her father is. So maybe keep that in mind when deciding who to prank?"

"Yes, ma'am," says Tristan. "Although the fact that she's a Junior Agent even after failing the tryouts is a pretty clear reminder of just who her father is."

Agent Fiona frowns but doesn't reprimand him. Probably because deep down she agrees. We all do. It's not fair.

Tristan cuts his eyes to me and whispers, "Sorry about this. It's nothing personal."

I have no idea what he's apologizing for. Then he raises his hand again.

Agent Fiona sighs as she looks up from her papers. "What is it now, Davies?"

He turns to look at me full-on now. "I think many of us, including myself, are wondering how it is Peters got the gold star for Supernatural Investigations."

The room mumbles their agreement. *Seriously?* He knows perfectly well how I got the gold star.

"Settle down, the lot of ye," says Fiona. "Who can tell me how gold stars are given out?"

A girl's voice answers from somewhere behind me. "The Junior Agent who has the most impressive accomplishments at the end of camp is awarded a gold star pin."

"You've all seen the video of Amari and Dylan Van Helsing." Agent Fiona shrugs. "Seems pretty cut and dry to me."

That confident smile of Tristan's finally wavers. "No offense, instructor, but that happened before Chief Crowe promoted her to Junior Agent at the end of summer camp. It shouldn't count. Meanwhile I single-handedly took down a whole herd of mist monsters in the Famished Forest—"

Fiona looks to me now. "You want to tell him or should I?"

"Well," I begin. "I *first* made Junior Agent before the whole Dylan and Moreau thing. Agent Magnus promoted me in his office. Director Van Helsing demoted me back to trainee, like, right after, though."

Tristan deflates. "That means you only had to finish the summer as a Junior Agent for your achievements to count.

Which is what happened when the chief promoted you again."

Fiona grins. "Satisfied now, Davies?"

He just nods. "I can't believe I finished second. *Me!*"

"Oh, stop your pouting," says Fiona. "It's still your third star in a row. Nobody thinks any less of ye. Now, I assume I can count on ye to help Peters be the best she can be?"

Tristan smiles, but it doesn't reach his eyes. "You can count on me."

Not very convincing.

"Now that that's settled," says Agent Fiona, "let's get these schedules sorted."

"Have fun making a fool of yourself all summer," Tristan mutters to me under his breath.

So he was perfectly fine being my partner when he thought that he was getting the gold star pin, but now that I have it, he's gonna act like that?

My hand goes up.

"Yes, Peters?"

I clear my throat. "So the gold star gives you special privileges, right? Like picking your partner?"

Amusement flickers across Agent Fiona's face. "That's correct."

"Then I'd like to choose a different partner." Murmurs fill the room and I turn and scan the faces of the stunned Junior Agents seated behind me. They've all got partners already and I only know a couple of them anyway. They seem just as unhappy as Tristan that I beat them out.

Tristan spins around in his chair to have a look and seems to reach the same conclusion. A smug grin lights his face.

I turn back around to Agent Fiona and bite my lip. I'm tired of people pushing me around. "I'll choose . . ." I lift my chin. "Lara Van Helsing."

The room erupts, and doubt creeps into my head. Did I really choose the girl who hated me more than anything last summer just to make a point? The girl who literally tried to bash my face in?

Beside me, Tristan stares, his mouth hanging open. "I'm going to be without a partner?"

"Quiet," calls Agent Fiona and the room falls silent again. "Are you sure about this?"

Not at all. But it would be cruel to change my mind now. Besides, one thing I do know is that Tristan would be an awful partner.

So I nod.

"Very well," says Agent Fiona. "For now, Davies and Van Helsing, switch seats. I'll talk it over with the Deputy Director and see if there's a solution that makes sense."

Tristan stands, furious. The look that boy gives me could melt ice. A few seconds later, Lara takes his seat, looking totally confused.

Making an enemy of the best Junior Agent on my first day wasn't something I'd planned.

Agent Fiona leaves her desk and steps to the dry-erase

board at the front of the classroom. "*Now* then, maybe we can go back to the schedules. For those of ye who are new, open up your laptops and simply hold down the *S* key for five seconds. Your schedule should pop up onscreen. Once you know what you'll be doing today, head on over to your first class. Ye lot are dismissed, but please come and see me with any questions." Her eyes seem to snag on me for a moment, then she looks away.

I follow her instructions, and my schedule pops up:

JUNIOR AGENT AMARI PETERS
SUMMER CAMP SCHEDULE

Day 1

Roll Call & Announcements (Junior Agent

Room):   **7:45 a.m. to 8 a.m.**

Current Events Class (Youth Classroom):

                          8 a.m. to 10 a.m.

Sky Sprints—Aerial Acrobatics (Training

Gym A):   **10 a.m. to Noon**

Lunch: **Noon to 1 p.m.**

Private Tutoring: **1 p.m. to 3 p.m.**

Dismissal (Junior Agent Room):

                          3 p.m. to 3:15 p.m.

Welcome Social: **6 p.m. to 8 p.m.**

Three classes in one day? As a trainee we had two, max. And what's this private tutoring after lunch? I turn to ask Lara, but she's already on her feet, rushing toward the door without so much as a word. *You're welcome*, I think.

One by one, the other kids start to pack up their laptops to leave too. Once I'm the only kid left, I head up to Agent Fiona's desk to ask about my schedule.

"Peters," Fiona says, briefly glancing up from her papers. "Report to Briefing Room Seven after lunch. And tell absolutely no one where you're going."

"But—"

"Heavens, lass," she cuts in. "Just follow orders for once. I promise it won't kill ye."

That answer seems like all I'm going to get, so I turn to leave.

It's not until I get to the door that Fiona repeats, "Tell absolutely no one."

I frown and nod. What in the world is going on?

☙ 12 ❧

"WELCOME TO CURRENT EVENTS, WHERE WE'LL TAKE what's happening in the news and dissect it to help us better understand the supernatural world around us. While we may disagree on some things, debate is important. So let's keep things civil and polite." Agent Addison, the training agent in charge of this class, isn't one I've met before. But hopefully her cheery smile means she won't hold being a magician against me.

I've settled into one of the seats near the front with Lara in the chair next to me. I can't help remembering how she told the other trainees not to sit beside me in Supernatural Immersion class last summer. I felt like such an outcast.

What was I thinking, choosing her as my partner?

Tristan and Bear sit together on the opposite side of the room. Which is fine by me.

Agent Addison leans back against her desk at the front of the classroom. "Who wants to choose a news story to discuss?"

"How about our new Prime Minister canceling the welcome ceremony this morning?" calls Bear.

Agent Addison's smile falters. "Yes, that was . . . unexpected."

"But it's the right thing to do," says Tristan. "We've got to protect ourselves. Merlin was way too soft on UnWanteds. And don't get me started on magicians—our ancestors would be turning over in their graves if they knew we've got them working at the Bureau now."

I almost can't believe my ears. He didn't seem to mind me being here back at the Club Fair. I wonder how he'd have answered if things had gone differently.

Agent Addison's eyes flick to me, then back to Tristan. "Everyone please be respectful of your classmates. Let's keep things polite and educational." She turns her attention back to the class. "Now then, one of the most pressing issues of our time has been the status of the UnWanted community since the Ancient War. Technically they've been banned from society since the 1300s, but as times changed this was enforced less and less, so that almost no one even uses the term "UnWanted" anymore. The descendants of those who fought on the Night Brothers' side are now productive members of our society."

A girl on the other side of the room raises her hand.

"Go on," says Agent Addison.

She clears her throat. "I just think it's horrible how they're considered, like, second-class citizens. UnWanteds should have the same rights other supernaturals have. Even our new Prime Minister is technically an UnWanted."

I didn't think about that, but she's right. Wraiths like Bane are the creations of magicians, just like other UnWanteds. They were made using the Living Death curse. And yet Bane is the one leading the charge against other UnWanteds. It doesn't make sense.

Agent Addison nods. "Does anyone disagree with that statement?"

Tristan's hand goes up.

"The floor is yours, Davies," says Agent Addison.

"Wraiths might've been created by magicians, but they were human first, and they didn't fight for the Night Brothers, so they don't count. As for the *real* UnWanteds, I don't mind them having a place in the supernatural world, as long as it's separate from the rest of us."

Every time that boy speaks, I realize how I lucky I was to get away from him. Now that I can see what kind of person he truly is, I'm positive he only wanted to be my partner to make himself more popular.

"Well, where are UnWanteds supposed to go now?" asks another boy. "As soon as Bane took over, he restarted the ban so that UnWanteds aren't allowed in the known world, and most of the hidden supernatural cities won't let them in either."

This time it's Bear who speaks up. "Not our problem. It's a shame the Supernatural World Congress got frozen, 'cause my dad says they were about to vote to finally crack down on the UnWanteds for good."

I sit up straighter in my chair. The Supernatural World Congress was meeting to discuss UnWanteds when the time freeze happened? That could be the whole reason they were frozen. And if we know *why*, then maybe we can figure out *who* too. I pull out my phone and message Elsie beneath my desk.

From Amari_Peters ◆ :
Els, any way to check what the Congress was meeting about when frozen?

The answer comes back quicker than I expect.

New Message from Els_the_Inventor:
Maybe? Stuck in a lecture. Library for lunch?

I send a quick "yes" and tuck my phone back into my pocket before Agent Addison notices. Except, when I glance up, she's looking right at me.

". . . it seems that our classroom is just as split on the issue of UnWanteds as the rest of our world is. But one voice we haven't heard is that of the Bureau's very own magician. Amari, is there anything you wanted to say to the class?"

My cheeks burn from being put on the spot, and I'm tempted to just shake my head so we move on to another topic. But how can I *not* say something?

I blow out a breath. "I—I guess I'd just ask you to imagine that you were me. I didn't *choose* to be a magician, I was born this way. I know the Night Brothers were awful—my own brother is stuck in Supernatural Health because of Moreau. But I'm not the Night Brothers. I haven't done anything to anyone, but so many people and supernaturals have already made up their minds about me anyway. It's not fair, and I don't deserve it. And neither do any of the UnWanteds."

It's quiet for a moment before Tristan lets out a mocking, "Aww, poor Peters."

Anger surges through me as arguments break out around the room. Who does that boy think he is?

"You're just being a jerk," shouts Lara. "You were my sister's biggest fan before you learned she was a magician."

"And *you* would've been saying the same things I just did until you found out that big sis is exactly what you used to bully your new partner for," Tristan replies.

Lara pales and cuts a glance at me, then looks away.

"Enough," says Agent Addison. "Perhaps it'd be best to move on to another topic."

I don't say anything else in class. I just sit there, my whole body tense with irritation. It's so easy for some people to dismiss others' experiences because they don't have the same problems.

Once class lets out, Lara follows me into the hallway. I watch her speed-walk past me, stop, then turn back, red-faced.

"I, uh, just wanted to apologize for—"

"Don't bother," I interrupt. "Okay?"

I leave her there and start toward the gym for Sky Sprints training. I immediately feel guilty but also justified for what I said—honestly it's so many emotions at once. I can only imagine what Elsie would say if she could see my aura right now.

The study rooms are all reserved when we arrive at the library. Seems lunch is the time lots of juniors choose to get a jump start on their studies. But one look at my Elites pin and the librarian, Mrs. Belle, taps a button and a bookcase swings open to reveal a secret study room.

"Okay, I wasn't jealous before," laughs Elsie. "But that's starting to change. This place even has refreshments?"

It's true. All the other study rooms are just two chairs, a computer, and a desk. This place has three different computer stations to choose from, two drink machines, and a giant bowl of chocolate chip cookies on a small table.

The sign clearly says *Elites Only*, but Mrs. Belle has always had a soft spot for me and Elsie. "Y'all go on inside," she says, "'fore anybody sees."

She doesn't have to tell us twice. Elsie and I take the computer farthest from the door, in case another Elite comes in.

"Do you think the Supernatural World Congress was really meeting to discuss UnWanteds?" I ask. "Or was it just Bear pretending his family is *so* important like he did back at Whitman Prep?"

"He does like to stretch the truth, but his dad is a pretty high-ranking Senior Agent. What if the Congress was frozen *because* they were discussing the UnWanteds?"

"That's what I was wondering too," I say. "Maybe whoever froze the Congress didn't want them passing any new laws on UnWanteds."

Elsie nods, and I can see she's just as excited as I am—nothing gets her going like discovering the answer to a tough question. "Since this is a library computer, we should be able to search every supernatural newspaper and magazine at once. If it's mentioned, we'll find it."

She clicks the search button, and the loading screen appears. A moment later:

No results

"Not even one?" I say.

Elsie looks genuinely confused. "But how is that possible? Surely someone in the whole supernatural world reported on what our most powerful leaders were meeting about."

"Is there anywhere else we can search?" I ask. "Maybe the government website?"

"Worth a shot." Elsie pulls up the page. "Bingo! The official schedule."

She clicks on the link, but this time we get a message asking for a username and password.

"Another dead end?" I ask.

"Maybe not," says Elsie. "Please don't tell anybody what I'm about to do."

I raise an eyebrow. "What *are* you about to do exactly?"

My best friend pulls a tiny metal spider from her lab coat and sets it down on the table. She presses a button on its head and the thing springs to life, folding until it's small enough to fit into one of the computer vents and crawling inside. "I'm assisting the Senior Researchers in the Gadgets Room with literal computer bugs. I'm not supposed to take them out of the lab, but I figured it might come in handy."

"Elsie the Hacker." I grin. "Do they put hackers in Blackstone? Or is it straight to the Sightless Depths?"

Elsie buries her face in her hands. "Oh gosh, don't even joke like that."

"It's working." I give her a nudge as one by one, the username and password sections are filled in.

She presses Enter and an *Access Granted* message flashes. We're in!

Suddenly the screen begins to dim and Elsie scrambles

for her phone. She just manages to snap a photo of it before the whole thing turns black and a message pops onscreen in bright red letters.

This Information Has Been Deemed Confidential
by the Department of Half Truths
and Full Cover-Ups

"Harlowe," says Elsie. "She clearly doesn't want anyone snooping around this website. I'll bet she's also the reason we didn't get any results on our search before."

"You don't think she'll know this was us, do you?"

Elsie shakes her head. "These computer bugs are untraceable."

"Good. Let's see what you got on the phone."

My best friend lays the phone down so we can look together. She got a really good shot of the webpage.

"They *were* meeting about UnWanteds," I say. "Bane was leading the Ban All UnWanteds side, and Merlin was on the side of giving UnWanteds equal rights."

Elsie sucks in a breath and points to the screen. "Look who was scheduled to speak."

BAN ALL UNWANTEDS CAMPAIGN GUEST
SPEAKER: Elaine Harlowe—To deliver the sad tale of how her adoptive parents were lost in one of Moreau's careless attacks.

"Moreau killed Harlowe's parents," I say. "That's got to be why Bane has given her so much power. She believes the same things he does."

"The part that stands out to me," says Elsie, "is that both Bane and Harlowe were supposed to be in the Congress Room that day. They should be frozen like everyone else."

"Are you saying they knew the attack was coming?" I ask. "You don't think they caused the time freeze, do you?"

Elsie shrugs. "All I'm saying is it's an awfully big coincidence, don't you think?"

"But neither of them can cast a spell," I say. "Even if they could, that doesn't explain why the time freeze didn't affect me."

"Well, they're definitely hiding something," she says.

"That we *can* agree on."

After a pretty eye-opening lunch, it's back to training for both of us. For me, that means discovering just what's up with the private tutoring on my schedule.

On my way I stop to peer into the training room where the rest of the Junior Agents are. As far as I can tell, they've all got Supernatural Ability practice right now. Inside, kids do incredible things like lift weights with one finger and stretch their arms like rubber bands to grab things on the other side of the room. There's no sign of Tristan, though. What's the golden boy's ability?

Then I look up.

Tristan can *fly*. And fast too—like a real superhero. I grimace. It figures that he'd have the coolest ability. He whizzes overhead, diving through the air at blurring speeds. He doesn't even need Sky Sprints. I leave before he can see me watching.

If I remember correctly, the briefing rooms are located near the Operations Bay. They tend to be really small. And private.

A guess pops into my head that causes the smallest spark of hope to flicker inside me. If the others are practicing *their* supernatural abilities, does this mean what I think it does?

The thought scares me as much as it excites me. I stick to the illusions I know because they're safe. I'm in control. Truth is, I didn't mean to call down lightning against Dylan, I only wanted to stop him somehow. My magic took over and did the rest. But what if next time it does something I don't want?

The thought of someone getting hurt because I can't control my magic terrifies me.

I move down the hallway, ducking past two very serious-looking agents stepping out of Briefing Room 6. I pause in front of the next door and take a deep breath. *Here goes.*

I give the door a knock and it opens almost immediately. Maria Van Helsing appears in the doorway, and relief floods through me. Finally. "I've got so much to tell you."

"I know," says Maria, and she pulls me inside. After a quick look both ways down the hallway, she shuts the door.

The briefing rooms are just as I remember. There's

enough space for a small metal table, a few chairs, and little else. Maria steps past me into the room, flashing one of her big, warm smiles. The kind that almost makes me forget I've been trying to speak with her for the last two days.

"I wanted so badly to reach out to you," she says. "But I was under house arrest until yesterday morning. They took my phone and locked my Eurg account."

"Did they think you had something to do with the time freeze?" I ask.

"I don't know," Maria says. "My dad said it was out of his hands. The order came straight from Bane himself, and Harlowe managed to keep it out of the news."

"Harlowe and Bane are definitely up to something." I start to explain what Elsie and I found on the computer at lunch, but Maria holds up a hand.

"You're doing another investigation?" she asks.

I nod. "To figure out how to end the time freeze."

"*Amari*," says Maria. "It's not your job to save the world every summer."

"I don't have a choice! The League of Magicians might go to war . . ."

"I know all about the League. But let me handle that, okay?" Maria pulls a tattered brown leather book from inside her gray jacket. "*This* is why I've brought you here. I'm going to teach you magic."

I force down my frustration about Maria not listening to me. If she really does know all about the League, then she must know about Cozmo's offer to give me the Crown. If she can convince the League not to go to war, shouldn't I let her? It would make life so much easier for me.

I nod and focus on the leather book instead. The same worry I always get at the idea of exploring my magic sends butterflies fluttering through me. "The Bureau is allowing this? Even with Bane in charge?"

Maria doesn't quite meet my eyes.

"The Bureau *is* allowing this, right?"

"So . . . ," Maria begins. "Prime Minister Merlin sent down orders for me to teach you the basics of magic weeks ago, in the hope that you could use it to help the supernatural world. Like I have."

"And Prime Minister Bane?" I ask again. "What does he think?"

"Bane doesn't know."

My jaw drops.

"As long as we don't advertise what we're doing, we should be fine." Maria's lips press thin. "Bane is only *Acting* Prime Minister. He can't overrule a direct order from Merlin."

"Then why are we hiding it?" I ask.

"Because Bane hates magicians," she answers. "He'd try to punish you in some other way. It's okay if you'd rather not risk it, I understand. Just let me know."

"No," I say. "I am curious about what I can do." With Maria here to help me, it doesn't seem quite so scary. "I just worry about losing control again. Everyone sees a hero when they watch that video of me and Dylan, but I see a girl who isn't in control of her magic."

Maria nods. "With power as great as yours, there's always the risk of it getting away from you. But that's why I'm here, to show you how to always be in control. What do you know about magic already?"

"Not much," I say. "I've been really nervous about using new spells."

"Being able to show restraint is a good thing. It's the hardest part of being a fair magician."

"Can you tell me more about fair and foul magick?" I ask. "I'm not sure I totally understand it."

Maria flicks her wrists and a small flame bursts into life in the palm of her hand. "Nature is neither good nor bad. And neither is this flame. It simply is."

"But doesn't fire burn things?"

Maria nods. "Certainly. But it also warms you up on a cold day."

"So it's not so much what the spell does, but how you use it?" I ask.

"That's mostly correct," says Maria. "It's probably too complicated to fully explain in one lesson, but essentially fair magick is self*less* where foul magick is self*ish*. Fair magicians seek to use magic to benefit the world around us. Foul magicians use it for their own gain, at the expense of others."

"I've, uh, used foul magick before." I know it was foul magick because that's how it was listed in the spell book Dylan gave me. "But it was to defend myself against a bully who wanted to beat me up. Does that mean it's still wrong?"

"Some spells can *only* be used to hurt or punish, and we call those foul magick spells," says Maria. "For a fair magician, self-defense means defending yourself, but it stops short of punishing your attacker."

I think back to last summer. That spell didn't just stop Lara from punching me, it went further than that. Much further. It cast an illusion of her worst nightmare, bad enough to bring her to tears.

"I understand," I say in a small voice.

Maria shifts uncomfortably, her voice pained. "Lara told me what happened between you two. What's done is done."

She flicks her fingers and the flame becomes fiery butterflies that fly smoky circles around the room. It's the same thing Dylan used to do. A question pops into my head. "Does the League of Magicians practice only fair magick?"

"We do," she answers. "It's why we never joined Moreau. Even though we were founded by a Night Brother, we saw the error of their ways and decided to take a different path. But it's not always easy. In fact, choosing to be good is the hardest decision you can possibly make—especially when you possess magic as great as your own."

"Why?" I ask.

Maria flicks the light switch, and the room goes dark save for the glow of a tiny flame dancing in her palm. She leans forward, holding it closer. "Think of this flame as you. You're burning with the will to be a good magician. But look around at the darkness surrounding the flame.

It's always there, tempting, waiting for your resolve to falter. Being good is a choice, Amari. And it's one you have to keep making, again and again. No matter how hard it gets. However tempting it is to let the darkness win."

I know what kind of magician—no, what kind of *person* I want to be. Someone Quinton would be proud to call his sister. "I *will* be a good magician. Even if I'm forced to wear the Crown."

"Crown?" says Maria. "What crown?"

I'm confused. "I thought that since you're part of the League, you knew about Cozmo's offer."

Maria's flame flickers out, and a moment later the lights are back on. She leans forward and takes hold of both my hands. "*What* offer, Amari?"

"It's what I was trying to tell you. Why it's so important I end the time freeze."

I tell her everything.

"He had no right to ask that of you." Maria is red-faced and furious. "And then to threaten you! You aren't ready for magic like that—it's too dangerous. You're too young." She looks at me seriously. "Promise me you'll let me deal with Cozmo."

I've never seen her like this. I nod and say, "I promise."

≋ 13 ≋

TURNS OUT, LEARNING MAGIC ISN'T NEARLY AS FUN AS IT sounds. Maria spent the rest of the class teaching me to concentrate. Which I thought I was already pretty good at, but with magic it's not so much your thoughts you have to control, but your feelings. Controlling your emotions is the key to controlling your magic.

Once our last class of the day is done, all Junior Agents are supposed to meet back in the Junior Agent Room for dismissal. But since I'm the only person who wasn't in Agent Fiona's Supernatural Ability practice, I'm the first one there. As I wait for the others, I think about what Maria had to say about the Crown of Vladimir. Deep down, I knew something seemed off about the whole thing.

I'm only thirteen. The League can't expect me to lead adults into a war against people I care about here at the Bureau. That's just crazy.

I feel so relieved—it's like someone's taken a fifty-pound weight off my shoulders. Maybe Maria is right, I saved the supernatural world once. I shouldn't have to keep doing it.

I decide to let Cozmo know that I can't accept the Crown. I'm not sure how he'll take the news, but I can't worry about that right now. I'm going to let Maria handle it, like she said.

I take out my phone and send off a quick reply to Cozmo's text message.

From Amari:
I can't accept Vladimir's Crown. I'm just not ready.

I follow it up with this:

From Amari:
You'll have to talk to Maria from now on. I'm really sorry.

The reply is almost instant.

New Text Message from Cozmo:
I'm sorry too

What's that supposed to mean?

The other Junior Agents start to file in. So I tuck my phone into my jacket as Agent Fiona goes up to the dry-erase board at the front of the room to write out something about tomorrow's schedule.

If anybody missed me in Supernatural Ability class, no one mentions it. Most everyone is talking about the Welcome Social tonight.

Lara comes in last and takes a seat next to me. She keeps her head down, staring at the desk in front of us like she's counting down the seconds till we're dismissed. I wonder if the other Junior Agents continued their teasing in the training gym.

I should probably say something—she is my partner, after all. And I wasn't much nicer to her in the hall. I owe it to Maria to at least try to be kinder to her sister.

"Lara . . ."

Suddenly red bulbs flash brightly at the corners of the room, and *Red Alert* flashes on each of the monitors along the walls.

Lara jumps in her seat, then leans forward and flips open her laptop. "Something should pop up here really soon."

"Let's keep calm, everyone," calls Fiona, gesturing with her hands for us to stay in our seats. "We'll just wait and see what this is about."

Director Van Helsing's voice comes over the intercom. "Senior Agents and above report to the Operations Bay immediately. I repeat, Senior Agents and above report to the Operations Bay *immediately*."

"Everyone?" Lara whispers. "This must be something really bad."

Words flash across the laptop screen:

RED ALERT
Wanted criminal Dylan Van Helsing has escaped
the Sightless Depths.
He is considered extremely dangerous.
Current whereabouts unknown.

Reading those words sets the world around me spinning. I feel like I might throw up. How could this happen? It's got to be a mistake, right?

It takes me a moment to realize Agent Fiona is now crouched in front of my desk, calling my name.

"Peters!" She gives my shoulders a firm shake, snapping me out of my daze. "Are you all right?"

"I . . . don't know," I say truthfully.

"And you, Van Helsing? Dylan *is* your brother."

"Not anymore," says Lara bitterly.

Agent Fiona just nods. "You two stay put, okay? I'll be back with news as soon as I can." She gets up and heads through the door.

The room buzzes, and one by one the screens begin to show footage of a vast underground fortress shrouded in near total darkness. The Sightless Depths is a place for the worst of the worst criminals—located miles underground in the pits of the Goblin King, deeper than the lowest level of the Bureau and surrounded by all sorts of terrors, it's supposed to be even more secure than Blackstone Prison because it's more dangerous outside the jail than it is inside.

A question echoes in my head: How long before Dylan comes after the girl who put him there? I shiver.

"Looks like you'll be getting your old partner back." Tristan stops in front of me, flanked by Bear and a couple others.

"I'm actually pretty excited to see the rematch," says Bear.

I'm too shaken to answer, which just makes them bolder.

Bear steps forward and kicks my desk. "You hear us talking to you?"

Lara hops to her feet. "Back off, or my dad will hear about it."

Bear sneers and steps closer, but Tristan pulls him back.

"Leave it alone," says Tristan. "If there's one thing Lara here is good at, it's running to Daddy to solve all her problems. What an embarrassment the two of you are."

Tristan leads the others to the back of the room and Bear follows, sneering over his shoulder.

A million thoughts race through my head.

Lara turns to face me. "Uh, you all right?"

The intercom buzzes before I can answer. "Amari Peters, please report to Supernatural Health immediately."

My heart skips a beat. *Quinton.*

When I arrive in Supernatural Health, a Junior Curse-breaker is waiting for me, and I can tell from his expression that I was right to worry.

"What's wrong?"

"Um, I'm only allowed to say that Quinton's condition has worsened, and you need to speak with a Senior Curse-breaker."

He leads me through the hallways until we reach my brother's room, where we find him shaking in his bed.

I rush forward and take his hand. "Quinton, are you okay?" I turn around, frantic. "Is he okay? Please someone tell me something."

The Junior Cursebreaker pales. "T-the Senior Curse-breaker should be here any second."

I want to shout at him for not knowing, but I know this isn't his fault. Instead, I turn back to Quinton, tears in my eyes. What if this is it? What if I'm about to lose him?

I squeeze his hand tightly, and Quinton's shaking begins to lessen. Am I doing this? Is it magic? I don't notice that a Senior Cursebreaker has come into the room until I see him step past me to hook up a machine to Quinton's arm.

"The presence of family is always helpful with a curse like this, but I'm afraid that whatever relief you're offering, it's temporary. He's still worsening—though it doesn't make any sense. Just yesterday he was doing so much better."

I shudder. It may not make sense to the cursebreaker, but it makes sense to me. "Dylan Van Helsing just escaped." It can't be a coincidence. He must be doing this somehow. Maybe to get back at me. I ball my fists in anger. Quinton doesn't deserve this.

"I see." The Senior Cursebreaker nods to himself. "Initially my colleagues and I were split on whether Dylan took possession of Quinton's curse when he stole Moreau's magic. But this seems to prove that Dylan does in fact own the curse. You see, magical criminals are kept in magic-canceling cells. That may have slowed the effects of the curse. But now that he's free—"

"The curse is back to full strength." I've never felt so helpless. "How bad could it get?"

"As you know, only those with blood magic like Quinton's partner, Maria, can reach him. My fear is that if the curse progresses any further, well . . ."

The words are like a punch in the gut, hard enough to make me break into a million pieces. "If it gets worse, then we may not be able to talk to him at all?"

Pity fills the Senior Cursebreaker's expression, and he nods.

Fighting back a sob, I dash out of Quinton's room and sprint through the Department of Supernatural Health at full speed. I don't stop until I reach the elevators, where not even Luciano's song can calm me down.

I get out at Supernatural Investigations and don't quit running until I reach the Hall of Special Agents, where

Maria is coming out of her office.

I call her name, but she just says, "I already know."

"But Quinton—"

"I know that too," she says.

"There has to be something we can do."

Maria shakes her head, lowering her voice. "I'll contact the League. See if anything else can be done about the curse. It's a long shot, but—"

"We have to try!" I say. "*Please.*"

Maria nods and again that stupid intercom blares overhead: "Maria Van Helsing, please report to the Operations Bay."

"I have to go," she says, "but I promise we'll talk soon—we'll figure something out. For now, just go back to your room and try to stay positive."

"How am I supposed to do that?"

"Just try," says Maria. "I'll be in touch as soon as I can."

$\lessapprox$ 14 $\gtrapprox$

INTERNATIONAL LEAGUE
OF MAGICIANS

FLIP TO THE BACK FOR INSTRUCTIONS. THANKS!

IF I THOUGHT I WAS THE CENTER OF ATTENTION BEFORE, it's nothing to the looks I get when I arrive at the youth dorms. Everyone's curious to see how I'm taking the news that Dylan is free. Kids stare as Bertha clears a path for me down the hall. I keep my eyes on the floor in front of me and quickly slip into my room the minute we arrive.

Where's Elsie? I really thought she'd be here, especially with everything going on. I didn't realize how much I was counting on it until now. I could use someone to talk to, because it feels like my whole world is falling apart.

A knock sounds on my door. Which is strange because Bertha made it clear that nobody was to bother me. Well, somebody's asking for it. I'm *not* in the mood.

I yank the door open, and Jayden steps in wearing a black-and-white polka-dot suit. The dots swirl around in fancy patterns, jumping from his jacket to his pants and back again.

"Jayden!" I throw my arms around his neck. Then I realize what I'm doing and quickly let go.

Jayden just stands there stiffly for a few seconds before laughing. "Missed me, huh?"

"So much," I say. "Come in."

He steps inside, posing to show off his suit. "Whatcha think?"

I raise an eyebrow, grateful for a distraction. "How did you get a suit that's so *you* for the Welcome Social?"

He grins and shrugs. "It was just sorta hangin' in my closet when I opened it up. Think they'll let me keep it after? Shoot, if I hit the 'Wood in somethin' like this, nobody gonna be able to tell me nothin' at all."

Now I really do smile. "If you walk around our neighborhood in that suit, I want to be there to watch."

"Sure thing, superstar. Speakin' of, you really *are* famous 'round here, ain't you?"

"Don't remind me," I say, plopping down on my bed. "Besides, who cares about me? Did you guys end up having a late welcome ceremony? What supernatural ability did you get?"

Jayden nods and leans back against the door. "My way with animals became a *say* with animals."

"So you can, like, talk to them?" I ask.

He nods again. "Y'all might hear a bird chirp or a dragon growl, but me? I hear words now. And animals seem to understand me too. Haven't had much practice besides the folks at Creature Control letting me stop by for a few minutes to test it out."

"And you're trying out for Creature Control?" I ask.

"Yeah," he says. "It's crazy 'cause I used to like hanging out with the pigeons on top of our apartment building when it was just me up there. Always thought it would be nice to, like, work in a zoo or something, but you gotta go to college for that. And we don't have that kinda money." He smiles so wide it lights up his entire face. "So for this to happen is pretty cool, man. Guess I'm using all these words to say thank you. For seeing somethin' in me that I ain't even see."

I wipe at my eyes. "You don't know how badly I needed to hear that I'm doing *something* right."

"You're a hero, Amari."

"Doesn't always feel like it." Again I shift the focus back to him. "Do you have friends going to the Welcome Social with you?"

"Yeah, but . . ." The boy blushes so hard. "I was, uh, hoping we could go together."

"Oh," I say, and now my cheeks are burning too.

Jayden adds, "Then the whole Dylan escape thing happened, and I figured I should see how you were doin' and stuff. Trainees aren't allowed to come to the junior side of the dorms, but Bertha said you could use somebody—"

My phone buzzes.

New Text Message from Cozmo:
Your immediate presence is requested at the League
meeting grounds.

For a few seconds I just stare at my phone. Cozmo wants me to come to a League meeting? *Now?*

"You okay?" asks Jayden.

"I—I have to go." I've got to find Maria. I don't know where the League meeting grounds even are.

Jayden frowns. "But this the first chance we got to talk."

"I know," I say, "and I'm *so* sorry, but this is really important. I'll make it up to you, I swear."

I leave Jayden in the hallway outside my room and rush down a hall full of kids in fancy suits and magical dresses—they're so into one another's outfits they barely notice me now. I head straight for the elevators.

"*Amari,*" comes Elsie's voice from behind me. "Where are you going?"

I don't even remember passing her in the hallway. My shoulders droop—I don't have time for this. "I'll tell you everything the moment I get back."

"Back from where?" she asks. "I'm coming with you."

"No," I say. "You can't."

"But—"

"I'll tell you everything tonight." Before she can say anything else, I step into the first open elevator and take it up to Supernatural Investigations, then power walk through the hallway to Maria's office. The light's on, so I give the door a hard knock.

Seconds later, Maria's face appears in the glass window, and I hold up my phone to show her the message. She doesn't look happy but lets me in.

As soon as I'm inside, Maria closes the door and flips the lock.

"I got the same message," she says.

"Then why didn't you message me?" I ask. "To tell me where to meet you? I only guessed you'd be in here."

That's when I notice she's got the left sleeve of her agent jacket pulled back. And there's a transporter already strapped to her bare arm.

Realization strikes like lightning. "You were going without me."

Maria closes her eyes and pinches her temples. "This is the first full gathering of the League of Magicians that Cozmo has called in years. I'm sure he wants to discuss Dylan's escape—it's only going to give Bane another reason to hunt down as many magicians as he can. Maybe it's best if you stayed behind."

"I *have* to go. It's not just about the Crown. Maybe with everyone there, somebody will have an idea how to help Quinton."

She appears to mull it over, but I can tell her mind's made up.

So I say, "I've got just as much a right to be there as you do. If my brother doesn't make it and there was something I could've done, I'll never forgive myself. And I won't forgive you for leaving me behind."

"*Fine.*" Maria breathes deeply, looking tired. "But stick close to me so we can teleport out of there at the first sign of trouble, got it?"

"Definitely."

I wrap my arm around Maria's, and she taps away at the buttons on her transporter. Suddenly the world bends around us until we're no longer in her office but a large, dimly lit space.

It looks like the ruins of some ancient castle or something. Tall stone walls rise up around us, and starlight pours in through gaping holes in the roof.

A single candle flickers to life on a dusty table a few feet away. An old lady cloaked in shabby robes hunches beside it, staring at us.

Super creepy.

Maria takes a step forward. "You know why we're here."

"Do I?" the old lady's voice squeaks. "And who have you brought along with you, Maria Van Helsing?"

"One who is born to the magic," says Maria. "It's all the introduction she requires."

"Quite right." The old lady grins, revealing a mouth full of yellowed and rotting teeth. She lifts a hand and waves it in front of us. "Dispel."

Nothing happens.

"Good to know you are who you claim to be." The old lady reaches over to put out the candle with the tips of her fingers, then steps away. "I require proof of magic."

Maria snaps her fingers, and the candle lights up again. The old woman simply nods and, with a wave of her fingers, sends a gentle breeze to put it out. Her attention turns to me. "Amari Peters, I demand proof of magic."

Maria starts to speak, but the woman raises a hand to cut her off.

She must want me to light the candle too, but I don't have the kind of magic that starts fires. Or if I do, I'm not sure how to use it. But what I can do well is create illusions, so I open the palm of my hand and blow on it, breathing to life a fiery bird that swoops and dives through the air until it explodes atop the candle, seeming to light it.

My fire may only be an illusion compared to Maria's actual flame, but the old lady claps.

"A flair for the dramatic, I see. An artistic soul. Then perhaps you'll appreciate a performance of my own." With a graceful flick of her wrist, great big torches blaze to life around the space, chasing away the darkness. But the light does so much more than simply brighten the space. Walls that were chipped become whole, and cracks in the floor close up completely. What looked like a neglected ruin has suddenly become a grand throne room.

Finally she snaps her fingers and is no longer a hunched old lady, but a beautiful actress I recognize instantly. Priya . . . Kapoor, I think? Me and Mama binged her Bollywood movies on Netflix a few months back. She curtsies with a flourish, then gestures to figures lining the balconies above us, wearing bright red cloaks. "It is my pleasure to formally introduce you to the League of Magicians."

As I gaze at the hundreds of faces staring down at me, I realize something. "So many of them look familiar." One guy is like a CEO or something—he does the annual press conference where they announce the newest version of my cell phone every year. Another guy is Elsie's biggest crush and favorite singer in the world—she would freak if she knew he's a magician. And I'm pretty sure one lady is chancellor of some European country. My government teacher at Whitman Prep has her picture on the World Leaders wall.

"That does not surprise me," Priya replies. "After all, the best place to hide is in plain sight."

I still can't believe my eyes. I thought League magicians all lived like Cozmo—alone in impossible-to-find places like the bottom of a lake. I never imagined they could be some of the most famous and powerful people in the world.

"Please, Amari, follow me." Priya leads us farther into the room, where a massive high-backed throne of polished black wood reaches ten feet or so into the air. Intricate designs are carved into the surface, and shimmering gold accents sparkle in the torchlight. As grand as it looks, it would probably be super uncomfortable if not for the thick velvet pillow that rests on the seat. What had Cozmo called it back at his lake house?

The Midnight Throne.

Where he wanted me to sit.

Beside the throne is a much smaller chair of stone—the steward's seat. It's there that Cozmo is perched, eyeing me closely. A grin tugs at his lips. "Come, come. We've been awaiting your arrival."

"Take my hand, Amari," says Maria.

I want to remind her I'm not a little kid, but I did promise her I'd stick close. The worry in her voice spooks me. I put my hand in hers and we walk toward the empty throne. A hum of murmurs breaks out among the magicians seated above us on all sides. I honestly don't know what to think about any of this.

I came here to ask if there was anything that could be done to help Quinton, but just like my visit to Cozmo's lake house, I get the awful feeling that I've stepped into something I shouldn't have. My heart thumps loudly in my chest. Something feels off about this whole thing, and I don't know what it is.

Maria brings us to a swift stop. "I would like you all to meet Amari Peters. On behalf of her brother, Quinton—"

My brother's name draws a wave of angry hisses from the people gathered. It startles me, though I guess it shouldn't. My brother hunted magicians. He went right along with the idea that we're to be feared and locked away. But I have to think that's only because he didn't know about the League, or that his own partner is a magician.

He didn't know about *me*.

Cozmo holds up his hand until the room falls silent. "Now, now. That's no way to treat our honored guest."

I swallow. "Moreau cursed my brother with a spell that he's never woken up from. And ever since Dylan escaped, he's been getting worse. I was hoping that someone here might know how to help him."

"You heard her." Cozmo gets to his feet. "Does anyone have an answer?"

The room remains quiet. Of the sea of faces above us, hardly anyone looks sympathetic.

I pull my hand free of Maria's. "You're supposed to be good magicians. Why won't you help him?"

Cozmo shrugs. "Choosing the fair path does not mean being a fool. You cannot expect us to provide help today for someone willing to hunt us tomorrow."

"Quinton hunted *bad* magicians. Moreau and his apprentices terrorized the supernatural world for centuries . . . it's not like any of you did anything to stop him."

My words draw grumbles from the magicians above, and even a few hisses. I ball my fists at my sides. Why did I come here? They aren't even willing to try.

"I have my own question," says Maria, stepping forward.

Cozmo looks annoyed. "And what might that be, Maria?"

"My brother, Dylan Van Helsing, escaped an inescapable prison this morning. The only way that's possible, the only thing that makes sense"—Maria lifts her head, looking up at those in the balconies—"is if he had help. I demand that those responsible make themselves known."

A commotion breaks out above us, shouts echoing around the room. That didn't seem to go over well at all.

Then I hear Maria gasp. But it's not until I lower my

gaze to Cozmo that I understand why. He's raising his hand, a small smile on his lips. "It was me."

"Interference!" calls someone from above. Many of the magicians have gotten to their feet, while others wave fists in the air.

Maria has gone beet red. "Vladimir made it very clear that we weren't to do anything to influence what happens between Dylan and Amari."

The League's strange rule about how special Dylan and I are as born magicians was the main reason I was so hesitant to join in the first place. They've got all these big plans for us. There are certain things not even Maria could tell me, because it would mean breaking some code.

Priya steps to my other side. "*Cozmo?* How could you?"

"How many times have you yourself lectured us about the rules?" someone calls from above. Murmurs of assent echo through the room.

"It was a last resort!" he answers. "Do you not think that I, who once stood at Vladimir's side, understand what his intentions were? He cast his illusions into the future and saw the Night Brothers' defeat. It was with this knowledge that he entrusted me to look after all of you until the next pair of born magicians emerged. Have I not done this?"

The magicians stare in silence. It's the same thing he told me at the lake house. As steward, he was only supposed to lead the League until he could offer the Crown to either me or Dylan.

And now that he's freed Dylan—

Oh *no*.

"What Vladimir didn't see," Cozmo continues, "what he couldn't have known, was that his own cruelty would create beings more vengeful than this world has ever seen. Bane and his wraiths have always wanted magicians wiped out. And now that he is Prime Minister, he's got his chance, doesn't he? He's made it very clear that he intends to hunt us all down."

"You're going to offer the Crown to Dylan," I say. "That's why you freed him."

"You don't get to choose who wears the Crown!" yells someone from the balcony.

"I am as impartial as I ever was," answers Cozmo. "Why, I first offered the Crown to Amari on the grounds that she'd already bested Dylan once."

Priya starts. "Is that true?"

Every eye in the room shifts to me, the weight of their stares making me uncomfortable.

"I-it's true," I say.

"And you turned it down?" The shock is clear on Priya's face.

My heart drops into my belly. "I couldn't—I wasn't ready . . ."

"She asked for more time!" shouts Cozmo. "The one thing we don't have."

"Only to give myself a chance to figure out a way to end the time freeze," I say desperately. "It's the only thing keeping Bane in power."

The magicians turn to one another, considering my words. But what if it's too late? What if me turning down the Crown is the reason Dylan gets everything he ever wanted—all that power, all that magic . . . an entire army to lash out against the Bureau with? What if I've screwed this all up?

Maria takes a step forward. "She's barely a teenager. Leading the League, possibly into a war against the Bureau and maybe even the entire supernatural world, is not a choice a kid should have to make."

As much as I'm grateful to Maria for having my back, I *did* make that choice.

Priya steps away from us now, concern lighting her expression. "The League decided long ago that we would not follow in the Night Brothers' cruel ways. It's why we never joined Moreau. We mean to be good, decent people and not exploit the power we've been given. But whatever disagreements we may have had with the Night Brothers, we are sworn to uphold Vladimir's rules about protecting the next generation of born magicians. It's this mission that the League was founded on. We were never to interfere. We were to allow Dylan or Amari to chart their own path to the Crown. If it was *refused*, though . . ."

But why not just tell me that to begin with? I hadn't even heard of the Crown before a few days ago.

"*Priya*," says Maria. "You can't really believe it's okay to put all that on a teenager? Imagine if it were your daughter. Imagine—"

"Stop speaking for me!" I say.

Both Maria and Priya turn to look at me. There's hurt in Maria's expression, and annoyance flashes in Priya's.

But it's Cozmo's smug face that chills me most of all. He warned me that turning down the Crown would have consequences.

Still I ask, "What can I do to stop you from giving the Crown to Dylan?"

"Simple." Cozmo leans forward in his chair. "We call for a Game. It's the only way."

"A . . . game?" I ask, confused. "What kind of game?"

My voice is quickly drowned out by shouting from above.

Beside me Maria shudders, her voice ragged. "That's a last resort! Only in case of an emergency."

"Prime Minister Bane *is* that emergency!" shouts Cozmo. "He has laid down a challenge that demands an answer. We must have a leader who *wants* the Crown and is capable of wielding the full might of the League."

"And I *definitely* want the Crown," comes a raspy voice that raises the hairs at the back of my neck. "How about you, Amari?"

15

MARIA AND I TURN TO FIND DYLAN BEHIND US. HIS face has gone deathly pale, with dark circles beneath eyes I no longer recognize. Gone are the blue eyes I smiled into so many times last summer. They've been replaced by a deep red that makes him look unnatural.

Like a monster.

My feet feel rooted to the floor. I can't speak. This wasn't supposed to happen so soon. I wasn't supposed to see him again for years . . . decades. And now the boy who betrayed me—who tried to take my magic and destroy me—is right there.

Maria has gone still, her face stricken. "Dylan . . ."

"Maria," he calls. "You seem disappointed to have

your little brother back."

I say the only thing I can think to say. "Dylan, please release the curse on Quinton. *Please.*"

Dylan practically growls when he speaks. "I don't owe you anything, *partner.* You're the reason I've spent the past year in the Sightless Depths. Stuck in the dark, day after day. It was a nightmare."

I shake my head. "You did that to yourself."

"Did I?" he mocks. "So I trapped myself in a cage of lightning?"

I ball my fists and step closer. "Help my brother. Or I swear I'll—"

"You'll what?" He steps forward to meet me.

Priya puts herself between us. "Stand *down*, you two. This throne room is considered neutral ground. Only words may be used against others within these walls."

How can I be calm when the key to helping Quinton is right in front of me?

Dylan throws his arms open, turning to gaze up at the magicians in the balconies overhead. "If you offer it to me, I will humbly accept the Crown of Vladimir. It's time to show the supernatural world that magicians won't be pushed around. What would Vladimir think of you all, cowering in your little castle, afraid of your own shadows? The Night Brothers struck fear into the hearts of all who dared to cross their path. I'll teach Bane the lesson he should have learned the first time he attacked our kind. I'll return us to our proper place in the supernatural world."

A few anxious seconds pass, then a cheer goes up. A few magicians even chant "Crown him!"

My belly flips. Just like that? They're ready to give him all that power just so they don't have to feel afraid anymore?

Cozmo raises a hand. "Bring forth the Crown!"

A figure in red emerges from a doorway, carrying the glass case that holds the shimmering black crown, then places it on the Midnight Throne.

"Vladimir was kind enough to leave us a message for this occasion." Cozmo steps over and strikes the glass hard with his hand, the pieces shattering across the floor. Immediately winds kick up throughout the room, blowing so hard I have to cover my face. It's not until they die down that I'm able to see that a shimmering ghostly illusion of a thin man with a twisting beard now sits on the throne.

Count Vladimir—one of the most infamous criminals the supernatural world has ever known. Even if it's just an illusion, this can't mean anything good.

Immediately the entire League drops to one knee. Only Dylan and I are left standing. I won't bow to a Night Brother, and Dylan seems to come to that same decision because he just crosses his arms. I do my best to hide my trembling hands.

The booming voice of Vladimir's illusion echoes throughout the throne room. "When I cast my illusions into the future one final time, I saw that our righteous cause would end in failure. I would soon fall, and in time so too would Moreau. So I took steps to share my magic and preserve the existence of magicians through the creation of the League. In my final hours, I poured what magic I had left into a Crown, in the hope that one day a new generation of born magicians would wear it and take up the fight that Moreau and I were destined to lose."

I glance to Dylan and he smirks.

"But only one can inherit the power," Vladimir continues. "Moreau and I chose to share our magic, and that was our great mistake. For two halves can never be as grand as one whole. So I ask: Who here dares to wear my Crown? Who thinks themselves worthy of my magic?" The illusion vanishes.

Dylan steps forward anyway. "I do."

"And you, Amari Peters?" calls Cozmo. "Would you now fight to possess this Crown?"

"I . . ." Deep breath. "Dylan can't be allowed to have it."

"What would you do to stop him?" Cozmo prods.

I can't believe I'm about to say this, but what choice do I have? If Dylan has the Crown, he'll start a war, and countless people and supernaturals would get hurt. I'm the only thing standing in his way. Again.

"Amari . . . ," Maria warns.

My voice comes out as a shaky whisper. "I'd accept the Crown."

Cozmo smiles. "If both of you want the Crown, then there is only one way to settle this. The Great Game. The winner shall wear the Crown—and determine the fate of magiciankind."

"And what does it cost to join?" asks Dylan.

"*Everything!*" says Cozmo. "You must pledge all but a drop of your magic to the Crown, and the winner shall walk away with the magic of three born magicians. An unstoppable force of nature!"

My heart races in my chest. If I win the Crown, then I'll get Vladimir's magic and Dylan's too. I'll be able to end Quinton's curse. But if I lose . . .

"And what is the Great Game?" I ask. "What will we have to do?"

"What it is not, is a contest for the timid or weak of heart. Either you must play—or forfeit the Crown."

Cozmo answered Dylan's question but danced around mine. It's hard not to believe that he'd rather Dylan win than me. But before I can say anything further, a shelf extends from the base of the throne.

The steward walks over and pulls out a platform that holds two golden rings. He brings the rings to Dylan. "Nature relies on balance, and magic is no different. Fair and foul. A force that is both kind and cruel—that both gives and takes. You two represent that balance. But know this: to wear this ring is to commit yourself to the Game. Once it is placed on your finger there is no going back. Do you understand?"

Dylan takes the first ring, which instantly flames up, giving off dark smoke. If that hurts, he doesn't let it show. Instead he grins before quickly sliding the ring onto his finger.

I take the second ring. The moment it touches my skin,

electricity sparks over my fingers. Just like back at Mrs. Walters's apartment.

"Amari, wait. Please! You don't know what you're doing." Maria steps closer, but Priya pulls her away.

I glance at her, then back at the ring. What am I agreeing to? But I don't have a choice anymore.

I close my eyes and slide it onto my finger. *This is how I save my brother. This is how I save the world.*

"It appears we shall have a Game!" Cozmo roars, and the League cheers.

My legs wobble, and I open my eyes to find Maria staring back at me. She looks as scared as I feel. But I can't think about that right now. I need to find out just what I've gotten myself into.

Dylan's smile widens. "Looks like I'll be taking that magic of yours after all."

"Not if I can help it." I take a giant step away from him so that he's not breathing down my neck anymore. I hold up my hand to get a closer look at the ring—but it's vanished. The only reason I even know it's still on my finger is that I can feel it there, cold against my skin.

"The Game is first and foremost a duel," Cozmo says. "The rings you wear are Game Rings. Each is imbued with special magic—you have only to squeeze it tightly and you will be taken to a dueling ground where a Victor's Ring can be won."

I swallow. So these rings act like transporters too? What if I squeeze the ring by accident while I'm asleep?

Cozmo looks us over carefully. "Five times the Game Rings will call for a contest by warming on your finger, with each Victor's Ring more difficult to obtain than the last. The first to claim three Victor's Rings will be declared the winner and have the Crown appear to them. *However*, the Game can end at any point should one magician successfully steal the magic of the other. If this occurs, then that magician shall be declared the winner and worthy of the Crown."

I shudder, remembering Dylan stealing Moreau's magic last summer—the old man dissolved into ashes. "But won't that destroy the other magician?"

Cozmo nods. "As I said, the Great Game is not for the weak of heart."

I glance to Maria again, unable to imagine what she must be thinking. She may have promised Quinton that she'd keep me safe, but Dylan is still her brother. I make a promise to myself that no matter how bad it gets, I won't try to steal Dylan's magic. I won't become a monster to win.

From the way Dylan is looking at me, I can't say that he feels the same. He's already tried to steal my magic once. And that was *before* he blamed me for sending him to the Sightless Depths.

"There is one final order of business before the Game can commence. And that is a vow of secrecy. Neither of you may reveal the existence of the Game to anyone who is not present here tonight. Agreed?"

"Agreed," says Dylan.

"Agreed," I repeat, though I don't mean it. I'm telling Elsie everything.

"Then take heed. Once you leave this room, the Game is officially underway. Be careful, and be brave. Prove yourself worthy of the Crown."

Dylan steps right up close to me. "Watch your back, Amari. One way or another, you're going to pay for what you did to me."

A chill runs down my spine. I know he means it.

Then Dylan takes a step backward and vanishes.

When Maria and I arrive back in her office, neither of us says a word for the longest time. I think we're both feeling overwhelmed by what happened.

I bite down hard on my lip. Maria made it pretty clear she doesn't want me in the Great Game. "Maria, I know you're mad, but—"

"Just give me a moment, Amari." She falls heavily into a chair and covers her face.

"I'm going to win," I say anyway. "And I'm going to do it without stealing Dylan's magic, so you don't have to worry."

"I *do* have to worry," she says. "Don't you get it? This isn't some Bureau tryout where the worst thing that can happen is you get sent home for the summer. Vladimir believes the Night Brothers lost the Ancient War because they didn't go after one another's magic—they chose to join forces. He doesn't mean for there to be two magicians left at the end.

The contests will happen in impossible locations. You could *die*. And there's nothing I can do about it."

For a moment I go quiet under the weight of her words, then I ask, "Would you rather Dylan get the Crown and start another war? If that happened, way more people would get hurt than just me. I know you promised Quinton you'd look after me. But you've got to let me do this. If I can win three rings, I can help Quinton *and* prevent a war."

Maria tilts her head back. "You're *thirteen*, Amari."

"I can do it," I say.

"So what do you want me to do?" Maria asks. "Just go along with this?"

"I want you to give me a chance to win," I say. "You've already started teaching me magic. So teach me how to use it to defend myself."

Maria shakes her head, tears shining in her eyes. "I'll help as much as I can. But I'm scared for you. I'd have done anything to keep you from this."

"I'll be fine." I try my best to smile. "Don't underestimate me."

I make my way out of Maria's office and back through Supernatural Investigations to the elevators. I'm lucky to get Lucy.

"Is something wrong, Junior Agent Peters?"

"Rough night," I say.

"Is there someone I can call for you?" she asks. "Maybe Agent Magnus or Agent Fiona. Someone you can talk to?"

"No," I say. "It's up to me now. It's all on my shoulders."

16

WHEN I GET BACK TO MY ROOM, ELSIE IS SITTING ON my bed with a look that says, "Tell me everything." And that's exactly what I plan to do—vow of secrecy or not, I'm not keeping things from my friends like I did last summer. Especially something this big.

I sit beside her. "So you probably want to know where I've been."

Elsie nods. "Your aura is super yellow. What's got you so scared?"

I take a deep breath. "It's a long story, but basically—" The invisible ring starts to dig into my finger and my voice cuts out completely. I sit there, opening and closing my mouth—but the words won't come.

"I can't talk," I say.

Elsie raises an eyebrow. "You literally just did."

I try again to tell her about the Great Game. Same result—my ring tightens and my voice stops. Trying to force the words out only makes my throat hurt. With every attempt the ring squeezes my finger a little more. It hurts.

Elsie stares, clearly confused. "Are you okay?"

I feel like I could scream. Because I realize that Vladimir has taken the choice out of my hands. My ring's reaction isn't a coincidence—it's preventing me from breaking my oath to keep the Great Game secret.

I try pulling off the ring, but it won't budge. "It won't come off!"

"What won't come off?" Elsie asks. "What's going on?"

"I'm trying to tell you but I can't." I groan, frustrated. Frantic, I look around for a pen and paper. Maybe I can write it down.

"This isn't funny," says Elsie. "I'm worried about you. First you wouldn't tell me where you were going, and now you're acting like you can't talk at all."

"I'm not acting, Els. I really can't." I spot a pen hanging from Elsie's lab coat and reach for it. I'll write on my hand if it'll make her understand.

But Elsie gets to her feet. "I thought we were done keeping secrets. You did that last year and it helped Dylan get away with stealing the Black Book."

It takes me a few seconds to realize what she's saying. "You're seriously blaming me for that?"

"Of course not." Elsie sulks, her voice going quiet. "I didn't mean it the way it sounded."

"Really? Because it sure sounded like you think keeping Dylan's secret about being a magician helped him steal the Black Book. Even if that's true, I'm also the one who stopped him."

Elsie shakes her head. "I'm not trying to pick a fight. I just want to be there for you. I can *see* that something is scaring you. Is it the magicians you were telling me about before?"

I try to nod but can't—the vow of secrecy won't even let me do that. I'm *so* annoyed.

It's clear from Elsie's expression that she doesn't understand. She thinks I'm just deciding not to tell her. Or being funny.

But that's not true. She's my best friend, of course I want her to feel included. There's literally no one I want to talk to about this more than her.

"Fine," Elsie says, going back to her bed. "Some best friend you are."

My frustration boils over. "Well, you didn't have any problem keeping Oxford a secret, did you?"

Elsie whirls. "Maybe that's because the thought of leaving is hard for me too. Did you ever once stop to think about that? Everything doesn't revolve around how *you* feel."

My jaw drops. I really hadn't thought about that, and it makes me feel worse than I already do. "Just leave me alone."

"Fine!" she shouts. "If that's how it's going to be, then fine."

The lights cut out and tears streak down my face. I don't know what to do or even how to feel, other than alone and in over my head.

Maybe I should apologize? The words are on the tip of my tongue when I realize that Elsie being mad at me might be the best thing that could've happened. Because she'd only keep trying to figure out what it is that I'm not telling her. And then she'd want to come along to find the Victor's Rings. She'd want to help me, no matter the danger. And that's just something I can't allow. This is for me to figure out. I can't let Elsie get caught up in all this. Friends protect their friends.

And Elsie's the best friend I've got.

My best friend is already gone when I head out for breakfast the next morning. That means I'm the last one to arrive at the food court. I decided on the way here that the only way to keep Elsie safe is to keep her at a distance.

So when I grab my tray and spot her coming in my direction, I purposely turn and head the other way. Elsie hates conflict, so she'll probably want to talk things out, but even if we did, I still wouldn't be able to tell her about the Great Game. Which would just lead to another fight.

Even so, the look on her face breaks my heart. I keep telling myself it's for her own good.

But who am I supposed to sit with if not Elsie? The Junior Agent table isn't a possibility with Tristan and Bear already seated there. I hate that this summer is already starting to shape up like last year.

My phone buzzes.

New Message from VanQuish_Maria ✔️:
Spoke with Priya this morning. If we can end the time freeze and oust Bane as Prime Minister, she'd be willing to call a League vote to cancel the Great Game. Many don't want a war.

I type a quick reply.

From Amari_Peters ✔️:
That's great news! Does that mean you'll be willing to help?
Maybe figure out how to get around Harlowe and Bane?

I don't have to wait long for an answer.

New Message from VanQuish_Maria ✔️:
I'm on it. We'll talk more in tutoring

I find a spot alone at the far end of the food court, near a restroom that's always out of order. It's the one the yetis like to use whenever they visit, and no bathroom survives that bunch. But the upside is that there's no one nearby pretending not to stare or coming over to ask me questions about Dylan's escape. It gives me time to think.

Maria's message means that ending the freeze is still the surest way to keep the Crown out of Dylan's hands. And with her help, maybe I can actually pull it off. It's almost the perfect solution. Except that it doesn't help Quinton. But maybe showing the magicians I'm on their side will make them change their minds about helping him. Right now, they've got no reason to trust me, but I can change that.

Of course, none of that matters if I die in the Great Game. What will these challenges even be like? Maria says they'll be dangerous, but I'm sure she can help me prepare somehow. I just need to make sure Dylan can't end the Game early by stealing my magic and leaving me a pile of ashes on the floor.

"I'm going to win the Great Game." When I told Maria that yesterday it was more about making her feel better. But this time, I repeat it to myself until I believe it too. I've already beaten Dylan once. After the first challenge, win or lose, I'll at least know what to expect.

I look up as Lara Van Helsing slides into the chair opposite me and blurts, "I don't know why you picked me for a partner, but I asked Agent Fiona about switching and she won't let me."

"I did you a favor and you really tried to ditch me behind my back?" I ask.

"I hate this," she says. "If even *you* feel sorry for me—I

don't need anybody's charity. I'm good enough to be Junior Agent without anyone's help."

"I don't feel sorry for you," I say.

Lara looks confused. "You don't?"

"Not at all." I pour syrup over my waffles. "You're stuck up, you're spoiled, you're just plain mean—"

"*Okay*, I get it," she cuts in. "I was pretty awful to you last year, and karma is real."

I can't help a small smile, and surprisingly, Lara flushes and grins too.

"So why *did* you pick me?" she asks.

"Honestly, it was mostly just to rub it in Tristan's face. That boy is not a fan of yours."

She frowns. "Fair enough. But . . ."

"What?" I ask.

"It's just that I *need* to do well this summer or my dad will be furious. He's practically disowned Dylan and Maria since learning they're magicians. That means it's up to me to carry on the Van Helsing tradition all on my own. And as much as I hate to admit it, I do need a partner. Since it looks like we're stuck together, I thought maybe we could help each other out."

"Help each other how?" I ask.

"I need the chance to prove myself as a Junior Agent since the whole world knows I failed the tryouts on a silly technicality. That's going to be nearly impossible without a partner. And I figure *you* can use someone to help you keep up with the older Junior Agents in class. I've been training my whole life for this."

I lean back in my chair. That's not a bad deal, but when I look at her, it's hard for me to see anyone but the bully she was last summer. "That would mean I'd have to trust you, and I don't know if I can do that."

Lara winces. "All right, fine. Ask me anything and I promise to tell the truth."

I lean forward and rest both my elbows on the table. "Anything?"

She swallows and nods.

"How *did* you make Junior Agent after failing last summer's tryout?"

Lara groans. "My dad forced me to transfer to a school in Australia so I could try out again when their summer break came in December. As soon as I passed, he brought me back to the States. And before you ask, no, I don't want anyone to know that I passed a Junior Agent tryout, because the fact that my dad took things that far is, like, ten times more embarrassing than failing in the first place."

"Is that even allowed?" I ask.

"Not at all." Lara sighs. "I fully expected Chief Crowe to demote me as soon as I showed up. I was counting on it. But my dad went over her head and asked for special permission from the Prime Minister's office. No response for months, and then suddenly we get a new Prime Minister and the request gets approved. So here I am, a total fraud."

No wonder she's been so grumpy.

"Hmm." I tap on the table between us. "You said I could ask anything, right?"

Lara looks like she's going to be sick. "Anything."

"Who painted that dead magician mural in my dorm last summer?"

"That really wasn't me," she says quickly.

I'm not convinced.

Lara must see it in my face because then she adds, "But . . . it *was* my idea. I wanted to scare you into quitting. I had no idea my partner, Kirsten, would actually go through with it."

"And where is Kirsten?"

"She's trying out for Junior Spy this summer. Said she didn't want to be in the same department as two magicians. We haven't spoken at all since Maria and Dylan were outed. In fact, all the people I thought were my friends have totally ghosted me."

Part of me wants to rub it in, because she's getting just a taste of what I got last summer, mostly from her. But becoming a better Junior Agent might also help me in the Great Game, especially if she can help me improve with my Sky Sprints and Stun Stick.

Plus, I owe it to Maria to make an effort with Lara.

I take a deep breath and meet Lara's eyes. She's clearly expecting me to turn her down. "I can't promise we'll be friends, but I do promise to be the best partner I can be."

Surprise lights up Lara's face.

"I'm going to do my best to trust you, Lara. Please don't make me regret it."

Lara just cocks her head to one side, a smug little grin on her face. It's the first time she's looked like herself all week. "Let's do this."

≋ 17 ≋

O NCE LARA AND I ARE DONE WITH BREAKFAST WE take Whispers the elevator up to the Department of Supernatural Investigations. Lara explains that at some point over the past year, Whispers decided to focus on his dream of becoming a comedian. As if his name wasn't funny enough already.

"WHY DON'T EGGS TELL JOKES?" Whispers shouts at his usual headache-inducing volume.

"I don't know," I say. "Why?"

"THEY'D CRACK EACH OTHER UP!"

Lara uncovers her ears and fights back a laugh. "That's so bad it's actually funny."

I shake my head. "Is it though?"

Once we finally arrive at Supernatural Investigations, we head through the lobby and into the main U-shaped hallway. Today's our first day of Field Training, which means we get to go out into the world and start doing agent stuff. Our schedule says we're supposed to head to the Operations Bay to meet our agent mentors and get our first assignment.

Every Junior Agent knows that the Operations Bay is the most important room in the whole department. It's where the director and deputy director oversee all the missions being carried out by their agents. The place is full of people sitting at long tables topped with computers. It's always reminded me of a NASA control room, with all the big monitors covering the walls. Usually the giant screens show at least three different missions at once, but today each shows the same hulking creature.

The Carcolh is its official name, but most folks in the Bureau call it the Doomsday Snail. That probably sounds like a joke, but I promise it's not. It's the second most dangerous of the seven great beasts—only the abominable snowman is worse.

Seeing the thing in action, I totally get it. It's pretty much the biggest, most fearsome dragon that ever lived . . . that also happens to be covered in slime with a great big snail shell on its back. And the fact that it can shoot a beam of white-hot radiation from its mouth equal to an atomic bomb? Well, that makes it even more terrifying.

Lara and I squeeze in next to all the other anxious-looking Junior Agents lining the back wall.

"No sense in looking afraid," calls Agent Magnus from the center of the space. He's sporting a new silver name tag on his jacket that he didn't have when I saw him in Quinton's room the other day.

Only deputy directors wear silver name tags. When did Magnus get promoted?

"I'd planned on givin' you kids an easy first day," Magnus continues. "Ease you back into the agenting spirit. Seems the morning had other plans! With most agents around the globe conducting a worldwide manhunt for Dylan Van Helsing, it's left a shortage of folks able to respond to the Carcolh slithering out of hibernation. So you'll be backing up the European agents and Creature Control teams as they try to turn the thing back to its cave before it reaches the surface."

Even if I could tell anyone that I've seen Dylan since he escaped, the vow of secrecy wouldn't let me give any details. Not that simply telling someone would be much help anyway—he could be anywhere in the world by now.

"Isn't the Carcolh supposed to be invincible?" whines Bear. "That's what the books say!"

Magnus nods. "The Carcolh is covered in a layer of slime ten feet thick. The goal isn't to hurt the thing, 'cause that's impossible. Its only weakness is that it moves about as slow as a regular snail. So we mean to annoy and harass the thing so much it gets bored of fighting with us and returns to its underground lair. Preferably without blowing anything up."

Bear shivers. In fact, a lot of the Junior Agents seem

nervous. Even Lara looks spooked.

"What's the matter?" Magnus bellows, a big grin on his face. "You all wanted to be real-life superheroes, right? Well, now's your chance! When I call your name, come down here to meet with your agent mentor. Follow that agent's every instruction, understand?"

Agent Magnus begins to call our names, teaming up each pair with a Senior Agent. My heart thunders in my chest as I wait for my own name to be called. I don't know about Lara, but when I got up this morning I wasn't planning on picking a fight with one of the seven great beasts. We all jump as the Carcolh's screech blasts through the speakers.

One by one, the Junior Agents are assigned mentors until, finally, only Lara and I are left.

Magnus folds up his list and stuffs it into his jacket. "You three will be with me today."

"Three?" I ask, whipping my head back and forth. I don't see any other Junior Agents.

Lara looks just as confused as I am.

"This summer we're gonna be doin' things a bit different," Magnus adds.

That's when Tristan gets up from one of the desks, looking far too pleased with himself.

My eyes narrow. "But—"

"It's an order straight from Director Van Helsing," Magnus continues, cutting off my protest. "So don't go pouting at me. Besides, with an odd number of Junior Agents this year, one team had to have an extra member."

Lara and I both glare at Tristan. Why does the director care who my partner is?

Tristan ignores us to address Magnus, floating a few inches off the floor. "I can fly above you and provide an aerial view of the Carcolh."

Lara scoffs. "Well, I can run a lap around the Carcolh before *you* even get airborne."

"As if," says Tristan.

I look between them. They're gonna try to outshine each other all summer and I'm gonna have to listen to it.

Magnus sighs. "Listen up, you three. 'Cause I got bad news. With Dylan being free, the new Prime Minister feels it's important we protect Amari here as much as possible by keeping you all's assignments within spittin' distance of the Bureau."

Tristan deflates like a balloon. "Are you saying that because of Peters, we don't get to battle the Doomsday Snail? That snail only shows up once a decade!"

"That's exactly what I'm saying," says Magnus.

Lara crosses her arms. "So what *will* we be doing, then?"

Magnus suddenly looks a bit sheepish. "We've received report of an UnWanted hiding out in a local apartment building. With the Prime Minister's ban on UnWanteds, it'll be our job to get it to leave the city."

"You mean deport them?" I ask.

"Well, it *is* the law," says Tristan. "They aren't supposed be in the city."

"And what happens when the Prime Minister decides I'm no longer welcome either?" I ask. "Will you send me away too?"

No one volunteers an answer to that question. Even Tristan looks away.

Finally Magnus says, "How 'bout we go see what we're dealing with, then we'll decide what to do about it."

Tristan and Lara both nod. Realizing I don't have much choice, I nod too. I can't help feeling guilty about the disappointment on the others' faces. This assignment isn't something any of us wants to be doing.

"We'll need to make a quick stop first." Magnus moves toward the door. "Follow me."

The three of us catch up to him. Unlike me whenever I step into the main hallway, Agent Magnus doesn't make any effort to stay out of the way. He walks right up the center of the hall, and everyone else moves to give him space. Must be nice to be the boss.

"So do we call you Deputy Director now?" I ask.

"Agent Magnus is fine," he says. "Bein' deputy director will always come second to agentin'."

That's when Agent Fiona steps out of a doorway and notices us. Well, it's not us she's got eyes for, it's Magnus. The moment they lock eyes, Agent Fiona goes pink, then ducks into another hall.

Lara and I look at one another. I don't think I've seen the Red Lady blush before. Ever.

It makes me curious. "Agent Magnus?"

"Yeah," he calls over his shoulder.

"Are you and Agent Fiona still partners now that you've been promoted?"

"Well, no." Suddenly, Agent Magnus's neck goes bright red. "It, err, just so happens that Agent Fiona and I have decided to become partners in life, if you can believe it. We're getting married."

Lara gasps. "You proposed?"

"And she said *yes*?" I add.

"Well, there ain't no need to act so darn shocked!" Agent Magnus huffs. "I'm well aware she's beautiful and smart and one of a kind . . . and I'm just, well, *me*. But I mean to prove myself worthy of her. Don't you worry a lick about that."

"*Aww*," Lara and I say together.

"How did you ask her?" asks Lara.

"Was it really romantic?" I join in.

"More importantly, how big is the ring?" adds Lara.

Magnus runs a hand through his hair, flustered. "If you must know, I took her back to where we had our first date. With her parents' blessing, I got hold of the family ring—"

"No offense, sir," Tristan cuts in. "But shouldn't we be focused on the mission?"

"Oh, err, right." Magnus clears his throat and straightens. "Let's concentrate on the task at hand. Our door is up ahead."

Welp, that was a nice distraction from deporting some poor UnWanted while it lasted. The door is marked

Department of Magical Science, and inside is a spiral staircase that leads to the floor above us. "Are we going up to the Gadget Room?"

"That's right," says Agent Magnus. "Need to get you and Lara field ready."

Excitement swells inside me. I've never actually been to the Gadget Room, but I've heard all about it from Elsie.

Elsie. My eagerness fades. The Gadget Room's official name is the Agent Support Division of the Department of Magical Science, and it's where Elsie most wants to use her Mastermind Inventor supernatural ability.

What are the odds Elsie's up there right now?

I'm last to climb the swirling staircase. The Gadget Room is much different than I expected. It's a lot like being in a jewelry store, with long glass display counters running the length of each wall. All kinds of gadgets are here, each with a little video screen that demonstrates what they do.

I see pens that shoot tranquilizer darts, watches that activate temporary force fields, even electronic mosquito attack drones. There's also freeze grenades, coins you can snap in half to create a thick getaway fog, and hats that expand into tents for agents who find themselves stranded without a roof over their head.

"Over here," says Magnus, waving us toward the main counter. He rings the call bell.

"Be right there!" comes a voice that makes my stomach drop.

Elsie.

A few seconds later my best friend comes stumbling out of the back room and up to the counter, her usually curly dark hair standing straight up and her glasses tilted sideways. "Sorry!" Elsie straightens her frames, a grin on her face. "Believe it or not, that explosion was on purpose. The electrical storm that followed was pretty unexpected, though."

"I'd ask for details," says Agent Magnus, "but I've got a feeling I wouldn't much understand the explanation."

Elsie's grin widens. "Probably not. What kind of gadget are you looking for?"

"Nothing fancy," says Agent Magnus. "Just a couple Restitchers for Van Helsing and Peters. First day in the field."

At the sound of my name, Elsie's eyes dart around until they find me at the back of our group. As well as she can see other people's emotions, her expression has always been just as easy for me to read. Right now, there's anger in her face, but mostly there's just hurt. I drop my eyes guiltily.

This is for her own good, I tell myself.

Elsie's attention goes back to Agent Magnus. She's cheerful again, even if it's a bit forced. "Two Restitchers coming right up."

Magnus glances back in my direction, eyebrows raised. He gives his beard a good scratch. "Everything all right between you and Rodriguez?"

I shrug, and he turns back to the counter as Elsie returns with two tiny boxes.

"Two Restitchers," Elsie says, sliding them across the counter.

Agent Magnus scoops up both boxes and tips his hat to Elsie. Then he turns, tossing them to me and Lara. "Open 'em up."

Inside the tiny box is a single black button. It doesn't look like anything special to me.

Elsie steps from behind the counter. "Place the button right here, near the end of your sleeve, so that it blends in with the other buttons."

Lara and I both do as we're told. The moment the button touches my sleeve, black stitching leaps out, fastening it to my jacket. "Whoa," I say.

"Restitchers are easy to use," Elsie continues. "Just press the button and call out whatever outfit you need to change into. Over ten thousand are programmed in there."

"Thank you, Rodriguez," says Magnus. "I'll show them the ropes on the way."

Elsie nods and disappears behind the counter.

"All right, everybody link arms," Magnus calls. We do, and Magnus pulls up his sleeve and begins to punch buttons on his transporter armband. The world around us begins to bend. . . .

I don't know where I thought we'd end up, but it certainly wasn't some dingy alley. By the looks of Tristan and Lara, I'm not the only one.

"Sir, what's the disguise?" asks Tristan.

Magnus strokes his beard before pressing his own

Restitcher button. "Pest Control." New threading springs from the button, traveling up his sleeve, transforming the material as it moves. Bright orange replaces dark gray until suddenly it's an entirely new uniform—orange coveralls with two small patches on the chest. One says *ACME Pest Control*, and the other says *My name is Beauregarde*.

Lara and Tristan go next, and I follow.

"We aren't really going to be fighting any pests though, right?" Because I'm not the girl you want on your side if one of those flying roaches jumps out at us.

"Of course not." Tristan rolls his eyes. "Honestly."

Lara does her best to stifle a laugh, which is a lot more than she'd have done for me last summer. My cheeks burn with embarrassment. Gold star pin or not, I'm so far behind her and Tristan when it comes to knowing anything agent related.

"Probably not, Peters—but I once tried to arrest a giant roach that knew karate." Magnus rubs his hip. "Tossed me around like a rag doll." He turns and waves us after him. "Anyway, where we're headed is right around the corner."

The building is one of those fancy high-rises covered in reflective glass. One look through the sliding glass doors and the doorman rushes us inside, half in panic. "Please be discreet. If word got out that the Millennium has a pest problem . . ."

"We'll be in and out," says Agent Magnus. "We're very good at what we do—have been for a very long time."

The doorman shakes his hand. "Bless you, mister." His eyes narrow as he takes a closer look at me, and then Tristan and Lara. "Are those teenagers?"

"Special summer internship," Magnus answers. "Never too early to begin an exciting career, I always say."

The three of us play along, nodding enthusiastically.

"Oh," the doorman says, looking puzzled. "If chasing rodents is you kids' idea of fun, who am I to disagree?"

The four of us move quickly through the wide lobby, passing beneath a sparkling chandelier. The building is fancy—the kind of place with a reputation to protect. No wonder the poor guy at the door was so nervous.

We round a corner and head into a tiny room marked *Authorized Personnel Only*. It's dimly lit and full of wires and switches. It also feels like it's a thousand degrees in here. Whatever we're doing, I hope it won't take long.

Magnus puts his ear to the back wall and knocks three times. I jump as three knocks come back from the other side. Magnus knocks three more times, then says, "Deputy Director Beauregarde Magnus, here on account of your UnWanted problem."

We sweat it out in this sweltering room for what feels like forever before a sliver of the wall slides away, revealing another dimly lit room.

A tiny person around six inches tall marches out of the gloom. The little guy has a thick handlebar mustache and is covered head to toe in battle armor that looks a lot like . . . a Pepsi can? He's even wearing a bottle cap as a helmet.

I cover my face to hide my grin. Even after a year in the supernatural world, you can still be surprised by what's beyond the next wall.

The tiny man lifts his right arm in salute. "I am Sir Percival, the Knight of Pepsi."

"Is there a Knight of Coca-Cola too?" The question is out of my mouth before I can stop myself.

Magnus and Tristan both shoot me a look, and Lara buries a laugh in her sleeve.

"The ever-valiant Knight of Coke has already gone after the foul beast," says Sir Percival. "I stayed behind to await aid from the Bureau."

"And just what are we dealing with?" asks Agent Magnus.

Sir Percival pales. "Oh, a beast most terrible. A shadowy creature with nasty glowing eyes. A terror of the highest order!"

"Unfortunately, that describes a whole lotta things." Magnus strokes his beard. "Show us the UnWanted's last known location and we'll take a look around."

"We greatly appreciate the assistance," says Sir Percival. "Follow me."

Sir Percival turns and marches back into the darkness. Magnus and Tristan both crouch low to follow. Then Lara. She waves for me to hurry before disappearing into the next room.

I drop to my knees and crawl forward into the dark.

"Turn up the lights," calls Sir Percival. "These are friends."

A loud click echoes, like a switch being flipped. And suddenly thousands upon thousands of glowing Christmas lights brighten up the space—they've been taped to the sides of pipes that twist and bend and crisscross around us, disappearing into holes in the walls.

My eyes follow a pipe through the wall. I'm looking directly into someone's apartment. Strange.

Suddenly the opening darkens as something rushes out toward my eye. I lean back just in time for a tiny lady—in a dress that looks an awful lot like a sock—to come sprinting out clutching a crayon.

She races along the pipe just in front of my face, giggling in delight. "Finally got the green one!" She slows to a stop when she catches me watching her. "Who do you think you're staring at?"

"A tiny person?"

"*Person?*" the woman exclaims, her little face going red. "We are fairies, thank you very much."

"But don't fairies have wings?"

She nearly drops the crayon in indignation. "We're *flightless* fairies! Proper, working-class fairies, mind you. Not like those vain hippies in the forest with their buzzy wings and twinkly 'Look at me' skin." She glances at the crayon over her shoulder. "Although some do refer to us as borrowers on occasion."

"More like keepers." Lara snickers over her shoulder. "You don't actually give anything back." My partner starts crawling again and I follow.

The fairy joins us, hopping from pipe to pipe. "Not true! If we can't use it or trade it at the market, we do return items. And we don't just trade for ourselves. Each fairy family is assigned to an apartment, and we do our best to look after the folks who live there. Ever catch a cold and swear you're out of cold pills only to find there's somehow one left in the bottle? You can bet a borrower did that." She puffs up a bit. "Heck, the number of fires we've put out on humans' behalf is more than worth whatever we borrow, I'd say."

I can't help thinking about all the times I haven't been able to find something in my room, whether it's a matching sock or my favorite pen. "And do all apartments have fairies?"

"Most," she replies. "Though not all buildings have a setup like this one. Welcome to the traders market!"

She points ahead through the maze of pipes to where the space opens up, revealing a miniature town made of household items. Tall buildings made of cardboard boxes sit next to upside-down buckets with little doors and windows carved into them. Great big tents made of pillowcases and sheets fill the center of the space, with fairies carrying all sorts of items. Toy train tracks rise and fall in every direction, and fairies sit atop train cars, a few reading the latest issue of *Pee Wee Guide*.

Even from here, I can hear a fairy arguing that a shiny penny is worth more than a rusted nickel. The other fairy doesn't sound convinced.

We keep to the edge, following the Knight of Pepsi to another wall, where a panel slides away and the Knight of Coke shivers in his red and white armor.

"Did you find the foul beast?" Pepsi asks.

Coke nods. "Came right up behind me and didn't make a sound. Barely made it back with my life, I did!"

"And you saw it on the other side of this wall?" Agent Magnus asks.

Another nod from Coke.

Magnus reaches inside his jacket and peels off what looks like a transparent Post-it Note and slaps it against the wall. "Pocket Windows always come in handy." I'm not sure what he means at first, but looking closer, I realize I can actually see through it to the room on the other side of the wall. Magnus tugs at both ends of the thing and it stretches until it's wide enough to squeeze through.

"Cool," I whisper.

"Follow me." Magnus goes first and we follow him through to an area marked *Keep Out*. "These here are the Mechanical Rooms. Lots of dangerous equipment, so try not to touch anything."

"We should probably split up," Tristan suggests.

"Good idea," says Magnus. "I'll go this way, and you three go that way. Davies has got the most experience, so he'll be in charge. Any of you run across the monster, keep your distance and give a holler so I can get to you as soon as possible. You're not to try taking the UnWanted down on your own. Understand?"

We all nod.

Magnus heads toward a sign that reads *Danger: Electrical*.

Tristan laughs. "You don't win a gold star by sharing credit." He winks and dashes off alone. "Good luck!"

"Unbelievable." Lara darts off in the opposite direction.

Splitting up when there's a terror on the loose? I don't know how I feel about that. But with Tristan going off on his own, and Lara eager to prove she's every bit as good as him, it doesn't leave me with much choice.

Flicking my Stun Stick to flashlight mode, I turn and step into a space full of giant tanks and even more pipes. Machinery hums in my ears.

Thankfully, I make it across the room without any trouble.

I've just decided to recheck a few spots when a shadow moves across the wall. My whole body stiffens as a low growl fills the room, drowning out the machine noise.

The shadow moves in my direction, and I duck around one of the tanks to hide. For a moment I consider calling for help, as Magnus instructed, but that would give my location away. And there's no way the others could get to me before whatever's doing the growling will.

The growl grows louder, echoing through the room. It's close now, maybe just around the corner.

You can do this, Amari. I flick my Stun Stick to stun and wait, hands trembling and heart thundering in my chest.

Next thing I know, it's right there. It's now or never.

I jump out. "Freeze!"

18

"DON'T SHOOT!" A TOWERING SHADOW WITH GLOWING white eyes lifts both hands in surrender. Thick black smoke wafts from its body and I have to cover my face to keep from coughing.

I may not have heard of a flightless fairy before today, but every Junior Agent trainee has had to study up on the various types of supernaturals created by the Night Brothers during the Ancient War.

"What's a NightWalker doing here?" I ask.

He flashes me a card:

Permit to Terrorize

Department of Supernatural Licenses and Records

Area:	Darkened Alley Beside the
	Millennial Building
Fright Times:	Midnight–Dawn
Name:	Newton FearDrinker

"Newton?" I ask. "Seriously?"

The NightWalker sighs and folds the permit back into his shadowy body. "My mother insisted I was too cute to have two terrifying names."

He might look like a horror movie villain, but he's got the voice of a scared teenager. I lower my Stun Stick—he doesn't seem like much of a threat to me.

I look back over my shoulder to check that none of the others are close and then say, "But that doesn't explain what you're doing back here. Your permit says you're supposed to keep to the alley and only come out at night."

"I'm in hiding!" Newton shrieks. "Bane sent agents to my alley last night to deport me. I won't be sent to the Sightless Depths for some bitter old wraith's grudge." He shivers. "There are *real* monsters down there."

"That's the same reason I'm here." I shake my head, fuming. "I'm supposed to turn you in."

The giant shadow trembles and starts to sniffle before suddenly going still. "Why do you look familiar?" Its glowing eyes narrow. "You're the magician girl!"

I nod.

"Well, I won't join the magicians either," Newton says.

"I want no part in the fight against the Bureau. Leave me out of it."

I just stare. "What fight against the Bureau?"

Now he stares at me. "You don't know? A magician sent out the call just this morning for all UnWanteds to fight for magiciankind as our ancestors did—"

"A magician?" I interrupt. "Are you sure?"

Newton nods vigorously. "Who else would make such a demand? It was written in shadow. Just as the Night Brothers used to do."

Could it be Dylan? Is he so confident he'll win the Great Game that he's already gathering an army? He's studied magiciancraft since he was little, collecting as many magician relics as he could. It wouldn't surprise me if he knows how to write in shadow.

"This is bad," I say.

"Very bad," he agrees. "Things are just like they were seven hundred years ago. Magicians and the supernatural world gathering forces, everyone made to choose a side . . . even a time freeze!"

Wait, *what*? I step closer. "Are you saying the time freeze in the Congress Room isn't the first?"

"That's exactly what I'm saying!" Newton whispers, his glowing eyes darting around nervously. "The Night Brothers. But you didn't hear that from me!"

The Night Brothers? Was Director Fokus wrong about a time freeze spell being impossible? She had to be, especially if it's happened more than once. Maybe the agents were right after all; magicians *are* known for doing the impossible.

"There's nothing here!" Tristan's voice in the distance makes me jump. I want to ask Newton more questions, but I can't let Tristan see him. Why should this NightWalker lose his home just because Bane says so? If he were causing any trouble, there's no way the Bureau would've given him a permit in the first place.

"Go before the others get here," I say. "Hurry!"

"But where can I go?" Newton asks, voice high and panicked.

"Can't your kind walk through walls?" I ask.

"Yes," Newton replies. "But my pet shade can't. I wouldn't be able to take it with me."

Tristan's voice sounds closer now.

"Just go," I say quickly. "I'll figure something out."

"You really are a hero," says Newton, melting into the wall. "I won't let anyone say different."

I wave and smile, then notice a small shadow the size and shape of a baseball—the shade. The thing stares back at me with glowing white eyes.

"What am I going to do with you?" I drop to a knee and scoop the little guy up. It's surprisingly cold to the touch. The shadow bounces happily in my hands, its big eyes making it look like something out of a cute cartoon.

"Good question," comes Lara's voice.

I whip around and the little shadow hops from me to

Lara, who startles but still manages to catch it.

"H-how long have you been standing there?" I ask.

"Long enough to watch you ignore orders," says Lara. "We should've brought that NightWalker in for questioning. A magician summoning UnWanteds, and some centuries-old time freeze no one's talking about—that's huge! Imagine what else we could've learned."

"And Bane would've thrown him into the Sightless Depths for his trouble," I say.

"You don't know that."

"Lara, your sister and I wouldn't even be here this summer if it were up to Bane."

Lara frowns.

I blow out a long breath, my heart pounding. If Lara decides to turn me in, I'll be in so much trouble. "Are you going to tell Magnus what I did?"

"And get us both in trouble now that it's gone? I think not."

I blow out a heavy sigh of relief. "Well, what if . . ."

Lara raises an eyebrow.

"What if we didn't turn the shade in either? It's just a pet, it can't tell us anything."

My partner stares down at the little ball of shadow in her hands, the corner of her mouth lifting. "It *is* a cute little thing, but—"

"Any luck?" Tristan calls.

Lara jumps and stuffs the shade into her jacket.

"Nope, didn't find anything," I say, meeting Lara's eyes.

She sighs but gives the slightest of nods.

"What a tremendous waste of time," Tristan huffs.

Magnus walks up next. "Y'all strike out too? Only thing I found was Davies here chasing *my* shadow."

Tristan winces. "To be fair, sir, your shadow does fit the description." Magnus shoots him a look, but the boy just shrugs.

"S'pose whatever was here is long gone," says Magnus. "Probably for the best. Can't say I'm much of a fan of the Prime Minister's new orders. We'll head back and let the little ones know their monster problem seems to be a thing of the past."

As we start back toward the traders market I glance at Lara, who looks stiff as a board walking with the shade still tucked into her jacket. She shivers, and I remember how cold it felt in my hand.

Maybe she had a point about questioning that Night-Walker. Was there really another time freeze? If there was, why doesn't the Bureau seem to know about it? Or do they know but are ignoring it for some reason? It wouldn't be the first thing Harlowe has buried. I need to find out more.

Up ahead, I can just make out the Christmas lights leading back to the traders market when a sudden burst of heat flares up on my right hand.

My Game Ring!

The realization makes me stumble. The Great Game, it's beginning!

But how am I supposed to leave in the middle of Field Training?

"Um, Agent Magnus? I think I left my Stun Stick behind. Do you mind if I run back and get it?"

"No you didn't," says Tristan. "It's right there in your jacket pocket."

Even Lara looks at me strangely.

"Oh, right," I say, wishing I'd thought up a better excuse. "Thanks."

"Headin' back's the fun part," says Magnus. "Amari, I'll give you the honor of addressing the building's elders. It will be good practice speaking in public—it's a necessary part of the job."

I nod and fake a smile. "Great." My mind races for another excuse but nothing comes.

So I just take off running back the way we came. The others are so stunned, they don't even come after me. The moment I round a corner, I squeeze my ring.

What happens next isn't like using a transporter, where everything bends around me until I'm someplace new. This feels more like I'm falling through shadows—everything goes dark and I'm totally weightless. . . .

Until suddenly I'm standing at the edge of a cliff, beneath a blazing sun. I stiffen and yelp at the steep drop before me, the forest below impossibly far. Nothing could survive that fall. I take one giant step backward, putting some distance between me and the edge.

Grabbing my Stun Stick, I turn to look for Dylan, but I

don't see him anywhere. Though I do see a golden pedestal *far* on the other side of the canyon—that must be where the Victor's Ring I'm supposed to claim is located. But how do I get over there?

My Sky Sprints!

I click my heels to turn them on, but nothing happens. I try again and still nothing.

That's when I notice words etched into the rock near the cliff edge:

EYES CLOSED, STEPS BOLD BELIEVE

What's that supposed to mean? Just believe I can make it over there and I will? My eyes dart desperately around the rocky canyon, looking for trails that might lead down and back up the other side. There aren't any.

I've got to try what the message suggests—there's no other way. And if I wait any longer, Dylan could show up. He made it clear he's out for revenge; he'll have no problem hurting me to win.

I bounce from foot to foot to build up my nerves. *You can do this, Amari.*

When I'm ready, I step right up to the edge, knocking a few pebbles over the side that skip down the ragged cliff face and into the trees below. The winds kick up, blowing my hair. My heart beats so fast. I'm ready to throw up.

Now or never. I take a slow, deep breath and shut my

eyes tight. Then step off the edge—

My foot lands on something solid, and I gasp, relief pouring through my limbs. I take another step, and another. Each more confident until I'm moving at a quick, steady pace.

I can't believe it's working! I'm crossing the canyon.

"Turn back!" Winds begin to whip around me, carrying voices. *"Open your eyes! You're going to fall, Amari."*

I shake my head and keep my eyes closed. I know where I am now—the Whispering Canyon. Home of the Whispering Winds.

A wind gust hits me so hard I almost lose my balance. It swirls around me, taunting, *"Do you honestly think you can win the Great Game? You're frightened of your own magic! Turn back!"*

The truth of the words makes me hesitate, but not for long. I do fear my magic, but Maria is helping me overcome that. "I know what you're trying to do, and it won't work. I'm going to cross this canyon no matter what you say."

"We only want you to live!" sing the winds. *"It's such a long way down."*

I keep putting one foot in front of the other.

"Just take a peek, you're nearly there."

I sure hope so. With my eyes closed, I can't tell how much progress I've made—it feels like I've taken a hundred steps already.

The winds kick up into a frenzy. *"Dylan is here, you're in trouble now."*

My heart skips, but I shake it off. The winds are trying to trick me, but I won't let them.

"*What's he doing?*" whistles the wind.

"*That's not allowed!*" howls a breeze.

I shiver as the voices sound more and more urgent.

"*The boy can fly? Impossible!*"

"*Horrible boy! You are not above the rules!*"

My heart hammers in my chest. What's happening? Is Dylan really here?

"*Leave her alone,*" the winds wail in unison.

I go still, bracing for an attack I can't see coming.

"You should've listened to the winds, Amari," comes Dylan's growling voice, directly behind me.

My eyes snap open, I reach for my Stun Stick and spin around . . .

To find nothing.

I let out a scream as the slender bridge of rock crumbles beneath my feet and I begin to fall.

Laughter echoes through the canyon. "*So gullible!*"

Panicking, I squeeze hard on my ring—and when I open my eyes I'm back at the Millennium apartment building, behind the walls.

For a few seconds I sit shivering on the floor. Dylan was never there—it was all a trick. The winds must've imitated his voice, knowing that I'd react.

Knowing that he scares me enough to make me open my eyes.

"Found her," Tristan calls, before folding his arms and

staring down at me disapprovingly. "What were you think-ing running off like that?"

"I—I thought I saw something," I say quickly, still shak-ing. "Wanted to check it out."

Magnus and Lara come next, and I get a long lecture about working as a team and how I've still got a lot to learn. I'm barely listening, because it's really sinking in just what I've agreed to by joining the Great Game. That was terrify-ing. Will every challenge be like that?

By the time we finally leave the miniature city behind the walls, my ring has gone ice cold. If the ring going warm means the challenge has begun, then cold must mean it's over. Dylan must've claimed the first Victor's Ring. A ring that could've been mine.

I'm so disappointed in myself.

It's already lunchtime when we arrive back to the Bureau, so Field Training is technically over for the day. Tristan grumbles and marches off to find Director Van Helsing to complain about having his gold star chances impacted by being stuck with me. Unfortunately for him, the Direc-tor is off helping the Senior Agents and Junior Agents get deslimed from the fight against the Carcolh.

Lara heads downstairs to drop off the shade in her room. I volunteered to keep him, since bringing him back was my idea, and it might be nice to have a secret I can actu-ally share with Elsie, but Lara insisted her room would be best since she doesn't have any roommates.

After lunch I've got another Private Tutoring class with Maria. The second I'm inside the briefing room I blurt out, "I've already lost the first challenge! But only because it tricked me into thinking Dylan was there. There's no way I could've prepared for that because how *do* you prepare for something like that?"

Maria just stares for a moment before saying, "There's been a challenge already?"

I nod.

"Then I'm just glad you're okay!" Maria is on her feet in an instant. She comes over and throws her arms around me. "I can't believe the Game's already begun."

I'm confused. I know Maria's not thrilled about me being in the Great Game, but I did think she at least wanted me to win. After all, it's my best bet to save Quinton and stop Dylan from getting the Crown.

I frown. "Shouldn't you be mad at me for losing a ring?"

Maria releases her hug and looks me in the eyes. "I'm more relieved that you didn't actually come face-to-face with Dylan. You're not ready for that—not even close. You got the best of him last summer, but that's mostly because he underestimated you. He won't make that mistake again."

"You don't think I can win." It's more of a statement than a question. And the thought hurts. "That's why you didn't want me in the Great Game. You think I'm going to lose."

Maria's face falls. "It's not that I don't believe in you,

Amari. Dylan just has such a head start. My brother has been studying magic *since he was seven years old*. He's obsessed with everything there is to know about magicians. His collection of spell books and artifacts would be impressive for a small museum."

"I know all that," I say. "It's why the Whispering Winds were able to trick me—I'm terrified of Dylan. What am I supposed to do?"

"We get you prepared like we planned," she says. "Starting with you learning how to defend yourself. Take a seat."

I slip into a chair at the small table, and Maria fumbles inside her bag. Her face is flushed, her fingers quivering slightly as she retrieves a beat-up-looking leather-bound book.

"Are you okay?" I ask.

Maria looks up and tries to smile. "I made a promise to Quinton to do my best to look out for you. And Dylan—even with everything he's done—he's still my little brother." She sighs. "Having you two in competition like this, it's hard. I thought we'd have more time to prepare . . . to solve the time freeze and get this awful Great Game canceled. I'll be honest, I'm a bit out of sorts right now."

I don't know what to say, so I just whisper, "I'm sorry."

"I'm the one who should be apologizing to you," Maria says. "You're as much a victim of Dylan's lies as anyone."

"It's not your fault Dylan turned out to be a monster," I say quickly.

Maria shakes her head. "That's the thing—he wasn't

always. Dylan used to be this sweet kid who followed me around like a lost puppy. But his magic didn't stay hidden like yours did, and when suddenly he could turn on the TV with just a snap of his fingers, it scared him. And it scared me too. Because Van Helsings made their name by hunting magicians."

"But you were a magician too," I say. "There have been Van Helsing magicians for centuries, and they didn't go bad."

"Because we weren't born with magic like Dylan was," she answers. "We Van Helsing magicians have always known how dangerous it is to have magic in a family of magician hunters. When our magic is secretly passed down from one generation to the next, it's always to someone who can handle that burden. I was nineteen when my uncle gave the magic to me, and only after we'd had countless conversations to ensure I understood what I was accepting. Dylan was never supposed to have magic, and certainly not as a kid."

"So what happened to make Dylan join Moreau?"

She opens her mouth a few times without saying anything. Then tears fill her eyes. "When Dylan needed me most, I was too busy being famous. I'm sure you've noticed just how much he hates me, and I can't say he's wrong for that. I should've been his safe place, but I wasn't able to come home every weekend to comfort him. I'd get frustrated when he'd message me late at night to say that he was worried about Dad or Lara finding out about him after a close call. Growing up in that house had to be a night-mare for him. But I was too busy being on magazines and winning awards and hanging out with the supernatural celebrities. Being part of VanQuish became my priority. So Dylan found someone else to have his back. Raoul Moreau."

I hate that part of me feels sorry for Dylan. Because none of that excuses what he's done. So many people got hurt because of his attacks on the Bureau last summer. But I also remember something Quinton told me once, about why he never took it personal when this kid he was mentoring blew up at him for the smallest reasons. *Hurt people lash out because pain is what they know.*

"When I win the Great Game, and I have Dylan's magic, then he won't be a threat anymore. Maybe it'll help him go back to the person he used to be. That kid you remember."

Maria reaches over and gives my hand a squeeze. *"You're* a pretty amazing kid, Amari Peters." She leans back and slides a book onto the table. "Let's get you prepared for what's to come. First things first: we need to figure out what your secondary magic type is."

"Wait, what?" I scoot forward in my chair. "I have another kind of magic?"

"Most magicians do," she says. "Did you ever wonder how Dylan creates illusions *and* manipulates technology? Or how I can use blood magic to speak to Quinton *and* create flames in the palm of my hand?"

"I guess I thought that some magicians were just lucky. No one ever told me I could do anything else. I mean, everything I know I learned from Dylan . . ." I trail off as it hits me how stupid that must sound. Didn't he lie to me all last summer?

"Dylan would've told you exactly what he wanted you to know." Maria points to the book again. "If your secondary magic is what I think it is, I doubt he'd have wanted you to be capable of using it against him or Moreau."

Just one more lie on top of a whole mountain of them. I ball my fists in my lap. To think I ever considered him my friend.

"Secondary magic," she continues, " is never as strong as your primary magic. But when you're as magical as you are, it can still be pretty formidable." She flips open the book to a page with an intricately drawn circle. The opposite page is filled with symbols.

I lean in to have a better look.

"Watch closely." Maria places the palm of her hand onto the circle, facedown. The symbol with an outline of a human body begins to glow, and then a second symbol starts to shimmer—a picture of a flame. "I'm not just a blood magician, but an elemental magician as well. Fire, to be exact."

"That's how you were able to light the candle," I say.

She nods, and flames flicker over her fingers. "Now your turn."

Butterflies flutter in my belly—but good ones. I'm nervous, but also excited to explore my magic with someone I really can trust.

I step to the book and place my hand down onto the circle. I glance over the page full of symbols, wondering what they all mean. The image of an eye shines super bright, then a few seconds later the picture of a cloud begins to shimmer.

"Like I thought." Maria smiles. "A weatherist—you can create storms."

"That's how I was able to summon lightning last summer!" I say. "I thought the illusion did it, but you're saying it was really me?"

Maria lets out a small chuckle. "What you did was combine your magics in one spell."

"Whoa."

"Yeah," says Maria. "Pretty cool stuff, huh? And from what I know about weather magic, it's very reactive to your mood and what you're feeling. For that reason, it can also be very subtle—it's possible to use the magic and not even realize it. It would seem like an ordinary change in the weather. Something as small as a much-needed breeze on a hot day or—"

"Or making a bad storm worse!" I think back to the bus ride just before the time freeze. Hadn't I felt uneasy, and suddenly those storm clouds began to thunder and lightning?

That realization brings another: and why that spark skipped across my fingers during the Witch's Spades game . . . because I can control *lightning*. "That's kind of terrifying actually."

"Understandable," says Maria. "But it also means you've

got magic you can use to defend yourself. Illusions are pretty to look at, but they're lousy for self-defense." She reaches back and pulls a thin book from her bag, then hands it to me. "I borrowed this from Priya, our friend in the League. I want you to start with controlling the winds."

THE RESPONSIBLE WEATHERIST
Environmentally Safe Spellcasting
for Every Situation

Something must show on my face because Maria asks, "What's wrong?"

"Dylan gave me my first illusionist spell book last summer," I say. "This kind of reminds me—"

The door flies open and agents storm the room, followed by Harlowe, who grins widely. "Caught red-handed."

19

HALF A DOZEN STUN STICKS ARE POINTED AT MARIA and me, and we raise our hands in surrender. This is bad. Really bad.

Harlowe sniffs the air. "The place reeks of magic." She steps up to the table and flips through the spell book. "Practicing magiciancraft inside the Bureau is strictly forbidden."

"We have permission," says Maria. "Prime Minister Merlin—"

"Is sadly frozen at the moment," Harlowe interrupts. "And Prime Minister Bane has made his position on magicians crystal clear. Curious timing, this *lesson*. Trying to recruit young Amari here for whatever you and Dylan are planning next, are you?"

I lean forward to protest, but Maria beats me to it. "That's not what's happening, and you know it."

Harlowe waves a dismissive hand. "I've heard enough. Take her away, please."

"Wait!" I say. "You can't!"

The agents escort Maria to the door anyway. She gives me one last look and mouths the words "the winds" to me over Harlowe's shoulder.

Director Harlowe smiles and takes the seat opposite me.

I shake my head, my hands balled tight in my lap. "You can't be serious about arresting Maria Van Helsing."

Director Harlowe purses her lips. "I'd be far more concerned with yourself, young lady. Practicing spells inside the Bureau, that's a big no-no."

"It really was an order from Prime Minister Merlin," I say. "That I be taught magic to help the supernatural world and prove magicians can be good." Not to mention it will give me a chance to win the Great Game. "It's actually really important."

"You don't need magic to do either of those things," says Harlowe. "So why is it *really* so important? Anything you want to confess?"

As if I'd tell her—talking to her might as well be talking to Bane. I grit my teeth and say, "It just is."

"*It just is,*" Harlowe repeats, then sighs heavily. "Honestly, I blame myself. I thought by making you an Elite you'd be grateful. That you'd come to value and honor this wonderful institution as I have, not befoul it with that awful magiciancraft."

"My magic isn't awful," I say. "At least, it doesn't have to be."

Director Harlowe shrugs.

"You don't even care," I snap. "Because of what happened to your parents, you'll always see magicians as the bad guys."

Harlowe's eyes flash, but it's quickly replaced by the pleasant act she does so well. She folds her hands and smiles. "Please keep Lord and Lady Harlowe's names out of your mouth."

"I only meant that what happened to them was terrible, but that was Moreau, not me or Maria. You're arresting her for nothing!"

She raises an eyebrow. "The Prime Minister needed *someone* to be guilty, dear, and we decided on Maria."

"B-but that's wrong," I say. "I'll tell people what you're doing."

Harlowe pouts her lips mockingly. "And who'll believe you? Maria is the only way you have to speak to your brother, is she not? So it stands to reason that you'd be oh-so-desperate to keep her from going away . . . maybe even desperate enough to lie?" She grins and leans in close. "See how easy that was?"

How can she twist the truth like that? "You're horrible."

"Horrible?" Harlowe just shakes her head. "If it weren't

for me, Bane might've pinned it all on you. But I stuck my neck out, even let you become an Elite! Though I'll admit that wasn't entirely selfless. You've become popular. The *Good* Magician."

"If that's what you care about, then Maria is way more popular than I'll ever be. She's a member of VanQuish!"

"True," says Harlowe, "but with Dylan being on the run, the Van Helsing name is a mixed bag. The family has always been so staunchly antimagician, yet *two* Van Helsing magicians were hiding in plain sight. The public feels lied to, and not even Maria's good deeds and pretty face can make up for that. Her star is on the decline. But yours, dearest girl, is still poised to ignite!"

"What are you saying?"

"I'm saying that despite whatever disgusting magician-craft was happening in this room, I'm willing to forgive you."

"Forgive *me*?" I ask, incredulous.

"I can make you a *star*," she continues. "It's perfect. The poor Black girl who comes to the Bureau and learns she's a magician—the enemy of the supernatural world—only to save us all from Dylan's awful plot! Why, it's positively *marvelous*! Movies aren't written so well!"

I can only stare at her. "You're . . . serious?"

"Deadly serious." Suddenly that bright smile of hers seems sinister.

"I don't want to be your star," I say. "I want you to let

Maria go free. She was just framed for the hybrid attacks last summer and now you want to blame her for this too? It's cruel."

"And ruin tomorrow's big headlines?" Harlowe laughs out loud. "Supernaturals want to feel safe, and if they believe the culprit behind the time freeze has already been captured, they will. Prime Minister Bane is going to look like a leader who keeps his promises. And you're going to help the people trust him even more."

Who does this lady think she is to tell me what I'm going to do? "And how am I going to do that?"

"By being the good little magician girl everyone's already rooting for, of course. You are an influencer, Amari, and by the time I'm done with you, there will be no one more trusted."

I look Harlowe right in the eye so she knows I mean what I'm about to say. "I won't help you lie to the supernatural world."

Harlowe stares right back. "Not even to save sweet Maria from the Sightless Depths?"

The words slam into me. I lean back in my seat, my eyes searching Harlowe's. The lady means what's she's saying— she'd really send Maria to that horrible place.

"If you cooperate," she continues, "I'll see to it that she's only transferred to some far-flung outpost where she'll remain out of sight. How does that sound?"

I lower my eyes to the table, desperately searching for

a way out of this. But I'm trapped. The only way to help Maria is to do what Harlowe wants. "Cooperate how?" I answer in a small voice.

"Just be ready to return the favor when I ask."

I snatch the spell book from the middle of the table. "If I agree, then I get to keep this. It's, um, sentimental."

Harlowe frowns. "Very well. But don't let me catch you doing any more spells. Not even I can save you a second time."

As she escorts me to the Junior Agent Room for dismissal, Harlowe tells me to be ready, that she'll be needing me very soon.

I ignore her and step inside with the others. Bear makes some comment that causes a roar of laughter, but I'm focused on Lara sitting at the front of the room, bent over her laptop.

I slip into my seat. "Lara, have you heard? About Maria?"

"What about her?" My partner looks genuinely puzzled.

I hesitate. How do I say this in a way that won't freak her out?

"So, um—"

The Junior Agent Room door swings open. "You guys gotta see this! Maria Van Helsing's in handcuffs!"

Lara is up and out of the room in an instant, her superhuman athleticism allowing her to move at a blurring pace. I run after her as fast as I can, skidding to a stop to avoid crashing into the wall of bodies crowding the hall to watch.

Maria walks with her head down, flanked by the two agents with Director Harlowe out front.

"I know this must come as quite the shock," Harlowe calls. "But not to our wise Prime Minister. He worried that letting magicians back into the Bureau could compromise the time freeze investigation. It's why he took over. But magicians are crafty, aren't they? Our computer technicians discovered stolen time freeze files on Maria's computer."

That's the real reason Harlowe is doing this to Maria, I realize. To stop Maria from looking into the time freeze. Which she was only doing to help *me* get the Great Game canceled.

Shocked murmurs fill the hallway.

"I *know*," Harlowe continues, her voice dripping with fake sorrow. "But it gets worse. Today, Maria Van Helsing was caught not only secretly practicing her forbidden magic inside the Bureau, but she was trying to recruit young Amari Peters to her side."

Every eye turns to me and I freeze. This can't be happening.

"Tell them," Harlowe insists. "It was *you* who turned her in, after all. I can't imagine what a sacrifice it was for you to stand up to someone you admire so greatly. But that's why you are one of my Elites, because you show the strength of character befitting the club."

I just stand there until someone shouts, "Well, is it true?"

A dozen others echo the question.

I look first at Lara, whose eyes are furious. Then at Harlowe, who seems smug. Finally I meet Maria's eyes, and I can see she understands what's happening. I'll bet Harlowe couldn't wait to tell her she'd be using *me* to send her away.

Maria gives me the smallest nod.

This is the only way to keep her out of the Sightless Depths, I remind myself. I take a slow deep breath. "It's true."

The hallway erupts. Lara springs into action, running up to Maria and snapping one of the handcuffs with her bare hands before an agent drags her away.

"Now, now," calls Harlowe. "Let's not forget that freeing a prisoner is a crime."

Director Van Helsing steps into the hallway. "What's all this commotion?"

"Daddy!" Lara shouts. "They're trying to blame Maria!"

Director Van Helsing's face goes quickly from shock to disgust. He lifts his chin. "A magician is no daughter of mine."

≈ 20 ≈

A T DINNERTIME I SIT ALONE IN THE FOOD COURT, EYES on the table in front of me, trying to pretend like Maria and I aren't the topic of every conversation. I tried to explain things to Lara, at least, but she wasn't in her room.

I finally look up when someone plops down at my table. It's Elsie. With everything that's happened, I'd almost forgotten about our argument last night. I'm sure she's heard about Maria by now too.

I glance up at her, expecting her to look angry or disappointed, but . . . *oh no*. She's far too pleased with herself. I know that look—it's the face she makes whenever she's figured out a tough problem.

I just hope that problem isn't me.

Elsie waits till I drop my hands before she reaches into the pocket of her lab coat and places a small sheet of paper on the table. She pushes it in front of me.

I recognize it instantly. It's from one of the very first bets I lost to her, last school year.

I, Amari Peters, promise to grant Elsie Rodriguez one favor.

"Els . . . ," I groan. This is what I get for constantly losing bets to my best friend.

She grins and points to the paper. "You didn't read the second line."

I lower my eyes and read. "No matter what."

"No. Matter. What." She leans back and crosses her arms. "All I want is for you to answer my question. Where'd you go during the Welcome Social?"

"It's not that I don't want to tell you," I say. "It's that I can't. Like, I *literally* can't."

Elsie looks skeptical.

I've got to find a way to show her what I mean since my words aren't working. "Give me a pen," I say. "I'm going to write down what happened when I left you."

She grabs a red one from her lab coat and hands it to me.

I flip the sheet of paper over and attempt to write out the words *Great Game*. But the pen doesn't budge, even as my hand trembles from the effort. "See what I mean?"

I can see the moment it clicks in Elsie's head.

She grabs my arm. "Amari, tell me you didn't agree to a magical vow of secrecy?"

I nod.

"What in the world have you gotten yourself into?" Her face falls. "Sorry, that's the same question, isn't it?"

"Yep," I say. "Just trust me, okay? I know what I'm doing." After failing the first challenge so badly, I'm trying to convince myself as much as her.

Elsie frowns. "I wish I could help somehow."

"It's Maria I want to help," I say.

Elsie looks lost. "What happened to Maria?"

"You really haven't heard?"

She shakes her head. "I've been in the Gadget Room all day dealing with Carcolh slime. They make juniors clean up the equipment that gets turned in after missions."

I explain everything I know, including my suspicion that Harlowe went after Maria because she agreed to help me with the time freeze investigation.

"How did Lara take it?" Elsie asks.

"Not great."

My phone starts buzzing in my pocket.

New Message from The_Lara_Van_Helsing◆:
Help!
Come to Room 149!
Hurry!

We don't waste any time getting to Lara's room in the youth dorms. I only knock once before she appears in the doorway.

"I know you're mad about Maria, but I didn't have a choice—"

"I'm not mad anymore," Lara interrupts. "My sister got her one phone call and she used it to call me and explain what happened. I know Harlowe was just using you."

"I only did it so she wouldn't get sent to the Sightless Depths."

Lara nods. "I figured it had to be something like that when they didn't put her in prison, only transferred her to the Antarctic Outpost."

I nod. "You said you needed help?"

Lara opens the door fully to let us inside. It looks like a bomb went off. Clothes and shoes are everywhere, the mattress is hanging off the bed, and her dresser is lying on its side.

"What happened?" asks Elsie.

The answer bounces happily from beneath an overturned shoebox and into a pile of clothes before disappearing out of sight.

"It's been destroying my room ever since I got back." Lara plops down on the edge of her bed and rubs her temples. Her eyes are still red from crying. "I thought I could just slide it under my bed and go on with my day, but it won't stop bouncing!"

I bite my lip. "Yikes. Have you tried putting the shade in a drawer or something?"

Lara shakes her head. "To do that I'd have to catch it first. I've got superhuman athleticism, but I'm still not fast enough."

Elsie puts her hands on her hips. "Between the three of us, I bet we can do it."

"I've had enough bad luck for one day," she says. "If you two want to take turns looking silly, go right ahead."

Silly might be an understatement—Elsie and I fail miserably, again and again. If the shade had a mouth, it would probably be laughing at us. Every time one of us gets close, it hops a bit faster, or a little higher, just out of reach. After five minutes of flopping all over the room like fish out of water—with nothing to show for it—we decide to both go at it together. Me on one side and Elsie on the other.

The result? Elsie and I run straight into one another, banging foreheads and falling backward.

"*Ow*," I say. "Is your head made of stone or something?"

Elsie winces.

The only good news is that our bloopers seem to cheer Lara up. At least she's able to laugh a little. "I *did* warn you."

"What are we supposed to do now?" asks Elsie, rubbing her face.

"You're the genius," I say.

Elsie's face suddenly lights up. "You're right. And part of being brilliant is knowing when to ask for help. I'm messaging Jayden."

Why didn't I think of that?

It only takes five minutes for him to knock on the door. But it's five minutes that the three of us spend watching helplessly as the shade ping-pongs around the room having the time of its life.

"*Whoa.*" Jayden does a double take when he sees the state the room is in. "Elsie said this some kinda emergency or somethin'?"

All three of us point at the ball of shadow bouncing happily atop the overturned dresser.

Jayden just smiles. "Come here, lil dude." The shade bounces right into his arms.

"I'd say you need to chill out, but you already freezin' cold. No more bouncin', a'ight?"

The shade goes still, and Jayden pats it on the head.

"You made that look way too easy," I say.

"I didn't even know it *could* stop bouncing," groans Lara.

Jayden shrugs and flashes a sheepish grin.

"When did you learn about Jayden's supernatural ability?" I ask Elsie.

She and Jayden look at one another and laugh. "We hung out after you ditched us before the Welcome Social."

"Shoot, we even formed a club," Jayden laughs. "Triple A."

"Do I even wanna know what that stands for?" I ask.

Elsie answers anyway. "The Amari Abandonment Association."

My cheeks burn and I glance between them. I don't like that nickname, but I can't really be mad either—I did abandon them. "Sorry about that."

"Where *did* you run off to so fast?" Jayden asks.

How am I supposed to answer? "I . . ."

"I'm sure she would've been there if she could. Right, Amari?" Elsie shoots me a knowing look and I nod. Now that she knows about the vow of secrecy, she's got my back just like she always does. I honestly don't deserve a friend like her. Still, there's enough worry in her eyes that I'm kind of glad she doesn't know exactly how much trouble I'm in with Dylan and the Great Game.

I turn to Lara. "Any chance the shade can stay here?"

Lara practically growls at me.

"Let's take turns," Elsie suggests. "We don't have any other roommates, so no one would have to know."

"Y'all don't have to worry about Shadow creating no more messes." Jayden gives the shade a gentle pat. "Ain't that right?"

The shade wiggles happily.

"Shadow?" I say. "You've named it already?"

Jayden shrugs. "Fits pretty good."

Lara sighs. "If you can promise me that thing—"

"*Shadow*," Jayden cuts in.

"*Okay*," says Lara. "If you can promise me *Shadow* will behave, then we'll take turns. I don't want it sent to the Sightless Depths, even if it is a little terror."

"Sightless Depths?" asks Jayden.

"Deep underground," says Elsie. "Where most of the *really* scary things live. It also happens to be where supernaturals are sent when they do something awful enough to be banished from the supernatural world."

Lara adds, "Only the Supernatural World Congress has the authority to banish people, but since the only congress member not stuck in the time freeze is Bane, he can pretty much banish anyone he wants." She frowns. "What if he ignores your deal with Harlowe and sends Maria there anyway?"

"We won't let him," I say. "If we can figure out who really caused the time freeze, then he'll have no choice but to let Maria go."

"Is our investigation getting a few new members?" Elsie asks.

I nod. "Maria needs us."

"So y'all were already investigating the time freeze?" Jayden asks.

"You know me," I say. "Always trying to save the world."

"But *how* do we investigate?" asks Lara. "Bane has already closed the case."

"Bane and Harlowe were already blocking anything to do with the time freeze before today," I say. "They wouldn't even let the Bureau investigate. So we're just going to have to bend the rules a little."

"If you're serious about this," says Lara, "then count me in."

Elsie shrugs. "You already know I'm down to help as best I can."

"Me too," says Jayden. "I don't really know Maria like that, but I ain't a fan of deporting folks." Something flashes in his expression, but it's gone too quick for me to guess what it is.

"Then it's official." Elsie moves to the center of the floor and waves for us to gather around. She reaches inside her lab coat for a small notepad. "What do we know so far?"

I quickly explain to everyone what the NightWalker told me about the Night Brothers supposedly using a time freeze like this seven hundred years ago.

"If that's true," says Lara, "it's a good starting point for us. I think we should treat this like the real deal—that means gathering more evidence. If this were an official Bureau of Supernatural Affairs investigation, we'd be doing stuff like checking out the scene and learning all we can about the crime."

"Leave the research part to me," says Elsie. "I've been looking into everything time related at the Bureau every chance I can, and I've got a couple leads. The hardest part will be getting anywhere near the Congress Room."

"Unless y'all planning on sneaking out." Jayden laughs.

We all look at one another until I break the silence. "That's exactly what we should do."

"The Congress Room is beneath the Georgia State House," says Elsie. "It's not like we can just walk up to it. And we'd need permission to teleport there."

"What if I could get my hands on one of my dad's transporters?" Lara asks. "Directors can go pretty much anywhere, no questions asked."

"Could you?" I ask.

"I would have to go to see my parents," says Lara, "and we aren't exactly getting along right now." She sets her jaw and meets our eyes. "But I'd do anything for Maria."

"Then that's how we'll check out the scene of the crime," I say.

"So I guess we've got a plan then?" asks Elsie. "A bonkers, totally dangerous plan for sure, but at least a plan?"

"I think we're on the right track." I glance around at the others and grin. We just might be able to pull this off.

Elsie nods and returns my smile—no doubt she can see from my aura how much better I'm feeling. "How about we meet back here after we've each done our part so we can figure out what comes next."

Lara crosses her arms. "We can't keep meeting in here without somebody noticing. I'm honestly shocked that Bertha hasn't come to check on us already." She glances up at Jayden. "Especially with a boy in here."

Jayden scratches the back of his head, looking awkward. "I know a spot we can use."

We all look up, surprised. He's only been at the Bureau a few days.

"When I chose Creature Control, I kinda wandered off the tour. Ended up finding this little place that I don't think many people even know about."

"Great," I say. "Elsie can research the other time freeze, Jayden will make sure the new meeting spot is secure, and Lara and I will work on sneaking out to the Congress Room. We'll meet again in a couple days. But let's try to do it sooner if we can."

Because there's another secret I'm keeping even from my friends—the Great Game. The second challenge could come at any moment, and I may not make it back.

≈21≈

LATER THAT NIGHT, I FOCUS ON THE GREAT GAME. There's no way to know what the second challenge will be, but I can still learn to defend myself in case I come face-to-face with Dylan. It's why I'm sitting in bed hunched over the *Responsible Weatherist* spell book. I've got one of Elsie's best inventions, the sneakandle, right up against the wall. Anyone more than three feet away can't tell the twisty green candle is even lit. Not only does that keep Elsie from waking up, but there's no light shining beneath the door to let Bertha know I'm up after curfew.

To say that I'm completely lost would be an understatement.

With illusions, it's easy—well, not easy, but at least straightforward. Do this gesture, say these words, and believe it'll work.

And then it works.

But with weather magic it's all *Be the wind, feel the wind, know the wind* . . . What's that even mean? And if I'm being honest, all thinking about the wind does is remind me of the first challenge where the Whispering Winds tricked me into falling into a canyon.

I blow out a sigh and read the passage again.

WIND TAMER

You must first understand that winds are a primal force of nature. As such they can never be controlled, only tamed, and only for a short period of time.

You must convince the wind that you are its master.

That you are even worthy to be its master.

This can only be accomplished through strong emotion and sheer force of will.

I concentrate on the air around me and will it to move.
Go!
Do wind stuff!
Not even a slight breeze. I close my eyes and try again.

By the time morning comes, all I've accomplished is making myself so drowsy that even if I did manage to control the winds at some point, I'd be too sleepy to remember.

I do my best to stay awake as Lucy zips us to the food court, where we find a table as close to the elevators as possible.

"Why are we here so early again?" I yawn.

Elsie rolls her eyes playfully. "I already *told* you. Following up on one of my leads. If it pans out, this could be huge. Like really huge."

I know my best friend well enough to tell when she's unsure about something. And she doesn't look confident at all. "*If* it pans out?"

"I'd say there's about a fifty-fifty chance."

"So wait," I say, a sudden realization making me slightly more awake. "You're saying we might've gotten up at the crack of dawn for nothing?"

"Maybe?" She smiles sheepishly. "Think of it as a stakeout. We're scoping the scene for a potential witness who could help us crack our case."

"Using fancy cop-movie words doesn't make what we're actually doing—which is trying not to fall asleep next to a taco stand—any more exciting."

"Think happy thoughts," says Elsie cheerfully.

An entire hour goes by and nothing. I feel myself drifting off to sleep when Elsie shakes me awake.

"Oh good! He's here."

I turn to look. "Who's here?"

"VanQuish's *second* biggest fan," she says. "Come on!"

Elsie tugs me in the direction of a couple of Junior

Fortune-Tellers. Because their department is only open at night, our breakfast overlaps with their dinner. Director Horus allows his juniors to wear whatever makes them feel happiest, so one girl is dressed as a giant teddy bear, and her friend wears a flowing red cape like something out of a comic book. Does Elsie think having our palms read will get us the answers we're looking for?

But she leads me right past them. Instead, we step to a boy in glasses wearing a brown suit and matching bow tie.

"Arthur," says Elsie. "Allow me to introduce you to my best friend, Amari Peters."

Arthur's eyes already look large behind his thick glasses, but somehow the mention of my name makes them grow even bigger. "I didn't think . . . I mean, sure, Elsie promised, but I just never imagined . . . you're really *her*."

"Yeah." I cut a glance to Elsie. "I'm really me." I don't know what else to say.

He shakes his head in disbelief and blurts, "Holy wow!"

"I promise I'm not that big a deal," I say.

"Don't listen to her," says Elsie. "She totally is."

"Of course she is!" he says, looking offended by my words. "Your brother is one of the best agents of all time. And you!" He shakes his head in awe. "Imagine coming to the Bureau and trying to fill those big shoes. But you're doing it! You're amazing!"

My cheeks burn with embarrassment. How are you supposed to react when somebody gushes over you like this? "I hope you never visit my Sky Sprints class, because that might change your mind."

"Anyway," says Elsie. "We need your help, Arthur."

His eyes narrow. "What kind of help?"

Elsie lowers her voice. "What do you know about a time freeze before this one?"

He flinches. "How do *you* know about that?"

"Then it's true?" I lean in. "Please, tell us if you know something."

Arthur glances around to make sure no one's watching. "It's been said the Night Brothers might've conjured one back in the Ancient War. But that's really all I know. You'd have to talk to Director Wenn—he's the expert on all things time related. Unfortunately, Prime Minister Bane sent him away on some special assignment, and I haven't seen the guy since camp started."

"Who's Director Wenn?"

"He runs the Department of Time Management," says Arthur. "His talent for timeliness got enhanced to time*less*-ness, so he's like a hundred and fifty years old but doesn't look a day over forty."

"That's a department?" I ask, stunned.

"It's a restricted floor," Elsie answers. "Like Black-stone Prison. You won't find it listed in *Ins and Outs and In-Betweens of the Bureau.*"

I just stand there gawking at my best friend. We're investigating a time freeze, and this girl never thought to mention a floor in the Bureau that *manages time* before now?

Elsie reads my expression and quickly adds, "I only

learned about it yesterday. Thing is, just like Blackstone, you need special permission to go there. And with Director Wenn gone, there's no way to get it." Her eyes flick to Arthur. "Unless maybe *you* could let us in to search the archives for information about the other time freeze? Maybe in exchange for Amari's autograph?"

He shakes his head. "No way. If we got caught . . ."

"What about a picture of us to post on Eurg?" I ask. "I'll post it to my page too."

His excited eyes fill up his glasses. "You mean it?"

I nod. "Absolutely. Anything you want."

"Then there's really just one more thing," he continues. "Elsie also has to admit that I'm the biggest VanQuish fan ever."

Elsie scoffs. "As if!"

Arthur crosses his arms. "You'd only be admitting what we already know. I'd put my VanQuish stash up against yours any day."

"I'm not a member of VanQuish," I cut in.

"Not officially," says Arthur. "But many serious collectors include you in the extended collection. VanQuish 2.0."

A shudder passes through me. That's the nickname Dylan and I gave ourselves last summer. Before he betrayed me.

"That's not me anymore either," I say in a small voice.

"Sure, but with you teaming up with Lara now, VanQuish 2.0 is technically still in effect. Although there is some debate on the online forums as to whether VanQuish 2.5 is a better name for this new phase."

"Casuals," says Elsie. "No serious fan would ever—"

"*Els*," I cut in.

"Right," she says. "Get us into the Time Management archives and I'll say you're the bigger fan, okay? That should tell you how important this is. As in, save-the-world big."

He looks between us. "How soon did you want to come?"

"As soon as possible," I say.

We hop on an empty elevator and Arthur types in a special code that sends us straight to the Time Management floor without stopping.

The elevator doors open to a giant clock face set into a wall of black steel. Arthur adjusts the hands to 11:59. "Just have to wait until the clock strikes twelve."

While we wait, I decide to ask, "So you aren't upset about me turning in Maria?"

"The online VanQuish forums were *furious* with you yesterday," says Arthur. "But Elsie explained that you were really just helping her stay out of Blackstone or the Sightless Depths. And since Elsie is a Level 10 Platinum member, nobody dares question one of her posts."

"Oh," I say. "Level 10 Platinum, huh?"

Elsie beams. "That's going on my tombstone as my proudest achievement."

"So how do you try out for a restricted floor?" I ask.

"You have to be chosen," says Arthur. "Two summers back, at the end of the departmental presentations, a fidgety guy came over and told me that my supernatural ability made me perfect for his department."

"And what supernatural ability is that?" I ask.

"My talent for guessing the time became the ability to *know* the time. Basically I can tell you what time it is without looking at a clock."

I try to keep my disappointment from showing.

"It's okay," he laughs. "I know it's pretty basic compared to kids with fancy badges."

I glance at the second hand as it rounds the nine. I can squeeze in one more question. "How did Elsie figure out your department?"

"Because I told her." His face reddens. "It was either that or give up my super-rare, still-in-the-box Junior Agent edition Quinton Peters action figure."

Elsie just grins. "I keep telling people not to make bets with me, but they never listen."

As the clock strikes twelve, a loud click sounds and the clock face swings open like a door, revealing the entrance to a ticking room where clocks of all sizes cover the walls. Arthur leads us inside, and my head whips around at all the clocks, each with a shiny gold plaque underneath.

"Welp," says Arthur. "This is the clock room. Every major city has its own clock, and by watching them we can tell if there's been a disturbance in that city or the surrounding areas. The clocks are really precise and will even alert us to something as small as a freeze grenade going off for a few seconds."

"You call it the clock room?" Elsie asks. "Not very imaginative."

Arthur shrugs. "I tried to get the old man to start calling it the Temple of Time, but no luck." He points to the hallway in the back. "The archives are that way."

Elsie and I follow him into the twisting hall, past a room with a faded clock face etched into a giant slab of stone. Instead of numbers it's got strange symbols around the dial.

"What's that?" I ask.

"The Master Clock," Arthur answers. "Legend says that stopping the hands on that clock would cause the planet itself to stop spinning."

"Really?" asks Elsie.

Arthur shrugs. "Who knows, honestly. It's so old that no one even remembers how the claim originated. And it's hardly worth risking the end of civilization to find out."

"Agreed," I say.

We continue down the hallway and take the next left into a complete mess. This is the archives room? Books and scrolls and diagrams litter the floor, and scattered piles cover tables and shelves. The far wall is completely hidden behind tall stacks of books so awkwardly placed they seem one good sneeze away from collapsing.

"How are we supposed to find anything in this?" I ask.

"Sorry." Arthur tugs at his sleeve. "When you're a department of only two, keeping things neat isn't high on the to-do list."

"Well, we'd better get searching," says Elsie. "We could be here for a while."

The three of us each take a corner of the room and start

going through every book that even looks like it might have the info we need. Unfortunately, since everything here is related to time, that's a lot of books. We're lucky that Arthur seems to have read through many of the texts, so he lets us know what's worth skipping.

I literally stumble across a book written by Director Wenn himself, a stained copy of *Titans of Time*, and we all gather around it. Arthur says he's only read parts of the book, so we do a quick search through the index for anything about the Night Brothers or a time freeze.

Nothing.

"Well, that's disappointing," says Elsie.

Arthur nods. "That was probably our best bet."

I blow out a frustrated sigh. "Point me to a restroom?"

"Right around the corner," he says.

I get to my feet and step into the hall while Arthur and Elsie keep searching. Turns out there's actually two doors right across from one another. One is the restroom, but the other has a faded sign on the door that reads *Director Wenn*.

Curious, I press my face up against the glass panel of the door to get a look inside, and my weight pushes it open—the door wasn't all the way shut. For a moment, I consider locking the door and pulling it closed, but again my curiosity wins out. What if there's something in there about the special assignment Prime Minister Bane has him doing—and it's something to do with the time freeze?

So I slip inside. The office is pretty boring, just a desk

and a wall full of diplomas and certificates. But then I notice a book open on Director Wenn's desk. I step over to read the title:

TITANS OF TIME, VOLUME II:
SWINDLERS & SCAMS
Frauds & Hoaxes Ranging from Stupidly Simple
to Extraordinarily Elaborate
By Timothy Wenn

Frauds and hoaxes? I flip to the index.

Night Brothers—*see Thomas Fletcher, p. 348*
At first glance, disgraced werewolf Thomas Fletcher would appear to confirm a folktale popular among certain UnWanteds. He claims that his werewolf pack caught Vladimir and Moreau in a surprise attack and would have succeeded in capturing them both had Moreau not stopped time and frozen the entire wolf pack in place. The spell supposedly had no effect on Moreau and Vladimir, and so they were able to escape.

A chill runs down my back. The spell had no effect on the Night Brothers, just like it had no effect on me. Whatever happened back then is the same thing happening now.

～ 22 ～

AFTER SLEEPWALKING THROUGH MY MORNING CLASSES, the plan was for me and Elsie to come back to our dorm at lunch to take a nap. But while Elsie's over there snoring away, I'm not so lucky. Every time I close my eyes, thoughts of Thomas Fletcher and the Night Brothers race through my head.

Elsie and Arthur both sided with Director Wenn when I showed them *Titans of Time, Volume II*. They think it can't possibly be a true story, because if the Night Brothers had powers like that, wouldn't they have gone around freezing time whenever they got into trouble? They'd have easily won the Ancient War.

And they've got a point. But I keep thinking about

Thomas Fletcher's claim that the time freeze was magician-safe just like the current freeze. No way that's just a coincidence.

I think the reason it worries me so much is because it would mean a magician really did cause the time freeze. And if that's true, then who could that magician be?

Since I can't get to sleep, I sit up and pull out the *Responsible Weatherist* spell book. Only instead of flipping directly to the Wind Tamer spell, I start at the very beginning. There's got to be something I'm missing.

Turns out I'm right. There's a warning on the very first page:

Introduction by Gustav Whend

Weather magic responds most to all-consuming emotions like fear and anger. But be warned, young magicians, for those same emotions pave the way for foul magick. A fair magician knows that self-control is the key to remaining selfless. For when we give in to fear and anger, is not our first instinct to be selfish? To put ourselves first and lash out at whatever is causing our discomfort? The only way to truly master the weather is to first master yourself. It's true that foul magick is the quickest path to achieving the impossible, but take heed: To delve too deep is to lose yourself entirely. You risk the magic becoming your master instead.

I bite my lip—I'm sure I can control my emotions. I can stop myself from going too far. So I'll test what he says.

If my choices are fear and anger, then I choose fear, because I know exactly what scares me most. Dylan. The Great Game. Quinton never waking up. I keep those thoughts in my head, even as they make me squirm with unease. Fingers trembling, I point across the room, demanding the wind obey me. *Go!*

And then jump as a breeze ruffles Elsie's hair.

After lunch break, I make it to the training gym just as Agent Fiona is shutting the door.

"Cutting it close, Peters," says Fiona.

"Sorry." I duck inside.

Lara is on the far side of the gym, sitting cross-legged on the training mat with the others. She's already got my Sky Sprints out of my locker for me, so I plop down beside her. I'm right in the middle of explaining what Elsie and I learned about this Thomas Fletcher guy when Tristan comes up behind us.

"Heard people are calling you two VanQuish 2.0," he says with a laugh. "Given how VanQuish 1.0 ended up, is that really such a compliment?"

Lara whirls around to face him, jabbing a finger into his chest. "You ungrateful jerk! They were your mentors and now you talk about them like that?"

"Back off, Van Helsing," calls Agent Fiona. "There'll be

plenty of chances to make googly eyes at one another after class."

Tristan and Bear howl with laughter.

Lara is red-faced as she watches them cross the gym to take spots next to their friends. "I hate him so much."

"He's pretty hateable," I say.

"All of ye pay attention," Agent Fiona shouts, her voice ringing off the walls. "Self-defense is an essential skill for a Junior Agent. The baddies ye face during Field Training won't care that you're only teenagers. That's why your Stun Sticks and Sky Sprints are so important—"

The doors swing open and our heads swing around to find Director Harlowe leading a large group of supernaturals holding cameras and microphones into the gym. It must be more folks from the press. "Amari, dear!" She waves me over.

I glance to Agent Fiona. Her expression is sour, but she just sighs and says, "Go on, Peters—see what the buzzard wants."

My shoulders slump and I keep my head down as I go. Out of the corner of my eye, I can see Tristan fuming at the attention I'm getting. Like this is something I want—I'd trade places in a heartbeat.

Harlowe steps forward to throw an arm over my shoulder, pulling me close before leaning in to whisper, "Remember to play nice, or there will be consequences. Now *smile*."

I grit my teeth and grin. Cameras flash in my face.

Harlowe clears her throat. "Some have accused our Prime

Minister of carrying out a grudge with his new policies. But that couldn't be further from the truth. All evidence points to the fact that magicians can't help their selfish, and often dangerous, impulses. But through his steady leadership and guiding hand, Prime Minister Bane has shown that not all magicians are a lost cause. And Amari here is the proof. She is Supernatural Investigations' brightest young star!"

I want to call Harlowe the liar she is—the only reason she and Bane care anything about me is that I'm popular. But telling this lady about herself would only make her angry, and that would only mean more trouble for me and Maria. So, as much as I hate it, I keep smiling.

"Good, good," says Harlowe, patting me on the head. It takes everything in me not to knock away her hand. "Go back and join the others."

"I'd love to see Amari in action," shouts a reporter.

The crowd oohs.

"How about a duel?" blurts Tristan.

Fiona scoffs and waves him off.

Even Harlowe seems eager to avoid it. "Come now, we've interfered with the lesson enough already."

But Tristan, seeming bolder, gets to his feet and suggests, "I'm sure these reporters want to see what Supernatural Investigations' *brightest star* can do. Bear and I will take on . . . what do you two call yourselves? VanQuish 2.0?"

"We don't call ourselves that!" I say.

But the press is already scribbling excitedly on their notepads.

Agent Fiona shakes her head. "That's hardly a fair match. Davies has more experience than the both of them combined."

"Not to worry, instructor," says Tristan, "I'll go easy on them. In fact, I'll keep one hand behind my back the whole time. Unless they're scared, of course."

"You're on!" shouts Lara, standing to meet the challenge. I agree with Agent Fiona and Director Harlowe that this is a terrible idea, but I'm supposed to have my partner's back. So I get up too.

Harlowe frowns. "I'm afraid I really must insist—"

But Tristan starts twirling his Stun Stick around his fingers and posing, and the reporters start to cheer him on.

"Peters? Van Helsing?" Agent Fiona puts her hands on her hips. "Are ye sure about this?"

I pull Lara aside before she can answer. As much as I don't want to put on a show for these cameras, I also don't want Tristan's smug face to shine either. "We can still back out."

"I don't *want* to back out," she hisses. "You heard what he said about Quinton and Maria. We can't let him get away with that."

"But—"

"If we don't stand up for our siblings, who will?" Lara cuts in. "Are you with me or not?"

I blow out a sigh. "With you."

Lara nods, and we turn to face the others. "We're in."

"Very well," says Fiona, shaking her head.

Harlowe has come over now. She yanks me away from the others and whispers, "Don't you dare embarrass me. You'd better win, *or else*."

I swallow. "Or else what?"

No answer comes.

Turns out duels take place in midair over a giant ball pit. The rules are simple: don't get zapped by an opponent's Stun Stick. Agent Fiona gives us five minutes to plan a strategy.

Tristan saunters over and grins. "You two are new, so I'll let you in on a little secret—I never lose."

"First time for everything," I mutter.

Lara nods. "Remember those words when I'm dancing over you."

Tristan nearly doubles over laughing. "This is going to be so much fun."

Once he's back on his side of the ball pit, Lara asks, "You know the Helsing Technique, right? From last summer?"

"Kinda," I say. "I only did it once, and we were on the ground."

"Don't worry, it's the same steps. Just leave Tristan to me."

I doubt the Helsing Technique will be as simple in the air. But the girl is determined, so I'm going to give it my best shot. Not that I've got much choice with Harlowe and these reporters watching.

Each team climbs the tall ladders at opposite ends of the ball pit. I reach down, power on my Sky Sprints, and then step out onto open air, Lara taking a spot beside me. I glance down at all the cushy colorful balls below. How long will it be before I'm crashing down into them?

I shake the doubts from my head. *We can do this.*

Once Tristan and Bear take to the air on the other end, Agent Fiona blows her whistle to begin.

Lara and I start the Helsing Technique, her family's Stun Stick strategy—it's constant motion from side to side so your opponent can never get a clear shot at you. It's tricky because the footstep patterns change at odd times. So once your opponent thinks they can predict where you'll be, suddenly you're headed in a different direction and you can zap them instead.

But the thing that only dawns on me as Tristan begins to float higher and higher is just how much of an advantage flying gives him. It's no wonder he wins all the time. We can only move side to side, but he can move in any direction.

Bear realizes at the same time we do that Tristan is completely abandoning him to take up a spot near the ceiling. His own supernatural ability, which allows him to understand any language he hears, isn't much help in a duel. He screws up his face, staring helplessly as Lara and I move closer. Outnumbered, he charges at us, running through the air at full speed.

But Lara's superhuman athleticism allows her to sprint past him before he even realizes what's happened. She lands a perfectly aimed Stun Stick blast right in the center of his back.

Bear's muscles lock up and he tumbles down into the ball pit below, howling with laughter as the tickling power takes effect.

One down, one to go.

Now that Bear is out of the way, Tristan descends to a height just above us. The only downside of Lara's sprint to take down Bear is that now we're on opposite sides of the ball pit, with Tristan right in the middle of us.

It might feel like we have the advantage—if only Tristan wasn't grinning so hard. And suddenly I realize our mistake: Lara and I can't do the Helsing Technique if we aren't anywhere near each other.

Tristan begins to twirl in the air, faster and faster, sending out Stun Stick blasts one after the other. They come so fast that it's all Lara and I can do just to dodge them.

The only thing saving me is that most of the shots are aimed at Lara. Which makes sense because she's clearly the bigger threat. As he spins closer and closer to her side of the room, shots stop coming my way entirely. They're all aimed at her.

Soon even she can't move fast enough to avoid them. I try to aim a few shots at Tristan, but I'm so far away they don't even come close. Seconds later Lara goes tumbling into the ball pit below and my heart sinks.

Tristan stops spinning and strikes a pose for the cameras. "*I'm* the next star of Supernatural Investigations. Peters is just a phony who'll never get out of her brother's shadow."

I point my Stun Stick, and this time I'm the one charging. If I'm going down, I'm going down trying.

Tristan waits until I get right up close, letting me fire my Stun Stick. He drops below me and the shot sails over his head. Next thing I know, he zips around me and rips off my left Sky Sprint. I lose my balance and flip upside down, hanging in the air by the one Sky Sprint I've still got on.

Worst of all, my Stun Stick slips out of my hand and falls into the ball pit. I'm stuck, dangling in midair. Tristan points to laugh at me, then it feels like the whole training gym is joining in. I've never felt so embarrassed.

I let out a loud, angry shout—not just for this failure, but for *everything* that's gone horribly wrong this summer. I've already lost a Great Game challenge. I'm still nowhere near ending the time freeze, even with today's progress. My best friend is leaving me behind. Quinton may never get better. And maybe worst of all, I'm a total fraud—a smiling face that Harlowe and Bane can use to justify their cruelty.

Stop laughing at me! I ball my fists and suddenly warmth fills my chest—the way it does whenever I cast an illusion.

Someone screams.

Swirling black clouds swell to fill the air above us. Booming thunder nearly makes me jump out of my skin, and bright flashes of lightning charge the air. Wind howls through the training gym, carrying equipment through the air.

I'm too shell-shocked to even move.

"Peters!" calls Agent Fiona from the edge of the ball pit. "Are ye doing this?"

Still hanging upside down by one Sky Sprint, I nod, dumbstruck.

"Well, can ye make it stop?"

I close my eyes. *Storm, please stop. Like right now.*

BOOM! A crack of lightning strikes the lockers on the edge of the room so hard my heart skips. That's when I'm forced to admit the truth. "I don't know how."

"Was afraid you'd say that," she replies. "Take off the other Sky Sprint and drop into the ball pit. We're evacuating to the hallway."

I do what I'm told.

Once I'm down, I grab my Stun Stick and crawl to the edge of the ball pit to follow Agent Fiona. We sprint across the rain-soaked floor into the hall, where the other Junior Agents stare. Along with a soaking wet Director Harlowe.

Camera flashes light up the hallway. I can only imagine how I must look, dripping water.

"I have never been so humiliated in my life!" hisses Harlowe. "What were you thinking, performing a spell like that *inside* the Bureau?"

I don't have an answer, so I keep my mouth shut.

"Thought you'd show me up, did you?"

"I wasn't—"

"Let the lass alone," says Fiona. "Her magic clearly got away from her."

"Then perhaps we need to reevaluate our arrangement,"

says Harlowe. "Why don't we let the Prime Minister decide what's to be done?"

I sit in the chief's office, arms folded. Chief Crowe isn't here yet, but Director Harlowe has been in and out, giving me a disapproving head shake each time. As angry as I am at this whole situation, I'm equally scared.

When she finally comes in and takes a seat behind the large desk, I decide I've had enough. "I wasn't trying to show you up. Agent Fiona was right, I just lost control."

"So you say," she says calmly. "But I think you can't help that rebellious streak inside you."

"What are you going to do to me?" I ask.

"I'm not going to do anything." She leans forward. "I've tried to set you apart as useful to the Prime Minister's cause, Amari. But if we can't rely on you to toe the line, what good are you to us?"

How did things get this bad? At lunch I could barely stir up a breeze, and now I've set off a whole storm? Why can't I control my magic?

My next thoughts are for Quinton and Maria. "Please don't punish anyone else for what I did."

Director Harlowe doesn't react to my words. She just points to the large screen on the wall behind her chair. "The Prime Minister will be with us shortly."

I start to sink into my seat but go tense at a warming sensation on my ring finger. No, no, no . . . This is the *worst* possible time. The last challenge was literally yesterday morning—will there be one every day now?

"Are you listening?" barks Harlowe.

I blink and she's staring at me, goat ears raised. "Um, yes, sorry."

"*Good*," she says. "See to it that it stays that way. Now then, as I was saying . . ." A cell phone rings and Harlowe reaches down to grab it off the desk.

I can't wait any longer. The moment her eyes leave me, I squeeze my ring and vanish.

~ 23 ~

I N A BLINK, EVERYTHING GOES DARK. AND STAYS DARK.

It takes me a few seconds to realize I've arrived at wherever the second challenge is. I force down the rush of panic that brings. *Okay, okay, okay . . . this is really happening.* I fumble through my jacket until I find my Stun Stick and turn on the flashlight mode.

I'm on a stone staircase, except the path upward has caved in. The only way to go is down. Into more darkness.

So that's what I do. Slowly at first, but then I remember Dylan could arrive any moment and start to run, skipping two and three stairs at a time. I continue until I reach the bottom and emerge in a dimly lit room so vast my footsteps seem to echo forever.

I freeze, a nasty chill spilling down my back. If Dylan beat me here, then I've just announced myself.

Gotta be careful.

I wave the flashlight around, taking in the sight of enormous columns as wide as houses, each covered in books, reaching up like skyscrapers into the gloom above. Golden balconies circle the massive bookcases, a staircase on each level leading up to the next. A web of arching bridges stretches from column to column, eventually disappearing into the outer walls of this massive room. And here I thought the library at the Bureau was huge; this place is practically an indoor city.

But where am I?

I move farther inside, swinging my flashlight back and forth looking for any sign of Dylan. A dozen steps in, my feet land on a large, slightly raised plaque set into the floor. The inscribed words are written in some other language.

If I hadn't needed a spell to quickly translate the Spanish homework I forgot to do over winter break, I'd be out of luck right now. I may have been anxious about trying new magic, but that wasn't nearly as terrifying as the thought of telling Mama why I'd received a zero on an assignment that would count for 10 percent of my final grade. I drop to one knee and place the palm of my hand against the stone, whispering, "Translateur."

An illusion of shimmering words comes floating up from the stone.

Beware all those who tread here
This is the Living Library of Alexandria
Curated and preserved by those born to magic
Continue at your own peril

The Library of Alexandria . . . As in Alexander the Great from world history class? The ancient Greek king who conquered like half the world? What's he got to do with the Great Game?

Unless . . . he was a magician too?

Have we really been around for that long? I take another look around me. And what's it mean by *living* library?

As if in answer, the faint hum of music sounds in the distance.

My neck starts to feel sweaty. What if this is another trick of the Great Game to hurt me? Or worse, Dylan's trying to lure me close enough to steal my magic and win? He won't care that it would kill me.

But there's also a chance this song is the key to finding the second Victor's Ring. I've got no choice but to see where it's coming from.

It doesn't help my already jumpy nerves that every so often I'll hear a strange shuffling sound, but whenever I whirl around to have a look, nothing's there. The farther into the library I go, the more I hear it. I'm not alone—I'm sure of it. And with every step the "something" seems to grow more and more restless.

"D-Dylan?" I whisper, flicking my flashlight around frantically.

No answer.

Heart hammering, I do my best to stay calm and continue deeper into the library. At some point it becomes clear that the music I'm hearing is actually a voice—someone's humming a gentle melody that hits me right in the feels even though I can't understand the words. It makes me think of Quinton and how much I wish I could go back to before he was cursed.

When I'm close enough, I peer around the next column of books to where the singing seems to be coming from. Just like with the shuffling sounds—nothing's there.

I can't keep waiting for whatever's in here to reveal itself. Dylan could arrive at the library any minute—if he hasn't already.

Please don't let this be another trick. I swallow and step out into the open, following that soothing voice right to the next column of books. My breath catches as I realize the song is coming *from* a book. I pull it down from the shelf and feel the melody vibrating through my fingertips. I lay my palm against the cover to translate the title.

MELODIES OF REMEMBRANCE
A Songbook

"You're singing because you're a songbook," I say quietly. "A literal book of songs."

The book responds by opening halfway to reveal a papery tongue, sticking it out at me and then wriggling free of my grip to hop back onto the shelf. The books around it start to move too, shuffling up to the edge of the shelf to have a look at me.

A dusty old book plops into my hands. It clears its throat, the cover opening and closing as it begins to belt out an opera song. The sound of violins pours out of another book and seconds later the whole column is singing, or playing music, or even just tapping out a beat—a hundred different melodies all at once. Books twirl and dance across the shelves.

I laugh, feeling like I've stumbled into a Disney movie. So that's what that plaque meant by a Living Library. All that shuffling I heard before . . .

"These books are alive!" I stare up at the columns in wonder.

"Incredible, isn't it?" Dylan's voice echoes, making me jump. "This is one of the secret libraries of Alexandria—Alexander the Great being the most famous magician who's ever lived. Not that anyone but his closest generals knew that about him."

I shudder and quickly set the opera book back on the shelf. "W-where are you?"

A torch flickers to life in the distance, showing a figure in a bright red cloak. At the sight of Dylan's sneering face glowing in the firelight, the books fall silent, many of them shivering on the bookcase.

"All these magical books stored away," he continues. "You couldn't read them all even if you had a hundred life-times. But that's what it means to fully devote yourself to the Foul Path. To reach your full potential, you must be selfish. Give up everything in the name of power."

"Is that what you've done?" I ask. "Have you chosen foul magick?" I still remember a boy who created rainbow forests and helped me conjure an Amari Blossom. "There's still good in you, I know it."

"Good?" The figure in the distance vanishes. Too late, I realize it was just an illusion—the real Dylan is only a dozen feet away, hands exploding into flames. He hurls them at me, great big fireballs, one after the other. I yelp as I duck and scramble on all fours to get away.

The books look on as I sprint around bookcase after bookcase, my head whipping back and forth trying to look in every direction at once. I'm so tempted to squeeze my Game Ring and get out of here, but that would mean Dylan gets a second Victor's Ring. If I lose another challenge it'll be nearly impossible for me to win the Great Game.

I have to find that ring.

I take off again and don't even see the next fireball coming. The only reason it doesn't hit me is that I trip on a book and the blaze goes right past my face, into a bookcase behind me. The column erupts in flames.

The noise of rustling pages fills the air. It's not a happy sound.

Desperate, I try to summon a wind to put out the fire,

but I'm rushing and fail. A shower of books comes crashing down around me as they leap down from the bookshelves to safety, some from impossible heights.

As bad as I feel for them, I've got to keep moving. Books leap off other columns now, but this time it's not for safety—they're *aiming* for me. As more and more books dive at me, it's all I can do to dodge them. "I didn't start that fire!"

I only barely manage to avoid a giant tome as tall as I am. It hits the ground with a *BOOM!* that sounds like a bomb just went off. If that book had landed on me, I'd be done for.

The books begin to bang on their shelves in unison, louder and angrier each time. It almost sounds like a war drum. The clatter echoes throughout the library, making me shiver. I notice that it's not only me they're after—the books are going after Dylan too. But he isn't just avoiding them like I am. He's aiming fireballs at them.

Which only irritates the library even more. Books on a nearby column open up to release a hail of arrows that whistle toward us, forcing both me and Dylan behind columns. I have to cover my ears after a cannonball fires from the next book. If the first column I approached held books about music, then this one is clearly the warfare section. Which means I need to keep my distance.

Dylan responds with more flames. As much as my heart breaks for the books he's torching, there's nothing I can do. I've got to get out of here.

I sprint for the opposite end of the library, looking for

any sign of the Victor's Ring or even just an exit. I'm already breathing heavy from all this running and ducking when I finally spot a door on the opposite wall.

At the same time I hear fluttering directly above me. I tilt my flashlight upward to find a cloud of shapes descending out of the darkness. These seem to be books too, covers flapping like wings. Except between the pages are very real fangs that gnash at the air.

They're coming straight for me—and fast.

I pick up my pace, legs burning, rounding column after column.

Maybe I'm a terrible weatherist, but what I *can* do well are illusions.

I dash behind the next column and send an illusion of myself running back around the other side. When I peek around to have a look, I see dozens of books crash into the floor trying to take her out. In a matter of seconds, a tall pile fills the space where my illusion had been. If there was any doubt what this library's intentions are, that settled it.

I sprint to the next column and repeat the same trick. But this illusion Amari doesn't make it five steps before a fireball blazes right though her chest.

"You can't hide from me!" Dylan calls.

Now what? I've got a cloud of angry books floating to my left, and Dylan coming from my right. I'm trapped here behind this column. Whichever reaches me first, I'm still toast.

Maybe I could turn invisible, but Dylan has clearly

thought of that too. He's casting Dispel every few steps. If I step out and he dispels my invisibility, I'll be left out in the open.

I slump to the floor, fingers hovering over my ring, my jaw quivering as I realize that I've got to get out of here—it's my only choice. I'm not good enough to beat Dylan. Not even close.

Something nuzzles my leg. I jump, realizing it's a book, and immediately aim my Stun Stick at it. But unlike the others, this one isn't flashing fangs. Probably because it's wrapped in a tight leather strap. Faded Chinese characters are etched into the cover.

I pick it up and cast my translation spell.

FIREWORKS FROM THE FAR EAST

The book wriggles in my grip. If a songbook can sing and books on war can fire arrows, does that mean a book about fireworks might create a distraction for me? It's worth a try.

"Can you tell me if the ring is through that door over there?" I ask.

The book shivers in a way that feels like yes. At least I hope that's what it means.

"If you buy me like ten seconds, then I can get through that door and Dylan will probably chase me. He won't hurt any more books."

At that, the book does an excited flip.

"Okay, I'll give it a shot." I undo the straps and, with one giant heave, slide it out into the open. Great big pops sound and white sparks shoot out from the pages, creating a dazzling display overhead.

The other books begin to crash down around it, and I can hear Dylan's footsteps moving away from me now, headed back toward the fireworks.

I bolt for the mysterious door, stopping only to slip off my gray jacket and smother the flames on a silvery book that's in my path. Once the fire is out, I take off toward the door again. I do a quick translation of the words etched into the door to get a sense of what I might be walking into.

Book Handling Gloves

Gloves? I give the door a hard shove that sends me stumbling inside.

But I don't see a ring. Just a bunch of gloves and a bowl—

Dylan appears at the entrance to the room. He stalks forward, and I shrink away.

"Wait!" I'm as scared as I've ever been in my whole life. "Please don't . . ."

He lobs a fireball directly at me, and I panic.

"No!" I thrust my hands forward and feel warmth in my chest. Swirling winds surround me, like a miniature tornado, swallowing up Dylan's fire and creating a barrier of gusting wind. I reach out and send a current of wind in Dylan's direction, knocking him back into the wall.

"S-stay back!" I shout. "I'm warning you."

"So you *have* been learning." He holds up both hands as if to surrender. "Truce?"

But I'm not listening. I can't worry about Dylan right now. I've got to figure out how to win this Victor's Ring and get out of here.

A second glance around the room gives me a better look at the gloves. All kinds hang from little hooks on the walls—shimmering gold, plated metal, even jeweled gloves that look like they could belong to some great queen or empress. At the center of the space is a pedestal with a wide glass bowl attached—it's filled with boiling liquid that crackles and sizzles.

At the bottom of the bowl is something small and shiny.

The ring! We've got to reach into the bowl and grab it—except the liquid doesn't look safe at all.

That must be why we need the gloves. But with so many to choose from, how can I know which to pick?

I continue to look around the room and stop in my tracks when I notice Greek letters inscribed on the floor. I crouch down to translate with my magic, careful to keep my eyes on Dylan, who watches me with a smirk on his face.

The Strongest

"Those were Alexander's last words," says Dylan. "After his generals asked him who should inherit his empire. Spoken like a true foul magician."

The strongest? Is that a clue? I glance around the room. Which of these gloves is the strongest? How are we supposed to know that?

I look over my shoulder to find Dylan just as baffled. Thank goodness.

I pick up a glove made of polished wood and compare it to another of rusted silver, all while keeping one eye on Dylan on the opposite side of the room. For now, it seems like he's focused on getting his hands on the ring instead of me.

I move a bit farther down the wall and hear Dylan laughing behind me. He's got on a glove that looks like it's made of twinkling diamonds.

My belly knots as he lowers his gloved hand into the boiling liquid. The second it makes contact, thick smoke rises from the bowl and Dylan yanks his hand away.

"Ouch!" Dylan snatches off the glove, shaking his hand. "It doesn't make sense! What's stronger than diamond?"

What *is* stronger than diamond? My eyes flick between a glove of shiny bronze and one of stained wool. And then I catch sight of the mural painted above us on the ceiling. It's Alexander and his army, facing down the Persian emperor on a battlefield. It's one I've seen before, in history class when Mr. Green marveled at how he fought at the head of his men, not in metal armor but in folded linen. While Alexander charges courageously, the emperor is fleeing.

I realize the answer.

And come up with a plan.

As Dylan ruffles through glove after glove on the opposite wall, I grab a linen one and ease my way to the bowl. The only problem is that I've got to let my protective winds die out completely to keep from splashing that boiling liquid everywhere.

Thankfully Dylan doesn't seem to notice until I'm right next to it. His eyes narrow. "*That's* your choice?"

"Yep," I say, pointing up to Alexander on the mural. "It's the same material he used for armor, so it's gotta be what he trusted most."

Dylan smirks and shakes his head. "So very clever. It almost feels like we're back in the tryouts again, except we were on the same side then."

I shove down the rush of emotions those memories dredge up.

"Suppose you're right?" he continues, a fireball forming in his palm. "You don't really think I'll let you claim the ring?"

For a moment we just stare at one another. Then I throw the linen glove toward the door.

Dylan's eyes widen as he dives to catch it. At the same time, I plunge my bare hand into the boiling liquid. And then I'm laughing, because it tickles.

"I don't understand," Dylan says, clutching the linen glove tight.

"What's stronger than diamond?" I ask.

"Nothing."

"Exactly!" I say, pulling out my hand and wiggling my bare fingers. "Alexander would've found strength in courage, not armor. He fought at the front of his army—where all the danger is—not at the back."

I extend my finger to slide on the Victor's Ring.

Dylan starts toward me and I throw up another small tornado to protect myself. The magic really does feed off my emotions, I realize—it's working now because Dylan scares me so much.

But he only smiles and raises a hand in front of his face. Shadows rush through the swirling winds, coiling tight around my legs and arms, my neck, and even my mouth, so that I can't move or even speak. The dark tendrils pry the ring from my grasp. My winds die out around me.

No!

I stand there, helpless, as the roiling shadows both hold me still and carry the ring back to Dylan. He wastes no time putting it on, and the moment he does, my Game Ring turns ice cold on my hand. Since when can he control shadows?

"It didn't have to be this way," Dylan says in a low voice. "Last summer I had already won. I had the Black Key and the Black Book. I could've simply walked out of there, and you would've let me. All you cared about was getting your brother back.

"I never planned on stealing your magic back then," he continues. "Not really. I only wanted to scare you, to push you to realize the depth of your power. To see what we're capable of when we draw on one another's magic. But you did more than that, didn't you? You let them send me to the Sightless Depths, where I was alone, surrounded by terrors you can't even imagine. What if I told you that I found another magician in that place? One of Moreau's old apprentices thrown away to rot in the dark. That's what the Bureau does to people like us. That's what it thinks of magicians."

Dylan steps right up close. "So I did what I had to. I stole her magic—seems she'd been able to survive because she was a master of shadows. That power is mine now. In the Sightless Depths I learned what it truly means to fully devote myself to foul magick. I realized I'd only been playing at it before. I became more monstrous than anything around me—until I became the thing to be feared. Whatever bits of me that cared for you are gone now, Amari. I smothered them."

He turns to leave. "The last time I played at stealing your magic, it lashed out and things didn't end so well for me. Let's leave things like this instead. So long, *partner.*" He glances over his shoulder and smiles. "Maybe I'll come back to visit you when you're nothing but bones."

I watch Dylan squeeze his Game Ring and vanish. Now that he's gone, I'm able to see just how much damage those fireballs have done out in the library. The books have somehow managed to put the fires out, but even through the smoke I can see the charred columns and bits of ash in the air.

Horror rips through my whole body. How am I supposed to squeeze my ring if I can't move?

The answer is simple, I can't. I'm stuck here and there's no way to save myself.

A tear skips down my face. My friends and family won't even know what happened to me.

I notice a book at the room's entrance. How long has it been there?

As it wriggles its way across the floor I realize it's the book with the silvery spine that I put out when it was on fire. It leaps, slamming shut around my ring.

A moment later I'm back in the chief's office, sitting in the very same chair I left from, this strange book still in my hands. Dylan's hold on me is gone now, his shadows fading away. Thankfully the office seems to be empty.

I hug the book super tight. "Thank you." It must've been watching long enough to see Dylan squeeze his ring to leave. If it hadn't followed me to that glove room, I wouldn't have made it out of there.

But even my relief at being saved can't stop the crushing disappointment I feel next. I lay the book gently on my lap and bury my face in my hands. That was *my* ring. It was practically on my finger, and Dylan just took it from me. His magic—he can do things now that I didn't even know were possible. Last year he could only do illusions and control technology, but just now he took away my ability to move with a wave of his hand. Not even my winds could stop those shadows.

There's just no way I can possibly compete. He's too strong. Is that the power of foul magick?

I'm going to lose. Dylan's going to get the Crown of Vladimir and gain control of the League. He'll have his war against the Bureau and the supernatural world. And it's going to be all my fault.

≋ 24 ≋

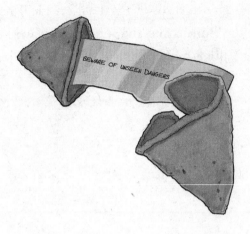

BEWARE OF UNSEEN DANGERS

FRANTIC VOICES REACH ME FROM THE HALLWAY.

"No, my office does not have any secret escape hatches," says Chief Crowe. "Do be serious."

"Then how do you explain the girl's disappearance?" comes Harlowe's voice. "One moment she was sitting right in front of me, the next she was gone."

I tuck the book behind me on the chair, unsure what to do. I should've realized that after disappearing like that, people would be looking for me. "I'm right here," I say, startling both ladies as they come through the office door.

The chief looks relieved. "All your blustering and Peters never left the room."

But Harlowe is furious. She stomps up to me and pulls

back both my jacket sleeves. "Where is it? Where's the transporter you've been hiding?"

"I don't have one," I answer. "Junior Agents aren't allowed to have their own transporters."

"Don't play smart with me," says Harlowe. "How did you manage it? Where did you go?"

Even if I wanted to tell her the truth, my vow of secrecy wouldn't let me. So I just say, "Oh, you know, here and there."

Not a good answer—not by a long shot. If Harlowe looked angry before, she looks ready to explode now.

"You know," Harlowe begins, straightening her skirt suit. "I honestly thought you were different. That you were like me—an outsider seeking to prove herself. You could have been a shining example of the Prime Minister's generosity and compassion, a model for others to follow—"

"Oh, give it a break," says Chief Crowe. "There aren't any cameras around. You don't have to peddle that nonsense here."

I'm with Chief Crowe. Is this lady for real?

"Quiet," says Harlowe. "It just so happens that I spoke with the Prime Minister while you were gone. He's decided to oversee this matter *personally*." She taps away at her phone and then stands back.

A ghostly figure appears on the screen at the back of the office, and I swallow. This isn't the first time I've seen Bane, but it still makes me queasy. There's no color to him, as if it's all been bleached away, and just like during his press conference he flickers and fades, going blurry every few seconds.

"Go on," Bane finally says, "have a good look at the horrific consequences of magiciancraft."

If watching him sneer was unsettling, it's nothing to watching him speak. His expressions freeze on his face, so that they don't always match up to his words. It's like trying to watch a lagging video with a bad connection. It's so creepy.

"I . . ."

"You what?" says Bane.

"I'm sorry," I say. "I can't imagine what being a wraith must be like."

"No," he says coldly. "I don't imagine you can. Being ripped from your body is a fate I wouldn't wish on my worst enemy." He grins, a moment late. "Then again, maybe I would. It's a special kind of horror to see your body age and die without you. Forced to live on forever, only half existing."

I can only shake my head. "That's awful."

"Don't pretend to feel pity for us." He's sneering again. "Not when you've got all that cursed magic inside you. It's because of you wretched magicians that wraiths no longer remember what it's like to feel the wind on our faces. Or how the woods smell after a spring rain. I can't recall the taste of my favorite meal, or the love of the wife who would prepare it for me. Only the anger remains. It's all that's been *allowed* to remain."

I don't know what to say to that, so I don't say anything. He sounds so much like Dylan, his voice full of nothing but rage.

Bane continues. "If I had my way, I'd throw you and every magician I can find into the Sightless Depths and never let you out. The only way to cure the world of evil is to root it out and banish it forever."

"I'm *not* evil," I snap. "I'm a good person."

"So everyone tells me," says Bane in his disjointed voice. "Your proximity to VanQuish and your heroics last summer have convinced so many that you are the exception. The Good Magician. Enough that I can't even kick you out of the Bureau without taking a public relations hit at a time when I cannot afford the negative press. It's the only reason you were permitted to come and certainly the only reason you've been allowed to continue."

"Because they're right," I say. "I'm proof that being a magician doesn't make you bad. And so is Maria."

"You both certainly play the role very well. But we'll see how long you can keep up the act—it's only a matter of time before you decide you don't have to play by the rules." Bane grins in slow motion. "Harlowe, what have we decided the girl's punishment shall be?"

"We may not be able to get rid of her," says Harlowe. "But we can certainly make it as difficult as possible for her here. Kill off this reputation for heroics she's built." Harlowe rips the Elites pin from my jacket and follows with my moonstone badge.

"Those are mine!" I shout, reaching after them, but it's no use.

Harlowe digs into her pocket and pulls out an enormous bright red badge. *Dangerous* is written across the front in giant letters. She shoves the thing at me. "You will wear this at all times and are hereby banned from interacting with anyone other than those you can't avoid. From here on out, you are to be seen and not heard. Understood?"

"T-that's not fair!" I stammer.

"How is she supposed to train under those conditions?" asks Chief Crowe.

"Perhaps Amari should have thought about that before her little stunt today," says Harlowe. "No one makes a fool out of me. Be thankful the Prime Minister is allowing you to train at all."

I look to Chief Crowe, but she doesn't say anything. Then again, what *can* she say?

Bane's smug voice comes through the screen. "Do feel free to quit if you can't perform under these conditions. It would be music to my ears." The screen cuts out.

I ball my fists at my sides and turn to Harlowe. "I won't ever quit."

"We'll see about that, won't we?"

A small dark cloud forms over Harlowe's head and begins to pour down rain.

"I—make it stop!" Harlowe dances across the office trying to escape it, but the cloud just moves with her. "How dare you!"

I go totally stiff. I didn't mean to do that.

Hiding a smile, Chief Crowe shoos me toward the door. "Get out of here while you can."

I scoop up the Living Library book and do just that.

"Unbelievable!" says Elsie, pacing around the study room.

After I left the chief's office, I messaged Elsie to meet me in our old study room. It's not like I can use the Elites study room anymore.

Elsie is supposed to be in her last class right now, but she got here in minutes.

"Of all the mean, totally inappropriate things they could've done, this is the worst. They have *no* right to take your moonstone badge. None at all."

My best friend is fuming, and it hits me just how much I'm going to miss her having my back when she's in England next year.

"What's wrong?" Elsie asks. "Your aura just went blue."

I shake my head. "Nothing."

Elsie looks concerned for a moment, but then continues. "They're trying to set you apart, to make things like they were last summer. But you can't let them get to you."

"I know," I say. "I told them I won't quit. But it did feel nice getting to wear that Elites badge and have people just automatically be nice to me." I shrug. "And now it's like I'm right back where I started. I know I can handle it, but that doesn't mean I'm looking forward to being the camp outcast again."

Elsie sits and blows out a long breath. "I'm supposed to visit the London Bureau this weekend and meet Director Ansers, the English Director of Magical Science . . . but I can totally stay if you need me to."

I meet Elsie's eyes and can tell she means it—she really would cancel her trip if I asked. It's also clear that she *really* wants to see what things will be like for her next summer. "I'll be fine, you should go and have fun. Besides, Jayden is staying, so I'll have someone to hang out with."

"Are you two allowed to hang out?" Elsie nods toward my new *Dangerous* badge.

I shrug. "We'll figure something out."

Elsie nods, but her eyes snag on the little book peeking out of my jacket. "What's that?"

"Oh," I say, dropping my eyes. "I found it . . ." The rest of the words won't come.

Elsie leans forward, whispering, "The vow of secrecy?"

I nod and set the book onto the table. "Believe it or not, the book is alive."

She raises an eyebrow.

"It's okay," I tell the book. "You can show her."

The little book hops so that it's standing up. Elsie jumps in her seat.

"Is it okay if I translate your title?"

The book rocks back and forth. So I lay my palm flat against the cover and say, "Translateur." Once again, shimmering words drift up into the air.

A COLLECTION OF LOOKING GLASSES

"Open it up," says Elsie excitedly.

So I do. Thin plates of glass are set into the pages above the same type of writing on the cover. But when I stare through the glass, I don't see my reflection—I see me and Elsie huddled over the sneakandle and listening to a radio she built from scratch back in our old trainee dorm.

"What do you see?" I ask.

"Us," says Elsie. "The night we first met last summer."

"Me too."

I cast my translation spell again on the small words beneath the glass and it reads:

Where you've been . . .

"That's pretty cool," says Elsie. "Are there more?"

I flip the page and find another. This time I translate the words before gazing into the glass.

Where you'll be . . .

Another image of the two of us appears. Elsie's breath hitches beside me. This one shows Lara pointing a Stun Stick at me and Elsie. Our hands are up.

"Maybe we're practicing?" I say quickly.

Elsie frowns.

"Let's keep going." I turn the page, and the next translation reads:

What you most want to see . . .

This time I'm sitting next to Quinton's hospital bed as his eyes blink open. He smiles up at me. My heart feels so full at the sight.

"What do you see?" asks Elsie.

I tell her and then ask the same question.

"I see myself as a full dragon," she says in a hushed voice. "It's *incredible*."

"It's going to happen," I say, and give her hand a squeeze.

My phone alarm sounds. I set it for the end of class so I'd know when it would be safe to head back to the youth dorms without Bertha getting on our case about cutting.

"One more," Elsie begs. *"Please?"*

I flip to the next page.

What you most need to see . . .

Elsie is back—but in the background this time. It's our last Soup Club meeting. The one where Elsie gave us the real fortune cookies. The message written on that strip of paper in bright red letters is front and center.

Beware of unseen dangers.

"It's showing me the fortune I got from your fortune cookie," I say.

"I'm looking at the message from my fortune cookie too," says Elsie. "About my hard work paying off."

"Is that really what we most needed to see?" I ask.

Elsie shrugs. "We can talk about it at dinner later."

I nod and tuck the book back into my gray jacket. Together, we leave the study room, following the little hallway that leads back to the main library.

We both stop cold at the sight of Lara and Director Van Helsing stepping out of another study room up ahead. Director Van Helsing leans over to whisper in Lara's ear, and she nods. But I can't see her face clear enough to tell how she feels about whatever her dad is saying. They turn and leave together without looking back.

Elsie raises an eyebrow. "Maybe Lara's just making up with her dad to get his transporter?"

"That's gotta be it." Still, I can't get the image of Lara aiming her Stun Stick at us out of my head.

THAT NIGHT I GET MY FIRST TASTE OF WHAT LIFE WILL BE like wearing my new *Dangerous* badge. Harlowe makes an announcement letting everyone know that I'm to be avoided at all costs—an order directly from the Prime Minister.

This means having to catch rickety old Beauford to the food court because no one else will let me ride the elevator with them. Tristan and Bear get a kick out of pretending to run into me then acting surprised that I'm still here.

It's a relief to finally get back to my room. Since it's Friday, most kids will be going home tomorrow for the weekend. And even better, no classes—which means I'll have at least a couple days of freedom to work on my investigation.

I'm sitting in bed skimming an othernet article about how the thunderstorm in the training gym was my first step on the road to villainy. The worst part is that this is the same magazine that called me a hero at the beginning of camp. Harlowe's right about one thing—the media can turn on you in an instant.

My phone buzzes:

New Message from The_Lara_Van_Helsing ✔:
Got my dad's transporter

That makes me sit up. Finally, some good news.

From Amari_Peters ✔:
We should sneak into the Congress Room tonight

Lara doesn't reply right away, and I wonder if maybe she'd rather hold off. But now that I've lost the first two rings, I can't afford to wait. The next challenge could come at any second, and if Dylan gets the third ring, it won't matter what we can prove about the freeze—the supernatural world and the League of Magicians will already be at war.

Elsie comes back from her Junior Genius Society club meeting and I wave her over. She takes the spot next to me on my bed.

"Lara was able to get her dad's transporter," I say.

Elsie looks relieved. "So maybe she really *was* meeting with her dad about getting it."

"Seems like it. But I'd be lying to say I'm not worried she might be setting me up too."

"Gosh I hope not." Elsie pales. "What we saw in the looking glass—it did look an awful lot like she was turning us in. And you're already in trouble with Bane and Harlowe—if you get caught sneaking into the Congress Room . . ."

"I've still got to try—too much is riding on me solving this."

Elsie lowers her eyes, and my phone goes off.

New Message from The_Lara_Van_Helsing✅:
Sorry, my mom called. Long story. I'm in.
My room. Tonight.

Lara and I agree to meet in her room just before curfew. It's not far, so I was sure I could get there without being seen, but Bertha has some kind of kid radar or something and stepped around the corner the moment I left my room. Word around the youth dorms is that her supernatural ability lets her literally sniff out trouble, and I believe it. Half panicking, I made up a story on the spot about needing to practice my footwork for Sky Sprint class on Monday. Even I knew it was a pretty weak excuse so I threw in that Lara was feeling lonely in her room all by herself and that I'd planned to sleep over. Since Lara is my partner, she's one of the few people Harlowe's new badge allows me to interact with.

Bertha gave me a look but let me pass, so long as I promised that there wouldn't be any actual Sky Sprints used inside the dorms and that once curfew struck, I'd stay there till morning. She really does seem to have a soft spot for juniors that she never showed for us as trainees.

I take a slow breath before I knock on Lara's door. If I'm being honest, that trip to Time Management yesterday really did a number on my hopes that a magician wasn't involved. Who but a magician would create a time freeze spell that *doesn't affect magicians*?

What if solving the time freeze only makes things worse? If it was truly a magician that did this, even if Merlin returns to being Prime Minister, Bane would still be proved right about what a danger we are. Dylan's words about finding an old Moreau apprentice in the Sightless Depths echo through my head. *"That's what the Bureau does to people like us. That's what it thinks of magicians."*

I give the door a good knock and Lara pulls me inside.

"You okay?" I ask, watching her pace around her room.

"I think it's finally hitting me just what we're doing." Lara looks a bit flustered. "We're *literally* sneaking into an off-limits location during a lockdown when we're both connected to the magician who Bane's got everyone believing is responsible for the time freeze. How's it going to look if we get caught? What if people start to think *we* had something to do with it?"

"Trust me," I say. "I'm freaking out too. I know it's a big deal. I can probably go by myself if you don't want to risk it."

"No. I said I'd help and I will."

The way her hands tremble tells me a different story. "Only if you're sure."

Lara nods. "I can do this. We need to prove that my sister's innocent."

She doesn't *sound* like she's setting a trap for me, but Elsie's warning won't stop echoing inside my head. "I'm just going to come out and ask: You aren't trying to get me in trouble, are you?"

Lara narrows her eyes. "Why would you think that?"

"Elsie and I saw you in the library—with your dad."

Lara makes a face and crosses her arms. "My dad wanted to talk things out, so we did."

"And you're still on our side?" I ask.

"You're here, aren't you?"

"I'm trusting you," I say. "*Please* don't let me down."

Lara lifts her chin, but when she speaks her voice is soft. "I'd do anything for Maria. Even if you don't believe me, you should know that's true."

"I do." It surprises me how relieved I feel. "Let's go over the plan."

"Right," she says. "You turn us invisible, then we teleport to the Congress Room. When we get there, you head inside to look for clues while I keep an eye out for guards. Easy enough."

"Let's hope it's easy," I say. "Ready?"

Lara nods. "Let's do it."

I take Lara's hand and whisper, "Invisbil." In seconds,

we both begin to fade away. The last thing I see of my partner is her wide eyes as she watches herself disappear. Once we're completely invisible, I hear Lara type in the code for the Congress Room.

A robotic voice sounds on the speaker. "Be advised, you are attempting to teleport into a restricted area. Authorization required."

My eyes dart toward Lara.

"Just wait," she whispers. "It should recognize my dad's transporter."

"Director Van Helsing . . . Permission to transport is granted."

The world around us bends and a moment later we're standing in a large curving hallway. It wraps around an enormous circular room with stairs leading down to a podium at the center.

This is it. The Congress Room.

It's so quiet I can hear myself breathing. All around us is bright yellow crime scene tape and *Off-Limits* signs in big red letters. The magical science equipment brought in at the start of the time freeze is shoved in a corner beside a stack of boxes. The entire area is roped off.

So how exactly is Bane investigating how to end the time freeze?

But then, why would Bane even want to? As long as Merlin and the Supernatural World Congress remain frozen, Bane's emergency powers give him total control over the supernatural world.

The coast seems clear, so I drop Lara's hand and she immediately pops back into view.

I let my own spell fade away, then gulp. Because I never thought about cameras. And there's one aimed directly at us.

"Lara!" I say, and point.

She takes a quick look and says, "Don't worry, they aren't on. Those are the same kind we use on our estate." She walks up closer. "If it was working, there'd be a red light flashing on the side."

"Do you think these cameras were on during the time freeze?" I ask.

Lara shrugs. "Beats me. But check this out." She reaches up and pulls off a tag I didn't even notice, then waves me over.

"What is it?" I ask.

"Standard procedure," says Lara. "The agent who checked the cameras leaves a tag so other agents know that some-one's already working on this part of the case. This is Agent McKenzie's tag. She must've been assigned to the cameras before Bane kicked the Bureau out."

"But how does that help us?" I ask.

"Because . . ." Lara scans the hallway until her eyes settle on the boxes beneath the magical science equipment. "There!" She sprints over and I follow, not sure what she's so excited about.

Lara looks through the boxes until she finds one marked *McKenzie*. "This'll have all her reports. My dad's super old-school and insists on everything being put on paper before it gets scanned into the computer."

We grab the file marked *Cameras* and open it up. There's only one page inside, so I pull it out.

Agent: Samantha McKenzie

Case Notes: Unable to get anything helpful from the camera system. The footage seems to cut out just moments before the time freeze began. Strangely, the footage we have doesn't show anyone tampering with the cameras or even anyone out of the ordinary entering the surveillance room. Even the hidden cameras, which only a handful of supernaturals knew existed, were turned off. And those individuals are all frozen right now.

Lara sighs. "I guess we shouldn't be surprised. If the cameras were working, the Bureau would've known right away who came in and performed the time freeze spell."

"But who's capable of shutting them all down without being seen?" I ask.

My partner shrugs, and we sit in silence a moment, trying to think this through.

What had my fortune cookie said? *Beware of unseen dangers.* What if it meant a danger that went unseen by these cameras? Someone capable of stopping time.

After all, hadn't I asked the fortune cookie what I most needed to know? It would make sense for the answer to be about ending the time freeze. Solving that would also solve nearly all my problems this summer.

Lara breaks the silence. "Any guesses?"

"Dylan's primary magic is tech magic," I say. "He can control any kind of technology. I'm sure he'd be able to sense where all the cameras were and use his magic to shut them off."

"But he was still in the Sightless Depths when the time freeze happened," says Lara.

"Unless maybe he wasn't?" I ask.

"So he, what, escaped the Sightless Depths, froze the Congress Room, and then went back?"

"Yeah, that's the part that doesn't make sense."

Lara glances down at her phone and then looks over my shoulder. "We'd better go check out the Congress Room before it's too late."

We duck under the crime scene tape and go right up to one of the open doorways leading inside. The two of us stare out at the rows of seats and desks that form their own orbits around the huge podium.

Lara steps up beside me. "It was spooky enough onscreen, but it's so much worse in person. They're just stuck like that—time completely stopped around them. Do you think they can feel it? Being trapped?"

"Elsie says we can't feel time, even when it stops. That's probably the only good thing about it."

Even so, I can't help feeling sorry for everyone inside. Great big giants and bulky trolls stand close to the walls, while all the regular-sized supernaturals are seated at fancy little desks. Elves and goblins and dwarves and on and on. Above us, a few winged and aerial supernaturals perch near desks situated high on the walls.

"Don't get too close," I say, remembering something Elsie said just before I left her for Lara's room. "If any part of you gets caught in the time freeze, I won't be able to pull you out."

Lara takes a giant step backward. I stay put.

I move closer, sticking my hand inside the room and wiggling my fingers. Just like before, the time freeze doesn't affect me at all.

"I'll let you know if there's any trouble," she says.

I nod and turn to step into the room fully. If I thought it was quiet in the hallway, it's nothing to how eerily silent it is inside the Congress Room. It reminds me of how strange it felt back on the bus when the time freeze covered the whole state.

I search as hard as I can for anything that seems unusual, looking behind and underneath desks until I'm sure I haven't missed anything. If there are any clues to be found here, I'm not seeing them.

What if there's nothing to find?

Anxious, I head down to where Merlin, the true Prime Minister, stands in his dark blue congress robes behind a large podium of shimmering moonstone. It's an amazing sight. The elf king is beyond ancient, his tree-bark skin lined with age and covered in dark spots. And yet, even with time stopped, the power of his magic radiates from him. It's like standing next to the heater on a cold day.

That's why the sight of him frozen there, clutching at his chest, a mixture of shock and terror etched onto his face, scares me so much. Merlin is one of the most magical beings in our world. And unlike me, he's in full control of his powers.

Who could possibly scare him this badly?

I follow his eyes. They seem to be staring at nothing. I look to the next face, and the next—every one of them staring in the same direction. Every one of them terrified.

They all must've seen who caused this. And for everyone here to be scared—it would've had to be someone they all recognized. Somebody dangerous. But that rules out anyone from the League, because those magicians keep their identities secret. And if it wasn't me or Maria, there's only one other magician it could've been.

Dylan. Especially since his tech magic is the best explanation we have for how the cameras got turned off. I think about the shadow magic he stole from that magician in the Sightless Depths, and another realization comes.

That NightWalker didn't say which of the Night Brothers caused the first time freeze. What if it was Moreau? What if in stealing Moreau's magic last summer, Dylan got much more than my brother's curse—what if he stole the power to stop time too?

But Lara's right, it doesn't explain how he was able to cause the time freeze *before* his escape from the Sightless Depths . . . unless that wasn't his first escape?

I shudder.

Flashlight beams appear in one of the entrances above me. At the top of the stairs leading back to my entrance, Lara waves her hands frantically. I can't hear what she's saying, but that makes sense—we learned in science class that sound travels by waves, and those waves would definitely be frozen in here.

The panicked look on Lara's face is all the warning I need. I sprint back up the stairs as fast as my feet will carry me.

"Someone else is here," Lara tells me once I'm back in the hallway. "Security or something."

"You there!" comes a voice from far away. "What are you doing here?"

The screech of an alarm blares in my ears.

"Let's get out of here!" Lara and I lock arms, and she reaches inside her sleeve to tap the reverse button to take us back to the Bureau. In an instant we're back inside her dorm room.

"That was close," I say.

Lara nods.

A booming knock sounds on the door.

A Bertha knock.

"Bed!" Lara whisper-shouts.

I jump into the empty bed and pull the covers up to my neck.

A key turns in the lock, and I shut my eyes just as Bertha leans inside.

"It's as I told you," Bertha tells someone. "The girls are right where they're supposed to be."

A deep voice says something I can't hear, and Bertha scoffs. "These girls have it hard enough without you pulling them out of bed after curfew because of a hunch."

The voice speaks again in a much harsher tone, but Bertha doesn't back down.

"Then come back once you've got proof, is that clear?"

There's a snarl and the door shuts again. Did Bertha just save us from being caught?

We both keep quiet for a few minutes before Lara whispers, "My dad didn't get to be the Director of Supernatural Investigations by luck—if they know enough to come to my room, then it's only a matter of time before they'll be able to prove it was us tonight."

"Then we need to solve the time freeze before that happens."

"Did you find something in there?" she asks.

"I did," I say, and quickly explain what I found. I pause before finishing, because I know she won't be happy about what I'm about to say next. "I think it's Dylan. I'm not sure how, but it has to be."

Lara is silent for a long time. Finally she says, "Every time something bad happens, it's always my brother. I hate him, Amari. So, so much."

≫ 26 ≪

ELSIE IS SET TO VISIT THE LONDON BUREAU EARLY THE next morning, so I rush through the hallways of the Department of Supernatural Licenses and Records to meet her by the group transporters. I was supposed to be there at six a.m. to see her off, but since no one can ride an elevator with me because of my badge, I had to keep getting off every time someone else got on.

The large transporter Elsie's supposed to be taking is empty when I arrive and my face crumples. I was supposed to be here for her like she's always shown up for me. But just when I turn around to sulk back to my room, I hear Elsie's voice.

"Amari!"

I turn to find her and that giant duffel bag full of half-completed inventions peeking out from behind the control panel. "I thought you were gone."

Elsie laughs. "And I knew you'd be late, just like biology class and every single Soup Club meeting I've ever called. So I told you six o'clock when I'm really leaving at six fifteen."

"You know," I say, "you really *are* the smart one."

"Did, um"—she glances over her shoulder—"everything go okay last night?"

I nod and quietly update her on what we learned in the Congress Room.

"I agree that Dylan makes the most sense," she whispers. "But if he really was able to leave the Sightless Depths whenever he wanted, why would he ever go back?"

I don't have a good response to that. Because if it wasn't Dylan, then who else could it be?

"All aboard!" a man calls. "Transporter loading up."

Elsie looks suddenly nervous. "So I guess this is really happening, then?"

I nod, fighting back tears. "Don't forget me, okay?"

Elsie shakes her head. "It's only for the weekend."

"I'm saying this now in case I'm not able to say it later. I didn't have friends before I met you last summer. Quinton was missing, Mama and I were fighting all the time, and me and Jayden had grown apart. That Amari was miserable. But then I came here and met you and I . . . well, you were just you. Silly, and kind, and brilliant, and I'll miss you *so* bad."

"Oh gosh," she says, wiping her eyes. "I knew you were going to make me cry. You're not so bad yourself, you know. I watch you be brave, like, every day, and it makes me want to be that way too. I think it's the only reason why I'm able to do something like this at all—because leaving scares me to bits, but you inspire me to face my fears. So that's what I'm doing."

"Do I really have to say last call?" the man says. "You're the only traveler scheduled."

Elsie and I laugh and hug, then she turns to walk up onto the platform, lugging her giant duffel bag. She gives me a little wave and I wave back.

Then she's gone.

On the way back to the dorm, I get a message from Elsie's Eurg account.

New Message from Els_the_Inventor:
Forgot to tell you I left something under your pillow!

Turns out that "something" is a bright green *Nobody's UnWanted* badge with flashing lights and sound effects if you press down on it. I literally laugh out loud when I see it. She must've stayed up last night to make it for me.

It already feels strange not having her here. The dorm room seems even emptier somehow knowing she won't be back for a couple days. Lonelier.

Elsie isn't the only kid gone for the weekend. Even with

the Bureau on lockdown and Dylan still on the loose, most kids chose to head home. I don't mind too much. It's certainly a lot easier taking the elevators.

After breakfast Jayden messages me about meeting up to visit Quinton. At first I reply, "Maybe tomorrow," because my focus needs to be on Dylan and the time freeze, but if my suspicions are right, there's not a whole lot I can do right now. Every Bureau in the world is already looking for him.

So I ended up messaging Jayden to meet up after all. I still can't get used to him being on Eurg, since he's one of the few kids I know who doesn't have any social media accounts in the known world. That boy didn't even have a phone until he started hanging out with the Wood Boyz, a gang from my neighborhood. Thankfully, he kept his promise to give all that up before coming here.

Non-relatives have to be escorted by a family member to visit patients in the Intense Curses Unit, so Jayden's waiting for me in the lobby of Supernatural Health when I get there. I can't help but smile seeing him in his tan safari gear with his hair braided down neatly. A copper badge is attached to the front of his tan vest. Go, Jayden. Almost looks like a different person.

We stop at the front desk for weekend passes, then head toward Quinton's room.

"Surprised you didn't bring El Smooth with you," says Jayden.

"El Smooth?" I ask. "Please don't tell me that's what you call Elsie."

He grins and shrugs. "Whatever nickname pops into my head is what I use."

"Well, Els isn't even in the country right now," I say, and explain about her being accepted to the special program for geniuses at Oxford. "That school is a really big deal."

Jayden shoots me a look. "I know what Oxford is."

"My bad," I say. "Didn't think you cared about famous schools."

He just shrugs. "Look who judging a book by their cover."

I stick out my tongue at him and he laughs.

"How you feelin' about her leavin' you behind?" Jayden asks.

I bite my lip. "I'm not sure how I fit in at Whitman Prep without her. Sometimes I don't even know if I belong *here*. I'm always going to be the magician girl, and no matter if people think I'm wonderful or hate my guts, it feels like I'll always be separate from everyone else."

Jayden just nods along. "I made a few friends who explained the whole magician thing to me and how it's unfair they're making you wear that badge. But maybe you *need* to be on your own to figure out where you really fit in. I ain't gonna lie, when Ms. P dropped me off I was extra nervous. But it also kinda forced me to find my own way too, ya know? Like maybe I would've hid out next to you if we'd come here together. 'Cause that would've felt comfortable."

Now I'm nodding because I have pretty much only hung

out with Elsie both at Whitman Prep and here. She's been my safety net this whole time. "When did you get all wise?"

He strokes his nonexistent beard. "I'm an ancient wise man trapped in a thirteen-year-old body."

I burst out laughing. "*Sure* you are."

We pass the sign that says *Intense Curses Unit* and split up to walk on opposite sides of the hall to let an agent pass by. He glances at my *Dangerous* badge and frowns but doesn't say anything. I'm already used to it.

Once he's gone I drift back closer to Jayden. "So, first week is done. Did you have your first tryout yet?"

He nods and grins. "Nailed it too. We had to take care of a golden goose egg until it hatched. Lots of kids cracked their eggs the very first day, but not me." The boy whistles, and a tiny bird with a shiny gold beak pops up from behind his collar.

"That might just be the cutest thing I've ever seen," I say.

"I call her Fancy."

"Fancy, huh?" I can't help shaking my head at this boy. "All these years and I didn't know you loved animals so much."

That grin of his gets wider. "I'm kind of mysterious like that."

That makes me laugh. So much that I almost walk past Quinton's room. But it's hard to keep up a smile when we get inside. Because just being here is a reminder of the Great Game and how much is at stake. I didn't agree to participate just to prevent a war. Part of me honestly thought I could win. That maybe I could take Quinton's curse away from Dylan.

But I'm not winning at all. I'm failing so bad.

"You okay?" Jayden asks.

"Yeah," I say. "Just wishing my brother was better."

Jayden nods and steps farther into the room. He stands next to Quinton's bed, his expression turning somber. "Don't seem real, seeing him like this. He always seemed invincible to me. Like nothing could ever hurt him."

"That's what I always thought too," I say. "What was your nickname for Quinton?"

"Mr. Untouchable." He smiles then, adding, "Shoot, I remember this one time I didn't show up to a tutoring session because I was afraid to walk down the street where some bad dudes were bothering anybody who came by. And when Quinton came to see where I was, I told him that. So what did he do? He put his arm around me, and we walked right down that road. He told those guys I was with him and he didn't ever want to hear that they were messing with me again."

I raise an eyebrow. "What was he going to do if they did mess with you?"

Jayden laughs and shrugs. "Don't know—they never did. Quinton said something about how facing your fears is half the battle, and when bullies realize they can't scare you anymore, you take away their power."

"My brother always keeps a good saying handy," I say.

Jayden chuckles. "Maybe he's the *real* wise man."

"Do you, um, have any more stories about Quinton I haven't heard?" I ask.

"I'll tell you mine if you tell me yours," he says.

"Deal."

Me and Jayden spend hours laughing at old Quinton stories. When my belly starts grumbling for some lunch, I ask if he wants to come with me.

"So I kinda had another reason for wanting to meet up," says Jayden. "Besides just checking on Quinton."

"What's up?" I ask.

"There's this girl I know—you know her too, I think. Julia something? Goes to the department with all the ghosts and zombies and stuff?"

"Wait, you know Julia Farsight?" I ask.

"Not that well," he admits. "My roommate is her cousin and they were talkin' about doing a livestream fundraiser for UnWanteds. Guess they're getting deported unfairly and I wanted to help—so I might've said you'd make an appearance, since you're such a big deal around here?"

"*Jayden.*" I point to my *Dangerous* badge. "They could get in trouble for even talking to me."

He shrugs. "Seemed pretty excited when I mentioned your name. Think they'd planned on asking you anyway. Don't seem like they cared about breaking rules all that much."

I frown. "I still don't know if it's a good idea." After all, it's not just me Harlowe might punish. The reason I cooperate with her and Bane at all is to keep Maria out of the Sightless Depths.

"Please," he asks, putting on these big puppy-dog eyes that I hate to admit are kind of cute. "It'll make up for you ignoring me when we first got here."

Guilt gnaws at me. "Fine, but I'm not promising to be on the livestream. I'm already on Bane's bad side."

Jayden and I turn in our weekend passes at the desk and head to the Supernatural Health lobby to wait for an elevator.

Lucy arrives and opens her doors to a laughing Lara Van Helsing at the back of the elevator. I give her a little wave, but the moment she spots me, her face flushes bright red and the smile drops off her face.

It's not until Jayden and I are fully inside that I see Director Van Helsing standing in the corner. Jayden glances between us, sensing the tension.

"Young man," says the director. "I do believe the announcement was very clear about keeping your distance from Junior Agent Peters."

"Uh, yes, sir, it's just that we grew up together—"

"No exceptions!" Director Van Helsing barks. "If you are not her roommate or her partner, then you should not be associating with those who've been deemed dangerous."

Jayden glares, but I shake my head. I don't want him getting in trouble for me.

The rest of the ride is short, but quiet—no one speaks.

I keep glancing at Lara, wondering what her deal is, but the girl refuses to meet my eyes. She told us that she only made up with her dad to get her hands on the transporter, but if she really is angry about her sister being punished for a crime she didn't commit, then why is she laughing it up with the man who did nothing to stop it?

I mean, I get he's her dad. But if it were me, and Mama betrayed Quinton like that, I don't think I could ever forgive her.

Lara keeps her head down as Jayden and I step out into the youth dorms. As soon as the Van Helsings are gone, we immediately catch a different elevator back up to the library. We do our best to look like we aren't together, even stand on opposite sides of the door. When the elevator opens, I let Jayden go first, then follow a few steps behind until we reach the study room.

Jayden gives the door a special knock and none other than Arthur from Time Management pokes his head out. "Amazing! Hurry, come in!"

We slip inside to find the room covered in posters with messages just like what Elsie put on her fancy green badge. They say things like *Speak Up/Speak Out* and *Everyone Belongs*.

Julia still has on her Junior Undertaker cloak, and a pair of large silver headphones. Her phone is mounted on a desk stand. There's at least a dozen people crammed in here, none of whom I recognize.

When she sees us, Julia smiles that drowsy-eyed smile

of hers. "Hiya, guys," she says to the stream, "I've got some friends who want to say hello." Jayden heads right over, but I hesitate and stay close to the door, because I know the moment I appear onscreen, there's no turning back. I've been warned about crossing Director Harlowe too many times to think of openly defying her like that.

Jayden looks disappointed, but he sits down next to Julia anyway. He seems nervous, but he's really doing it.

Julia doesn't miss a beat, introducing my friend in her singsong voice. "You guys already got to meet my cousin, Sebastian. Well, this is his roommate, Jay. Say hi to Jay, everyone!"

I move closer, enough to see the messages that pop onscreen. I blink at the 2.1K viewers they've got. That's pretty impressive.

"Anything you want to say?" Julia asks Jayden. "It's okay if you only say hello, I know you're new to the supernatural world."

Jayden nods and seems to find his confidence. "So . . . something a lot of people don't know about me is that my dad got deported when I was younger. He was in the country illegally and one day they told him he had to leave. I don't come from a whole lot, and Ma has a hard time keeping things together, so him getting sent away hurt, man. It's like . . . sometimes I wonder what my life would be like if he was still here, 'cause he was everything to me, ya know?"

He laughs. "Y'all probably wondering what that has to do with anything, but I guess what I'm sayin' is, these

UnWanteds—they mean something to somebody too. And Bane is sending them to a place that ain't safe, all because of something they can't even help. It ain't right. And I guess I just wanted to speak on that real quick."

Julia beams. "Seems like the people agree!" And it's true, the likes and comments come so fast, there isn't even time to read them.

When my eyes go back to Jayden, he's looking right back at me. And I know what he's silently asking.

I shake my head.

He nods, smiling at me the same way he does when he calls me "superstar." Because he believes in me more than I do. Just like Quinton always has. And suddenly the thought of letting him down, of him looking at me different because I didn't step up—it scares me more than Harlowe and Bane do.

I shake out my nerves and take a seat next to him.

Julia perks up. "I don't think there's anyone who doesn't recognize Amari Peters, my friend from Whitman Prep. You all know her as the magician girl."

I give a little wave. If I thought the likes and comments were coming fast before, now it's a blur. And the viewer count jumps to 3.3K to 5.6K and keeps climbing until it hits over ten thousand viewers. So much for this going unnoticed.

"Wow!" says Julia. "This is our biggest live ever!" She looks to me, excited. "Was there anything you wanted to say, Amari?"

I glance at Jayden. This is my last chance to chicken out, but something inside me just refuses. Not anymore. Weren't Jayden and I just talking about facing down our fears and not letting bullies control us? Well, that's exactly what Bane and Harlowe are to me—bullies. This is my chance to stand up for Maria too.

I pull Elsie's badge out of my pocket and pin it to the other side of my jacket. "I'm sure a lot of you have seen me with Director Harlowe, while she goes on about what a great leader Bane is . . ." I take a deep breath. "But that's all a lie. Bane and Harlowe blamed Maria Van Helsing for the time freeze just because they could. The only reason I didn't say anything is because they threatened to send her to the Sightless Depths if I didn't cooperate. I want everyone to know that UnWanteds don't deserve the way they're being treated and I'm sorry for making it seem like I agreed with Bane, because I don't." I point to Elsie's badge. "Nobody's UnWanted."

It's quiet for a few seconds, then the whole room starts clapping.

Jayden nudges me with his elbow. "I think Quinton would be proud of that."

≋ 27 ≋

I SPEND ALL SATURDAY EVENING CONVINCED THAT AT ANY
moment I'll be hauled in front of Bane and Harlowe
again to answer for that livestream. It's not like they don't
know about it.

Within a few hours, thousands of supernaturals posted
comments under the Bureau's Eurg account about Maria—
it even made the trending page. Harlowe had to put out an
official statement:

> The Bureau and Prime Minister would like to state
> that there is no truth to the claims made by one of
> our Junior Agents today.
>
> It pains us deeply that Maria Van Helsing

stands accused of such awful crimes.

More evidence will be provided in due time.

—The Office of Half Truths and Full Cover-Ups

But all that did was highlight how flimsy Harlowe and Bane's case against Maria is. The only thing they can prove is that Maria opened files about the time freeze and tried to teach me magic. But why wouldn't a top Special Agent look into the biggest case in the world? And someone at the Bureau leaked a copy of the order from Merlin to teach me magic. My phone buzzes nonstop from being tagged in #BringBackMaria and #TheGoodMagician posts.

By the time Sunday morning comes, I'm pretty sure I'm in the clear. And that means it's time to grab Elsie's whiteboard and get to work on the investigation again.

WHAT DO I KNOW?

Crime: Time Freeze

-NightWalker says Night Brothers caused one 700 years ago.

-Harlowe blocking info about this on computers. Which means it must be real!!!

-Titans of Time Vol. II says Thomas Fletcher, a werewolf, was a witness—too bad he's been dead for centuries.

-I visited time freeze at the Congress Room. Everyone looks scared.

-They were all staring in the same direction too. Recognized the magician?

Suspect: Dylan Van Helsing? Got the magic from Moreau?

My guess how he did it:
—Used tech magic to shut off cameras? Even the hidden ones?
—Used invisibility spell to enter Congress Room unnoticed?
—Revealed himself, then cast time freeze spell and fled?

Problem:
Dylan hadn't escaped Sightless Depths yet.

I sit back and look it over. This is everything we've learned in the past week, plus my guess for how Dylan pulled off the time freeze without getting caught. If he actually did it, that is.

But now I'm stuck. So without any more leads, I set my sights on preparing for the third challenge of the Great Game. The first two were so close together, it's honestly been a relief to have a few days of nothing trying to kill me. I only wish I had some idea what the next challenge might be.

Still, if the first two challenges taught me anything, it's that they can start at the most inconvenient times. As long as I stay out of trouble, it's really only during classes that I have to worry. So I spend a good hour perfecting my skills at pretending to be sick in the mirror. Telling your teacher you have to throw up nearly always gets you out of class, so I hunch over, rub my belly, and scrunch up my face until even I'm convinced I'm under the weather. I even change my voice to sound more pitiful.

Once I'm satisfied with how I'll get to my next challenge, it's about surviving it. The biggest threat will always be Dylan, so I flip through *The Responsible Weatherist* for spells stronger than Wind Tamer. I've got to find something I can use to defend myself. The spells at the back of the book each seem to summon storms more severe than the last. Thunderstorms. Hailstorms. Tornadoes. Out of curiosity, I turn to the very last page. The spell there has been x-ed out.

~~CALAMITY OF THE SKIES~~

~~Included only for thoroughness.~~
~~No magician has ever come back from summoning this weather magic.~~

What's it mean by "come back"? But then I remember what the introduction said, how weather magic feeds on emotions. What happens when it asks for more than you can give? Is that how you lose yourself?

Is that what happened to Dylan?

Knowing I can't afford to waste a whole day, I decide to pay a visit to Supernatural Investigations to see Agent Fiona and Deputy Director Magnus. With so few kids here, Lord Kensington lets me sneak a ride from the youth dorms so we can catch up. That elevator is just as snooty as ever—he can't shut up about his fancy new touch screen.

The main hallway is as busy as ever when I arrive—a reminder that only trainees and juniors go home for the weekends. Fighting supernatural crime is an every day job. Still, I know from checking their profiles that Magnus and Fiona both have desk duty on Sundays from noon to four.

I keep out of the way, following the hall toward the fancy offices located just before the Operations Bay. Magnus's door is marked *Office of the Deputy Director*. Only there's a sign on it that says *In Training Gym B if needed*.

I debate whether I should interrupt, but I'm also curious what kind of training a deputy director does.

Arriving at the training gym, I barely open the door when I see Agent Magnus high in the air, decked out in a full tuxedo. He's hand-in-hand with Agent Fiona, who wears a fancy white blouse and pants.

They're dancing in Sky Sprints! Twisting and twirling, spinning apart and then back together again. This must be for the wedding—I bet that's why they're all dressed up. No way is this their first practice; they both look so graceful.

I lean my head on the doorjamb and watch for a bit. Even from here, I can see Agent Fiona's huge engagement ring. Just how much do deputy directors make?

Agent Magnus accidentally steps on Agent Fiona's toes in midair, bringing the dancing to a sudden stop.

Fiona grins and gives his beard a tug. "It's two spins, not three, ye lovable klutz."

Magnus goes pink and leans in for a kiss.

"Hi, guys," I say quickly, stepping into the gym fully. "Sorry to interrupt."

They jump at my voice, but don't seem upset. Fiona turns and adjusts her Sky Sprints so that she slowly descends, like she's walking down an invisible staircase. "What brings ye by, Peters?"

"Advice?" I say.

Fiona's feet hit the floor. "Would that be about the investigation ye aren't supposed to be carrying out?"

My jaw drops. "You know about that?"

Magnus's rumbling laughter reaches me from overhead—he's still practicing his dance steps. "Couldn't have been more obvious if you'd posted photos to your Eurg page! Did you really think you were getting away with it?"

"Maybe?" I say, cheeks burning with embarrassment.

Fiona chuckles too. "I wondered at ye picking the Van Helsing girl as your partner over Davies, but serves me right for underestimating ye. Funny how the director suddenly stopped caring about who snuck into the Congress Room once he realized it was *his* armband got used."

Magnus lands with a thud. "Best advice I got for you now is to lie low for a while. Director Van Helsing may have kept your sneaking out quiet, but from what I hear, Bane and Harlowe are spittin' mad about the livestream."

I wince. "I thought they might be."

Magnus strokes his beard. "What's your best guess on who caused the time freeze?"

Fiona shoots him an elbow. "Ye aren't supposed to be encouraging her."

Magnus gives me a stern look. "Peters, I want you to follow the rules when you leave this here room, understand?"

I nod.

Then he grins. "Learn anything useful in the Congress Room?"

I stare between the two of them. "Is it okay to answer? You're my instructor, but he's my mentor. So I'm torn on who I should listen to here."

Fiona rolls her eyes at Magnus, then turns to me. "Just pretend I'm not here."

"I think it was Dylan," I say, and explain my theory.

Magnus nods. "We've got Dylan pretty high on our list too. Just don't make sense with the timing of his escape."

"Same problem I'm having," I say. "What do real agents do when you're out of leads and you aren't sure about your prime suspect?"

"Ideally, ye want to bring that person in for questioning," answers Fiona. "Get 'em talking and hope they tell ye something useful—something ye didn't already know."

"Good luck with that," says Magnus. "No one's seen hide nor hair of Dylan since he got himself free from the Sightless Depths."

My mind races. Maybe nobody knows where Dylan is hiding, but I at least know where he'll be the next time my ring turns warm—the third challenge. Why didn't I think to just question him myself last time? Well, aside from the fact that he was trying to make BBQ Amari.

I bite my lip. "But how can you tell if someone is telling the truth?"

"Can't say I've run into that problem," says Agent Fiona. "When people know that your supernatural ability lets ye see their intentions anyway, they tend to be a bit more honest."

Magnus laughs. "For the rest of us, we have to rely on our instincts. Body language nearly always tells the story. Do they meet your eyes? Are they suddenly real fidgety? Don't you worry, we'll come across a few baddies during Field Training this summer and you'll see what I mean."

"Thanks," I say, "that's actually *really* helpful."

"What's that look, Peters?" asks Fiona. "Cause I'm not sure that I like it. Don't you get any idea of going after Dylan yourself."

"Don't worry about me," I say, but Fiona doesn't look convinced. So I try changing the subject. "That's a pretty cool-looking engagement ring."

Fiona glances down at her hand, where a large moon-stone shimmers faintly. "Been in the family for ages, this thing. Since the Ancient War. Story has it, my ancestor Douglas Fiona was surrounded by magicians and managed to take down all three. Nicked this ring off one of them as a trophy. It's a bit delicate, so I don't wear it all the time. Pa must like Magnus something fierce to let him propose with me late mum's ring."

Magnus puffs up a bit. "Man obviously recognizes quality when he sees it."

Fiona grins and I smile and start for the door.

I get two steps before Fiona grabs me by the wrist. She's not smiling anymore—she looks scared. I don't know how to react because it's not something I've seen before.

"Ye take Magnus's advice about lying low," Fiona says. "Harlowe's been around for over a century, so she's had plenty of time to master that pleasant act she does so well. But I've seen the real faun behind the mask. When I was no more than a wee trainee myself, same day I touched the Crystal Ball and learned I could read folks' intentions, Harlowe cornered me. Said if I ever use my ability on her, she'd hurt me in ways I didn't even know existed. Said that to a twelve-year-old girl—and what's worse, I knew she meant it."

I swallow at that. "Do you know what her supernatural ability is?"

Fiona shakes her head. "Whatever it is, Prime Minister Merlin took drastic measures to keep her in check. And now he's frozen. Makes ye wonder who's holding her leash now."

Most of the kids who left for the weekend return on Sunday evening, but Elsie sent a message saying she was staying an extra night. She's still not back on Monday morning when I head to the food court for breakfast, but Lara finds me the second I sit down.

"Are we okay?" she asks. "I mean, I know it was really awkward in the elevator with my dad."

"Sure." I remember what Agent Fiona said about Director

Van Helsing burying the investigation of who snuck into the Congress Room. "You were staying on your dad's good side, right? Since he's covering for you about the Congress Room?"

Lara exhales, looking relieved. "Right! Obviously, I couldn't say anything with him right there. He knows I took the transporter, but he thinks I'm doing my own investigation. I told him I wanted to do something to stand out like you did last summer and he totally bought it. He did take away my phone as punishment, though. But I should get it back soon."

I grin.

"Thanks for trusting me, okay?" she says.

"Hey, we're partners, right?"

Jayden messages me that we should be good to use his secret spot to meet for lunch. First though, Lara and I have to sit through Supernatural Immersion class, where we're introduced to a new supernatural that's famous for munching on lost adventurers—a creature from the Black Lagoon. What's worse is we've got to climb into a tank of boiling black sludge in order to talk to him. He turns out to be pretty nice, and tells great stories, but even wearing special protective suits, it's hard to shake the uneasy feeling that we're all in a giant teenager-flavored stew.

When we get to Creature Control at lunch, we follow Jayden's instructions and head through an archway marked *Enchanted Gardens*. It's dark here, and we emerge into gardens that come alive as we pass. Great big flowers begin to shimmer, leaning over the railing to nuzzle our faces. Smaller glowing flowers change colors with every step we take, so that they almost look like multicolored Christmas lights.

"Firework flies!" Lara exclaims, as tiny bugs zip into view and explode in bright sparkles before re-forming again.

We keep going until we get to a bend, and a hand reaches through a patch of tall grass. "Over here," comes Jayden's voice.

Lara and I step through the grass to find a tiny meadow. There's a small pond with fish that glow in the dark.

"What do you think?" asks Jayden.

"Definitely cooler than a study room," says Lara.

We find our spots in the low grass and Elsie stumbles in about a minute later. Except she isn't alone.

"Hi, everyone!" says Arthur, looking extremely glad to be here. "Oh, this is exciting. I'm right in the thick of things! Wait till the VanQuish Fan Club hears about this!"

"And why did you bring him, exactly?" asks Lara.

Elsie gives a half-hearted smile. "He kind of figured out what we were up to from our visit to Time Management. Tracked me down and insisted on being part of the investigation."

"I'm no Director Wenn," says Arthur. "But I do know a lot about time. I can help."

"Well, you're already here," I say. "Just wait till we solve the time freeze before you tell anyone. We aren't supposed to be looking into this."

Once everyone has taken a seat in the grass, I stand up. "Thanks for skipping your lunches for me. And Jayden for skipping class. Wait—how are you here anyway?"

Jayden shrugs. "Second week of Creature Control is all about campin' out in the wilderness to get an appreciation for it. So technically I'm *in* class right now."

"Fair enough," I say. "We should start by going over everything we know." I explain the whiteboard I made on Saturday and how Dylan is still the most likely suspect. I wish I could tell them about my plan to confront him at the next challenge, but they'd just have questions that my vow of secrecy won't allow me to answer.

"So . . . ," I continue. "Any ideas?"

Arthur raises a hand.

"Oh," I say, a bit surprised. "Go ahead."

"This might be a dumb question." Arthur gets to his feet. "But have you tried speaking to Thomas Fletcher? Maybe he remembers how the Night Brothers cast the time freeze spell."

"He's dead," Lara says matter-of-factly. "Has been since the Ancient War."

"Believe it or not, I had the same idea," says Elsie. "I checked the Afterlife Undead Census right after Amari and I visited Time Management. Thomas's name wasn't listed."

"Right," says Arthur, puffing himself up proudly. "But that census is done every ten years. I happen to know for a fact that Thomas Fletcher applied for ghosthood only two years ago. Director Wenn wanted to interview him for the second volume of *Titans of Time*."

Elsie sits up straighter. "We do have a friend at the Department of the Dead. If Amari can learn the time freeze spell from Fletcher, maybe she can cancel it."

"I don't know if I have the right magic," I say. "But I'm willing to try. And, honestly, just learning what spell was used might help us figure out a way to end it." Because I could take it to the League of Magicians and see what they know—surely Priya and the other anti-war magicians would volunteer some info.

"I say let's go for it," says Lara.

"Me too," I say. "I'll ask Julia about speaking to Thomas's ghost tonight."

"Not to take all the credit," says Jayden, "but seem like my lucky spot came through for us in the clutch."

"Or . . ." I laugh. "Maybe it was having Arthur here to let us know about Thomas Fletcher's ghost?"

"It was both," says Elsie, grinning.

"Honestly," Lara chuckles. "Who knew boys could be so useful?"

"Oh, you got jokes?" Jayden crosses his arms. "Just for that, think I'll let Shadow know he can go back to bouncing."

Lara's eyes go wide. "I take it back!"

BECAUSE THE MEETING WENT SO WELL, ELSIE AND I ARE able to catch an elevator to the food court to grab a couple hot dogs before lunch ends. She fills me in on all the incredible things she did over the weekend, and there is so much excitement in her voice, and on her face, that it's pretty clear that leaving is what's best for her.

"... and Director Ansers is such a fan!" Elsie exclaims. "I didn't even think she knew who I was, but apparently she's had her eye on me since last summer. And get this, she's going to give me my own Inventor Lab! *No* junior gets their own lab."

"That's awesome," I say. I'm surprised to realize I kinda mean it.

Elsie must read the change in my aura. "You're happy for me."

I nod, remembering what I told Jayden about her being my safety net. "You shouldn't have to give up on your dreams just because your best friend depends on you too much. You deserve every good thing."

"We depend on each other," she says. "But we'll always keep in touch, no matter what."

"Promise?" I ask.

Elsie nods with a grin. "Who else is gonna lose all my bets?"

Afternoon classes come and go, and then it's dinnertime. Elsie is staying late in Magical Science to catch up on everything she missed while in London. That means I'm on my own for dinner, but that's okay because I'm not here just to eat. I've got a medium to find.

I shouldn't have to wait much longer. The food carts have already started shutting themselves down and rolling off on their own as breakfast stations take their place.

Since Julia Farsight's department has nighttime hours, I'm hoping she'll be down any minute for breakfast. Who knew the food court would turn into such a great place to recruit help with the investigation?

As I finish my last slice of pizza, I can practically hear Elsie's voice in my head telling me I need a more balanced diet. "Pizza and tacos aren't vitamins, you know," she'd say. But no self-respecting teenager gives up free pizza every day for broccoli or brussels sprouts. Just the thought makes me shiver.

I'm returning my plates when I notice Julia skipping through the food court with her own *Nobody's UnWanted* pin on her Junior Undertaker cloak. Since the livestream, lots of kids have created their own versions and are pinning them to their uniforms outside class. Unfortunately, just as many *I Support Bane* badges are popping up too. Nearly everyone in the food court has chosen a side.

I rush to catch up with Julia at the Belgian waffle booth.

"Hi," I say, taking the spot beside her.

Julia glances down at the bright red *Dangerous* badge but ignores it. "Hiya, friend."

I walk a few steps with her. "Could I maybe ask you for a favor?"

"Sure." She smiles, her sleepy eyes crinkling. "I'll charge you one waffle."

"But the waffles are free," I say. "You can get as many as you'd like."

"True," she says. "But things taste better when someone else gives them to you."

At least it's a price I can pay. "Deal."

We grab waffles and head back to my table.

"So," I say. "You're a medium, right?"

"Oh, I hope so." She glances down at her Junior

Undertaker badge, where *Department of the Dead* is engraved above the image of a tombstone. "Wouldn't that be awful if I suddenly wasn't and no one told me?"

"Definitely," I say. "But since you are, that means you can talk to the dead and stuff?"

"Usually," she says. "They do have to be *willing* to talk. And many of them aren't. Most quite resent being dead, in fact."

I bite down on my lip and think for a moment. "Could you help me speak with someone who's been dead for a really long time?"

Julia tilts her head to think. "How long?"

"Like seven hundred years?"

Julia shudders. "As in someone from the Ancient War era?"

I nod.

"Those ghosts can be scary." Julia swallows. "Most of them had pretty gruesome ends."

"Could we try, at least?"

Julia sighs. "You *did* give me this tasty waffle. And if they decide to haunt someone, it'll probably be you and not me, so . . . okay. Meet me in the Department of the Dead lobby tonight."

By the time I'm ready to meet Julia in the Department of the Dead, Elsie's back from catching up on the classes she missed this morning. Neither of us is excited about breaking curfew, but we wait until the elevators are clear and hop inside Mischief, the service elevator who more than earns his name. He knows me well enough to understand that I only use him when I'm up to something. I had to promise him a favor in exchange for him keeping quiet, but hopefully this will be worth it. Although the sneaky little laugh he gave after we made the deal does worry me.

The lobby of the Department of the Dead changes every so often, but no matter what form it takes, it's always *super* creepy. The last time I saw the place, it looked like the inside of a haunted house, with dusty furniture, flickering lights, and boarded-up windows. The time before that, it was a graveyard covered in thick fog, and something kept howling.

Tonight we arrive at a spooky forest so dark that no one with any sense would dare step foot inside. And yet Julia is right there in her Junior Undertaker cloak and hood. She smiles and gives us a wave.

Elsie and I look at one another.

"Don't be afraid," says Julia. "If something snatches you, I'll make whatever it is give you back."

She smiles like she's just said the most reassuring thing ever, but I'm not so sure. Still, Elsie and I step into the forest.

"There aren't any actual ghosts or ghouls in here, right?" asks Elsie.

"Of course there are," says Julia. "Much like the wilderness in Creature Control, we construct an environment where dead and undead creatures of the night can feel welcome. And the whole department has a permit to terrorize, so you really come at your own peril."

Elsie doesn't say anything, but she does stand really close to me after that.

"Ready to come inside?" Julia asks.

"As ready as we're going to be," I say.

We move deeper into the woods. Julia's right—just like Creature Control upstairs, this is the real deal. Grass crunches beneath my feet, and these trees are actual trees. The air is unusually cold, and mist parts around us as we go. Glowing eyes peek out from behind tree trunks as things scurry around our feet, but I refuse to look down.

"We're here." Julia opens a bright red door that seems to hover in the middle of a small clearing.

We end up in a dimly lit hallway. It's bright enough that I can tell it forms the same giant U shape as most of the floors in the Bureau. Relieved, I begin to thank Julia again for her help, but she puts a finger to her lips.

"Shh," Julia whispers. "We mustn't disturb the dead."

Just how many dead things are walking around in here? Now I kinda wish I could ask.

We round the hallway past a door that isn't a door at all, but a painting of a door on a solid wall. A plaque beside it reads *Ghosts Only Beyond This Point*. We take the next hallway, which is marked *Visitation Booths*. This leads to a large room with lots of little booths blocked off by curtains.

"In here," Julia says, leading us inside. "This is where I'm training."

The room reminds me of those visitation rooms you see on TV when somebody goes to visit a loved one in jail. There's that same thick glass wall separating the two sets of chairs.

We each take a seat with Julia sitting closest to the glass.

"Tell me his name again?" she asks.

"Thomas Fletcher," I say.

"And tell me as much as you can about him."

We tell her everything we've learned so far about the first time freeze and how he lost his entire werewolf pack.

Julia nods, and with a flick of her fingers a cell phone with a ghostly shimmer appears in her hand. "Once I start dialing, the number just sort of comes to me."

Elsie and I watch as Julia dials and then lifts the phone to her ear. After a moment, she grins and says, "It's ringing!"

Something huge shimmers into existence on the other side of the glass. A massive wolf appears, the size of an elephant, and slams its heavy paws against the glass, flashing fangs. "I'll huff, and I'll puff, and I'll *blow* your house down—"

Julia quickly hangs up and the wolf vanishes. "Seems I focused a bit too much on the wolf part and dialed up a big bad wolf by accident."

Julia clears her throat. "Why don't we try that again?"

A few seconds later, she exclaims, "Somebody's picking up!" But just as fast her face falls. "He says he knows why you're here, but he doesn't feel like talking."

"Please, it's really important," I say.

Julia repeats my words but shakes her head. "He claims he's already spoken about this twice before. Once with Director Wenn, and a second time when he was tricked."

"But that doesn't make any sense," says Elsie. "Nobody else took him seriously. Director Wenn listed his story as a hoax in the second *Titans of Time*."

Julia starts to lower the ghostly telephone. "He says his decision is final."

"Wait!" I say. "Tell him that we aren't trying to trick him. We just want to learn as much as we can about the first time freeze."

But Julia shakes her head. "I'm sorry, Amari. He's— hold on . . . yes, she is *that* Amari . . . Right, Amari Peters."

Julia's eyebrows lift so high she almost looks fully awake. "He says he's coming."

Sure enough, a moment later, a tall muscular guy with a wild beard shimmers on the other side of the glass. He picks up a ghostly telephone of his own.

"You are Amari Peters?" he asks.

Julia hits the speaker button on the glowing phone and I answer. "I am."

"I've read about you in *Dearly Departed*," he says. "You did what I could not."

"You mean confronting Moreau?"

Thomas shakes his head. "It's that sneaky Dylan Van Helsing I'm referring to."

"I did stop Dylan," I say. "But how do you two know each other?"

Thomas Fletcher covers his face. "You're not the first to come looking for me. Last summer, Dylan Van Helsing sat right where you are sitting now. I do not know how he was able to contact me without a medium, but he said he needed my help . . . and I believed him."

"What did he want?" I ask.

"He said he needed to know what happened the night my wolf pack went to face the Night Brothers. Claimed he was afraid Moreau might try to use that power again. He was a Van Helsing—the family is known for their great deeds. I never imagined he might be working with the enemy. I'm so very sorry."

"You don't have anything to be sorry for," says Elsie. "He tricked everyone."

"Can you tell us what you told him?" I ask.

"I wish I could remember," says Thomas. "He didn't just want to hear the memory—he used a spell and stole it right out of my head."

"Do you remember what words he spoke?" I ask. "The name of the spell?"

"That," he says, "I could never forget. The boy grinned and made two fists. Then he sat back in the chair and said, 'Dreamcatcher.'"

≈ 29 ≈

THE MOMENT ELSIE AND I GET BACK TO OUR ROOM, I dig through my things for my first spell book. I set it down onto the floor, with Elsie crouching on the other side. Shadow wiggles happily on my bed, its big glowy eyes seeming perfectly content with life.

This spell book isn't exactly what you'd think a spell book would look like at all. It looks more like a diary than anything else. It even has a gold key and lock.

This book has secrets too, and thankfully I learned them both last summer. I wave my fingers in front of it and whisper, "Dispel."

Suddenly the thing starts to shake furiously between us, shivering and expanding, the cover shifting from black to bright red. Words begin to appear on the front:

So You Want to Be an Illusionist?
The Spells and Musings of Madame Violet, Foremost Illusionist of Her Era

I open the book and flip through the pages and pages of spells meant for illusionists like me. Fair magick spells. The kind I've tried to stick to doing. But there are other spells in here too—foul magick. Dylan's kind of magic.

I flip to the very last page, where the words *The End* are written. But this is an illusion too. I cast it away just as I did the first. Again the book begins to shudder until it's suddenly twice as thick. This page isn't the last anymore but closer to the middle. More words appear.

The End
of
Fair Magick
and the Beginning
of
Magick Most Foul

On the next page is a warning:

That you have found these pages speaks to a willingness to wield more than what fair magick can provide. However, this pursuit comes with a dire warning. The foul magick contained on the following pages is not for the faint of heart. As I learned in their creation, uttering these spells will cost you. For once innocence is lost, it cannot be regained.

"Are you sure about this?" Elsie asks. "Remember the last time you used a foul magick spell?"

I do remember. Magna Fobia—a spell that takes a person's worst fear and creates an illusion out of it. When Lara was bullying me last summer and tracked me down an alley for a fight, I used that spell to defend myself. The result was so awful that I swore to never use foul magick again. Not even when Dylan threatened to steal my magic later that same summer.

"We're not going to use any foul magick." I say it to myself as much as to Elsie. "We just need to know what the Dreamcatcher spell does exactly."

Elsie nods, but I can see the hesitation in her face. She's worried about me, but I know what I'm doing.

I flip through the second half of the book, reading only the names of the spells and nothing more. I'd be lying if I didn't admit that a couple are mysterious enough to tempt me to read more about them, but I don't let myself.

"I was just thinking," says Elsie. "These spells Madame

Violet created . . . the words you speak all seem to have some relation to Latin, don't they? Even if it's just a play on words."

"I guess," I say.

"But *Dreamcatcher* sounds like plain old English," says Elsie. "In fact, that's what the Bureau calls people who work in the Department of Dreams and Nightmares."

That's when I catch on to what she's suggesting. "You don't think Madame Violet created that spell."

She shrugs. "Just an educated guess."

"But that would mean, what, that Dylan did?"

"Maybe?"

I bite down on my lip and flip through the pages much faster, until I reach the last few, all blank. I get a strange feeling deep in my gut. What if this book has a third secret?

I wave a hand over the top of the first blank page. "Dispel."

The book doesn't shake this time; instead words appear, etched in pencil. *Whoa.*

Whom do you serve?

Elsie frowns in confusion.

"I think I have to answer as Dylan would," I whisper. Then I clear my throat and say, "Raoul Moreau."

The words vanish and for a moment I think I've guessed wrong. But then more words appear.

Whom do you truly serve?

I'm tempted to say magiciankind. That's what Dylan is always going on about, protecting magicians and putting them where they're supposed to be. But if that were true, he wouldn't have betrayed Moreau. Not when Moreau and Dylan had the Black Book and the Black Key, and he had the power to do whatever he wanted. He betrayed Moreau because he wanted *me* for a partner.

In the end it wasn't about magicians as much as it was about getting what he wanted. And something tells me you can't lie to your magic.

Again I answer the book as I think Dylan would. "Myself."

In an instant, the pages fill with doodles and diagrams and spells scribbled on the pages. At the very top it reads:

**The Secret Spell Workings of
Dylan Van Helsing
Born Magician
and
Follower of the Foul Path**

The words give me a chill. Had I figured this out last summer, I wouldn't have gotten tricked. But I didn't realize he was working with Moreau till it was too late. There's no way I would've answered those questions correctly.

Scribbled in the bottom corner of the next page, in tiny writing, is the spell I'm looking for.

DREAMCATCHER

With much practice I've finally mastered a spell to protect myself should someone discover I'm a magician. It allows me to steal the memories right out of their head. I think I might even be able to store them as Wakeful Dreams. Stare into your opponent's eyes and ball both fists up tight. Without breaking eye contact, shout *Dreamcatcher!*

Note: This is a last resort. The victim will know that I've messed with their head.

No solution to that problem just yet.

"Dylan stole Thomas Fletcher's memory of that first time freeze," I say. "It's why Fletcher's ghost said he could no longer remember it."

"But why would Dylan want *that* memory?" asks Elsie. "Unless—"

I nod. "Unless he was trying to figure out how the Night Brothers did it the first time. Maybe Dylan didn't steal the time freeze magic from Moreau. Maybe he learned the spell from Thomas's memory."

"But couldn't he have just asked Moreau for the spell?" asks Elsie. "They were working together last summer."

I shrug. "Maybe Moreau wouldn't tell him. They may

not have been as close as we think." Hadn't Dylan himself pointed out that selfishness was behind the Foul Path?

It's quiet for a moment before Elsie says, "So you really think it was Dylan who froze the Supernatural World Congress?"

"It has to be," I say. "Everything we find seems to point back to him."

"There's still the fact that Dylan was trapped in the Sightless Depths at the time. How could he have done anything from there?"

"I don't know the answer to that yet," I say. "All I know is when Lara and I snuck into the Congress Room, all the supernaturals frozen there looked frightened. Even Merlin. Who could scare him like that but someone as powerful as Dylan?"

"So what do we do about it?" asks Elsie.

I startle at the sudden heat around my finger. My heart starts pounding.

Elsie looks up at me. "Amari, what's wrong? Why did your aura suddenly go yellow?"

I stare down at my hand. I'm out of time. The third challenge has begun. "I—I have to go."

"What do you mean?" asks Elsie.

"I can't answer that," I say. "I'm sorry."

"But—wait, hold on, okay?"

I can't hold on. Every second I wait here is one Dylan could be using to beat me to the Victor's Ring. I get up, wondering if my Game Ring works when I'm not alone.

Maybe I could sneak into the bathroom and shut the door if I had to.

But Elsie spreads her arms wide, blocking my path. Shadow jumps down onto the floor with us, looking agitated. "This has something to do with the vow of secrecy you made, doesn't it?"

I shake my head in frustration. "Els, not now. Please move out of the way."

"No."

It takes the word a few seconds to register. "What do you mean, no?" I ask.

"I'm not letting you do something that scares you this badly. As your best friend, I'm saying no."

"Let me go, Elsie. I mean it. I don't have much time."

Elsie bites her lip, something she only started doing because I do it so much. It would make me laugh if the situation weren't so awful.

I can't wait any longer. I take a step back and squeeze the ring.

The surprise on Elsie's face is the last thing I see before I'm suddenly staring into the face of Dylan Van Helsing.

My heart skips and I scramble backward, instinctively reaching for my Stun Stick. I aim it at Dylan, only to realize he doesn't seem to know I'm standing here. His eyes have a faraway look, almost like he's looking through me.

Strange.

I glance at our surroundings. Wherever we are, it's a relatively small room. A giant mirror covers all four walls, and when I stare into it my vision seems to go fuzzy at the edges. I get that same dreamy feeling I got from the *Collection of Looking Glasses . . .*

The next thing I know, suddenly I'm back in my apartment.

I have to blink a few times from the shock of it. Is this real? I reach out to touch Mama's lumpy recliner and then move into the kitchen and swing open the freezer. There's pizza-flavored Hot Pockets inside. This *must* be real. But how did I get back home?

"You coming back or what, sis?"

My breath catches and I go completely still. "Quinton?"

"You lost the game fair and square," he says. "I expect my Hot Pocket delivered right to my room." I can hear the laughter in his voice.

I stop right outside his door and take a deep, slow breath. Then I poke my head inside.

My brother leans up from his bed, where he's stretched out lazily, earbuds in his ears. His grin fades and turns into that goofy look he makes whenever he pretends to be offended. "Now I know you didn't forget my Hot Pocket after you took that big ole L in rock, paper, scissors!"

I dash across the room and throw my arms around him, squeezing him tight. "I'm so glad you're better. *When* did you get better?"

He grins. "I thought we agreed you weren't going to do this 'hug me every time you see me' thing forever, Chicken Little. I'm good as new, and I'm not going anywhere."

"But when did you get better?" I ask again. "Last thing I remember, you were getting worse . . ."

He raises an eyebrow. "Do I look worse to you?"

I shake my head. "You look good—back to normal."

"Then why don't you take a seat on the floor and we'll listen to some music like we used to."

A sudden chill makes me shiver. "Is the AC on too high? You know Mama will lose her mind if she finds out somebody touched that thermostat."

Quinton's smile wavers. "The AC is fine. Not sure why you're so cold." He folds his arms. "This your way of trying to get out of hanging with your big brother?"

A grin lights up my face. "Only thing that would make me do that is if you try to play that old-man rap. Put on something from this decade, please."

Quinton rolls his eyes. "Fine, fine. Just get comfortable."

I stretch out on the floor, putting my hands behind my head. I don't know the last time I felt so happy. But there's this little nagging feeling, like maybe I'm forgetting something. Maybe even a lot of somethings.

And for some reason, I can't stop shivering.

"Quinton, was I supposed to be doing something?"

He laughs. "You were *supposed* to be making my Hot Pocket."

"That's right." Now I'm laughing too. "Oops."

"Don't you worry about it though. Just keep relaxing. It'll be over soon."

"What will be over soon?" I ask, but he doesn't answer.

That's when another thought pops into my head. "You know who else loves Hot Pockets? Maybe even more than you?"

"Who?"

"Elsie. I hope she's not too worried about me. I kind of left her to watch Shadow by herself—"

"Did someone say my name?" Elsie leans into the room, a great big smile on her face.

"You're here?" I ask.

Elsie raises an eyebrow. "Am I not allowed to be?"

I laugh. "Of course you are, you're my best friend. It's just that I could've sworn I left you behind a second ago . . ."

Mama's voice calls from the living room. "Got some fresh gumbo for anyone who wants it!"

"Gumbo!" I shout as the smell fills my nose. I can already taste it. But why do I still feel so cold, even with my Junior Agent jacket on?

"How about you let me get that jacket?" Quinton asks nervously. "We're not doing any agenting tonight."

I meet his eyes and start to take it off. Except something is moving around inside.

I reach into my pocket and pull out Shadow, that freezing little shade. But wasn't he back in the dorms with Elsie? He must've jumped into my pocket before I squeezed my ring to come here. He doesn't like loud noises, and Elsie and I were arguing about me leaving to come to the third challenge . . .

Dylan . . . those mirrors . . . *this* is the challenge!

I look at my fully awake brother and my heart breaks. "This isn't real."

I glance from Quinton to Elsie, then to Mama who's stepped into the doorway. "*None* of this is real."

Quinton steps closer. "It can be real if you want it to. Don't fight it, Amari. You can stay here with us forever. Doesn't that sound great? You can have anyone here you'd like. I'm awake here."

Elsie takes up my hand and gives it a squeeze. "And I'm not leaving you behind here."

"That's all I want," I say, tears skipping down my cheeks. "I don't want to be alone."

"Then take it," says Quinton. "Aren't you tired of fighting? Of things always being so hard?"

"Here, things are easy," says Elsie. "Don't you trust us?"

"I do," I say. "And I do want to stay."

"Then say you'll stay," Mama says over my shoulder. "That's all it takes. Just say you'll stay, and you won't remember anything from your life before. You just gotta make that choice."

"Just say the words?" I repeat. And I'll get everything I've ever wanted?

"That's all, Babygirl," says Mama. "Think about yourself for once."

"Maybe I will," I say. All I have to do is say the words and I can be happy. No more stressing myself out trying to save the world. That really does sound so nice.

Shadow bounces in my hand. "But how would I get this shade back to its owner?" And not only that, what will my real friends think when I don't come back? Or when Dylan wins the Great Game and starts a war. Is my being happy worth everyone else being miserable?

"I can't stay," I whisper. "People are counting on me. *Real* people are counting on me. Staying would be giving up, and I said I wouldn't do that anymore. I'm the girl who tries, who fights. And I have to keep doing that, no matter how hard it gets." I wipe my eyes, but a sob breaks through. "No matter what it costs me."

Quinton shakes his head. "If you do succeed in ending the time freeze and canceling the Great Game, I might never wake up. Is that a reality you want to go back to? Choose *me*, Amari." He gestures to Elsie and Mama. "Choose us."

"I'm sorry," I say. "But I can't—I *don't* want this."

And just like that, the illusion vanishes and I'm back in the mirrored room. Quinton's words still float through my head, but I have to believe my real brother would understand why I'm trying to end the time freeze. Why I can't risk losing.

Dylan is standing a few feet from me, his mind still far away. Whatever he's dreaming about makes him grin. And his pupils . . . they aren't red anymore but blue, like they used to be. I don't know what to make of that, but I can't question him about it, or anything to do with the time freeze, if he doesn't even know I'm here.

Beyond him there's a break in the wraparound

mirror—the Victor's Ring must be through there. I rush over, turning sideways to fit.

Back here is another, much smaller room. A ring lies atop a pillow on a stone pedestal. I've never laughed and cried at the same time before, but that's how relieved I feel.

I don't waste any time sliding the ring onto my finger. It sends a jolt through my entire body, like fireworks going off beneath my skin.

Whoa.

Now I just need to get out of here. But not before my curiosity makes me glance back into the mirror room, where Dylan still stumbles around, entranced.

I should leave him. Just like he meant to leave me in Alexander's library. I check to make sure Shadow is still tucked safely in my pocket and reach for my ring. I'm just about to squeeze it when I hear, "Are you coming, Amari?"

His head is turned away, so he can't be speaking to me. At least, not the real me. *I'm* in Dylan's vision? But that doesn't make sense. He made it clear that whatever soft spot he had for me was long gone. Unless he wasn't being fully honest—with me or himself. Maybe there's some part of him that still thinks of me as his best friend.

Something moves along the ceiling in the next room . . . something long and scaly.

I lean farther in and, sure enough, a Living Nightmare slinks closer, its great big jaw opening wide enough to swallow Dylan whole. But the challenge is over, so why would it show up now? Unless it's here to gobble down the loser.

Didn't Maria warn me that Vladimir would want to make sure only one magician was left standing? If I did leave, it would solve all my problems. But it would also make me just as responsible for what happens to Dylan as Vladimir and that Living Nightmare.

Without another thought I dart back through the wall and send two quick blasts from my Stun Stick at the beast. It shrinks away for a moment, then lunges, its huge jaws snapping shut just above my shoulder.

I skid to a stop, hook an arm around Dylan, and squeeze my ring just as the Living Nightmare charges.

Next thing I know, Dylan and I are back in my dorm room, surrounded by Lara, Elsie, and Jayden.

Elsie screams.

≋ 30 ≋

Lara goes for her Stun Stick but Dylan does a quick series of motions with his hands and shadows surge into my friends. Each slumps to the floor, unconscious.

"Don't hurt them," I say quickly. "Please."

But Dylan's not concerned with them. He's turned his attention to me, his hands and arms erupting in flames. From this close, his fireballs won't miss.

"I couldn't abandon you," I say, backing up to my closet. It's all I can think to say.

His glare softens ever so slightly.

It keeps me talking. "And I know I was in your dream. We had the same dream, didn't we? To spend time with the people we care about?"

Dylan growls, but the flames go out. He lets out a frustrated shout and then turns back to me, looking hurt and angry and sad all at the same time. "What do you want? I know there's a reason you saved me, so what is it? And don't tell me it's because you care—because I don't believe that for a second."

"You were my friend," I say. "Part of me will always care, as much as I might hate myself for it."

"You're lying." He shakes his head. "Did Maria put you up to this? Did she tell you that if you pretend to care about me like she did, I'd let my guard down?"

Now I'm the one who's frustrated. "Remember what you said to me back in the Living Library? You told me that you'd already won last summer, that you had the Black Book and Key. Well, the same is true for me. I could've left you to that Living Nightmare and won the Great Game. But I went back for you, didn't I?"

I shake my head and wipe my cheeks dry. Then I add, "My brother could be awake right now, but I chose to save you."

Dylan doesn't have an answer to that. The eyes that seemed so red before are dull. "Then we're even."

"No, we aren't," I say. "I know you won't release the curse on my brother, but could you at least end whatever spell you're using to cause the time freeze? Help me get rid of Bane. You say you want to help magicians? Well, he's the one targeting us."

Dylan scoffs. "You really think I caused the time freeze?

It was all I could do just keeping myself alive in the Sightless Depths."

I watch his body language like Magnus said, but he looks confident in what he's saying. "I know you stole Thomas Fletcher's memories of the first time freeze last summer. There had to be a reason for that."

Dylan actually smiles. "Always so clever. I never said I wasn't interested in how they froze time—just that I'm not able to do it. That memory just confirmed it. But if you don't believe me, go and watch it for yourself in the Department of Dreams and Nightmares. My profile password shouldn't be too hard to figure out."

I risk a step closer, searching his face. "You're *really* not behind the freeze?"

"I've already answered that question." Now it's Dylan who moves closer, his eyes hard again. "Maybe I do miss the way things used to be. But we've both made choices, haven't we? I'll never forgive you for sending me to that place. The next time we see each other I won't show you any mercy."

He squeezes his ring and he's gone—back to wherever it is he's hiding.

It doesn't take long for my friends to come to once Dylan has left. I wait with them, wondering how I can possibly explain what they just saw.

Lara is the first to wake, and she's furious. "What. The. Heck. Peters? Why was *my brother* in your room?"

I wince and show her my palms. "I know how bad it looks. But it's a long story."

"You'd better get talking then," Lara snaps.

"She can't." Elsie rubs her head as she pulls herself up to her knees. "Whatever Amari is doing is protected by a vow of secrecy."

Lara looks incredulous. "Seriously?"

"Is it magician stuff?" asks Jayden, crawling into a squat.

"Vow of secrecy," Elsie repeats.

"This is what I *can* say," I begin. "Dylan told me something that will help with our investigation. Something big."

"I don't care what he told you," says Lara. "He's a liar. And a criminal—"

"Just listen, okay?" I interrupt.

Lara shuts up, though she looks ready to explode again at any moment.

"We're going to have to visit the Department of Dreams and Nightmares to see it."

The thing about the Department of Dreams and Nightmares is that you never actually enter the department, not really. In fact, it technically doesn't even exist. If you look on the blueprints or the floor plan it'll just show the department lobby.

That's because the rest of the department exists inside a dream. Seriously.

Since Jayden has an earlier curfew as a trainee, we decide

that me, Elsie, and Lara will go check out Dylan's profile.

The department lobby is a soft pink, and soothing lullabies play from speakers perched in the corners. Seemingly endless rows of cushy beds inside curtained booths fill the space. A few booths are large and fancy, like the director's booth, which has a golden tent around it. We each pick out a booth in the visitors section, where a robot waits inside.

I stretch out on the bed as the robot taps away at a computer.

"Good evening, Junior Agent Peters. I believe this is your first time visiting our department. Visitors can bring custom-made dreams to experience, search their mind for good or bad dreams they've had recently for interpretation, or even store important memories that can later be revisited as dreams. Would you like to set up a username and password to ensure that only you can access the dreams you store here?"

"What if I want to view someone else's profile?" I ask.

"In order to access someone's profile, you must have that person's express permission. If you can offer the password, then we can proceed."

"The name is Dylan Van Helsing." Here's the tough part. "And the password is Foul Path?"

"Incorrect," says the robot. "Two attempts remain."

I swallow. What's something he cares about? "Magiciankind?"

"Incorrect," the robot says again. "One more incorrect guess and you will be locked out of the system indefinitely."

Panic swells in my gut. I've come too far to blow this. Dylan said that I should know it . . . ?

An idea pops into my head—but it couldn't be that, could it? Then again, we *were* friends last summer when he set up the profile.

"Try Amari Amazing."

"Very good," says the robot. "Password accepted. If you'll just lie back on the pillow and close your eyes, I'll send you to the dreaming theaters."

It's the same password Quinton used—Dylan and I figured it out in order to get into my brother's computer last summer. I feel the strangest sense of satisfaction. I've felt like such an idiot this past year for falling for his lies. But maybe in his own twisted way, he really did care about me.

I do as the robot asks and feel the weight of the metal shades being placed onto my face.

"When you can no longer hear my voice, feel free to open your eyes. One . . . two . . . three . . . four . . ."

The robot's voice goes quiet, and I open my eyes to find myself inside a great big silver dome. It's empty and every step I take echoes. The sign on the wall says *Dreaming Theater 19.*

"One dream available for viewing," says the robot's voice. "Shall I proceed?"

"Hold on," I call back.

Where are Lara and Elsie? I whip my head around until I find a door set into the wall. I sprint over and open it up, poking my head outside. A long hallway stretches in both directions, but luckily my friends are wandering a few doors down. Probably looking for me.

"Over here," I call, and they come running.

Once they're through the door, I shut it behind them. Then I press down on a button that says *Do Not Disturb.*

"Okay," I call out. "I'm ready to see the dream now."

"Dream commencing."

In an instant, the metallic walls of the dreaming theater vanish and the three of us stand on a grassy hilltop, in the dead of night, overlooking a small stone building down below. Growls fill the air and Elsie yelps.

Large werewolves crouch low in the grass around us. Their gleaming yellow eyes glow in the dark.

"We'll end this war with one strike," snarls the largest.

"Alpha, brother, let me join you." Thomas Fletcher's familiar voice comes from behind us. Unlike the others, he's still in his human form.

"No," the alpha says. "One must stay behind, just in case. Someone must report back what happens here."

Thomas sulks but doesn't argue.

"Pack," the alpha wolf calls out. "The Night Brothers are down there, and we will make them pay for the misery they've caused. Future generations will sing songs of our victory!"

A howl goes up, and then they're all howling.

The wolf pack tears down the hill. There must be fifty of them in all.

Elsie and Lara step closer. None of us speak because we

know how this attack ends.

A light comes on in the building at the bottom of the hill, and two dark figures move frantically in the windows. The Night Brothers really were taken by surprise.

I start down the hill too, wanting to get a good look at exactly how the spell is done. But I'm only able to take a few steps before hitting some invisible barrier.

"This is a memory," says Lara. "We can only see what Thomas saw."

That means if Thomas stayed on this hill, then I have to stay up here too. I bite my lip and watch.

The wolves are almost to the stone house now, and the two figures move to the doorway. But they're still now, their stance confident. Not the least bit afraid.

"I don't think I can look," says Elsie.

The first row of werewolves leaps into the air to pounce, teeth bared and claws swinging. I step forward at the same time Thomas does, holding my breath.

One of the Night Brothers lifts an arm—and immediately time stops. The werewolves go completely still, some in midair, poised to attack, others in midstride coming down the hill.

Lara squints. "Is Moreau holding something in his hand?"

"Of course!" Elsie exclaims. "It's not a spell, it's an enchanted object. Like a superpowered freeze grenade."

Just like me, the Night Brothers are completely unaffected by the freeze. They move through the field of frozen werewolves, laughing so loudly we can hear them all the way up here.

But this doesn't make me feel better at all. Because even if it was some kind of magical stone that caused the freeze, and not a spell, it still means that whoever caused time to stop had to be a magician in order for them to escape. This proves it once and for all.

But every single magician I know has denied having anything to do with the time freeze—Dylan, Maria, the whole League of the Magicians too.

So who's not telling the truth?

≈ 31 ≈

CONFIDENTIAL
MEETING
IN
PROGRESS

T HE TRICK TO GETTING PAST BERTHA AFTER CURFEW IS looking really sleepy and carrying armfuls of books. With how much training there is, and how much learning we have to do, it's not hard to imagine some poor kid losing track of time or falling asleep in their study room.

But it's also a lot easier to pull off when it's just one or two of us trying to get back to our rooms.

Trying to convince Bertha that all three of us got carried away studying might be a stretch. But what choice do we have? We can't sleep in the elevators.

"Put on your best tired faces," Lucy the elevator laughs. "Now approaching the youth dorms."

It's just our luck that as soon as the elevator doors open,

Bertha is standing only a few steps away. Like she's been waiting for us or something.

We put our plan into effect. First I give a great big yawn. Then Elsie rubs her eyes and Lara pretends to stretch.

Bertha just shakes her head. "No need to put on an act tonight. You've all been summoned to the chief's office."

The three of us suddenly look a whole lot more awake. I swallow and ask, "Any idea why?"

Our dorm leader shakes her head. "All I know is the order came straight from Prime Minister Bane. I was told to make sure you got the message."

The elevator doors slam shut, and Lucy begins to descend with us still inside. "I'm sorry," she says, "but I can't disobey orders."

We arrive at the chief's office so fast that my head is still spinning from Bertha's words. What could Bane want? Does he know what we've been up to?

A dozen agents stand waiting for us in the lobby.

"Amari," Elsie whispers. "I'm scared."

"Me too," I say.

"Let's see what they want," says Lara. "Maybe it's just a misunderstanding."

Her voice sounds hopeful, but that's not what my gut tells me. Especially when I notice that neither Magnus nor Fiona is here. None of the adults who might be on my side. No way that's a coincidence.

Director Van Helsing *is* here, though. "Girls, follow me."

He turns into a hallway, and the three of us step off the elevator together. We follow him into the hall, the agents eyeing us closely—me most of all. The fact that they've each got one hand on a Stun Stick doesn't go unnoticed.

I try to put myself in their shoes. I *am* a magician, after all—and a powerful magician at that, even if it feels strange to admit.

Director Van Helsing waits for us to catch up before he opens the door to the conference room. The moment he does, that same staticky buzzing I felt last time I met Bane fills my ears. I hate that my hands begin to tremble, but the truth is I'm terrified.

I take hold of Elsie's and Lara's hands. Elsie's shivers even more than mine do. Lara's grip is strong, but I know her well enough now to see the worry in her face.

Together we enter the conference room.

Bane sits on the far end, absently passing a hand back and forth through the conference table until he notices us. The Prime Minister is actually *here*—in the same room with us. Two other wraiths stand just behind him, all three fading in and out in unison, dark expressions on their faces. Harlowe waits in the corner, arms crossed and eyes narrowed.

Great, the We Hate Amari's Guts squad is all here.

"Girls," says Bane. "Please do have a seat."

We each take a chair at the opposite end of the long table.

Director Van Helsing stays on his feet, finding a spot on

the wall to lean against. His eyes are on his daughter. Lara keeps her gaze on the conference table.

"I'll make this short and to the point," says Bane. "We know what you've been up to. So there's no point in trying to hide it."

A chill races down my back. How much does he know?

"I'll give you a chance to come clean and show some remorse for your actions. Be assured, you will only get one such chance."

I glance to Elsie and Lara on either side of me. My best friend's jaw keeps quivering while my partner sits as stiff as stone.

Bane sneers. "You had so much to say on Eurg Live, but now only silence. *Incredible.*"

Director Van Helsing clears his throat. "If Peters and Rodriguez have nothing to say, then I'm sure Lara will be cooperative, won't you?"

She glances to her dad, then to me. And nods.

My jaw drops.

"Lara!" whispers Elsie.

A wicked smile fixes on Bane's face. "We're all listening."

My jaw clenches as I wait for the inevitable. The looking glasses warned us about her, and I didn't listen. I feel so stupid.

Lara lifts her head. "At the beginning of the summer, my dad offered me a deal. He said I could keep the Junior Agent badge I earned in Australia if I agreed to keep an eye on Amari. And I took it because I honestly thought I deserved to be a Junior Agent last summer—"

"Yes, yes." Bane waves a dismissive hand. "I already know all about our arrangement with your father. What I want to know is what you've learned."

"No," I whisper. "Please don't . . ."

Lara ignores me. "Amari has been doing her own investigation into the time freeze, even though my dad ordered her not to. The two of us even snuck out to the Congress Room after curfew."

"*Expressly* against my orders." Bane leans closer, resting his elbows on the table. "And what did she discover?"

Lara hesitates before answering. "Amari was able to enter the time freeze and leave again without getting stuck. It doesn't affect her at all."

"Proof!" Bane slams his hand on the table. "It's as I've been saying all along. Magicians must be behind the attack. There's no other explanation."

Director Van Helsing steps away from the wall. "To think we've allowed magicians to join the Bureau. A disgrace to the organization and an embarrassment to our family name."

"There's more . . . ," says Lara.

What is she *doing*? Did she not just hear what her dad said about magicians? About Maria, the sister she claims to care about so much?

Lara goes on. "We found a memory that my brother

was hiding. He stole it from a werewolf who fought in the Ancient War. It showed the Night Brothers using magic to stop time. Except it wasn't a spell, it was some kind of . . . stone."

I glare at my so-called partner. She's really going to tell them everything.

Bane strokes his cheek. "A stone, you say?" He snaps his fingers impatiently at Director Van Helsing. "Put your best people on finding this stone. We need to ensure that nothing like this ever happens again."

I glare at Bane. I'm sure that stone will get buried just like everything else about the time freeze.

"The stone will be found." Director Van Helsing nods. "As soon as this meeting is over I'll—"

"*Now,*" Bane snarls.

Director Van Helsing bristles but dips his head. "As you wish." He gives Lara a proud nod before disappearing through the door. Harlowe comes and takes his place on the wall.

"Tell me, girl." Bane gets to his feet. "Why was your partner *really* investigating the time freeze on her own? What did she hope to accomplish?"

Lara spares me another glance before saying, "Amari figured that if she could learn what caused the freeze, there might be some way to undo it and put Merlin back in charge. She, um, wanted you to lose your position as Prime Minister."

I sink further into my chair. This really can't get any worse.

"Did she now?" Bane smirks. "Well, I happen to believe her motives were more sinister than that. I think our little magician here has finally given in to her evil nature. It's my opinion that Amari is looking to obtain the power to freeze time for herself."

"That's not true!" I say.

"Hush!" calls one of Bane's assistants.

But Bane himself just stares. It takes me a moment to realize he's looking at my *Dangerous* badge. Then his eyes shift to the one Elsie made for me. "I was wrong about you. You're more than just dangerous—you, girl, are a traitor. And it's time the supernatural world sees you for what you truly are."

I shake my head. "I'm not a traitor!"

Bane just sighs. "It's a shame, really. Such a talented bloodline. But in the end, you cannot help what you are. If it's any consolation, I do believe some part of you wishes to be good. But a wild tiger cannot simply shed its stripes. It will always be a threat to those around it, especially when it grows hungry. And magicians hunger for power. It's in your very nature."

"S-sir," Lara stutters. "What's going to happen to Amari now?"

"Director Harlowe," says Bane. "Kindly explain what will happen to Miss Peters and Miss Rodriguez?"

Harlowe steps forward. "We must make the most of

Lara's successful undercover work. I suggest we make an example of Amari and her witless friend. The supernatural world will know that under Prime Minister Bane's leadership, the centuries-long threat of magiciankind will end. He is the hero our world needs—the savior it deserves!"

Lara swallows. "Could I make a suggestion—"

Harlowe waves her off. "You are free to go, child."

Lara hesitates but gets to her feet. "But—"

"Leave," Bane interrupts.

"I'm sorry," Lara says, not meeting my eyes. She practically runs out of the room.

"Now then," says Harlowe. "We need to plan how best to play this. Unfortunately, because it's *you*, things must be handled more delicately than I'd like. But no matter, when I'm done, the world will believe you no different from the evil magicians of old."

"For now," she adds, "the wraiths will escort you both to your room, where you will be confined indefinitely. No one goes in or out. The Prime Minister and I have much to discuss. And one more thing, you've just lost dear old Quinton his spot in Supernatural Health."

"Y-you can't," I plead. "He didn't do anything."

"I warned you," says Harlowe. "Actions have consequences."

≋ 32 ≋

I T'S LATE WHEN WE GET BACK TO THE YOUTH DORMITO-
ries, Bane's two assistants leading the way. Elsie and I are
quiet. There's nothing to say, anyway. Lara sold us out and
now we're going to be called traitors no matter how untrue
it is.

We keep our heads down as we move through the halls,
but the staticky buzzing sound coming off the flickering
wraiths is loud enough that kids begin to peek out their
doors to see what's going on. Bear laughs as if this has just
made his entire summer.

Bertha steps from around a corner and raises a hand
to halt the wraiths. "Only members of the Bureau directly
involved in youth supervision are allowed in these halls. You

can wait up front near the elevators and I'll take the girls back to their rooms."

"We've got orders directly from the Prime Minister," says a wraith. "In case you've forgotten, he's in charge now."

"The Prime Minister doesn't get to rewrite the Bureau's rules," Bertha says.

This time the other wraith answers. "And who's gonna stop him? Some glorified babysitter? Move along."

The two wraiths push forward, shoving Bertha aside. I flash our dorm leader a grateful smile as I continue on. It's the least I can do.

The walk to our rooms feels like it lasts for hours. I can hear the whispers from kids who support Bane, pieces of conversations reaching us from behind their barely open doors.

"Knew this would happen."

"Should've never allowed a magician at the Bureau."

Eventually I just cover my ears. But that doesn't stop me from seeing Tristan's smug face. He gives the wraiths an exaggerated salute.

When we get to our room, Elsie goes in first and I follow. The wraiths wait by the door. "You're hereby confined to this room. You're not to leave for any reason, understand? Your meals will be brought to you."

"If you're even allowed any meals." The other wraith laughs. "I hear food is hard to come by in the Sightless Depths. I'd get used to it if I were you!"

The door slams shut, leaving Elsie and me alone.

I fall back on my bed. "Tonight couldn't have gone any worse."

Elsie plops down on her own bed and closes her eyes. "Things will turn around somehow. I believe that."

For once I'm not in the mood for Elsie's constant optimism. "And what if they don't?" I ask. "If Bane does manage to convince everyone that I'm a traitor, they really will throw us into the Sightless Depths like Dylan. What do we do now?"

Elsie answers in a small voice. "Solve the time freeze mystery before tomorrow morning?"

"Sure," I say. "It's only what we've been trying to do since before we got here."

"Well, we can't go down without a fight," Elsie breathes. "So let's think—what do we know now that we didn't know before?"

"Just that the time freeze was caused by some kind of stone and not a spell," I say.

"Right," says Elsie. "Stopping time requires a massive amount of magic. To keep it going for this long is way more than any magician could manage . . . *But* if you had a special stone that could *somehow* hold all that magic, it could act as a superpowered freeze grenade."

She stands and begins to pace. I keep quiet, knowing better than to interrupt my best friend when she's onto something.

"What if the reason the Night Brothers never used the stone again was because they *couldn't*? It takes freeze grenades months to recharge, and those only freeze a small area for a short time. A stone capable of freezing the entire state for several minutes and the entire Congress Room for a week—that must take centuries!"

"That must be why the Night Brothers used the stone in the first place," I say. "They didn't want to use it when they did—it was a last resort. In Thomas Fletcher's memory, the werewolves launched a sneak attack the Night Brothers didn't know was coming. The wolf pack made it right up to the house where they were hiding. Using the stone was the only way to save themselves."

Elsie nods. "And once they used it, the stone became useless because it takes so long to recharge. That's why they never froze time again."

"Until someone found it," I say. "Or maybe it was passed down to another magician, I don't know."

Elsie gasps. "Amari! I'll bet Bane sent Director Van Helsing searching for the stone because he doesn't understand how time enchantments work. If time is still frozen inside the Congress Room, the stone has to still be there somewhere!"

Now I'm on my feet too. "If I could find the stone and take it somewhere else, the Congress members would be freed!"

"Only one problem," says Elsie.

"What's that?" I ask.

"Lara has the transporter."

A familiar heat surrounds my finger. Not now! We're so

close to figuring out how to end this time freeze once and for all. "Els . . . I've got to leave."

Elsie swallows. "This place you keep going . . . will you have to face Dylan again?"

I try to answer her but can't.

Elsie goes pale. "I guess that's a yes."

I feel guilty for what I'm about to ask, but I've got to do it anyway. "If I don't make it back it's up to you to fix things at the Congress Room, okay? Promise me you'll try."

"I promise." Elsie gives me a hug.

The moment she lets go I squeeze my ring . . .

And suddenly I'm standing in a small living room. It's fancy, with plush furniture and gold-trimmed tables and lamps. Matching silk curtains cover one entire wall. A giant crystal harp sits in the corner beside a faded painting of a frowning dwarf in jeweled battle armor, a golden ax perched on his shoulder.

"He sure seems pleasant," I mutter.

"For dwarfkind, that's considered a smile." Dylan's muffled voice sounds close.

Too close. I turn to face him, but the room lurches beneath our feet, sending us stumbling.

Dylan smacks into something solid and groans. "This your doing?"

I shake my head. "I just got here."

He reaches for me, his fingers pressing up against something solid. "It's glass."

Glass? I stretch out my own hand. He's right, there's a

wall of glass separating us. But why?

Dylan's eyes widen and I follow his gaze above my head. The ring! We both leap to grab it and fail. The ring is *inside* this wall of glass.

Dylan throws fireballs and even shadows at the barrier, but it's no use. "How are we supposed to get to it?"

"Hold on," I say, noticing something for the first time. "Is it me or is this room vibrating?"

Dylan goes still. I rush over to the curtains and yank one of them back. Pitch-darkness fills the window—and bubbles. Where are we?

Dylan looks between me, the window, and that portrait on the wall. His expression turns grim. "This is Great King Olaf's train."

"I don't know who that is," I say.

"The dwarf who built Cibola, the city of gold beneath Las Vegas."

"Okay, but why does that matter?" I ask.

"Because he had planned to build a city made completely of silver too, but never got the chance after gambling away his fortune trying to create his own underwater trains to compete with the International Railways of Atlantis."

"Wait, we're on an underwater train?"

Dylan nods. "Turns out the old fool didn't know the undersea well enough to know where to put tracks and where not to. This was a train track that never should've been built." He laughs bitterly. "There's a reason it's unfinished."

"What do you mean, unfinished?" I ask. "These tracks don't lead to anything?"

"Oh, it's much worse than that."

I swallow. "How can it possibly be worse?"

The train starts to rock as it begins to ascend. Dylan glances out the window, his confident smirk wavering. "How about you look out there and find out?"

I do as he says. Outside, in the glow of the shimmering train, enormous white tentacles swish about in the distance.

"That *can't* be . . . ," I start.

Dylan grits his teeth. "The Devourer of Ships."

"The Kraken," I whisper. "One of the seven great beasts."

We both watch in silence as the train cuts wide circles around the edge of this giant cavern. The tracks take us higher and higher, until the creature's huge yellow eyes come into view. And here I thought the Carcolh was scary. "At least it seems to be sleeping—"

Suddenly the lights atop the train blaze extra bright, enough that I can clearly make out just how massive the Kraken is. It seems to stretch on forever.

The train enters a short tunnel leading out of the underground cavern onto the ocean floor. A terrible screech echoes, and the ground trembles so hard I can feel the train wobble on the tracks.

"The K-Kraken only turns white when it s-senses a threat," I say, in a low, trembling voice. All those hours studying for our Supernatural Knowledge test last summer taught me that. "It's going to come after us."

Dylan nods stiffly. "So the challenge must be who'll stick around long enough to claim the ring."

I shudder but ball my fists at my sides and meet his eyes. "I won't let you win."

He sets his jaw. "So you really mean to see this through to the end?"

"If that's the only way to stop you, then yes," I say.

Dylan's answer is drowned out by another screech.

We turn to peer out the windows, but even with the train's much brighter lights on now, there's just nothing to see. Emptiness surrounded by darkness.

Boom!

"That sounded close." Dylan tries to sound nonchalant, but I can hear the fear in his voice. "Just how far do you plan to take this?"

I step up to the glass wall. "A few seconds longer than you."

"You're impossible." He shakes his head. "We would've been such a great team."

"I told you. I could never be cruel like you are."

Dylan lifts his chin. "Nature itself is cruel. I won't apologize for it."

BOOM!

A giant tentacle slams against the ground just outside the window, throwing everything into chaos. My feet leave the ground, the train car twisting around me. But before I can even process what's happening, my head slams into something hard—

I blink a few times before I realize my eyes are open. It's that dark.

Ears ringing, I manage to sit up. "Dylan?" No answer. I can't see anything.

I reach into my jacket for my Stun Stick and flick on the flashlight. The train must've derailed. It's lying on its side, furniture strewn everywhere. That glass wall is still there, and Dylan pulls himself up to his knees on the other side of it.

The ring remains between us, still stuck inside the glass.

The lights flash and start to flicker back on, both inside and atop the train. I make the mistake of looking up . . . and scream.

Through the window that's now above our heads, enormous tentacles swish about, but at the center of the beast is its mouth—an endless pit of giant teeth that rotate like the blades of a chainsaw.

I gasp as the train jolts from the sudden impact of those massive tentacles crashing against it. The metal groans loudly, and I realize we're being lifted from the ocean floor. Dylan and I lock eyes, both coming to the same realization. If we don't get out of here, we'll be devoured.

I tremble as we hold one another's gaze, fighting down the urge to panic. How far *am* I willing to take this? How far is Dylan?

I can hear it now, the gnashing of all those teeth above us. But I won't look—I can't—because I know I'd lose my nerve.

But Dylan does. He pales, his jaw falling open—then he squeezes his ring to escape.

The moment he's gone, the glass shatters and the ring skitters somewhere between the overturned furniture. I dive over to where it fell, shoving things aside. A series of loud pops startle me as water starts spraying into the train.

This is so bad.

Soon those gnashing teeth are all I hear. I pick up the pace, throwing things aside to search for the Victor's Ring.

My whole body shudders. I can't stop shaking.

And then I find it. Jam the thing onto my finger.

And squeeze my Game Ring as the train begins to come apart around me.

≈ 33 ≈

AS SOON AS I REAPPEAR IN OUR ROOM, ELSIE DROPS
her phone and rushes over.

It takes me a few seconds to stop shaking, and Elsie pulls
the blanket from her bed and wraps it around me.

"I—I'm okay," I say.

"You don't look okay, Amari."

"Just give me a few minutes." I pull my knees up to my
chest and try to slow my breathing.

Elsie does what I ask, looking on with concern.

It's over, I tell myself. *I'm safe.*

Finally, I'm able to ask, "Who were you talking to?"

Elsie winces. "Lara called, like, right before you
showed up."

Anger fills in the spaces where my fear just was. After finally putting my trust in that girl, how could she sell me out? Especially when she knew how hard it was for me to trust another partner after Dylan.

"Let's just hear her out, okay? We need that transporter to get to the Congress Room." Elsie reaches back to grab the phone, then offers it to me. Reluctantly I take it. Lara's face fills the screen.

"You've got a lot of nerve," I say.

Lara shakes her head. "I know it seems like I betrayed you, but—"

"No, you *did* betray me," I say. "You told Bane everything!"

Lara shakes her head. "I didn't tell him about whatever you and Dylan are doing."

I open my mouth to refute that, but Lara's right. Of all the things she did say, that wasn't one of them.

Lara goes on. "So . . . it's true that my dad asked me to keep an eye on you after he learned we were partners. But I refused. I told him it's not how partners treat one another. As Director of Supernatural Investigations, he should know that better than anyone. But he kept insisting, so eventually I played along."

"Then why tell him anything at all?" I ask.

"Because it was the only way I could think to *save* you," Lara says. "Everything I told him was stuff they'd have figured out anyway. They caught us red-handed with Dylan's stolen memory. All they had to do was watch that dream for themselves to know that we were looking into the time freeze. In an active investigation, my dad wouldn't need Dylan's password."

That makes sense, but it doesn't explain everything. "Fine, but why tell him about me sneaking into the Congress Room with you? Or about my plan to get Merlin back in charge?"

"Because I had to give them something they didn't know," says Lara, looking apologetic. "Something to make Bane and my dad believe that I really was turning you in, so they would back off. Imagine if he'd called in Agent Fiona to tell them your intentions, or if they'd forced Director Horus to look into your past. Then they really would know everything."

"Oh," is all I can think to say.

Lara gives me a hopeful smile. "Now do you believe I was trying to help?"

I drop my eyes. "I think so."

"Good." Lara sounds relieved. "Because we've got much bigger problems. I overheard Bane and my dad talking, and Harlowe is planning a press conference tomorrow in the Underground Auditorium. They want to bring you two onstage and publicly accuse you of being traitors."

"Elsie too?" I ask.

Lara nods. "My dad was willing to let her off—he's known her since we used to have sleepovers in kindergarten—but Harlowe insisted. Said people would be more willing to turn on you if it looked like you were convincing other kids to join in your schemes."

Elsie shakes her head. "But he's got no proof we were doing anything suspicious. Even if he believed you, it's still just your word against ours."

"He's going to say Amari was trying to learn the time freeze spell," says Lara. "Plenty of agents will testify to the alarm in the Congress Room going off. Plus, Amari used Dylan's password to access the memory—it's going to look like they're working together."

I bury my face in my hands. "Even I would have a hard time believing me—it's too much of a coincidence. Lara, any chance you've still got that transporter?"

"No," she answers, but then grins. "I made a show of putting it back and then swiped a different one a few hours later—just in case. You thinking of sneaking out again?"

·"Hear us out," says Elsie. We explain our theory.

Lara looks worried but determined. "I'm down if you are. You'd just need to come to my room to use it."

"Except Tweedledee and Tweedledum are guarding our door." Elsie's face goes red at our shocked expressions. I don't think I've ever heard her insult anyone. She crosses her arms. "Excuse my language, but I don't like those two one bit."

I grin. "Good thing I can turn things invisible."

Fifteen minutes later, a series of explosions goes off in Elsie's duffel bag. The wraiths come gliding in through the door, and we sprint into the hallway, my invisibility spell keeping us hidden. Shouts ring out behind us and we move faster.

We're barely around the corner when we run directly into Bertha. I fall on my butt, the shock breaking my concentration. Our illusion vanishes and we're very much visible.

Bertha crosses her arms. "Sneaking about, are we?"

I open my mouth to give an excuse, but running into Bertha wasn't something we planned for. I've got nothing.

Bertha shakes her head. "Honestly, you kids got no imagination these days. When I was your age, we had all kinds of ways of getting out." She sighs. "On your feet then. Better get the illusion back up if you mean to get wherever you're going."

It takes me a few seconds to catch on. "You mean you're letting me go?"

"I'm tough on you kids," she says, "but I'm also fair. Don't much appreciate how Bane and his cronies have been carrying on. So maybe I can look the other way just this once."

"Thanks," I say. "I'm trying to fix things—"

"Don't need specifics," says Bertha. "There's a thing we adults call plausible deniability. Now skedaddle before those wraiths get wise."

Bertha pulls me to my feet, and I quickly recast my invisibility spell and rejoin hands with Elsie. We race the rest of the way to Lara's room.

Lara knows the plan, so she's not confused when she answers the door to find nothing there. Instead she pulls it open just enough for us to squeeze inside, then quickly shuts it again.

Dropping my invisibility, I plop down on the extra bed as Elsie rocks back and forth near the door. Shadow sits quietly on the dresser, big eyes moving between us. "Since when does that thing know how to behave?"

Lara rolls her eyes. "It's always calm after Jayden drops it off. He literally just tells it not to cause trouble and it doesn't."

"Sounds about right." I smile.

"We should get going while we still can." Lara pulls the transporter from under her bed and slides it over her forearm.

"Um, before we go," I say, "I just want to, uh, apologize . . . for accusing you of betraying me."

Lara shrugs. "Well, I needed my dad to believe me. So the fact that you fell for my act too just means I did a great job."

I smile. "Guess so. You know, if somebody told me last summer that you and I would be working together like this, I'd have told them they were crazy."

Her face goes slightly pink. "Same. I'm glad you took a chance on me."

"We're friends," I say.

Lara stiffens. "You mean that?"

I nod. "I do."

"Good." She grins. "Because if this doesn't work, at least I can say I got kicked out of the Bureau for a friend."

"Hey, positive vibes only!" says Elsie. "We're going to find the stone and fix everything."

Lara gives me a thumbs-up. We link elbows, and Lara wastes no time entering the coordinates to the Congress Room.

Then we're there.

Alarms wail.

"Go, Amari!"

I dash into the time freeze, that same eerie sensation washing over me once again, making my skin crawl. I'm instantly reminded just how enormous this room is. It could take all night and most of tomorrow to search everywhere.

And it's not like I didn't search the Congress Room the last time I was here—and found nothing. I glance up to see how Elsie and Lara are doing. They're already surrounded by agents who've responded to the alarm.

My heart sinks. If this is my last chance to save myself, it might just be hopeless.

Unless I get lucky.

No, unless I'm smart about this. The agents can't enter the time freeze like I can, so for now I'm safe. I just need to make sure I leave here with the time stone.

I stand and think for a moment. Someone came in here with that time stone and attacked the Supernatural World Congress. Looking at the faces of all the supernatural creatures, whoever showed up must've been awful, because everyone looks terrified.

If I follow their eyes, maybe I can figure out where this mystery person was in the room when they used the stone. I go up to a frozen cyclops. He doesn't seem to be looking straight ahead, but slightly higher. So are all the rest.

I follow their gazes to a spot high on the wall. But there's no time stone here. Another dead end.

Don't panic. There's got to be something I'm missing. Something I'm not seeing.

I start down the stairs just like last time, head swinging back and forth as I take in the scene. But it's all more of the same. It's not until I get halfway down the stairs that I remember Merlin. Even if I'm technically the most magical being in our world now, Merlin's mastery of his magic means he could run circles around me. And probably anyone else too. So why does *he* look so frightened?

I dash down to the floor of the Congress Room and walk straight up to the elf king. An idea pops into my head. What if I could see what he saw? What if I could look into his memory of what happened?

I ball my fists and look straight into Merlin's eyes. "Dreamcatcher."

Nothing happens. Is it because of the time freeze? I try to turn myself invisible, but that doesn't work either. My magic won't work with time frozen. So what now?

The agents at the entrance continue to look on, knowing I can't stay in here forever. I'm starting to feel desperate . . .

I gasp. That's exactly the word I'd use to describe Merlin's expression.

Just like the Night Brothers were the night the werewolves attacked! A strange thought pops into my head and I think back to Fiona telling me about her family ring. How her ancestor kept it as a trophy after defeating three magicians. What if he wasn't the only one to keep something from the Ancient War? What if Merlin kept the time stone, and it was used here for the same reason it was the first time?

A last resort!

I swallow, my eyes on Merlin's right hand clutched to his chest. Now that I know what I'm looking for, I reach out and slip my hands between Merlin's stiff wooden fingers . . .

And feel something hard. The time stone!

At my touch, a surge of magic goes through me, just like when I put on the Victor's Rings.

There's a loud crash, and shouts and growls fill my ears. It's all so sudden, I jump at the noise. Time is no longer frozen in here.

Merlin's eyes find mine. "Return the stone, child! Before it's too late!" He pulls the stone away from me, and instantly everything goes still again.

Too late for what? I wonder. *Why would Merlin want the Congress Room to stay frozen?*

As soon as I turn around, I get my answer.

Beware of unseen dangers.

≋ 34 ≋

I CAN'T BELIEVE MY EYES. WRAITHS. POURING THROUGH the ceiling, ghostly weapons in hand. There must be fifty of them.

I sprint back up to the stairs of the Congress Room as fast as my feet will carry me. My friends and all those agents stand at the edge of the room, looking every bit as stunned as I feel.

They clear a path for me to reach Director Van Helsing, who stands blinking in disbelief at the scene inside the Congress Room.

Buzzing fills the hallway as Prime Minister Bane and his two assistants shove their way over. All three flicker and fade together in that creepy way of theirs. "What's going on here? Why haven't these girls been arrested for trespassing?"

"Why don't you have a look?" I say.

Bane snarls, but then catches sight of what everyone is staring at—his wraiths frozen inside the Supernatural World Congress. On the attack.

For the first time, fear flickers across the Prime Minister's face. It gives me confidence that I've figured this out.

I step forward. "The Supernatural World Congress wasn't about to put *more* restrictions on the UnWanteds, I think they were about to lift them. And you and your wraiths were so angry, so blinded by your hatred for magicians and UnWanteds, that you betrayed everyone. *You're* the traitor. Not me."

Bane squirms under the accusation, but the faces of the gathered agents are grim. "This is just some elaborate illusion—can't you all see that? It's what she does. There weren't any wraiths in there before and now suddenly they're all over that room! It's a trick!"

"The wraiths were always here," I say. "They just weren't visible because Merlin happened to use the time stone at the exact moment they'd all flickered out of sight."

"I don't have to listen to these lies!" shouts Bane. "I'm leaving."

"You're not going anywhere," says Director Van Helsing. The agents in the room close ranks, forming a wall around us.

Bane cowers, and the director turns his attention back to me. He asks, "Well, what happened to make the wraiths appear?"

"I went in and took the time stone from Merlin," I say. "And that ended the time freeze for a few seconds. But Merlin saw that the wraiths were still a threat and snatched it back, restarting the freeze. Only this time, the wraiths weren't lucky enough to be faded out of view when time stopped again."

Murmurs break out among the agents. But I can tell most of them believe me.

Bane hisses, but he's sunk so far into himself he's practically crouching. "My wraiths are all out tracking down UnWanteds, not trapped in that room with the Supernatural World Congress. Would you really take the word of this—this *magician* over your Prime Minister?"

"If I'm lying, and this is just an illusion," I say. "Then tell your wraiths to meet you here in this hallway. If they aren't all trapped in that time freeze right now, then they should have no problem getting here."

All eyes turn to Bane, expectant.

"You loathsome little beast!" Bane lunges for me, but he's quickly restrained by three different agents. One of them slaps a pair of Spirit Cuffs around his wrists.

"Take him back to the Bureau," says Director Van Helsing, disgusted.

"Hmm, why don't we hold off on that?" comes a voice. "In fact, go ahead and release our dear Prime Minister."

What's Director Harlowe doing here?

We all turn to find Harlowe at the back of the hallway, pulling down her sleeve to cover the transporter on her forearm—all except for one agent who's busy uncuffing Bane. But why?

"What on earth are you doing?" shouts Director Van Helsing. "You answer to me, not to Harlowe!"

"Oh, Victor," says Harlowe. "I'm afraid *everyone* answers to me."

Bane crawls to Harlowe's side. She pats the top of his head. "I'm so sorry, Harlowe," he says. "The blasted girl figured it out."

"Wait," I squeak. "*You're* behind this?"

Harlowe shrugs. "Guilty."

A wave of Stun Sticks goes up, all pointed at her.

"Oh, put those silly things away," says Harlowe.

And they do. Every single agent in the room shoves them back into their pockets and holsters. Outraged voices fill the hallway as the agents stare at their own hands, utterly confused.

"Amari," squeaks Elsie beside me. "What's happening?"

I don't have an answer for her.

Director Van Helsing shakes his head in disbelief. "How are you doing this?"

Other agents shout their questions too.

Harlowe puts a finger to her lips and says, "Shh, it's my time to talk now."

The hall falls silent. I spin around, dread spilling over me. "Why are you all listening to her?"

"Haven't you figured it out yet?" says Harlowe. "You did such a fine job untangling the time freeze that my supernatural ability should be easy enough to guess by now. But if not, let me help you. Everyone, please aim your Stun Sticks at Amari Peters and Elsie Rodriguez. If they make any move to escape—zap them."

The sound of movement fills the room as the agents all rush to follow Harlowe's orders. One Stun Stick is only inches away from my face—my partner's.

This is what I saw in the looking glass.

Lara's eyes are wide and panicked, her face flushed as she strains to pull her arm down. But it's no use. She's under Harlowe's control, like everyone else.

I lift my hands in surrender.

"Your supernatural ability!" says Elsie. "You can control people."

Harlowe claps. "Very good! My talent for persuading people became the ability to *make* them do what I want."

"But why doesn't it work on me or Elsie?" I ask.

Harlowe frowns. "Unfortunately, my ability doesn't work on those with high levels of magic. A rather annoying limitation that makes a few supernaturals immune to my control. It's why I've chosen to operate outside the spotlight to protect myself."

"I don't have magic," says Elsie.

"Not as a human," Harlowe says. "But your dragon blood protects you."

Elsie and I glance to one another. How are we supposed to get out of this?

"Oh, come now," says Harlowe. "Surely you've got more questions? It's been torture ruling the supernatural world without being able to gloat to anyone. Me, an orphaned faun girl from the woods."

When we don't answer, Harlowe sighs and puts her hands on her hips. "Better speak up. You'll both be branded as traitors first thing tomorrow morning. After that, I highly doubt you'll ever be seen again."

I swallow. Maybe if I can keep her talking, we'll be able to find a way out of this. "What happened on the day of the time freeze? Did you know Merlin would stop time to protect the Supernatural World Congress?"

"Goodness, no," says Harlowe, who seems more than happy to hold us all hostage while she tells her story. "Irritable old Bane here was furious about Merlin wanting to formally lift the ban on UnWanteds. No one was even enforcing it anymore, but Bane and his wraiths were incensed by the mere suggestion. 'A slap in the face' they called it, 'to all those who'd suffered at the hands of the Night Brothers.' I simply suggested that if things didn't go the way they wanted, they should do something about it. Take matters into their own hands. And so we created a plan to attack the Congress Room and take control by force! Merlin was to be punished for such a betrayal."

"That's why neither of you was there," I say.

"Exactly!" says Harlowe. "Of course, Bane and I were just outside in the hallway with a couple of his wraith assistants. You see, I wanted to watch the great Merlin be taken down—to know the exact moment when my supernatural ability would be mine again to use whenever I pleased. But the old elf stopped time, trapping Bane's wraiths and saving all those in the Congress Room. A funny thing happened though—Merlin being frozen released his block on my supernatural ability anyway. And with the lucky break of Bane's wraiths being invisible to anyone who looked inside, well, I knew my time had come."

"And you don't mind being her pet?" Elsie asks Bane.

Harlowe gives him another pat on the head. "Oh, I've been in constant communication with Bane to make sure he gets a steady diet of new orders to keep up the ruse."

It's not that Harlowe was speaking for the Prime Minister all this time. She essentially *was* the Prime Minister—her promotion to director, the way that even in my meetings with Bane *she* was the one making the decisions . . .

"One more thing before I have you both dragged off. I want you to know that I wasn't exactly honest about dear Maria. I used my ability to force Director Horus to look into her past." Harlowe's hands go to her hips, her voice turning cold. "And wouldn't you know—he revealed magician after magician, all hiding in plain sight. Some might even call a group that large . . . a *league*."

"No!" Horror snakes through me. "What did you do?"

"What I promised, of course." Harlowe stands proud. "I sent agents after every single one of them."

My ring suddenly goes not warm, but white-hot, enough that I can't keep the pain from showing on my face. I shake my hand. *"Ouch."*

Harlowe narrows her eyes. "Zap them!"

I throw myself into Elsie and squeeze my ring.

N EXT THING I KNOW, ELSIE AND I LIE IN A FIELD OF
tall grass. A wide, clear sky stretches out above us,
sparkling with starlight. I get to my knees and take a quick
look around. I don't see a ring pedestal—it doesn't look like
anything's here at all. What kind of challenge is this?

Elsie pulls herself up beside me, rubbing her shoulder.
"Where are we?"

"No idea. Are you okay?"

"I'll be fine," she says. "Where's Lara?"

I shake my head, the weight of that question settling
over me. "There wasn't time . . . she had her Stun Stick
pointed at me. I could only save one of you."

My best friend looks stricken. "Harlowe has her?"

I nod. "And Jayden's still at the Bureau too. It wasn't supposed to turn out like this—"

Elsie gasps, her eyes snagging on something over my shoulder. *"Dylan."*

He's on the opposite side of the clearing. He whips his head back and forth, looking for the final ring, and maybe for me too.

I turn so that Elsie is behind me. "Stay down. No matter what happens, don't let him know you're here."

Elsie shivers. "You aren't going to face him, are you?"

"I have to," I say. "It's kind of the whole point."

As soon as I stand, Dylan spots me. For a moment we just stare at one another.

Dylan smiles at me, his hands erupting into flames. "This is it, Amari. It's time we settle this once and for all."

"Fine." This time I've got no choice but to fight. Squeezing my ring would only take me back to Harlowe, and besides, I can't abandon Elsie. I channel my fear into swirling winds, praying I can control them well enough to stay alive.

Dylan charges and I ball my fists, ready to stand my ground. The tall grass swirls around me.

Cozmo appears next, between us, carrying the Crown of Vladimir. The wind kicks up, blowing his bright red League of Magicians cloak around him.

Dylan stops short, his eyes narrowed.

"Cozmo!" I shout, stepping forward. "Harlowe knows about the League. She's sending agents after everyone—"

"I know all about that!" Cozmo snaps. "Dozens of magicians were already captured before a warning could be sent to the rest of us. It's why there will be no fifth challenge. The Great Game ends here and now. One of you will take the other's magic and earn this Crown. We must have a leader—a magician strong enough to protect the rest of us who are left."

"But magicians don't survive having their magic stolen," I say. "Why is this competition so cruel? Isn't it supposed to be about finding out who's the better magician?"

"But that's exactly what it *is* doing," Dylan calls. "Finding out which one of us is willing to do whatever's necessary to win."

"If you're unwilling to participate," says Cozmo, "then simply toss Dylan one of your rings and let us get on with the business of fighting back."

I shake my head. Either way it gives my magic to Dylan to use against the Bureau. "There's got to be something else we can do. Something other than war—"

"Enough talking!" Dylan shouts, lobbing a fireball in my direction.

I duck, and it sails over my head, starting a small fire where it lands. Quickly I put some distance between me and Elsie, who's still hiding in the grass. The farther I get from her, the less likely she is to get hurt. My heart hammers, and it feels like I might throw up.

But my fear is also how I know my weather magic will answer when I summon it. No more running. I've got to fight. And I've got to win.

I slide to a stop and stretch out my hands, great gusts of wind whistling in my ears as they whip through the tall grass. Dylan charges, his hands ablaze, and I hurl the winds in his direction.

The collision knocks him backward, so hard he flips in the air before landing with a thud.

For a moment I worry that maybe I overdid it, but Dylan slowly pulls himself up, teeth bared in a snarl.

"So you want to play rough, do you?" Dylan sends a wave of shadows, so fast I barely have time to react before they've coiled around my arms and legs. The shadows pull me to the ground, dragging me through the grass toward him.

No, no, no. I wriggle and twist, but it's no use—the shadows won't release me. Dylan heaves on them like rope, pulling me closer and closer.

And I know that if I don't do something right now, it's over. This boy who once claimed to care for me will do whatever it takes to get my rings. He'll kill me if he has to.

It's my own bone-deep will to survive that reacts. Electricity sparks in the air around me, shooting across my body like a live wire—and only then do the shadows recede. Unfazed, Dylan leaps on top of me, reaching to pry the rings from my fingers. We roll and twist in the grass, screaming and shouting, flames and electricity scorching the field around us.

But he's bigger than I am. Stronger too.

He wears me down until my body is too tired to keep struggling. Then he lifts me up and slams me into the dirt hard enough to knock the air from my chest. My vision blurs.

I feel him tug at one of my rings, trying to get it loose. My head's clear enough to ball my hand into a fist, but as he starts to peel my fingers back, I know it's only a matter of time before he gets what he wants.

Despair washes over me and it feels like I'm drowning in it. I think of Elsie still hiding in the grass, my friends trapped back at the Bureau, Mama and Quinton—my family. Everyone I care about, and none of them is safe because of Harlowe, because of Cozmo and this terrible game, because this boy who once called me a friend would break me to win.

Dylan nearly gets the ring off my finger, and in my desperation I bite down hard on his arm. He howls and I try to scramble away, but he tackles me. We struggle some more until he gets an arm around my neck and starts squeezing.

I can't breathe.

And then I feel *it*—panic followed by blinding anger. The wind begins to whip around us, the sky above darkening. A deep well of power opening in the pit of my belly.

The last page of the weatherist spell book flashes in my head. *Calamity of the Skies*. What do I have to lose? I summon everything I've got, channel these emotions into pure magic. No magician has come back from this spell? Well, those magicians weren't me.

My magic is strong, has always *been* strong.

Stronger even than Dylan. It's the reason I beat him last summer even with all his years of training.

And he seems to realize it too.

Thunder booms overhead, black clouds churning above like an angry ocean. Lightning flashes and Dylan scrambles away from me, his eyes wide and panicked.

Rain pours down around us, so thick all I can see is Dylan—it's like the whole world has been reduced to just us two. Slowly, I get to my feet, and he cowers, shielding his face from the downpour.

I feel myself start to lose control. I try to fight it but it's too much—my thoughts fade, my emotions growing so strong that they're all I am. Is this what happened to Dylan in the Sightless Depths? Did he give up control in order to survive that place?

My anger at all that's gone wrong and my fear of not being able to fix things shoves everything else away. A different Amari is forming inside me, the worst version of myself. This is what the spell book warned me about. What Maria explained in her very first lesson—the darkness waiting for my resolve to falter.

This must be what it means to lose yourself to foul magick. For emotions to take over and run wild. To not care what happens as a result.

I feel unstoppable. I feel limitless. And I want to bend

the whole world to my will.

Starting with that weak Dylan Van Helsing.

I lift my hand, and the clouds above flash with anticipation. Last summer I gave him lightning, and now I'm giving him the entire storm. All it would take is a thought.

"Amari!" calls Elsie. "Don't!"

My best friend's voice startles me.

I shake my head and summon forth the storm again. "I have to do this!"

"Please don't!" Elsie puts herself between me and Dylan. "You'll regret it."

Would I? Deep down, I know she's right. And yet I still have the urge to lash out, no matter the consequences. But the disgust I feel at the thought of hurting my best friend is so jolting it makes me stagger backward. It feels like waking from a trance . . . like I was sleepwalking.

Now that I can think clearly, I remember what else Maria said. *"Being good is a choice, and it's one you have to keep making."* So I do make that choice. I pull myself back from the edge.

"Finish this!" calls Cozmo.

I step past Elsie to Dylan, who's inching backward in the grass. And I get an idea. It's one I've had before, for something different, but maybe it'll work this time. I told Dylan once that I believe there's still good in him. Well, maybe I can help him find it.

I drop to my knees in front of Dylan so that we're eye to eye. He looks wary, confused. Then I ball my fists tight and stare him right in the eyes. "Dreamcatcher."

Dylan gasps, and his eyes drift shut. Suddenly tiny flashes of light are everywhere, fluttering and swishing around me like fireflies.

Each time I focus on a light I see a memory of Dylan's, as clear as if it were my own. I see moments of him snuggled up next to Maria as a kid, watching a movie. And I *feel* how safe he felt. Another shows him frustrated when she won't answer his texts. It burns in my chest too.

Finally I see him start to explore his magic on his own—angrily shorting out the electronics around the house with his tech magic.

When I see Moreau, the Night Brother who taught him to delve deeper into the Foul Path, to let his fear and anger control him, I do exactly what Dylan did to Thomas Fletcher. I pull those memories out of his head.

I can save Dylan Van Helsing. I can make him good again.

I've got to try.

I keep going until I find his first memory of the Sightless Depths. The unyielding dark of it, the cold chill, is unlike anything I knew could be possible. It's horrifying. I snatch the memories from his mind.

Finally, I find the moment when he gave up in there and let himself become this red-eyed monster, and I yank the memory free with all my strength.

Dylan's eyes open, as clear and blue as they've ever been. He looks at me and actually smiles. It isn't smug or angry. Not a sneer or snarl. It's like I'm meeting him for the first time. This is the boy Maria told me about. Who he could've been.

I'm so relieved that I burst into tears and throw my arms around him. And he hugs me back.

"Dispel," says Cozmo.

"No!" I cry out. I'd forgotten Cozmo was even here. The memories flash and zip back toward Dylan. Even the bad ones I kept separated from the rest. I scramble to reach for them, but it's no use. They're too many and too fast.

I can only watch as Dylan's regretful blue eyes meet mine. He whispers something I can't hear, and then those eyes turn hard again, as red as ever.

"Give him the ring, Amari," says Cozmo. "Or else."

"Never!" But when I turn to face him, I see that Cozmo's got his arm around Elsie's throat. He's taken away any choice I might've had. I won't let Elsie get hurt. I take off one of my Victor's Rings and throw it at Dylan's feet.

Dylan picks it up.

"Don't," I say. "Please don't take my magic."

He slides the ring on anyway. As the Crown appears on his head I feel my magic pour out of me all at once, a sensation that leaves me feeling hollow and slightly cold. When I call to my illusion magic, only a spark responds where it used to feel like a wildfire.

I double over, light-headed.

Dylan's entire face lights not with triumph, but relief.

"You don't have to use the League to start a war." I plead with him because there's nothing else left for me to do. "Please, just think of all the good you can do. You could introduce the League of Magicians to the supernatural world. *That* could be what makes you great."

But he's not listening.

Cozmo releases Elsie and she rushes over. "I'm so sorry, Amari."

"It's not your fault," I say. "Cozmo never wanted me to win."

"And why would he?" says Dylan. "You're pitiful. A simple threat, and you throw away your magic like it's nothing."

"Because I won't win at any cost."

"So you don't win at all." Dylan steps backward, his hands becoming flames.

"Amari . . . ," comes Elsie's panicked voice.

I grab Elsie's hand and we scramble to our feet.

We run. But the moment he aims those flames I know we aren't fast enough. Because it's not a fireball that comes but a wave of flame. I hook an arm around Elsie's and squeeze my Game Ring—it'll take us back to Harlowe but at least we'll be alive.

But nothing happens. Because the Great Game is over.

We aren't going to make it. Elsie realizes it too, and when our eyes meet, my best friend gives me a sad smile, then tugs her arm from mine.

Before I can stop her, she throws herself in front of me.

≈ 36 ≈

I T TAKES A FEW SECONDS FOR ME TO REALIZE THAT I'M not toast. Warmth heats my skin, but other than that, I'm fine. And so is Elsie. Even as she stands amid the flames.

Did I know my best friend was fireproof? She's not, though—I've seen her with burn marks on her hands after an experiment blew up in her face.

So then how . . . ?

I look closer. Elsie twitches once, twice, and again. Soon her whole body is shivering. Scales ripple over her skin, and bright red wings grow out of her back so large that for a moment, she's shielded from view. Those wings seem way too big—until my scaly best friend begins to grow into them, her once tiny frame becoming massive.

"Elsie!" I shout.

She turns, her brown eyes now bright yellow.

Elsie isn't just a dragon, she's a *dragon* dragon. With a roar that seems to echo in my bones, she unleashes a river of fire that scorches the entire clearing.

Even with all his newfound magic, Dylan wastes no time pulling back the sleeve of his robes to get to his transporter. He vanishes, and Elsie takes to the skies, wings carrying her higher and higher.

"Elsie!" I call out for her again, but it's no use. I drop to my knees. I've lost everything—my magic, my friends . . . What do I even do now?

"I *am* sorry, you know," says Cozmo, putting a hand on my shoulder.

I flinch away from him. "Harlowe has the Bureau, and Dylan has the League. There's going to be a *war*. And it's your fault."

"The war has already begun, child. All I did was give our side a fighting chance."

I shake my head. "Dylan is out of control. You'll regret choosing him."

"Perhaps," says Cozmo. "But at least I'll be alive to regret it."

I shake my head in disgust.

"You've every right to be angry," he says. "But your part in this is done now. Give me your hand, and I'll send you home."

The word "home" kills any protest I might've had.

Suddenly I feel so tired. I hold out my hand, and Cozmo removes the Game Ring. I didn't realize how heavy it felt until it's gone.

"It was all for nothing," I whisper. "Everything I did, none of it mattered."

"Then you weren't paying attention," he whispers back, offering the slightest of smiles.

It's not until Cozmo teleports me back to my apartment that I realize coming back here may not have been the best idea. Harlowe's bound to have agents searching for me, and this is the first place they'll look.

But it's quiet. I tiptoe through my living room but don't see anyone. I peek through the windows to the street; nothing seems out of place.

Strange.

I start toward my room, thinking about what's next. Do I stay here, or do I run? And what about Mama—what do I say to her? How can I possibly explain in a way she'd understand?

I step into the bathroom and almost don't recognize the girl staring back at me. There's grass and dirt in my hair, and my face is covered in scratches. My Junior Agent uniform is ripped in a few places, scorched in others. To top it off, I look exhausted.

I *feel* exhausted. But when I step past Quinton's room, I freeze. He's in there—lying on a hospital bed marked

Department of Supernatural Health. Harlowe really meant what she'd said about him paying for my mistakes. So much for running—I can't leave my brother to fend for himself.

I won't.

I grab a chair from the dining room table and sit it next to Quinton's bed. He shifts under the covers after I accidentally hit my knee on the side railing. I freeze, watching him for a few seconds. Okay, that was weird.

I plop down on the chair and take out my phone. Normally I don't pay much attention to news app notifications, but the name Priya Kapoor gets my attention.

I click on the link:

Famed Bollywood Actress among the Missing in Bizarre Disappearances Spanning the Globe
Authorities were called to the Manhattan apartment of Priya Kapoor, 37, after the woman's teenage daughter reported the actress missing. No signs of forced entry were found, but an unsettling message was left on the wall—the word "UnWanted" scrawled in angry red letters. It's the same message, Interpol reports, that has been found in the suspected kidnappings of high-profile individuals in more than twenty countries.

It's Harlowe, hunting magicians.

Beneath the article is a section called Local Headlines. And suddenly I know why there aren't any agents here looking for me—they've got much bigger concerns. A thumbnail video shows the Vanderbilt Hotel in flames— meaning the Bureau is in flames.

I click on the video, and a reporter appears onscreen.

"Hi, this is Amanda Barret from Fox 5, reporting live from downtown Atlanta where the famed Vanderbilt Hotel has suddenly caught fire. Police have blocked off surrounding roads as teams of firefighters from around the city arrive to battle the blaze and rescue anyone still inside. I have an eyewitness here who says this terrible event was no accident. Can you please introduce yourself?"

The camera pans to a man who looks far too excited to be speaking about something as awful as a fire. As soon as the reporter points the microphone his way, he snatches it from her.

"This is what we Watchers have been warning you about! The world within our world that you all told us didn't exist? Well, joke's on you, ain't it? All those big shots going missing, this building being burned, it's not random at all. If you'd been paying attention like we have, you'd know that a war has just been declared. And it's gonna get ugly—"

The video cuts out. This is a *nightmare*. I've got to believe my friends escaped, because if they didn't . . . I don't want to even think about that.

I close my eyes and lean my forehead against the edge of Quinton's bed. I was supposed to prevent this. And now look.

The sound of footsteps wakes me with a start—I don't even remember falling asleep. It's early morning now, and streaks of sunlight find their way through the blinds. I look to Quinton, still in bed, then to the hallway.

"Mama?" I call out.

The bedroom door swings open. But it's not Mama.

"Amari?" says Jayden.

I dash over and hug him. His tall self lifts me off my feet, spinning me around.

"How are you here?" I ask when he sets me back down.

"Juniors and trainees got evacuated as soon as the fire started," he says. "I been home since last night. Only snuck in here to borrow some clothes for El Smooth."

"Elsie's here too!" I'm so relieved it brings tears to my eyes.

He nods, grinning. "Found her on the roof when I went up there to think. Figured she must've did the whole dragon thing, 'cause she was passed out in some baggy coveralls from Mr. Bryant's maintenance closet."

"It was the most amazing thing I've ever seen," I say.

He grins, but then his expression changes. "They told us Harlowe had you. That we'd never see you again."

"That was almost true," I say. "Let's go get Els."

When Elsie's eyes blink open on my living room couch, she stares at me for a few seconds before saying, "Amari?"

"That's me," I say.

A happy grin lights up Elsie's face, but she's still squinting at me. "Why is everything so blurry?"

I laugh at that. "Your glasses didn't survive the whole dragon experience. And while I've got you here . . . scientifically speaking, how does one go from barely more than five feet tall to a hundred feet long and back again?"

Elsie's cheeks go pink. "I can't believe I did that."

"You saved my life," I say. "You literally threw yourself into the fire for me."

Now she's blinking back tears. "I just knew I didn't want you to get hurt. You're my best friend. I love you."

"I love you too," I say, and give her the biggest hug.

Jayden wipes at his eyes. "That's cool, man. Going through something like that, y'all more than just friends. Y'all sisters now."

I turn to Elsie and she nods. Sisters it is.

"But wait," I ask, turning back to Jayden. "Why are *you* crying?"

"Oh nah, you know, allergies be kicking in at the weirdest times. So, y'all gonna give me the full scoop on what happened or nah?"

Now that the Great Game is over and the Game Ring is off my finger, I'm finally free to fill them in on everything that's happened. Some parts they already knew, but most they didn't. By the end of the story we're all in a pretty somber mood, because it's not a happy one. Harlowe and Dylan are on opposites sides of a war that's just beginning, and not all my friends are here. I don't know where—or how—Lara is, and she risked everything to help me. And what about Agents Magnus and Fiona?

"What do we do now?" Jayden asks.

I shake my head. "What can we do? We're just three kids. I'm not even special anymore—I've lost my magic."

"Who says you need magic to be special, Chicken Little?" That voice.

My hands fly up to my mouth and I whip my head around, then suddenly I'm on my feet, diving across the living room to where Quinton stands in his bedroom doorway. I'm laughing and sobbing and trying to talk all at the same time and Quinton shakes with laughter, squeezing me tight.

"How?" I finally manage.

"I think it was Dylan," says Elsie. "When you were doing that Dreamcatcher spell, his aura turned white—he felt apologetic."

I think back. "He whispered something. He must've been releasing the curse."

So many emotions fill my head.

"I managed to catch most of the story as I was making my way out of bed," says Quinton. "Took me a while to remember how to use this body of mine after being asleep for so long."

I feel the deepest shame. "I'm sorry the first thing you had to hear was how much I screwed everything up."

"Sometimes things happen that are beyond our control," says Quinton. "All you can do is decide how you're going to respond now. You gonna fight to fix things or you gonna lie down and surrender? 'Cause it looks to me like you're surrounded by folks who still very much believe in Amari Peters."

I look to Jayden, who nods, and Elsie, who grins. In their faces I realize how true Quinton's words are. They do still believe in me, despite everything.

I take a slow, deep breath and meet my brother's eyes. In them I see love that makes my heart overflow. He's been telling me I can do anything my whole life.

Who am I to say they're wrong?

I smile through my tears. "I say we fight."

ACKNOWLEDGMENTS

If *Amari and the Night Brothers* was the book of my heart, then this has certainly been the book of my dreams. Once upon a time, the idea of getting to write a second book in this series seemed like too much to hope for, and I'm so incredibly grateful to be at this point. It's by far the most challenging book I've ever had to write (hello, deadlines!), but also the most rewarding, as I proved to myself that I've got more than one book in me. I hope you enjoyed it!

To those who've helped to make *Amari and the Great Game* possible:

The first thank-you will always go to God, who makes *everything* possible.

Thanks to my wonderful editors Kristin Daly Rens and Liz Bankes, who guided me through some pretty tough revisions and stuck it out with me when I needed extra time to get this book right. Kristin, this book couldn't have happened without you; not only are you brilliant editorially, but you give the best pep talks when talking your authors off the ledge! Liz, your notes and your insights were invaluable and made the book *so* much stronger. To all those who have already reached out about how much you love the ending, you can thank her for pointing me in the right direction!

Thank you to Gemma Cooper, superagent and all-around cool person! It was so great to get to meet you in person this year! You always have my back and I'm so grateful to have you in my corner. Truly you are a blessing in human form.

A huge thanks goes to my family and friends, who keep me grounded and sane throughout this crazy journey. Your unconditional love and unwavering support has meant the world to me and I'm so incredibly grateful to you all.

A BIG thank-you to Amari fans the world over who've made this past year so amazing. It's your excitement for Amari and the story that has made the book such a success in so many places. I love reading your messages and getting your mail! Your support means more than every award and bestseller list, and I hope to keep making books you enjoy.

Last but not least, thanks to my wife, Quinteria, my favorite person in the world. My Day One. I can't wait to go on so many more adventures with you.